Tears of an Angel

Nada Lubay

A catalogue record for this book is available from the National Library of Australia

Cover art: Consuelo Parra

ISBN-13: 978-1-923174-22-1

Linellen Press
265 Boomerang Road
Oldbury, Western Australia
www.linellenpress.com.au

Dedication

To our granddaughter, my sweet little Angel, who enriched and brought a new dawn into our lives beyond our wildest expectations.

To my husband, my unwavering moral compass in so many ways, who believed in me before I ever did, supporting me whenever I was overwhelmed by momentary doubts. He is the wind beneath my wings, made me feel that I can fly and reach the stars.

Disclaimer

This story was inspired by real-life events. However, it is a work of fiction – names, characters, places, and incidents are the product of the author's imagination or are altered to enhance the dramatic content.

Acknowledgements

First of all, I would like to express my sincere gratitude to my close friend and editor, Helen Iles, without whose invaluable advice and skilful editing, the publication of this book would have been difficult.

My sincere thanks also go to The Society of Women Writers, WA. The Society provided many amazing courses about writing, publishing, and launching a new book for aspiring writers like me, making my literary pursuit much easier. It certainly helped me to "find myself" as a writer.

I want to thank my other writing mentors, Rhuwina Griffiths, Creative Writing Facilitator at MALA, Christine Draper and Georgia Tingley who kept reminding me to stay true to my spiritual values and implicit beliefs, and Teena Raffa-Mulligan. This helped to enhance the intimate connections between the characters in my book thus enlivening their personalities.

Contents

Part One

The Early Years

Chapter 1

A Priest in Waiting

Aunt Pavica scolded the children climbing a giant fig tree in her courtyard, warning them not to startle the doves that had built their nest there.

"The tree serves as a perfect sanctuary for the dove and her chicks, protecting them from predators," she said. "In the mornings, before beginning fieldwork, I spread cornbread crumbs soaked in goat's milk for our dove and her young," Pavica described, pointing to the branches above her head. Reaching on her tiptoes, she picked ripe figs with her sunburned, wrinkled hands and invited the children to savour the sweetest fruits.

"My brother Andrija planted a fig tree in our shared courtyard. We cherished the moments spent under it enjoying the cool shade. At the same time, birds delighted in the sweet figs," Pavica recounted as she wandered around the courtyard, stooping occasionally as though looking for something.

The children crowded around her, eager to help. "What are you looking for?" one of the youngsters asked.

"I'm trying to find my brother Andrija's palm prints," Pavica said, scanning the courtyard. "When we poured cement into our shared courtyard, he pressed his hands into the wet cement to leave his mark. But I can't seem to find it now." She shook her head and smiled as her thoughts drifted back to her memories of Andrija just before the outbreak of the Second World War.

"Let's move closer to the kitchen so we don't disturb the dove's chicks." She pointed to a spot underneath the kitchen window. "Come on, kids, settle down so I can tell you another story."

Pavica fluffed her old pillow and settled against the stone wall to tell the children stories. She never wearied of gazing at the majestic, panoramic views of the stunning Croatian Adriatic Sea below, which shimmered magnificently.

⁂

Rtina, a small village in the hills, remained a hidden gem that was not easily spotted on maps. Yet, it burst into life each summer when city children came to spend their school holidays. They filled their days with swimming, diving, and scouring the jetty for seashells, their skin encrusted with salt and their hair interwoven. In the afternoons, they convened in Pavica's courtyard, their buckets brimming with seashells, which were then boiled in seawater and meticulously picked apart with crochet hooks and knitting needles.

Before sunset, neighbours gathered in the courtyard to clean the fish and collect their share of the day's catch. Anka and her girls, who shared the common courtyard with Pavica, started breaking large branches of dry grapevine stalks into small sticks, stacking them high to light a bonfire. Children gathered around the fireplace, roasting corn cobs on sticks, giggling at the corn popping and making crackling sounds. Some youngsters were restless, annoying one another while crunching on the tender sweet corn, often tossing the scorching hot corn from one palm to another as it was straight from the burning fire, or puffing and blowing the black soot from the golden ears.

As the sun set over the Adriatic Sea, Pavica ushered the children, including those from the adjoining courtyard, to wrap up in blankets and nestle into the cushions for the evening.

While their parents were absorbed in card games, the older villagers filled their pipes with tobacco, enjoyed glasses of wine, and mended fishing nets, the children gathered close, anticipating another captivating story from Aunt Pavica.

"What story will you tell us tonight?" one child asked impatiently.

"Ah, this story revolves around the Easter Celebration, a pivotal event marked by the villagers' participation in a procession and the enactment of Jesus' crucifixion and resurrection," she began. "My brother Andrija was chosen to play Jesus, a role he was ideally suited for. There were expectations for Andrija to be the next parish priest, you see, a path he never desired but felt compelled to follow. Our family were deeply devoted to God and felt honoured that Andrija, the eldest son, was chosen by the village elders to assume the role of the next parish priest ...."

The children, their young hearts empathising with Andrija's secret longing, sat spellbound as Pavica revealed his hidden desire to experience love and marriage. They understood the weight of his dilemma, torn between his parents' expectations and the village's traditions.

Venka, one of the curious children still awake, asked, "Why can't priests get married?"

"Ahh," Pavica waggled her finger, "in the Catholic faith, priests are not allowed to marry, as they are considered married to the church. Andrija was destined to become a priest.

"Before I begin, I would like to share something about the older generation before World War II ...." Pavica started recollecting her youthful times.

"We were so young then, but life was much simpler in those days; villagers helped one another. We worked hard ploughing the fields and planting crops from dawn to dusk, grinding wheat corn, and pressing black olives with a large stone pulled by donkeys and a few robust men. The poor donkeys were overloaded with heavy baskets, their legs barely visible as they climbed uphill back to the stables. Villagers depended on fishing, harvesting grapes, and selling olive oil.

"Preserving food for the chilly winter months was crucial for our survival. We picked fresh produce to sell in the city markets during summer. Getting up before dawn, we would load our donkeys with heavy baskets and walk twenty kilometres to Zadar. The group consisted mainly of women, some breastfeeding and walking with their babies strapped tightly to their backs.

"Village life centred around the quaint church atop the hill, constructed by our forebears. A skilled stonemason from Zadar sculpted a two-metre angel out of limestone. This majestic white stone angel stands guard at the church entrance, offering protection to both the church and its congregation. Villagers often touch the statue on their way to Sunday mass hoping it will bring them good fortune. The angel's grand wings, reaching towards the heavens, are admired by everyone in the village.

"The city of Zadar's Cathedral, Saint-Donat, donated two enormous bronze bells. The bells were deafening, echoing around the seaside village and beyond, alerting villagers to attend mass and the daily prayers."

Here Pavica paused and stood quietly to avoid disturbing others, and walked to the kitchen. Moments later, she brought back some cornbread, goat cheese, and pancetta, a jug of warm milk and sweet pumpkin cookies that the children adored.

"Thankfully, life has become much easier nowadays," she went on, "as our parish permits us to drive the old truck into the city."

Aunty Pavica sat down again, adjusted her pillow, covered her feet and savoured the sweet aroma of her mulled wine. The scent of cinnamon and cloves engulfed the courtyard as she continued with her story. The sound of nature's lullaby seduced some of the younger children to fall asleep, snoring on the rugged blanket Aunty Pavica had woven last winter.

"Tell us a love story," Milena said impatiently.

"This story will take time," Pavica whispered, trying not to wake up some younger children. "Young people fall in love and get married, but what happens after that is more important. This story is unique, and the entire story revolves around the Easter festivities. You must be quiet and listen, and I will speak softly so as not to awaken the youngsters already sleeping."

Collecting her thoughts, Pavica continued her story …

"Easter was the most important religious festival for the village elders, and the Procession was a source of joy for the children; they loved participating. Now nothing ever happened in our village without the priest's knowledge. Father Mateo was in charge of everything.

"The preparation started during winter; everything planned had to be approved by Father Mateo and the church elders. Men prepared smoked meats. Prosciutto had to be rubbed twice daily with fig leaves, sea salt, olive oil, herbs, and a special seaweed. Andrija was a skilful master; he had learned the craft of smoking meat from our grandparents.

"When the snow melted, the strongest men were assigned to climb the mountain to select the best oak tree and then cut the branches to precise measurements to build a large cross. Andrija, as a priest in waiting, was chosen to represent Jesus.

"The reenactment procession began on Good Friday with the crucifixion of Jesus. It was a solemn occasion during which Jesus was sentenced to death by the Roman General Pontius Pilate. Father Mateo led the procession to the church dressed in his finest robes, with a gilded belt and a shiny golden cross bouncing off his ample belly. The altar boys followed him, swinging brass holders with burning incense to ward off evil spirits.

"Our family walked alongside the church elders, and the

elderly who couldn't manage the steep hill were transported on donkeys."

Pavica smiled proudly. "Andrija carried the large cross on his back, stopping at the Twelve Stations of the Cross. The village women competed for the privileged positions of acting as Jesus' mother, Mary. Men wanting to impress their sweethearts walked behind dressed in robes resembling the apostles with whom Jesus shared the Last Supper.

"Andrija was nearly as strong as our donkey, but he kept shifting the heavy cross from one shoulder to another to ease his pain. While stopping to quench his thirst, village women rushed to his side to wipe his sweat, pressing the cloth to their hearts as if it were sacred. Andrija stumbled a few times before he reached the rocky hill, and collapsed with exhaustion on the church steps. He rested for a while as the village elders, acting as Roman soldiers, placed a thorny crown on his head. The old women rushed towards him, wiping blood and sweat that were pouring down his handsome, youthful face.

"The Good Friday procession service ended with Jesus' crucifixion. Village women dressed in black stayed behind, waving freshly cut olive branches for blessing, kneeling at the altar with their Bibles and rosaries, praying to God to forgive them for their sins."

Pavica stopped for a moment, crossed herself, and instructed the children. "Listen, children, remember that Jesus Christ died for our sins. One day, he will come down to earth to save all of us who have faith in him, so stay faithful and keep up with your prayers." She smiled broadly again and went on.

"On Easter Sunday, the celebration started in earnest. It was time to celebrate Jesus' resurrection by singing religious hymns, the sounds echoing off the interior marble walls. Our little church shone brightly, with its beautiful pink marble altar covered by a delicate white lace tablecloth. Candles glowed, and the scents of wild, fresh flowers filled the air. Villagers gathered in a grassy meadow below the church, where tables were full of festive, decorative ornaments. They indulged in a feast of exquisite delicacies: fish, meat, goat cheese, black olives, and stone-baked cornbread from the outdoor open fire. Over a period of weeks, the children had prepared the eggs, soaking the boiled eggs in seaweed beetroot, onion leaves, blueberries and grape juice, wrapped them in grapes and fig leaves, gifting the Easter Eggs to villagers and newlywed couples."

"How come kids got no chocolate eggs?" Donata asked.

"Well, my child, it may be difficult for you to grasp, seeing you live in a city where life is far more affluent, but here in the village, such comforts are unavailable to your grandparents. Yet, despite their lack of wealth, the villagers find happiness in Easter. It's a festive time for all the children, with celebrations that last into the night."

Pavica took a moment to reflect and shared that Easter signifies the arrival of spring, a season that brings new hope and opportunities for growth and renewal. "Even some stubborn individuals reconcile broken relationships and settle lingering disputes during this time."

Pavica smiled as she looked around at the children's faces; they were excited to hear the end of her story. "The matchmaking that occurred on Easter Sunday was the primary purpose of the celebrations for the young people," she told them. "It was the birth of new hope and love. Love among young lovers was born."

When Milena, Venka, and Donata started yawing, Pavica turned around and snapped, "Donata, stop mucking around; pay attention. This story concerns you the most." Then she went on.

"On Easter Sunday, the matchmaking occurred, and young people declared their love for one another. Young couples dressed in traditional costume, sang old folk songs and danced in a circle together to impress potential suitors, and eligible men chose their sweethearts for dancing. The priest then blessed the young lovers, and engaged couples no longer required a chaperone.

"It was on one such special occasion that I met my husband. It was love at first sight. Father Mateo approved and blessed our courtship, most probably because Josip owned the truck and fishing boat the church used."

She smiled. "I remember it as if it were yesterday. I spent the entire night dancing with my beloved Josip. He was my only love, and we were married until death did us part." She smiled more subtly, remembering the sweet love she had experienced with her husband, then adjusted her pillow, put her feet under the blanket, and lifted her mug of sweet wine. Sipping it slowly to soothe her pain, she wiped her eyes, trying to eradicate a few tears.

Pavica forced those sad thoughts away and instead shared happy stories with children, which kept her feeling joyful and youthful. She sipped her wine again and continued.

"The villagers gathered around the enormous bonfire at night, roasted a pig on a spit and drank the best vintage red wine. Young lovers listened to the harmonica playing in tune with the waves of the sea, which gently bounced a few small boats against the wooden jetty. The tapping in the distance sounded like nature's best drums.

"On that Easter celebration, my brother was the village celebrity. Young women wanted to touch his robes for luck and asked for his blessings.

"I was so proud of my brother, Andrija. He was indeed Jesus on that day."

Pavica yawned and, lifting her hands, prayed and crossed herself; she herself was ready to sleep. "Tomorrow, I'll have to rise before dawn. It is best to harvest red grapes early in the morning while it's still cool, which helps to make good vintage wine. After working in the fields, some women will pack fruit and vegetables to sell at the market. We will use the parish's old truck to transport grapes to Maraska Vinery in Zadar. It will be a long day, and I must get a good night's sleep," she whispered now as most of the children were already fast asleep.

As one girl in the group stretched and yawned, she inquired, "Did Andrija become the next parish priest, or did he fall in love, marry, and live happily ever after?"

"It is best to leave that story for another time. It is getting very late, and I must get up before dawn."

Pavica quieted the children and tucked them in for the night. She draped blankets over them and lay down beside them. Sleeping in her courtyard, enveloped by a woollen blanket beneath the stars on a warm summer night, with a hint of sea breeze blowing over them, contributed to the magical experience the children cherished. The crackling fire and the stars above produced a hypnotic effect, lulling the children to sleep, where they dreamt peacefully.

Pavica gazed at them and their innocence. They still believed in fairy tales, but she knew real-life stories rarely ended happily. Children shouldn't be forced to grow up too quickly, so she'd decided to keep some mature stories to herself. Pavica lay still, the crisp air and the gentle breeze fueling the fire's crackle. It was an ideal night for gazing at the celestial bodies that lit up the heavens.

Catching the sight of a shooting star, she closed her eyes as the moon slipped behind a cloud, wishing for sleep to come. But Pavica couldn't sleep, her memories surging her back to the days before World War II. It all began to unravel after the Easter Festivities.

Chapter 2

A Prosciutto for a Bride

When the Easter festival started to wind down, Andrija sat among the village elders, observing young couples holding hands and whispering sweet nothings to each other. He dearly wished to have what these young lovers had.

To distract himself from his melancholy thoughts, he stood up and began stacking chairs that needed to be stored in the parish hall then, lowering his head to conceal his tears, he wandered down to the beach. There, he watched silhouetted children playing happily with pebbles, which helped clear his mind and soothe his lonely heart. Being away from the old priest relieved him, as he feared the priest might discover his innermost secret.

He leapt when Pavica tapped him on the shoulder and asked him to assist her in carrying a few boxes of plates and cutlery back to her house. Andrija nodded, seeking an escape from the crowds. Returning to the village and picking up the boxes, he walked with his sister back to her home where he lit the wick of the kerosene lamp on the table, filling Pavica's modest kitchen with a warm glow.

The spring nights were still cool, so Pavica added another massive log to the fire to warm the house and bedroom where her two young daughters slept. She placed a large iron pot over the flames to warm up some of the remaining mulled wine. The cloves, honey, and cinnamon aroma soon soothed Andrija's emotional pain and calmed his nerves.

They sat together at the corner table, Andrija sipping mulled wine from a big clay cup that warmed his hands, the cup held close to his face hiding his feelings from his sister. But Pavica sensed her brother's hesitation and, after refilling their cups, moved closer and offered words of comfort. Andrija took a large gulp of his wine, his cheeks flushing as he leaned his head on his sister's shoulder and poured out his secret longings in hushed tones so as not to disturb Pavica's twin daughters sleeping in the adjacent room.

"Listen to me," Pavica said, gently holding his hands. "The old priest will never approve a marriage arrangement with any of the local girls. No girl would want to marry a priest-in-waiting, as it would be seen as a sinful act. Your chances of finding a girl from a nearby village are also impossible."

"I know that. That is why I will never find true happiness." Andrija lowered his head again and wiped away his tears. "I want to be as happy as you and Josip … and I want a family and a son to continue my line. I've been dreaming about what it would be like to experience the magic of love," Andrija said.

Burying his face in his sister's embrace, he sobbed as she caressed his dark, wavy hair. Then she lifted his head and looked into his eyes. "Oh, my poor brother, do not despair. I will help you, but it will be risky."

"What do you mean … risky?" Andrija asked.

Pavica then leant forward and also spoke in whispers. "You may find a girl on the other side of the bay, across the Adriatic Sea. This will be a courageous step, and you must think about this seriously."

"I understand your concerns, Pavica, but I do not want to become a priest! I desire to be married to a woman instead of the church."

"Do not lose hope then, brother. During our fishing trip last year along the Adriatic Coast, we met a family of sheep farmers. They had two daughters and hailed from the village of Sibuljna in the Velebit Mountains, close to Starigrad. Who knows, these two girls could still be free and not promised to anybody for marriage. If lucky, you may find what you are looking for, and God willing, all your dreams will come true."

She glanced at her brother, his smiling face reassuring her she was doing the right thing. "This will be your last chance to face your destiny, but it has to be now or never."

Andrija's brown eyes lit up like sparkling diamonds. He smiled widely, exposing his pearly white teeth. "I don't have to think about it. I will do anything to be happy like you and Josip. Please help me do this."

"Okay then, but we must move fast. There is no time to waste."

"Why, such urgency?" Andrija frowned.

"Last month, when Josip played bocce at the local trattoria, he overheard Father Mateo boasting that he would relinquish more parish responsibilities to you. On Christmas Day, he will announce to the church congregation that, when ordained, you will be our next parish priest. That is why we have no time to waste. After harvesting, we will go fishing and take a few cases of grapes to the Starigrad markets again. This will be our last fishing trip across the bay this year, and you will come along."

Andrija's heart raced with excitement and he leapt up and hugged Pavica tightly. "I want to be married and responsible for my life. I don't want my parents or the old priest to determine my future. Only God can choose my destiny."

"Okay then. It is settled. I will say nothing to my husband about this." She chuckled. "After a few drinks, Josip will spill all our secrets." Her mind ran with possibilities of how this would work. "On our next fishing expedition," she finally said, "you will come along in an official capacity."

"What do you mean?" Andrija asked, confused.

"Well, last year, when Father Mateo came with us on a fishing trip to bless the day's catch, the sea was rough with giant waves. Sometimes, the sea across the bay gets wild, and the poor old priest became seasick and green like seaweed, vomiting his lungs out and spending most of the time below deck." Pavica laughed.

"I am sure that if you volunteer to bless the fishing expedition instead of him, Father Mateo wouldn't object. That would be the perfect excuse, and nobody will suspect anything."

Pavica looked at her brother, waiting for him to comment, but seeing his determination was all she needed.

"Okay, I agree with you. I am sure God will forgive my sins," Andrija enthusiastically said.

"But listen well, my brother … your biggest obstacle is that these two prospects, who may or may not be available, come from a Serbian Orthodox family. We both know the ancestral hatred between Croats and Serbs – it has lasted as far back as the Ottoman Empire. Centuries of hatred and animosity continue from one generation to another. It will never end. Choosing a bride from a Serbian Orthodox family will be perceived by the church as the greatest violation. I just hope God will forgive my sins for helping you." Pavica crossed herself and continued to warn her brother. "You must be prepared for the backlash that will come your way. But once going down this path, there is no backing out."

"I am not worried, Pavica. God almighty is merciful."

"Yes, dear brother, that may be so but don't expect the same understanding from our parents. They invested and sacrificed so much for you to become the first family priest. They will probably disown you for betraying their faith in you, especially our mother; she will never forgive or forget!" Pavica could see it. "All hell will break loose. This is a potential disaster in the making."

Andrija lifted his hands, praying as if he was preaching to the faithful. "There is only one God, and he doesn't discriminate against any religion. And neither should we," he tried to convince himself. "I am ready for the backlash."

"Oh, my poor brother, you are so naïve. Father Mateo and our parents won't be as forgiving."

‽

As Pavica predicted, Father Mateo permitted Andrija to join the fishing expedition a few months later. He preferred to stay in his warm bed rather than experience Yugo Bura, a local name for the southern winds that were sometimes as strong as a hurricane.

Andrija assisted in loading Josep's boat with grape crates after the harvest, and the fishing trip proceeded as planned. The sailing was smooth on that particular day as they crossed the bay, the Adriatic Sea extremely calm, with only a gentle sea breeze that locals call the 'Maestral'.

As they were about to disembark at the wooden jetty below the mountain, Pavica decided to keep Josip in the dark until the matchmaking deed was done. She knew he would disapprove, so she suggested that, after he dropped the cases of grapes at the market in Starigrad, he should sail further into the deeper blue waters of the Adriatic Coast, where octopus, squid, and blue herrings were plentiful. He would return with his boat and pick them up before dusk.

After an excruciating walk on the steep rocky road, Pavica and Andrija eventually spotted a small house with a straw roof hidden amongst olive trees deep in the mountains. Before approaching the small dwelling, they sat on the rocky fence under an olive tree and rested briefly to cool off.

When they entered the front garden, they noticed a massive grinding stone in the middle of the yard. On it, villagers ground olives, corn, and wheat to sustain themselves during the winter months. The rest of the yard had olive trees, dark blue plums, corn, and vegetable patches on the sides.

Pavica stopped and confronted her brother, tightly gripping her fists and warning him through clenched teeth. "Now, you had better listen well," she warned him. "This is it. There is no turning back. When you step into this home, it will be a point of no return."

"I understand what you are telling me, but I am ready. God willing, this is my last chance to find a wife, and God is merciful," Andrija said.

"Yes, but don't expect miracles. You had better remember that the God we worship is biased, and I am sure he is Catholic, too." Pavica managed a slight smile. "Our village elders will resent your bride. They will blame her for taking you away from the church. A girl from a Serbian family will be perceived as impure and unworthy of joining our Catholic flock. Are you prepared to put your future bride through that?"

"I believe God will protect my wife," Andrija responded with conviction.

Pavica looked at her brother and responded sharply. "It is not God's job to protect your wife. That will be your job."

They entered the modest peasant dwelling, the kitchen pitch black, the ceilings scorched from the smoke of the open fire. The cement floor was covered with worn-out mats, and the adjoining room's floor was scattered with straw and dry corn leaves, where the domestic animals sheltered from the blustering wind from the mountain.

Pavica brought fresh fish, sardines, octopus, crabs, and a loaf of cornbread as a sign of a welcoming friendship. She recognised Slavka, the plump, short woman sitting by the stove, as they had met the previous year in the Starigrad markets. Slavka wore a worn-out jumper with a few holes in the elbows, a black scarf, and a few grey hairs on her forehead.

A tall man with bushy black hair stood beside a small table closer to the stove. He curled his dark moustache around his finger and introduced himself as Ilija, the girls' father. He firmly shook Andrija's hand and pulled out two wooden chairs.

The tense atmosphere in the room eased once Pavica explained the reason for their visit. Ilija removed his pipe and poured a glass of homemade Slivovitz, a brandy made from plums. Slavka rose and put a tablecloth on the table to cover up the scorched wooden edges from Ilija pipe. Then she lit a kerosene lamp, placed on the table clay plates, cups and a jug of fresh water she had fetched from the mountain stream that morning. Then she added a plate of dried figs, cornbread, and slices of goat cheese before grinding coffee beans to make a pot of Turkish coffee. The aroma of freshly roasted coffee beans filled the small kitchen as the guests began discussing matchmaking arrangements.

Both women kept quiet, as getting involved in the matchmaking business was not a woman's job. Instead, they occupied themselves with looking into the bottom of the coffee cups to read their fortune.

Andrija offered a Prosciutto as a gift in exchange for one of Ilija's daughters' hand in marriage. Ilija was pleased with the offer and poured another glass of Slivovitz to celebrate the special occasion. He then called his daughters into the room and encouraged them to introduce themselves to the prospective groom, his harsh, robust voice echoing around the kitchen.

He's displaying his daughters like sheep to the market, Andrija thought harshly.

The sisters entered the room holding hands. Both appeared to be in their late teens. Their sunburned faces were framed by long, dark brown, plaited hair. They were dressed in oversized homemade black dresses and worn-out aprons that hung on their bodies like soiled rags.

"Well, Andrija, what do you think of my girls?" Ilija asked.

One girl smiled, showing strong white teeth, while the other put her head down, not wanting to have any eye contact.

Andrija turned to Pavica and whispered," I prefer the one on the left; she has a friendly smile."

Ilija must have overheard and replied with conviction, "My eldest daughter, Angela, is no longer available; she has been betrothed to a respectable Serbian family, and we have already received a young ram as part of her dowry. Angela will wed and relocate to her husband's nearby village in a few weeks. We require a robust man to assist with our sheep. As I age, mountain life becomes more challenging, but we have little choice. Our farmland is barren and yields little, forcing us to depend on our goats and sheep for sustenance."

Our youngest daughter, Smiljana, has yet to be married. She is pretty and will make an excellent match for someone like you. I've heard that your Prosciutto is a valued delicacy. This is a good offer for my youngest daughter Smiljana."

Ilija then poured another glass, leant close to Andrija, and spoke quietly. "I think it's best if we keep this quiet because I don't want our neighbours to spread rumours that I am negotiating a marriage with a Catholic family from the other side of the bay. However, I understand that you made a long trip to get here, and it would be unfair to let you go home empty-handed."

Ilija stood up and packed his pipe, filling the small room with tobacco aroma. He stroked his moustache and wiped his greasy chin on his torn shirt, revealing his tobacco-stained, yellow teeth. "Get over here, Smiljana," he called to his daughter. "Don't be shy. You will never find a better husband than

Andrija. His family owns a vineyard and some fertile farming land. Now move closer and turn around," he shouted at her.

Smiljana moved slowly, her head bowed, her cheeks flushed, and her long, dark braids veiling her face. Ilija rose suddenly and swept his daughter's hair away from her face. His voice rose as though he was on the verge of bellowing; he then seized Smiljana's hand, twisted her wrist to unfurl her clenched fist, revealing her absent fingers.

"Look, there's nothing to hide. Please ignore Smiljana's hand; she was born like that. When she was born, the umbilical cord had wrapped around her fingers, and the village midwives had to cut off two of her fingers. However, it wasn't all for nothing; our cat had a good meal that day," Ilija said, laughing at his crude joke.

Nobody else found it amusing. Pavica stayed quiet and sat by the stove with Slavka, chewing cornbread with lard and anchovies. Both women remained silent as if mute and deaf, afraid to provoke further negative comments from Ilija.

"My wife Slavka and I are thankful that the umbilical cord wasn't wrapped around our daughter's neck. If it had been, Smiljana might not have made it. Sadly, we suffered a tragic loss with our newborn son that way, leaving us with two daughters. Sons are vital in helping families with their workload during tough times. Yet, even God has no mercy for us poor folk."

Ilija turned to look at his wife, but when Slavka remained silent, he muttered a string of offensive blasphemies related to God, his expression revealing the disappointment of that past event. Then he returned to promoting his daughter's best qualities. "There is no need to fret. Smiljana is still skilled at knitting and adept with a spinning wheel. She can shear sheep as fast and effective as any man.

Slavka then rose and walked to a wooden chest, and brought back some of her daughter's handcrafted items, showing a woollen blanket her daughter had woven from unprocessed sheep's wool last winter.

"Smiljana knitted the jumper I am wearing now, and she can cook a good mutton stew," Slavka said proudly, smiling at her daughter.

Ilija seemed eager to finish the matchmaking business and gestured towards Smiljana's robust physique. "Just look at her hips. Smiljana will give you many sons." He winked at Andrija as he poured himself another glass. "Let us have another drink. My Slivovitz is the best. I distilled it last year from the blue plums in our backyard. Well, Andrija, have you decided? I don't have all day. I must return to the mountain to gather my sheep or the wolves will have them for dinner." Ilija had suddenly become irritable and was now visibly drunk.

"Yes, I will be happy to marry your daughter. I ask your permission to make Smiljana my wife."

Ilija clapped his hands in excitement, offered his handshake, and poured more Slivovitz to celebrate the successful matchmaking deal.

Andrija then moved closer to Smiljana, worried about not startling his prospective bride-to-be. He gently lifted her hand, which she'd tried hiding from him, and placed it against his face. "Don't worry, Smiljana. I like you just as you are," Andrija said, nervously looking at Ilija, lest the man fire off another of his crude, hurtful responses.

Ilija became more agitated. "Move yourself, girl. Get packing, and don't waste time. It is getting late, and the weather may soon turn nasty. Their boat is leaving soon. No other will come this year if you miss the boat today."

"Great! The deal is sealed then. A Prosciutto for your bride and another for your firstborn son," Ilija said, shaking Andrija's hand and giving him a bottle of his homemade Slivovitz to take home. "This is my wedding present. It will keep you warm on your journey home, and make the sea look less menacing. I always take a bottle up to the mountain where the winds can freeze your bones," Ilija said.

"I promise to take good care of your daughter. On our next fishing trip, you will get the best leg of Prosciutto for Smiljana's hand," Andrija promised.

Ilija then hurried to the mountain to gather the sheep. Before he left, he instructed Slavka and Angela to go to the jetty and bring back some more sardines for dinner.

Slavka's distress at losing her daughter was obvious. Her husband, Ilija, spent summers in the mountains, and winters at home drinking excessively. As she bid her a tearful farewell, Slavka's heart weighed heavy with the realisation that she would never see her daughter again. The animosity between Serbs and Croats was as profound as the depths of the Adriatic Sea.

While Pavica's heart overflowed with joy at her brother's happiness, the distress on Slavka's face was heartbreaking.

Andrija waved farewell and strolled to the wooden jetty with his bride-to-be. His heart thumped loudly as though it might burst from his chest. He smiled, convinced that this was indeed a sign of love.

The boat glided across the bay in the late afternoon that day. Smiljana wept, waving her hand high above her head until her small home nestled among the olive groves vanished from view. At seventeen, she was embarking on a journey across the Adriatic Sea to a new world with her betrothed, knowing she would never return to her homeland.

Chapter 3

The Storm that Broke the Angel's Wing

Before Andrija and Smiljana's marriage could take place, Smiljana had to give up her Orthodox faith, get baptised, and convert to Catholicism. This required her to attend daily scripture classes with Father Anton in the nearby town of Razanac. During this time, she lived with the nuns on the parish grounds, wholly cut off from the outside world.

While she was gone, Andrija renovated a previously worn-out stone building that Pavica and Josip used as a smoking room. Having learned his construction skills by assisting with other villagers' homes, he now led the transformation of the smoking room into a cozy family abode. With the help of neighbours, Andrija added an upper floor with a terrace.

After the construction was completed, Andrija poured cement into the communal courtyard that he shared with his sister Pavica and a few adjoining neighbours and left his handprints in the wet cement. He planted a fig tree at the centre of the courtyard, just above the fresh stream of water, so the robust fig tree roots would grow strong, symbolising the family life they would share together.

After Smiljana's official conversion and First Holy Communion, she was welcomed into the Catholic Church, and their marriage was officiated in late autumn of 1937.

Smiljana faced difficulties settling in her new village, as she didn't feel welcomed by her immediate family. They blamed her for taking Andrija away from the priesthood. However, Andrija stood by her side and assured her that God would help them through these challenging times, as he had fallen deeply in love with his wife.

The following year, Smiljana gave birth to their first daughter, Anka, and their second daughter, Mara, a year later.

The religious tension between Serbs and Croats intensified during the end of the Second World War, straining their relationship. Smiljana gave birth to a daughter named Draga, leaving Andrija with an unfulfilled desire for a son.

ʘ

Smiljana felt deep disappointment and sorrow when she realised her new family didn't accept her. Despite her attempts to assimilate and win over her mother-in-law, Dora's insensitivity and malice remained unyielding. Dora's biting and spiteful words continually demeaned Smiljana, exposing her to relentless criticism and rejection.

Dora's reputation within the village was notorious, with the women avoiding conflicts with her. One churchgoer even remarked, "Where Dora spits, the grass will never grow again. Her vindictive nature and malicious gossip are deadly enough to kill a snake."

Ruling the household with an iron fist, Dora hypocritically clutched the Bible in one hand while conspiring with the Devil himself in the other. She adamantly blamed Smiljana for 'stealing' her son away from the priesthood, even praying for his salvation despite his marriage to a girl from the 'enemy camp'.

Bozidar, Dora's husband, knew better than to argue with her and realised it was pointless to challenge her. Instead, he sought solace in relaxation, sipping red wine and smoking his pipe.

Under the comforting shade of the grapevines, all his worries melted away as he dozed off.

Andrija's younger brother, Mirko, lived in the city, but visited their village during harvest time and religious celebrations. The brothers enjoyed themselves at the local trattoria, drinking and playing bocce. However, during family events, Mirko would often become tipsy and tell inappropriate jokes that insulted the religious beliefs of Smiljana's family.

Andrija's sister, Nevenka, had no children and also held a grudge against Smiljana for taking her brother away from the priesthood. She only returned to the village during Easter and Christmas, her long absences relieving Smiljana from her passive emotional abuse.

Smiljana tried to please her new family, but the more she tried the more complex the situation became. Eventually, she reached a point where she no longer made any attempts or cared about being accepted by them. She didn't belong anywhere anymore.

Consumed by guilt, Andrija held himself accountable for his family's problems. While he loved his wife and daughters deeply, he often prioritised the needs and expectations of others over his own family. In particular, he was terrified of his mother's disapproval, which left him feeling powerless to defend Smiljana against the verbal and emotional abuse she was subjected to.

After the old priest Mateo passed away, Father Anton from Razanac was appointed as the new village priest. Smiljana hoped Father Anton, who knew her and had taught her scriptures, would be more compassionate. However, she found him to be even more uncompromising than his predecessor. Father Anton strongly believed in preserving the purity of blood through the prohibition of mixed marriages. He preached such unions should be cursed on Earth and in the heavens. This only deepened Smiljana's sense of isolation and not belonging.

Despite her efforts, the family and the villagers never truly accepted her as an equal. She felt like an outcast, a *persona non grata*.

Despite witnessing her family's unjust and cruel behaviour, Pavica empathised with Smiljana's plight, yet felt powerless to enact change. At Sunday mass, she often distanced herself discreetly as she relied on the church for employment, and for the church scholarships for her twin daughters – their education was her highest priority. She privately supported Smiljana and would protect her daughters from harmful gossip. The families shared a common courtyard and relied on each other for various tasks, such as planting crops, gathering firewood, and fetching water from the nearby spring, all with the help of their hardworking and trusting donkey, Sule.

In the village, men fished while women baked bread and preserved food for the winter. As the sun went down, the shared courtyard was filled with various activities. Children played, ran around, and laughed. Men gathered to clean fish, enjoy wine, and sing folk songs. After dinner, the children would gather beneath the shelter of grapevine canopies and listen with rapt attention to Aunt Pavica's enchanting stories.

Andrija and Smiljana treasured their time together, finding comfort after a day's toil. They planned to produce and sell wine. At night, atop their rooftop terrace, affectionately called their 'Tower,' they gazed over the valley dotted with olive and fig trees and watched the grand sunset drape the coastline in vibrant golden tones, reflecting off the expansive azure Adriatic Sea.

ʘ

Post-World War II, the community and church demanded that women have more children, especially sons. Daughters were undesirable, as a dowry had to be paid. Families were impoverished, and women were blamed for giving birth to girls. During the occupation of much of Europe by Nazi Germany, Smiljana's Serbian ancestry was blamed for her lack of male offspring, exacerbating hostilities and conflicts.

Smiljana disagreed with this view. She believed that God was too busy helping the victims of war and easing poverty to feed children, including their own. She didn't want to bring more children into poverty – villagers had to work exceptionally hard to improve their lives. Andrija tended to his vineyard and livestock, while Smiljana looked after the children, handled domestic chores, laboured in the fields, grew vegetables, and preserved dried foods for the winter. She also joined the village women on trips to the Zadar markets, selling fresh produce to city folks.

During cooler months, Andrija worked as a contract builder in the city, returning home on weekends, leaving Smiljana to tend to all the home duties. Andrija wanted a son and urged his wife to pray that God would grant them one. Smiljana remembered her mother's words before her departure to marry Andrija. 'The wife's role is to warm her husband's bed, satisfy his manly desires, and produce healthy sons. Sons are highly valued.'

Eventually, after suffering a few miscarriages, Smiljana fulfilled her husband's desires and, after the war, gave birth to a son. Andrija was overjoyed, but sadly, their happiness was short-lived as their only son, Kuzma, died young from an undiagnosed illness. Despite another miscarriage and a stillborn son, Smiljana remained optimistic, believing that God would listen to her prayers, and, with her subsequent pregnancy, was confident she would have another son. But, instead, she gave birth to a daughter named Vera.

Time went on.

Smiljana became increasingly tired of being pregnant and having no chance to rest after giving birth. Selling fresh produce at Zadar markets while carrying her newborn strapped to her back was exhausting. She believed that God favoured devout Catholic mothers. She was a good wife and a devoted mother, and she gave birth to healthy daughters, but that was not valued as much. However, over time, Smiljana stopped caring about superstitious and malicious gossip. She adored her girls and believed that women held the family together.

While sitting on the roof terrace one night, Smiljana said to Andrija, "Let's stop chasing the elusive dream of having a son. We should grow more grapes to make some profit and educate our daughters." She wanted her girls to grow up as strong as steel and gentle as feathers.

Ș

With the dawn of a new decade, the early 1950s brought hope for prosperity and a fresh start. The promise of long-term peace and stability rekindled people's enthusiasm for success in villages and towns. During winter, Andrija worked in the city but longed to be with his wife and children. He looked forward to returning home on the weekends to be with his family. Once he was home and his girls were tucked in bed, he loved snuggling up with his beloved wife on a chilly winter's night. After all these years of marriage, Andrija still had an insatiable sexual appetite for her. However, without contraceptives, that desire resulted in yet another pregnancy. As much as they prayed for a son, another daughter was born. Smiljana named her Donata, after the St Donat church in Zadar. She teased her husband, saying, "It is not just that all the saints are named after a man … women who give life, carry the burden of raising children are not seem worthy to be called saints." She hoped that one day God would grant women sainthood, that they rightfully deserved to have.

Smiljana was unaware that, eventually, Donata's name would be shortened to Donna, a name of significance, meaning 'woman'. Surely, that would have put a smile on her face.

 CR

Approaching her forties, Smiljana never intended to get pregnant again. It was tough for her to work in the fields while carrying her newborn daughter on her back. However, upon Andrija's return, his sexual desire for his wife resulted in yet another unintended pregnancy. In the village, it was a common practice for midwives to terminate unwanted pregnancies; the church often turned a blind eye to this, especially when women gave birth to many daughters but no sons.

Midwives used traditional herbal remedies to end these pregnancies. They brewed teas with oleander and Pelin, a bitter herb found in fields. They would add rose petals and honey to make the unpleasant potion palatable. However, the potion was very potent and could be potentially lethal.

Desperate women chose desperate measures. Consuming such an awful concoction would make most expectant mothers feel incredibly sick, but it helped to bring on a miscarriage or stillbirth. If that poisonous remedy didn't produce the desired result, then old women acting as midwives would use knitting needles to poke and prod into the mother's womb to induce a miscarriage. For many women, such methods of abortion, when in the advanced stages of pregnancy often result in infection and severe bleeding. Without hospital intervention, many mothers died prematurely. Smiljana terminated her last unwanted pregnancy through this abortion method, which resulted in a positive outcome. She was sick for a few weeks, but that was all, so she decided to do it again.

Smiljana had faith in God, believing He would not take a mother away from her daughters. Unfortunately, this time, she wasn't so lucky, and the failed abortion had a tragic outcome. Superstitious village people believed Smiljana brought this upon herself. Removing an unwanted pregnancy was a mortal sin, and God had punished her.

As Smiljana lay in bed bleeding, the village women, ignorant of medical knowledge, kept putting hot bricks on her feet to keep her warm, but that only increased the bleeding. Abandoned by God, Smiljana lay motionless, bleeding to death.

Surrounded by her daughters, the mother felt her youngest child, Donna, clinging tightly to her bosoms as if her life depended on it. She held her baby close, finding solace in her presence, waiting for her husband to arrive. With her last breath, she placed Donata in her father's arms, and passed away peacefully.

Her untimely passing came before the last rites could be administered. Father Anton decided to maintain a low-key burial service, conducted without an obituary or the church's blessings for her soul's eternal salvation. Tragically, Smiljana found neither solace on earth nor in heaven.

The funeral procession was subdued. Andrija cradled Donata in his arms as the older daughters, clutching bunches of wildflowers gathered from the fields, followed in quiet solemnity. Only a handful of family members and villagers attended. Those who were absent attributed their non-attendance to the severe winter conditions. Smiljana relatives from across the bay were not informed, but even if they had been notified, they wouldn't attend.

Soon after, the mourners quietly dispersed and returned to their homes. Two aged gravediggers from the village interred Smiljana in an unmarked grave beside the unnamed soldiers of World War II.

Consumed by grief, Andrija could find no solace. He felt anger towards what he perceived as God's forsaking of his wife. Nevertheless, amidst his anguish, he recognised the necessity to return to the city to provide for his daughters.

Pavica comforted and supported her brother in these trying times and helped to run family farm.

Fortunately, some of Smiljana' daughters were much older and, therefore, were self-sufficient. Anka, the eldest, soon married a village fisherman, and she vowed to care for Donata until a suitable home could be found for her. A few months after the passing of his beloved wife, Andrija relocated to the northern part of Croatia. The tourism industry started to develop, and demand to build hotels and resorts was booming. Once he secured a new job and established himself, he intended to return for Donata, his youngest child and bring her to live with him in the new city.

☙

The winter marked by Smiljana's passing was characterised by fierce weather. Icy winds from the south lowered sombre clouds over the hill, enveloping the church and surrounding areas. Thunder and lightning assaulted the village with its celestial fury. Bolts of lightning electrified the church grounds and made the earth quiver.

The statue of the angel, carved from pristine white limestone, was hit by lightning; it toppled and one of its wings was broken. When spring arrived and the winter frost dissipated, Pavica and Anka visited the cemetery behind the small church to adorn a grave with fresh flowers. Unable to find Smiljana's resting place, they lit a candle and offered prayers for her eternal peace at an unnamed grave.

Smiljana had lived in a turbulent era and departed as though she had never existed. However, Aunt Pavica believed that

Smiljana's memory would be shared from generation to generation by telling stories and that her spirit would live on forever.

The Guardian Angel statue continued to watch over the church entrance, one wing reaching towards the sky, while the other remained irreparably damaged, a poignant reminder to the villagers of Smiljana's broken wings.

Chapter 4

Veritas Vineyard

When Smiljana died, Andrija had no time to grieve. He moved to a more affluent part of Croatia to seek permanent employment. In the early fifties, the Istria region started to develop its tourism industry, resulting in an increased demand for master builders.

Andrija secured a stable job in construction and settled in Kastav, a small town above Opatija, a bustling tourist city frequented by visitors from neighbouring Italy. This location seemed ideal for starting his new life. His financial situation improved, allowing him to send money to his eldest daughter, Anka, who cared for his youngest child, Donata.

Still grieving the loss of his true love, which caused him profound sorrow, Andrija knew he had to be practical and move on with his life. While visiting some local vineyards, he was impressed by the fertile land of the Istria region, which was ideal for growing wine grapes. This was the perfect starting point for him to establish a new life and a vineyard.

Now in his late forties, Andrija searched for a new wife and a substitute mother for his youngest child. The women he encountered were captivated by his handsomeness – his dark brown hair, soft brown eyes, and well-defined cheekbones that highlighted his wide grin – and he did not hesitate to marry when the chance presented itself. Zorka was the perfect match, a devout Catholic dedicated to God and the church. Andrija saw marriage to her as a path to redemption in God's eyes. Moreover, Zorka was a wealthy widow without heirs, and possessed vast fertile land ideal for grape cultivation. Andrija valued diligence and resilience, and was a traditionalist like his forebears. A true farmer, he found unparalleled joy in nurturing seeds into bountiful harvests. To Andrija, land was more precious than gold, and the prospect of expanding his vineyard on such an expansive estate surpassed his greatest aspirations.

After the honeymoon period, Andrija returned to his village the following year. However, he did not stay long in Rtina because the visit evoked painful memories. His primary reason for returning was to bring Donata, his youngest child, back to his new home.

Andrija was grateful for Anka's assistance in caring for Donata. With his devoted sister Pavica's support, Vera was placed with relatives in Slavonia, while Mara and Draga were sponsored to work in Germany. Andrija felt that Anka, who had become the family matriarch, should inherit the farm, livestock, vineyard and the 'tower' family home that Andrija built.

∞

When she came to live with her stepmother, Donata was five years old, arriving just as the festive holiday season began. Her first Christmas was a wonder, filled with the joy of playing in the snow. A freshly cut pine tree adorned with colourful ornaments of various shapes was crowned by a golden angel whose wings glittered in the night. Under the tree, flickering candlelight glowed, softly illuminating the decorative, religious nativities of a humble stable with animals where Jesus was born.

On Christmas Eve, after the family returned home from midnight mass, Donata discovered presents beneath the tree: a bowl with dried fruits, figs, chestnuts, walnuts, chocolates, oranges, and bananas from faraway, exotic places. She had never experienced such heavenly flavours and could not resist the luscious sweets. It was as if she had entered a fantasy world, yet her gaze quickly shifted to a slender rod hidden behind the grand pine Christmas tree, a lengthy, ornamental silver whip with a silver bow.

Curiosity got the better of her, and she asked in surprise, "What is that big stick for?"

"Christmas gifts always come with a whip used only for naughty children. If you are good, I don't have to use it; otherwise, St Nicolas will bring you a golden stick next Christmas," her stepmother, Zorka, explained.

Donata's first year was idyllic. The house was spacious and warm. They entertained well-to-do relatives and guests from Trieste, Italy. She received gifts, fancy, colourful dresses, and wooden toys. For Easter, she got a massive chocolate egg and enjoyed the heavenly chocolate all weekend. Donata felt like a princess living in a fairy tale.

Her step-grandmother, Franka, cherished and pampered her with chocolate cookies and warm honeyed milk before sleep.

To the outside world and outsiders, Zorka seemed the perfect wife and affectionate stepmother and thrived in a tight-knit Catholic community. For Sunday mass, she dressed Donata in delicate Italian garments and adorned her wavy brown locks with a silk bow. She frequently reminded Donata how fortunate she was to live with her family. She explained that Donata's older sisters had different opportunities to leave their village's poverty.

Zorka encouraged Donata to express gratitude and appreciate the blessings she had been given. And all the neighbours told Donata how blessed she was to live with such a well-to-do and respected family. Indeed, Donata was fortunate to have a stable home but yearned for more time with her father. He was tirelessly working on establishing his new winery and, as a result, had very little free time. Andrija believed Donata needed shelter, food, and a Catholic education. He couldn't understand why she would want anything more.

However, what Donata needed the most was love. Her stepmother was cold and distant, never offering her affection or hugs, and her father was too busy with his vineyard to notice his little girl's needs.

Zorka, in her mid-forties, miraculously conceived and gave birth to a son, which Andrija considered a true miracle. Zorka, a devoted member of her church, believed her generous donation to the church paid off when she received this precious gift from God. Zorka refused to share the experience of motherhood with anyone else, as she cherished her son and every moment with him. Andrija now had an heir, Emil, which reignited his passion for the vineyard.

Donata suddenly became the second-favourite child in the family, and with her father preoccupied with his vineyard and now his son, Donata felt ignored and unimportant.

That same winter, Donata's step-grandmother Franka died, but this sudden shift in dynamics took a turn for the worse, leaving Donata feeling even more isolated and neglected. Zorka, now preoccupied with raising her son, demanded that Donata do more chores after school, including gathering wood, feeding the animals, cleaning the kitchen, doing the dishes, and washing clothes, mostly in cold water by hand.

Her father was too focused on his vineyard to notice her feelings of displacement. At night, Donata would weep silently, wishing her mother was still alive to ease her loneliness and pain. She had lost her mother and felt invisible to her father. Donata's sole companion was her puppy, who provided her with the unconditional love she craved. He slept at the bottom of her bed and gently licked away her tears when she cried. She felt so fortunate to have him, so she named him Lucky.

◌

Spending all his time pursuing his winemaking ambition in the cellar, trying to achieve his ambition as a reputable winemaker, Andrija neglected his wife's requests to complete the home renovations, which resulted in frequent arguments. When Zorka threatened to stop financing his vineyard, chaos erupted, and Andrija reluctantly put his vineyard on hold, and refocused on the renovations instead, but this only led to resentment and animosity in his household.

Donata was given no time to spend with friends, as sometimes she would come home late from school after playing with them.

Zorka believed disciplining her would teach her respect and disobedience, but Andrija grew frustrated with Zorka, causing disagreements when she demanded punishment. He pleaded with her to be more patient with Donata, reminding her that she was just a child who should be allowed to play with kids the same age.

After coming home from Sunday mass one day, Donata was told to look after her stepbrother Emil while Zorka and her church-going friend lounged on the veranda, sipping Turkish coffee and gossiping about neighbours. Suddenly, Emil started to choke on a chicken bone from the soup Donata fed him, sending Zorka into a panic. Overprotective of her son, she overreacted and furiously used the gold stick with the bow Donata had received as a Christmas present. She whipped Donata so hard her legs turned black and blue, after which she was promptly sent to bed with no supper.

Donata resented being stuck at home with all the work she had to do and no free time to play and she became more uncooperative and spiteful towards her stepmother. In an act of defiance, she purposely mixed whites with colours in hot water while hand-washing a linen tablecloth. As a result, the snow-white handcrafted napkins and Zorka's best tablecloth were stained.

Zorka's rage erupted, and once again she resorted to using the gold whip. This, however, was not as bad as her father's dreaded homemade rubber belt, which she feared the most. Once, he had kept hitting her all over her bare legs, and she kept twisting and turning to avoid another hit. That rubber belt made whooshing sounds like the giant black snake her dog Lucky had chased away last summer. Her bruised legs were left with checkered marks, resembling the black and white chessboard she played on in the schoolyard.

Donata would not grant her stepmother the satisfaction of witnessing her tears. She covered her mouth firmly and balled her fists, resolving to suppress any sound that might slip through her teeth. This tactic dulled the sharp intake of breath from the pain. With every new onslaught, Donata mastered the art of burying the pain within herself, forbidding the tears to fall. Her tears were the only possession that was truly hers. She vowed to conceal her suffering and tears from everyone, particularly her stepmother. Zorka would never be privy to her tears, neither then, nor at any time in the future.

◌

On a few special occasions, when Andrija was cheerful, he occasionally took Donata to the stables to feed the animals. They would then spend time together in his cool cellar to converse and bond.

Once, he inquired, "Donata, my dear, why do you misbehave? Can't you be kind to Zorka? If you pleased her, I wouldn't need to discipline you so severely."

"But, Dad, you don't understand, Zorka hates me."

"No, she doesn't. She is trying to be a good mother, and you must try harder to get along with her."

"Why did you have to marry Zorka? She is such a wicked woman."

"I have a new wife now. We live at her home, and she funds my winery. Let's squash some grapes, my child." Andrija picked up his daughter and placed her inside the oak barrel. He then began squashing red grapes with his bare feet while holding Donata's hand.

"This is how I used to dance with your mother. God bless her soul." Andrija stopped stomping the grapes for a moment before he spoke again. "Sadly, your mother died before her time."

"What happened to her? Why did she have to die?" Donata caught her father off guard with the question.

"Only God knows why he took your mother away from us. Sadly, sometimes, life doesn't turn out as planned. You are too young to understand right now, but one day you will."

"Why don't we have any photos of our mother?" Donata asked.

"In our small village, nobody could take photos. That was something that only happened in the city. Your mother was the most beautiful woman in the town, with chestnut hair, brown eyes, a bright smile, and a lively spirit, just like you.

"Smiljana was such a good wife and a loving mother. She loved all of her daughters, but she loved you the most. You were her last child, and she adored you."

"Where are all my sisters? How come I never met any of them?"

"That's enough talk for today. When you get older, you will understand much more. Talking about the past is pointless; we must look forward to a better future. Let's keep stomping the grapes; that's more fun. When we pick more grapes, we will have to do it again on the weekend," her father said.

When Donata was exhausted, Andrija lifted her in his arms and climbed out of the barrel. After washing their hands and feet, he kneeled before her, hugged her, and said, "Promise to be a good girl. Don't upset your mother or she will make my life miserable. Then she will start demanding that I belt you again. It hurts me deeply that I had to punish you."

"Zorka is not my mother. I hate her, but I will try to be nice to her."

"Zorka is busy, you should help her, then you two will get along better," her father said, hoping she would obey him.

Donata cherished being lifted onto her father's shoulders and sharing laughter. Those precious moments held a special place in her heart, and she yearned for them to last forever. Jumping and squashing grapes in the vast oak barrel provided an escape from her pain. As she looked at her stained legs, coloured with hues of blue, purple, and crimson from the grape harvest, stomping grapes barefoot seemed to mask the bruises from the beatings as if they had never happened. The happiness she felt while stomping grapes with her father made her forget all the pain.

"Okay, I promise to do more chores, but can I go to the village this summer holidays? I love spending time with Anka and Aunty Pavica."

"Yes, I will talk to Zorka; I am sure she wouldn't object to you spending a few weeks in Rtina."

Joyful, Donata jumped and hugged her father.

ʘʀ

The summer holiday in her quaint village was unforgettable. Swimming on the beach with her sister Anka and her two daughters, Venka and Milena, and sleeping under the stars at night while listening to Aunty Pavica's stories were the most memorable school holiday experiences. She longed to return during the winter school break but Zorka objected; she needed Donata to assist with the household and farming chores and look after Emil while Zorka attended church choir practices. Donata figured if she became more disobedient, Zorka might want to get rid of her and send her to live with Anka and Aunty Pavica. However, that plan failed, and the beatings became more frequent.

When Zorka started to sell fresh produce at the market, Donata's resentment towards her increased, as did her work harvesting fruit and vegetables. With time, her animosity deepened. Driven by her growing anger, Donata released the chickens from their coop one night, hoping they would fall prey to foxes. Tragically, this mischievous act had dire consequences. By early morning, Lucky, her faithful dog, was barking wildly, battling the foxes to protect a chicken. Despite his valiant struggle, Lucky was gravely injured and, a few hours later, passed away.

Andrija laid Lucky to rest in the vineyard, leaving Donata bereft and yearning to lie beside her cherished dog. Lucky had been her loyal and attentive friend, easing her solitude by gently licking her tears. Rather than blaming Zorka, she felt divine retribution for her misdeeds, which led to her dog's eternal departure. Donata saw Lucky's passing as a result of her vindictive behaviour. Shattered by the loss of her most fabulous soul companion, she wept incessantly, and, consumed by guilt, believed she deserved the beatings.

Immensely angry, Andrija shouted and struck her with a thick black belt mercilessly, prompting Zorka to intervene and stop him.

"You are such a wicked child. I wish you were never born. Look what you have done!" And he hit her again. "Promise me you will change, or I will hit you again," Andrija shouted again and again, but not a sound escaped Donata's lips, nor did a single tear fall. That night, her father beat her so fiercely that he nearly killed her, and she wished he had done so.

As usual, they sent her to bed without supper, and she curled up into a small ball, clutching her legs, which had turned purple from the beatings. She wanted to cry to ease her emotional pain and release the negative energy, but tears eluded her; they had soaked into the ground beside her beloved dog.

That night, she dreamed of stomping grapes with her father, and her legs were stained so purple that she couldn't wash it off. Afterwards, she played ball with her dog. When she climbed a big cherry tree to hide from Lucky, he barked annoyingly, wanting her to climb down and play with him.

❧

As time passed, Donata grew angrier and more rebellious. Instead of becoming more cooperative, she became more disobedient, and no longer cared about the consequences; she was determined the beatings would never crush her spirit.

At night, while in bed, she prayed to God to rescue her from her miserable existence. She wanted to go back to her village.

Yet God must have listened to her prayers, for one day her wish came true. At the beginning of the school holidays, her sister Anka, Aunty Pavica and a group of villagers came to Rijeka city markets to sell their latest grape harvest.

Donata pleaded with her father to allow her to return with them, eager to spend more summer holidays in her village. This time, Andrija found no need to persuade his wife to let Donata go. Zorka was more than willing to give Anka some money so that Donata could spend the school holidays with them. Indeed, she would have paid any price to ensure Donata was no longer around.

Ecstatic when they came to pick her up, Donata grabbed her

rucksack, sprinted down the road, and leapt onto the back of
the old rusty truck. She sat on the box filled with onions, garlic,
and tomatoes that her sister Anka and Auntie Pavica were
taking to sell at the city markets. She couldn't resist indulging in
a tomato, which was just as sweet as the morning's strawberries,
not bothering that she stained her linen t-shirt. As the old truck
sped away on the winding road, she glanced back, seeing Zorka
and her father waving goodbyes. Donata's only wish was never
to return to live with her wicked stepmother.

ʘ

From then on, Donata returned to her village every school
holiday. Andrija put Donata on the bus. He arranged with the
bus driver to drop her off at the post office, where Anka would
wait. The six-hour journey was uncomfortable and tiring, but
well worth it.

Donata's heart smiled, she was so happy. Spending the
summer holidays in her village, where she received
unconditional love, was all she wanted. Anka's two daughters,
Milena and Venka, shared the courtyard with Aunty Pavica. The
best part of the school holidays was when children gathered
around the bonfire, sitting together at night and watching the
bright stars above, listening to Aunty Pavica's stories, which
transported them to another world and another place.

But the summer holidays always ended, and she had to return
to the home she didn't love to attend school.

"Why can't I stay in the village with you? I am so happy
here." Donata squeezed between Anka and Pavica, hugging
them dearly.

"Oh no, my child, you belong in the city. You must return
to school and be educated, just like my girls. I miss them too,
but it is for the best," Anka explained.

Controlling her tears, Pavica reflected on Donata's tender age and the upcoming lessons she would learn about life's challenges and how to gain the strength to overcome them. But right now, she should embrace her childhood.

Just before leaving her village, Donata grabbed some breadcrumbs from the kitchen to sprinkle under the fig tree for her little dove and her chicks. She had fed her every morning, and that pretty bird was not frightened of her, even picking crumbs from her palm. Donata watched in amazement when her little dove started flapping her wings, then hopping around and jumping on one spot, turning around as if performing a pirouette. Donata gently caressed the dove's soft, silky feathers with her other hand, whispering to avoid startling the beautiful bird.

"I will miss you, my sweet little dove. Please wait for me. I'll return next summer, and you will dance for me again."

When her little dove extended her wings, Donata noticed one of them was damaged, or broken, as she struggled to fly back to feed her chicks and hide behind massive fig leaves right at the top of the tree; she had the best views.

Donata's only solace was that she would return to her village the following summer, and her little dove would dance for her again.

Chapter 5

The Cherry Tree

During her tedious bus journey, Donata couldn't help but yearn to be transported in a time machine back to her village; this is where she belonged and where she had unconditional love.

Listening to the monotonous sound of the bus wheels and feeling the sun's warmth on her face, she drifted off to sleep. She was startled awake when the bus driver announced their arrival in the city. She spotted her father standing at the bus stop, smiling and waving.

☙

Zorka was not pleased to have Donata back. While she was away, Zorka's relationship with Andrija had improved, so she started planning to remove Donata from her home permanently. Andrija, however, did not accept the plan. He wanted Donata to study in the city, so sending Donata back to the village was out of the question.

While the tug of war continued between them, Donata was lonely; she didn't have many friends outside of school hours, and was nothing more than a servant in her home. She decided to run away. One day, when Donata had finished ironing the bed sheets and was putting them in the wardrobe, she noticed where Zorka hid her money. When Zorka left the room, Donata slipped one hundred dinars out from between the layers of sheets and she didn't feel an ounce of guilt for taking it. After all, she had done most of the household work and deserved pocket money as a reward.

However, she didn't realise it was the highest denomination of paper money. When she went to the shop, the shop owner, who knew the family, asked her, "Why are you buying so much?"

Donata's responded promptly, "I will return to my village next week. My sister Anka and my aunt Pavica are poor and have never tasted tropical fruits, oranges, grapefruits or bananas. My Aunt Pavica told me they never had chocolate for Easter. So, I plan to buy some chocolates for them, which will make them so happy."

Because Donata frequently went grocery shopping, the shopkeeper believed her and did not question her further. With the remaining money, Donata intended to buy a bus ticket and return to her village, never to return to this depressing life.

Donna's deception came to light when the bus driver informed her father. At ten years old, Donata couldn't buy a bus ticket without her parents' permission. She received another beating and was sent to bed without supper.

From then on, Zorka kept her money hidden elsewhere. She spread rumours around the neighbourhood that Donata was stealing from her. She refused to take her to Sunday mass, fearing that she would steal the church collection.

Her relationship with Zorka deteriorated further, and, desperate for a way out of the house, Donata made Zorka's life unbearable, praying she'd be sent to live with Anka and Aunty Pavica.

Next, seeking her father's attention, she sliced into his prized Prosciutto. When Andrija discovered maggots infested in the meat, he erupted, threatening that, when he got his hands on that naughty kid, he would kill her. Terrified, Donata hid until her father's rage subsided, climbing the cherry tree, finding refuge within its dense branches. As her father and stepmother's fury escalated, Donata figured she would get her one-way ticket to her village and be banned from returning home. The prospect of permanently living with Anka and Aunty Pavica was a silver lining.

With the onset of spring, the cherry tree burst into bloom with various colours, from pink to white to red, and some combined all three. There was a constant buzz of bees along its branches. Donna kept amusing herself. She could see straight through the kitchen window as her father and stepmother argued about what to do with that naughty child. Soon, it went completely dark in its canopy except for an occasional glimpse of moonlight through the dense foliage. She would never be discovered, and she listened intensely to her father's and Zorka's arguments.

"We have to send her away. I am concerned Donata will hurt our son. I don't want her in my house. I won't allow her to look after Emil anymore. Last week, she pushed him so hard that he nearly fell down the stairs. She did it on purpose, so you had better sort this out. I don't care how, but I want Donata out of here," Zorka demanded, hugging Emil tightly as if to protect him. She slammed the kitchen door and took Emil to her bedroom.

Donata watched the scenario unfold before her eyes. Her father paced nervously back and forth from the kitchen table to the window, then despondently sunk into a chair, put his hands on his forehead as if defeated, and wept.

Suddenly, he rose, opened the window, put his head out and called out into the night, "Please, Donata, come home. I won't punish you. Your daddy loves you. If something happens to you as it did to your mother, I may as well die, too. Please come home, my child. I know you can hear me; it is cold outside."

Andrija couldn't see Donata hidden among the thick cherry branches. But Donata heard everything. If her dog Lucky was alive, he would have caught her scent, barked at her to get down, and revealed her cover. Her father's voice echoed in the dark, chilly night and pierced her heart, but she couldn't speak. She put her hands over her mouth to stop her painful sobs from escaping. Oh, how she wanted to jump right into her father's arms. If only she could trust him. But Zorka owned him; she held the purse strings and, therefore, controlled Donata's future.

Donata held on tightly to the branch of the cherry tree as she started to doze. She longed for the affection and comfort of her sister, Anka, and Aunty Pavica. She would have done anything to live with them. Tears rolled down her cheeks; she hoped Zorka was so angry with her that she would send her away. Then she was startled, hearing Zorka's booming voice in the kitchen. Donna listened in on the colossal argument.

"Andrija, Emil is asleep. We need to talk seriously. You must return Donata to the village with Anka or your sister Pavica."

Hooray, Donata thought. I've won the gold jackpot. She felt ecstatic. I've got what I want, but her hope quickly faded when Andrija spoke again.

"No, I can't do that. Here, look at this letter I received." He threw an envelope down on the kitchen table.

"Anka sent me a letter; Donata won't ever return to the village," Andrija told his wife.

"Anka must have got tired of having Donata around every summer, but we can always give them more money," Zorka said.

"It doesn't have anything to do with money," Andrija explained further. "Anka's husband Nikola was offered a full-time job at the shipbuilding yard in Marseille. This will provide stability for their family."

"What about Pavica? She likes Donata. Why can't she live with her?" Zorka demanded.

"Pavica has responsibility for the farm and vineyard. During summer she also looks after her four grandchildren, and she is getting older. Besides, Donata needs to stay in the city to finish her education," Andrija explained.

"No way! I have had enough. If no alternative accommodation is found by the end of the year, Donata must go to the orphanage. That is my last word on the matter. You better listen to me, or you will never see another penny to finish your winery. I don't want her in my house. It is her or me, so you better choose fast," Zorka threatened, slamming the door behind her.

Andrija sat devastated, lost for words. His wife had given him no option; she had pushed him into a corner. Now Donata knew Zorka would get rid of her.

Donata grew tired holding on to the cherry branch. She heard every word and knew Zorka would win this argument and she would end up in an orphanage. Eventually, she climbed down and snuck back into her room where she barricaded the door with her bed to stop her father from barging in and belting her. Andrija heard her making a racket in her room but pretended to sleep. He chose not to punish her, believing his daughter had been punished enough.

Curling up into a fetal position, she cried silently, warm, salty tears heating her face as she drifted off to sleep. That night, Donata dreamt of her mother descending from heaven, like an angel dressed in a long, pure-white silk garment. She lay beside her, tenderly embracing her. When she had to leave, she couldn't fly, as one of her wings was broken. Flapping one wing frantically, a little dove came to the rescue, and they flew up into the sky.

Donata slept all night. When she awoke in the morning, she heard the familiar tune that only her dove could make: coo-coo. She felt safe listening to the familiar sound, which comforted her and numbed her pain.

Zorka relentlessly pursued getting rid of Donata and pestered Andrija to sign the documents to send her away. Eventually, he caved under the pressure and agreed to send his daughter to an orphanage.

Zorka and Donata attended an interview at the interim house to determine where she would be placed. The city orphanage's waiting list was long, and Zorka's application was unsuccessful. The only alternative was to put Donata in the orphanage on the island of Cres, which took children aged, ten to sixteen.

So Donata packed her belongings in a small cardboard suitcase and stayed in an interim house for a few weeks while waiting for a spot in the orphanage on Cres. While there, she befriended staff members who thought her stepmother's demands unreasonable, and she won their hearts with her kind nature.

At the end of the evaluation period, Zorka collected Donata and signed the release documents from the interim house. They then hopped on a bus to the pier and boarded the ferry to the island of Cres, an hour away from the mainland. The island was Croatia's largest and had a significant salt and salt packaging industry, an olive growing industry in the mountains, and was also a tourist hotspot known for its fishing, olive oil production, sardines, and anchovies.

Donna was going to live in the orphanage there from then on. *Just moving from one prison to another*, she mused dully. However, an eternal optimist by nature, she believed the orphanage was a better place than the home she had left behind.

Chapter 6

Collecting Olives

Donata arrived at the orphanage in Cres in the early 1960s when another war was imminent. The looming threat of the Cuban Missile Crisis cast an uncertain shadow over the world, leading many to fear the potential devastation of a nuclear war could create an Armageddon-like scenario.

The two-storied building had a tall copper and tin roof. The exterior walls were painted pink with arched windows, and iron bars covered the windows on the ground level. On either side of the cobblestone entrance, pencil-slim pine trees grew, and wild shrubs amassed in the front garden. A massive green iron gate with large spikes and a tall fence encircled the grounds. From the outside, the orphanage resembled a large hotel rather than a prison for disadvantaged and abandoned children.

As soon as Zorka signed all the required documentation, she grabbed her handbag, shoved the paperwork in the side pocket, and raced to the pier to catch the last ferry back to the city. As Donata turned, she could hear her stepmother's high heels on the cobblestones, disappearing in the distance.

Standing behind the colossal gate, Donata felt like she had just entered an island prison. What rotten luck! she thought. Now, instead of spending summer holidays with her sister Anka and Aunty Pavica in their pristine little village, she had ended up on this isolated island.

Now, just ten years old, she accepted the living arrangement of Cres Orphanage with a heavy heart. This would be her home for the next five years. Unloved, Donata found herself in a horrid place, and she couldn't help but wonder if this place would be any better or worse than the home she shared with her stepmother.

People at the interim house had explained to her why she was there: the orphanage catered to children who had lost their parents in the war, whose parents were too poor to look after them, and those nobody wanted. Donata had fallen into the latter group, feeling unloved and unwanted.

After registration, she was escorted by the nurse-in-charge to a room called the 'green room'; the walls were indeed painted in a deep green oil-based paint.

"My name is Radmila," the woman said, standing with her hands on her hips. "I am the orphanage nurse. Put that suitcase into the locker and strip your clothes to be washed."

Radmila gave Donata green pyjamas with no buttons. "Your mother told us you are a very disobedient child, and you tried to choke your little stepbrother."

"Zorka is not my mother! If she were, I wouldn't be here. What she told you is not true. I never ..." Donata tried to explain, clenching her fist in defiance.

"I know. Everybody says the same thing. I was told you also like stealing, so don't give me that innocent look." Radmila smiled widely, exposing two gold teeth. "Don't worry ... we will sort you out. After a while, you will be as good as a newborn lamb. Get your clothes off. I don't have all day," she snapped impatiently.

Donata stripped and stood naked, trying to cover her bosom with her hands, ashamed and scared in the unfamiliar environment. The big fat nurse quickly performed a basic medical check and wrote a health report in a journal. Radmila then handed her a bar of unprocessed soap, a toothbrush, and a stripy green towel.

Everything was green. Radmila turned on the tap and pushed Donata under the cold shower. "Hurry, get in and shower quickly; the only time the hot shower is available is at bedtime; now, brush your teeth and come sit over here."

"But I don't have toothpaste, " Donna said softly, trying not to upset the nurse.

"What do you think this is? A palace for a princess like you? You silly girl, use your soap to brush your teeth."

Donata scraped her toothbrush into the soap. It tasted revolting, and she nearly vomited. Then she put on her new pyjamas and sat on a steel chair.

"Now you know what will happen to you if you use foul or inappropriate language; we will wash your mouth with soap." The nurse laughed, then, without explanation, she draped a plastic towel over Donata's shoulders and fastened it with a wooden washing peg.

"Stay still or I may cut you with this shaver," Radmila warned.

"Please don't cut my hair," Donata pleaded.

"Stop moving; remain still; the blade is sharp, and it will cut if you are not sitting still. As part of our standard procedure, all new arrivals are required to have their heads shaved. This is done to check for contagious diseases, fleas, and lice. Since the orphanage houses over a hundred boys and girls, we cannot allow any infestations to occur. Otherwise, we would have to shave everyone to prevent the spread of such infestations," the nurse said sharply, then she started shaving Donata's head, moving her chin and twisting her head in every direction until she was bald. When finished, the nurse applied a strong-smelling ointment to her scalp. Donata looked down at the dark green tiles on the bathroom floor as her long brown locks, which used to flow past her shoulders, started to clog the drain.

"Here, stop whining! Your hair will grow back soon. Put this scarf on your head. It will keep you warm."

Donata put the scarf on and waited for further instructions, unsure what to do.

"Come on, don't stand there all day; follow me upstairs. You will share a room with five other girls; you will meet them when they return from school."

The room on the second floor was to become Donata's new home. She wanted to have the top bunk bed, but Sonja had already taken it, so Donata had to take the bottom bunk, close to the window. As she sat on the grey-striped mattress stained with dried urine, the sunken iron springs squeaked. Radmila gave Donata some bed sheets, one with a plastic lining, a woollen pillow, and two army-style dark green blankets.

"The other girls in your group are over ten years old and the two oldest will be over sixteen by the end of the school year. Milka is the oldest; her grandmother lives in Germany, so when she finishes her schooling, she may be sent directly to adult reform school. You'd better watch out so you don't end up like them. Girls like that are branded for life, and most end up selling themselves on the streets.

"You'll get your school uniform, shoes, and clothes tomorrow. You'll meet other children at dinner, but remember, the dinner bell only rings once. If you miss it, bad luck. There won't be any food for you."

Radmila stepped out and closed the door behind her.

Donata made her bed before putting her possessions into a rickety chest of drawers next to the bed. She sat at the edge of the window, watching the last ferry return to the city in the distance, leaving white waves and long, thin ripples in its wake. She stayed there for a while, watching sunlight glistening on the Adriatic Sea. The room had no privacy, and the orphanage heating was turned off at bedtime. The bunk beds, made from steel frames, some so old that the steel wires protruded through the mattress, squeaked all night, which made sleeping difficult, but not impossible. After sporting activities, exhausted girls fell asleep on any surface, steel frame or not, and sleep came easily.

The boys were placed on the left wing with uneven numbers, the girls on the right with even numbers, and two bathrooms occupied the middle. Orphanage rules forbade boys and girls from mingling, other than sharing the library, a space for homework and tutorials, a room for arts and crafts, and a large dining hall on the ground floor. The young teenagers found ways to sneak out to the movies, hide behind the laundry to smoke, and sometimes even steal their first kiss.

Upon Donata's arrival, it was customary for new children to receive a cake during their first year in residence. It didn't have to be on the same day or month; this was simply a welcome gesture. Blowing out ten candles made her feel she was part of group number four, which comprised boys and girls aged ten to sixteen and a few older ones who had failed their last school exams and needed extra tuition.

Donata quickly settled into her new home and became popular among her female dorm mates. Her extroverted nature made it easier to make friends with a diverse range of children. Most of the children came from dysfunctional or underprivileged families, and she had to learn quickly how to protect herself from bullies. One way was by acting like a 'tomboy.' This helped her hide from overzealous boys full of teenage hormones. She started hiding pocket money and stashing food under her bed, and when discovered, she found a new safe place to hide things. She had to fight for survival among her colossal family at the orphanage, and while sharing a bedroom with five other girls was tough, they all got along well.

Soveida, or Aida, became her best friend. The two clicked immediately because they came from the same hometown. They bonded like twins, walking to school together and attending the same art classes and sports activities. Aida had lost her parents in a car accident, and her Aunty Antonia was her primary legal guardian. When Antonia was contracted as a seamstress for different fashion brands in Italy, she couldn't take care of Aida, and, because she was a minor without relatives, she had to spend a few years in the orphanage.

Daily routines went like clockwork. If they didn't follow the orphanage rules, they would be punished. Children were smacked with a ruler, had their hair pulled, and their ears stretched so painfully that they looked like Bugs Bunny. However, standing in the corner of a room for hours was humiliating, and going to bed without supper or being deprived of outdoor activities or excursions was awful.

Early in the morning, the children walked five kilometres to school in the snow and blizzards. If it was raining, there would be splashing, jumping in puddles in black rubber boots, or playing in the snow. Sliding in the park on the frozen bench usually meant arriving at school late, which led to after-school punishments. The orphanage emphasised education, and receiving poor grades also resulted in punishment. If not performing well at school, students had to do more homework and miss out on outdoor play or fun excursions. Students who struggled academically had to attend tutorials and continue their studies during school breaks. After school and on weekends, each group had a roster of assigned chores: cleaning toilets, showers, and wooden floors. Cleaning the wooden floors was brutal. The parquet floor was scrubbed with a steel brush, resulting in painful splinters in hands and feet. If not treated, they became infected.

Destructive behaviours were punished with extra work in the

laundry room or cleaning blocked toilets that were usually stuffed with girls' menstrual pads or boys trying to hide condoms. Unblocking the toilets had to be done with bare hands and no gloves, the children rolling their sleeves up and shoving their hands into the excrement. When the drain was unplugged, children who vomited during the process had to clean that up, too. The orphanage supervisor inspected all the cleaning, and if they still needed to do their requirements, it had to be redone until it was completed to their satisfaction.

After homework, students were encouraged to partake in arts and crafts and play cards, games or chess. Participation in outdoor sports was a must, regardless of the weather. For Donata's first summer swimming lesson, she was thrown off the jetty into deep water to kick in her survival instincts. Luckily, she'd already had basic swimming lessons in her village, when she'd been thrown off the big jetty into deep blue Adriatic Sea. She had dog-paddled, kicking frantically, swallowing much seawater. When she managed to get out, the bullies pushed her back into the deep water again and again, until she learned how to swim on her own. Learning how to survive at a young age was solely up to her.

Achieving sports medals was highly valued, and Donata excelled in gymnastics and ran well. She challenged herself with marathon running, pushing through physical exhaustion and pain until she crossed the finish line.

There was time to relax after dinner when the children watched a small black-and-white TV that mainly broadcast communist propaganda. Throughout the sixties, the black and white TV was a huge novelty; boys would watch football and cowboy movies starring John Wayne or Gary Cooper, while the girls chose love stories like those featuring Doris Day and Rock Hudson. All the girls also watched the TV twice weekly for news updates, popular soap operas featuring Dr Kildare, Star

Trek, and Donata's favourite show, Bonanza. This western soap was set in a small town in Virginia, the Ponderosa Ranch and it was here that Donata first fell for Little Joe (Michael Landon). She fantasised about meeting and marrying her own Little Joe one day.

She was not the only one competing for the love of Little Joe; all the other teenage girl shared the same dream, physically fighting to grab the best spot to view the small TV screen.

Donata was fortunate to have Maria as her arts and crafts teacher, and immediately clicked with the young graduate teacher fresh from her university degree. In her mid-twenties, Maria was very approachable and had a great rapport with her students. During their class, she relaxed the rules of the orphanage and sometimes brought in her radio cassette player to play popular music from the fifties and sixties. Maria's favourites were Elvis Presley and the Beatles, whom the children enjoyed.

All the girls in the arts and crafts group teased Maria about her boyfriend. Maria's brother Guido and her boyfriend served their two-year compulsory service together in the Yugoslav army in Ljubljana. When given leave, they came for a short visit to the island. Guido played harmonica in the local band, and Maria's boyfriend practised drums. She'd nicknamed her soldier Ringo after the famous Beatles drummer and hoped that, after the army, they would get married.

Maria comforted and kindled Donata, helping her build her self-esteem. Donata was an excellent student, and her embroidery and tapestry were showcased as the best art and craft at the orphanage's annual open day.

As Donata's teacher, Maria was also a mentor; she taught Donata how to stay strong and positive, believe in her potential, and seize every opportunity. Donata honoured her mentor by achieving excellent results in school.

When public holidays arrived, the children excitedly celebrated the Communist Socialist festivities under Marshal Tito's authoritarian rule. Even though they were from diverse ethnic backgrounds – Serbs, Croats, Muslims – they all sang patriotic songs, dressed in their blue uniforms with red scarves and stars proudly displayed on their caps. The children were even more excited when visitors were invited: grandparents, aunties, or single mothers, who would bring fresh fruit, homemade cookies, biscuits, or new flannel pyjamas to keep their children warm during the harsh winter.

Donata was jealous of the children who had visitors. She had no visitors, even though her father and stepmother lived only one hour away by ferry. Other families travelled far: from Bosnia, Macedonia, Serbia, or Montenegro. Some families even came from Germany or Italy.

During the school holidays, the orphanage rewarded obedient children who worked and produced excellent school reports. Good grades meant children could go home if they had a home or spend time with distant relatives. During the summer school holiday, the almost empty orphanage was extremely dull; those who remained were tasked with daily chores. Donata missed her friends, especially Aida, who had returned to Optija for a few weeks to stay with her elderly grandparents. The usual staff had departed for the summer, leaving Donata with the unfamiliar faces of temporary or part-time staff.

Even though she had worked hard at school, especially enjoying geography and history, her stepmother didn't want her, and the feeling was mutual. Donata's distant relatives' lifestyle in the village had changed, too, and she couldn't visit them either. Sadly, she was all alone again when her sister Anka and her husband Nikola immigrated to France. Marseille offered new opportunities and prosperity for their growing family. Also, Aunty Pavica was getting old and sick. Donata missed their warm embrace and remembered the special school holidays she'd shared in their village; these two people were the only family she loved and missed. In that little village, she had found the abundance of love she desperately craved, but now that window of opportunity was closed.

Donata sadly accepted that she would never return to her village. The only thing she had left was the good memories, which would give her the strength to carry on. During her five years in the orphanage, Donata never returned to the village, and nobody from her family came to visit.

⋚

When Donata was fifteen, she experienced her worst summer holiday ever. The orphanage appeared almost abandoned, with most children returning to their parents, grandparents, or relatives, only a few children who had nowhere else to go remaining behind. As usual, they were assigned additional duties, one of them being to venture up the mountain to gather ripe black olives, which the orphanage sold to local olive oil producers.

The prospect of extra pocket money and a generous serving of chocolate pudding for supper excited the children. The olive-picking activity was transformed into a challenging and exciting competition. Returning with a bucket full of olives at the end of the day gave the children free time for swimming and increased their chances of being selected for special outings, which was the ultimate reward.

Donata was paired with Ned, who was in her class. He kindly tutored her in chemistry, maths, and physics, improving her grades. She had a crush on him, and fortunately, the feeling was mutual. Donata overlooked his occasional nervous stuttering, appreciating his kind nature and her sense of security when gathering olives together on the mountain.

Joining them were Donata's roommates, Milka and Sonja, who were a year or two older than her. Milka, an orphan, excelled in everything and received outstanding school reports. With her captivating curvy blonde hair and piercing blue eyes, her quiet demeanour starkly contrasted with Donata's talkative nature.

Milka was in love with Hussein, a handsome seventeen-year-old Muslim boy, but sadly he didn't feel the same way. Hussein courted an island girl but kept it a secret because the orphanage strictly forbade any relationship with the locals. Donata hated it when Bakovic came along with Sonja on the olive-picking excursions; he was a bully and targeted Donata constantly. Bakovic had awful handwriting and scribbled on the page like a cat with its claws out; he forced Donata to re-write all his homework and, if she didn't do what he ordered, he would kick her under the table with his boots, bruising her legs. Sometimes during dinner, he would take her chocolate pudding and fruit salad that she loved. At school when nobody was watching, he tripped her up, causing her to fall, or would clench his fists and threaten her so she would remember to do his homework on time. Bakovic threw stones at doves' nests, picked the chicks from the ground, and fed them to stray cats that prowled around the orphanage gardens. She hated him!

When they reached the mountain, the group of students separated, Hussein and Milka climbing further up to where there were more black olives to collect. They disappeared from view.

Shaking the trees, black olives fell to the rocky ground, and Ned helped Donna carry the half-full bucket of olives to another tree. When they were alone, he held her hand, and eventually gained enough courage to move closer and kiss her on the cheek. Donata's face flushed with a warmth she had never experienced, then paled instantly when she noticed

Bakovic and Sonja coming their way.

Moving closer, he shoved Ned away, grinning, exposing yellow-stained teeth from smoking unfiltered cigarettes. He shouted, "Hey, Ned, don't you want more than a kiss? You are such a sissy!"

Then Bakovic pushed Donata, grabbed up the bucket she held, and poured the olives into his bucket. Donata spat in his ugly face, standing so close she could smell his foul breath.

Ned stood frozen, but yelled, "Donata, run!" and run she did, scampering further up the mountain. Seeing her go, Ned also bolted and followed her up to another grove of trees, where they both stood watching. But Bakovic did not follow, and Donata realised they still had enough time to refill the bucket with olives before heading back. Bakovic and Sonja remained behind, sitting beneath an olive tree. As Donata continued picking olives from the ground, she heard Sonja and Bakovic arguing. Bakovic swore profusely, making Donata and Ned tremble with fear.

Nobody dared to mess with Bakovic, so they ran further up the hill to find Hussein and Milka, but they couldn't see them anywhere.

"Get away from me, you filthy, rotten bastard," Sonja screamed, her voice carrying in the stillness. "Get away!"

"Come here, you bloody bitch," Bakovic kept shouting.

"Stop! Stop it!" Sonja pleaded, then she screamed for help. But Bakovic didn't care. This was his mountain, and Sonja was his girl, so he would take what he wanted from her. Sonja kicked, scratched, and bit his lip but he still overpowered her, took her. Before she knew it, he was standing over her, zipping up his pants.

He called, "Hey, you lot, you can come down now. I am finished with that bitch. "Hey, Ned, the ripe olives taste the best," Bakovic smirked. "Come on, Ned, don't be shy; Donata wants to be kissed by a real man, not a sissy like you. Hurry, don't be scared. Girls like to see who the boss is, not a woose like you."

Ned didn't answer; he was too scared. He grabbed Donata's hand, and they both ran down the hill as if a hurricane roared behind them.

Feeling guilty for not helping her friend when Bakovic ravaged her, Donata immediately started looking for her friend when they returned to the orphanage. They had to report Bakovic. She found Sonja in the shower, crying.

"Let me go with you to the principal's office and report this," Donna pleaded with Sonja. "Bakovic can't get away with assaulting girls."

"No!" Sonja panicked. "Please don't! Please … you must keep this secret. Bakovic is a popular boy, especially among the supervisors."

Indeed, every morning, he and Hussein went with the supervisors to the city bakery by boat to collect fresh bread and return in time for breakfast. At night, they went fishing with the night watch porter. Therefore, nobody would believe Sonja's story, and there were no eyewitnesses. Donata knew she must keep Sonja's secret. And Hussein would defend Bakovic as they were best friends and would probably state that Sonja was a willing participant. Everybody in the orphanage knew Sonja had had a crush on him.

Sonja and Donata shared the same room. They were friends, and she promised they would never discuss the incident again. Sonja's anger, however, raged and she looked for retaliation, and when the opportunity came, her revenge was sweet. It happened a week later when Donata was assigned duties in the kitchen. She liked kitchen duties because she had much more freedom, and they were much more pleasant than unblocking a toilet or washing clothes in cold water. She worked with easygoing local women with whom she got along well, and at the end of a shift, there were often extra sweets.

Sonja was working in the dining area that day and fully supported Donata's plan and had promised to keep it a secret. If anything leaked, both girls would be punished. Like most evenings, after the main course and dessert, jugs of hot apple juice with lemon and vanilla essence were placed on each numbered table. When the cooks went outside for a quick cigarette break, Donata and Sonja urinated in two jugs and marked the jugs with the table numbers allocated to Bakovic, Hussein and his group of friends. The chocolate pudding and apple juice with vanilla, cinnamon, and lemon essence helped to hide the smell and salty taste of the hot urine. The boys drank the two jugs of apple juice and asked for more. When the girls couldn't pee anymore, they spat into the jugs. Sonja dissolved some laxatives she secretly used to slim down, and casually placed the jugs on the boy's table.

Later, while watching a TV show, Bakovic and Hessian boasted how special they were to receive more jugs of 'apple' juice. Sonja smiled widely, especially when she heard that Bakovic and Hussein had spent all night sitting in the toilet.

Nurse Radmila concluded the boys must have eaten too many black olives, Donata and Sonja had the last laugh. Nobody ever suspected anything, and the revenge helped a little to heal Sonja's broken heart.

Sadly, Hussein took advantage of Milka's love, but she was blinded by love and unable to recognise that Hussein didn't deserve her. She was a gentle spirit, intelligent, kind, and beautiful, and Hussein was not much better than Bakovic. Milka had been unable to resist Hussein's advances while picking olives on that day on the mountain, and, unfortunately, that passionate lovemaking with Hussein resulted in Milka falling pregnant. Hussein was Muslim, so the relationship was doomed, and marriage was impossible. Milka's only option was to have an abortion, but that would disgrace her Jewish grandmother, whom she adored and was her only living relative. When the olive picking season ended, one day, Milka didn't return.

The orphanage staff panicked and worried because students sometimes attempted to escape from the orphanage. Security during school holidays was still strictly enforced, so there was no way she could escape from this rocky island, which was guarded like Alcatraz. After an extensive search of the orphanage, staff and local volunteers also searched all the school grounds in the city. When the local firefighters searched the olive mountain, they found Milka's lifeless body. She had hung herself from the same olive tree where she had made love with Hussein.

That tragic day was indelibly imprinted in Donata's memory. She would have preferred to remember her friend as one of the lost souls who died in vain, an innocent girl who fell in love with the wrong man. She hoped Milka's spirit would live forever on that beautiful mountain full of olive trees, where birds never stop singing. Milka died so young, forgotten by many, but she would always be remembered as a gentle soul. Sonja, too, became subdued and depressed. Wishing to lose weight as she hated her body, her bulimia increased. During the night, Sonja talked in her sleep and sometimes screamed, waking the other girls.

The orphanage staff, oblivious to the girls' needs, never interfered to stop the bullies' brutality. Donata hated being frightened and felt helpless to stand up against the bullying and unable to prevent them from taking advantage of innocent girls. This left a void in her heart. She had learned a hard lesson after witnessing what happened to Sonja, Milka, and others who kept quiet due to shame and being alone.

Surviving in this harsh environment was challenging. She

learned at the early stages that showing vulnerability resulted in abuse and pain, and only strong girls were capable of navigating through these muddy emotional waters. She swore that, after leaving the orphanage, she would never allow another man to bully her again, and no man would ever dominate her.

These five years in the orphanage and the strict rules through her formative adolescent years shaped Donata, strengthening her iron character into pure steel. She became resilient, self-sufficient, and extra cautious in protecting herself from abusive men. She wanted to be educated and self-sufficient; that was the only way to keep her dignity and maintain her self-esteem.

Chapter 7

A Little Dancing Dove

Donata often sat at the edge of the window, wanting to paint the beautiful scenery from the top floor of the orphanage. In the afternoon, she sat watching the sun go down as the last ferry departed. Oh, how she wished to be on that ferry and run away, but there was no place to run.

During her last summer at the orphanage, Donata celebrated her fifteenth birthday. She hoped that one day she would meet one of her older sisters who would adopt her and take her from the orphanage and away from all the horrible experiences she had there.

But it wasn't to be.

Once again, she was alone and had to spend another summer school holiday at the orphanage. Most of her friends had moved away. Her best friend Aida went to live with her aunt Antonia in Italy, but they kept in touch by writing letters.

This summer, as usual, the orphanage was half-empty. The children who stayed behind this time had to sort out library books, clean and polish the wooden steps and floors, and tidy the outdoor gardens.

Sometimes, they would pretend to be sick, Sonja and Donata faking tummy aches, headaches, or period cramps to avoid doing chores. Sonja was bulimic, and showed Donata how she could induce vomiting. That scheme guaranteed the girls escaped work for a day or two. They congratulated each other when they convinced Nurse Radmila they were both sick. Getting extra hours to sleep in on the weekends was their greatest reward. Donata's lies came unstuck when she became ill one fateful weekend. She didn't have to pretend as she vomited profusely.

Nurse Radmila dismissed Donata's cries as she had done many times before. Children would resort to all sorts of mischievous behaviour to avoid unpleasant chores. She diagnosed Donata with food poisoning. She put a bucket next to her bed, gave her a bottle of water, and that was that.

However, by the following morning, Donata was seriously ill; she was in extreme pain, had a high temperature and needed urgent medical care. After further consultation at the central town surgery, the doctor on duty diagnosed Donata with a perforated appendix.

She was indeed in terrible shape and had to be transported to the mainland city hospital as soon as possible. Unfortunately, due to rough weather, the island's ferries, the only way to get to the hospital, were not operational.

By Monday, Donata's illness had become critical. Her trusted, kind teacher, Maria, had planned a quick trip to the city to meet with Ringo, who was on army leave that weekend. However, Maria postponed that meeting and volunteered to accompany Donata to the hospital, and she stayed with her patient below deck, comforting Donata as the high fever made her delirious. As soon as the ferry docked, Maria accompanied her in the ambulance that was waiting at the dock to the hospital for an urgent operation; she had legal rights to sign the medical documentation and stayed with Donata until her next of kin was informed.

After Donata had her first operation, the primary concern was to treat the infection that had spread into her lower intestines, bladder, urinary tract and fallopian tubes. If left untreated, she may never have children. Even with significant surgical intervention and several antibiotics, Donata's life continued to hang by a thread.

When her father and stepmother arrived, doctors told them to pray and be prepared for the worst. If the infection spread to the kidneys, it would be fatal.

The following day, Andrija came with a priest to administer the sacrament of the last rites. The only thing her father could do was pray, and only God could help her now.

During her stay in the intensive care unit, she witnessed many patients die prematurely. One young man also had a perforated appendix. He had the best view in the room, a vast window overlooking the park and the blue Adriatic coast.

Donata had thought she would recover sooner if she had a peaceful view. Sadly, her wish soon came true when the young man died from complications. Donata asked Nurse Rose, "Please, can you shift my bed closer to the window?"

The idyllic view from the window spurred her on to fight the infection, live, swim, see more sunsets, and fall in love. She wanted all that life offered, and refused to die.

Her father and stepmother visited a few more times. Once, they brought her stepbrother Emil along, too. However, the visits fizzled out, excuses followed, and nobody came.

While recuperating from the infection, Donata had a few more setbacks. When her condition deteriorated again, she ended up in the operating theatre for another emergency surgery.

She stayed in the hospital for many weeks and continued to soldier on. While painkillers helped, she was alone and cried silently. When she finally fell asleep, she dreamt her mother was alive and took her away from the hospital.

Nurse Rose was amazed by the improvement in Donata's health. Her fever had subsided, and she was finally responding to treatment. "Young lady, you are getting better. We all thought you might need some miracle to help you pull through. This morning, you are still delirious. We heard you talking with somebody."

"Yes, Nurse Rose, you heard right? I talked to my new friend, my divine little dove. She visits every morning and dances on the window ledge, but my little dove is shy; she comes just before sunrise." How Donata wished to have memories of her mother, but she was so young, and she imagined so beautiful, when she died.

Donata's hospital bed by the window was her only solace. She could never get enough of looking at the beautiful garden full of colour. The leaves were brown, yellow, and purple and blew around in the autumn breeze. She wondered where all the ships she saw on the horizon were sailing; she spent hours looking outside, observing patients walking around the hospital grounds. She wished she could go to the garden and say hello, but she couldn't; she was tied to the hospital bed with tubes in her arms, receiving intravenous fluids and antibiotics and tubes poking out of her abdomen, draining off the excess fluid. The only thing she could move was her head, so she kept staring out the window.

Then, one crisp morning, just after sunrise, a small dove landed on the edge of the window frame. It started tapping its tiny beak on the window, flapping its delicate wings to attract Donata's attention. When Donata looked at her, the petite little dove started hopping along, dancing, and then flew away. As the rising sunlight lit the dove's wings, she noticed that one of her wings was broken.

The following day, the little dancing dove came back again. Donata stared at the bird, wishing she could fly away with it. Then she remembered the little dove that she loved and had fed with cornbread. What if that was the same dove? It couldn't be;

she couldn't fly that far. Nevertheless, Donata wondered if the dove was indeed the one she knew already ….

Every morning, she felt excited and looked forward to her little dove arriving and performing another dance.

☙

"Well, my sweet child, if you think your little dove was a miracle that helped you recover, that's good enough for me." Nurse Rose smiled.

A few weeks later, the doctors announced Donata should start taking small steps and walk around the garden to get some fresh air.

"Please, Nurse Rose, can you get me some breadcrumbs so I can feed my dove?" Donata asked.

"Of course, I can, but don't stay long," Nurse Rose replied, still amazed at Donata's improvement in health.

Donata started looking for her little friend among the shrubs and flowers. She had to find her.

After a few days, she brought some bread and sat on the bench in the hospital garden when she spotted her dove. She came to her, hopped on her palm, picked at the breadcrumbs. Then she hopped off and started performing her little dance. One of her wings was shorter than the other, but she kept flapping her wings faster and faster, flying away … higher and higher.

The following day, her little dove was waiting for her. "Hi, my sweet little dove, I thought I'd lost you." Donata touched her silky grey and white feathers. "I missed you so much. I'm so happy we found each other again. Stay with me; don't fly away; you are my only friend."

During the night, Donata had the same dream again: her mother's spirit transformed into the dove. She was the guardian angel that spurred Donata to fight and survive; her little dove stayed with her during her most desperate hour.

For the next few weeks, the little dove knocked on her window, Donata's pain subsided, and she started sleeping without painkillers. While in the hospital, she often dreamt that her mother had descended as she embraced her baby girl, humming a lullaby. In another dream, her mother and her little dove merged into one. Her mother, Smiljana, had a human body, but her wings looked like the dove's.

When Donata was discharged from the hospital and put into her father's care, her little dove returned, frantically tapping the window glass with her delicate beak. Donata gently touched the warm glass window, not startling the little bird. Then, the little dove began flapping her soft wings as if waving goodbye. When Donata removed her fingers from the window, her little dove flew away into the blue sky and hid among the clouds, which looked as soft as cotton wool.

Because Donata had to continue outpatient treatment at the city hospital, she had to return and live with her father and stepmother again. However, she was not afraid anymore. Finding her little dove again made her feel optimistic about her future. When she felt sad or lonely, remembering her little dove dancing made her smile again.

Oh! How she wished that one day she could fly away with her little dove. But, not just yet.

Chapter 8

Hot Cross Buns

After her hospital stay, Donata never returned to the orphanage, and parting with her beloved teacher, Maria, made her sad, but they promised to write to each other. The outpatient hospital treatment lasted another six months, during which Donata's health continued to improve.

She hoped to reconnect with her friend Aida but Aida didn't know she was in the hospital. She wrote letters to Maria, and receiving a reply was extra special. In her last letter, Maria wrote that her relationship with her boyfriend Ringo ended when he moved abroad. However, she kept busy with her students, which helped heal her broken heart.

After five years at the orphanage, Donata was no longer filled with rage toward her family, which improved her relationship with her stepbrother Emil. She nicknamed him "Blondie", mainly because he looked like his mother, with blond hair, blue eyes, and white eyelashes, while Donata had dark hair and brown eyes, just like her father. The two siblings developed a bond as they began to play chess together.

After Donata recovered, she wanted to enrol in the School of Economics and Marketing, but her stepmother looked for a government-sponsored traineeship. Zorka insisted Donata take an apprentice job at the local bakery in the town centre.

Donata had no say in the matter. She had to get up before sunrise to work in a poorly lit, dusty bakery, where the wages were no more than pocket money. The local bakery was always busy, especially during Easter, when they were overwhelmed with orders for hot cross buns.

Vitomir, the bakery's owner, was a widower on the cusp of retirement. His singing in the church choir was well-known around town, and all the frequent church members respected him. He was bald with a larger frame, his belly protruding beneath his shirt like dough rising in an oven. His pants were sagging off his waist, held up only by a narrow brown belt and a big silver buckle.

At first, Vitomir was very polite. He gave Donata a white uniform, a netted hat, and a black apron. He showed her how to use a wooden rolling pin, dusting a wide oak polished countertop with flour, and rolling out the dough. She learned the essentials of baking and the importance of precise temperatures. As Easter approached, she became adept at combining white flour with yeast and sultanas and shaping them into balls to create delicious hot cross buns. Having all the baked goods prepared before lunchtime was necessary, as local customers eagerly queued up to purchase fresh bread and hot cross buns straight from the oven.

During Easter, the bakery made hundreds of hot cross buns sprinkled with icing sugar and cinnamon. It was the busiest time of the year.

Soon after Easter, however, Vitomir started behaving strangely, rubbing his body against her. The ugly old man was also a dirty old man.

One morning, when Donata arrived at work and put on her black apron, she watched Vitomir act strangely. As he was mixing flour with water, sugar, and yeast with his grubby hands, he smiled and started rolling the dough into a long stick, pulling and stretching the dough to recreate the male sex organ, smirking as he pulled and stroked the dough suggestively with his filthy hands.

Vitomir turned around and grasped Donata's hand, forcing her to help him roll the suggestively shaped dough. Then he started unzipping his pants, and started playing with himself. Grabbing her other hand, he tried to shove it down his pants. When she pushed him away, he grabbed her breasts with flour-covered hands, leaving his fingerprints on her dark apron. His foul breath was so near that it almost made her retch. She desperately wanted to vomit in his face, but instead, she thrust him aside and escaped to the toilet.

Terrified, she chose her moment, escaped the bakery, and ran home. She had nobody to talk to and confide in — such embarrassing topics were never discussed. This was a strictly taboo subject.

She had to get away. She was determined never to allow another man to bully her. She remembered Milka, who had died, and poor Sonja, who ended up living on the streets, picked up by the police and sent to reform school.

Donata hoped Vitomir would give her the sack so she would never have to return to the bakery, but her stepmother had other plans.

"Tomorrow, you are returning, and you will apologise to Vitomir. I worked very hard to secure this apprenticeship for you, and you must work if you intend to live here," Zorka snapped.

"No way! I will never, ever go back. I can't stand being around him. You can kill me first," Donata shouted at her.

"You see what your daughter has learned in the orphanage?" Zorka turned and faced Andrija, waiting for his response.

Donata stood her ground, willing to take any punishment. This time, her father knew that something was wrong, so he asked, "Zorka, why don't you go tomorrow and find out what happened? Why did Donata quit? Talk with Vitomir; find out what is going on. Then we will decide what to do."

Andrija looked at his daughter. He seemed tired and muttered, "Listen, my child, why are you giving us so much heartache? The only punishment today is that you will go to bed without supper. We will talk some more tomorrow."

Donata noticed her father's dejected demeanour. He looked tired and worn out, as though he had been defeated. Unable to sleep, she wondered why her father was so obsessed with his vineyard. She expected him to protect her and keep her safe. Why did he allow his wife to control his life? She was in charge of the entire household and ruled over him as if he were spellbound.

Donata's mind buzzed; she remembered overhearing a conversation between her stepmother and one of her church-going friends, while hiding on the top of the cherry tree. Zorka and Irma often got together, drank strong, pungent Turkish coffee, and chatted. "You can't blame me. I got rid of that disobedient brat. I waited long enough to get married and have my child. I deserve to be happy, don't I?" Zorka explained her reasoning as to why she didn't want to have Donata crowding her home life.

"I agree with you. It is best not to have any outside distractions. You did the right thing; you don't have to feel bad about sending her packing to the orphanage. I would have done the same. Besides, Donata is not your blood. I heard rumours that Donata's mother came from an Orthodox family. God forbid if our priest finds out. What will our neighbours say? You need to keep that a secret, or I won't be able to come around anymore.

"This is your time to be happy. You married a handsome man who works hard to establish a vineyard. Andrija is ambitious and has a big ego. Let him believe he will be the best winemaker around. That will make him happy."

"I've been married and widowed twice. You are so lucky to have a second chance, so make sure you keep him happy. I am older than you and can give you good advice about what every man wants." Irma lit another cigarette and turned Zorka's coffee cup around to read her fortune.

"And what would that be?" Zorka smiled.

"You must stay in control of your husband. One wise old woman once told me, if you stroke a man's dick, he will love you for one night. But if you stroke his ego, you will own your man for life."

Both women burst out laughing.

Donata didn't quite understand what she meant but finally figured it out. In her father's case, it was true. Andrija's ambition to establish his winery had blinded him. His enormous ego ruled his emotions and his life. Zorka had learned how to exploit it for her benefit.

CR

When the bakery was about to close the following day, Donata went with Zorka to face Vitomir. She was so nervous she wished she could just run away. It would have been much better to shame the old baker by writing a nasty article for the newspaper and punish the dirty old bastard forever. She was sure the sleazy old baker would never admit that he tried to molest a young girl. Vitomir had an excellent reputation among the tightly-knit Catholic community.

When they entered the bakery, Vitomir closed the front door. They went into his little office, and he spoke to Zorka charmingly. But Donata's anger rose, and she couldn't stand listening to that nonsense any longer; she had to say something.

"You had better pay me what you own me. I will never come back to work here. You make me sick, you filthy, dirty old man."

Donata's cheeks were flushed with rage. She looked at her

stepmother for support, but Zorka kept apologising. She pleaded with Vitomir to give Donata another chance.

Vitomir grew agitated and started retaliating. "You can't believe a word this stupid girl is telling you. It is all lies; she is trying to cover it up. Donata stole money from my register, and money was missing every week. Over Easter, we sold so many hot cross buns, and she skimmed the register. As God is my witness, I am telling you the truth. Donata has to pay back every cent that she stole." Vitomir remained calm and very persuasive. "And I demand an apology for these false accusations!"

Donata's jaw dropped open, and a cold chill washed over her. "No way. I don't want to work in this filthy place with a dirty old man who can't keep his pants zipped up," she yelled back.

But Vitomir was adamant. "I have a reputation to maintain. I am a God-fearing man and would never touch a young girl. She is making up all these vicious stories. My wife would turn in her grave."

Vitomir lifted his hands as if he were praying. "As God is my witness, I would never touch a girl."

Donata started screaming and yelling at him. "You are a filthy, dirty old man. I hate you. I'll tell everybody what you do with your grubby hands. Nobody will buy your hot cross buns from your bakery ever again."

Convinced that Donata was lying, Zorka turned on her. She had known the old baker all her life; they attended church on Sundays, and everybody liked him. Donata had made it all up to hide that she was stealing money. She said to him, "Yes, I believe you. Donata stole money from us, too."

Vitomir, now angry and feeling confident, insisted on involving the police. "Zorka, I did you a great favour in taking Donata as my apprentice. Now, look what she has done. She robbed me. I won't allow Donata to spread lies. I have a reputation to protect. When the police arrive, it will all be sorted out," he smirked as he wiped his hands on his big, fat belly.

When Donata attempted to run, he locked the back door. "You just wait, you lazy, no-good liar. You are not going anywhere. The police will come and take you to the juvenile detention centre."

Zorka, embarrassed and angry, refused to see the truth. "You need to learn a lesson and to not spread lies. Vitomir gave you a job, and he trusted you. Instead of being grateful, you stole his money, and now you are trying to ruin the poor man's livelihood."

When the police arrived, they all knew each other. They attended the same church and regularly bought bread and hot cross buns from the good old baker.

The police interview was brief. What put the final nail in the coffin was when Zorka affirmed that Donata had stolen money from her before. That confirmed that Donata was guilty of the same offence, and no further investigation into Vitomir's misconduct was listened to.

That day, Donata was taken to the detention centre, the same temporary residence she had stayed in for a few weeks, waiting for a spot to open up at the orphanage. However, when she was there previously, she was just ten years old. Now she was almost sixteen.

Zorka was determined to have Donata sent to an adult reform school; therefore, the initial interview at the interim house was short. Zorka completed the paperwork, stating that her stepdaughter was disobedient and an unmanageable teenager who stole money and spread lies that could ruin a man's reputation.

"I had to pay back the substantial amount of money that Donata had stolen from her employer; she stole money from us, too. My advice to you is to lock up your valuables."

Donata's thoughts raced. She knew there was no point in defending herself. She had stolen money from Zorka when she was a child, but she was only nine years old and didn't understand the value of money. She had never intended to take the highest-value note. That was a mistake, and she never did it again.

She also knew she was in big trouble and wished her father was present. Sadly, Andrija was preoccupied with his vineyard. He'd left his wife in charge.

Zorka signed the paperwork and didn't bother to say goodbye; she just slammed the door and ran to the bus stop.

Donata's face heated with shame when one of the interim house supervisors looked at her and said, "Oh, no, Donata, we are so surprised to see you back. We received positive reports about your progress in the orphanage, and we had such hopes for you. We never expected you'd be back. It shows you that sometimes we make a wrong judgment, too."

Donata dropped her head in shame and followed her supervisor to her designated room; she was given her pyjamas and a toothbrush, pillow and fresh linen. "Tomorrow morning, you will be allocated some duties. Next week, the committee will meet with your parents to decide what to do with you. Until then, you will stay with us."

Without another word, the supervisor turned around, locked the door, and walked away.

Not perceived as high risk, Donata was given a room on the ground floor, close to the kitchen and laundry, and shared a toilet and bathroom with other low-risk younger children. She wondered what would happen to her and was scared of ending up like some of the orphanage girls who didn't belong anywhere. Donata's best friend Sonja, had ended up in reform school. She had heard some horrid stories in the orphanage about students who ended up in a reform school doomed for life and branded by society as rejects. Donata never expected this would happen to her. Desperately fearful, she knew she could not trust her stepmother or her father.

While in the orphanage, she learned a lesson in survival. She must protect herself and find the solution to this life-threatening situation. Escape was her only option, but this was a monumental task. Nevertheless, she began to plan her escape. She recalled the advice her Aunt Pavica gave her, "If you want to make friends for your own benefit, you must be kind and nice. That will earn you favour, and you will go far in life. A gentle lamb has two mothers, her Aunt Pavica had said, using simple peasant language; her down-to-earth wisdom still echoed in Donata's mind.

So she started befriending the supervisors. She offered to work in the laundry, knowing nobody wanted to wash dirty linen. After a few shifts in the laundry, Donata's room was left unlocked, giving her a small opportunity to escape.

Donata was a gentle lamb, and the supervisors allowed her to hang sheets and towels on the washing line. One afternoon, while the supervisors sat in the kitchen, smoking and drinking espresso coffee, Donata rang the bell and asked to wash her clothes, towels, and sheets that were blood-stained from her period.

Perceived as a lovely young girl with low risk, the supervisors allowed her this extra freedom. As soon as Donata finished one load of washing, she kept the second load spinning much longer, the noise making it appear that she was still in the laundry.

However, as soon as she hung all the towels and her linen sheets on the washing line, blocking the supervisors' view, she quickly grabbed her wet jeans and T-shirt. Pulling on the wet clothing was difficult, even in spring, it was still cold outside. She had no jacket, shoes, or money, but she had to make do.

Underneath the outdoor terrace was a double garage frequently used by staff, and she could be seen. But the view was fully obstructed on the other side of the terrace; it was risky, though, because she had to jump down onto the road. With her hands sweating and her heart beating as loud as the church bells in her little village that she feared others might hear, she prepared to jump. *It's now or never!* She put her hand on her chest as if trying to stop her heart from leaping out. Praying, she thought, *What if I break my leg or get hit by a car?* She had to time her jump between the traffic lights, observing the red light to avoid being hit by a car, or it would be all over. This was her only chance. The light turned red. She must jump now. She had to be brave.

Then, as if in slow motion, she took a leap of faith, clenched her fists and jumped. She flew as if she had wings, just like her little dove.

On that fateful day, Donata believed her mother's spirit helped her fly. Her little dove wings softened her landing.

ℂℛ

Confident in her abilities – she was always good at sports, especially running and long jump, which helped a lot – she landed firmly on two feet, ecstatic that she had made it. Then she started running.

Without shoes, the asphalt was rough and hot. It blistered her feet, but her adrenaline was pumping, and she felt no pain. She ran faster than ever before. Her only thought was to get to the first bus stop and move to a safer place. She had no money, so she hopped onto a school bus and blended among the rowdy kids.

This was not just a tiny step but a giant leap into an unknown future. Yet she was so happy now. She was in charge of her own destiny.

Chapter 9

The Sound of an Alfa Romeo

When Donata jumped on the school bus, hiding among the students, nobody noticed her. She calmed down slightly, knowing the police never stopped a school bus. Now she tried to think of a safe place to go. Unfortunately, Aida now lived with her Aunt Antonia in Italy, but her school friend Gina lived with her mother in Opatija. Donata trusted Gina and ran straight to her home, where she intended to hide for a few days.

The two girls hugged and cried together. Donata was exhausted but felt safe to rest for a few hours. Gina's mother, Pierina, welcomed her warmly and offered her shelter, food, and a warm bed. After quenching her thirst and taking a quick cool shower, she lay on the sofa bed. Pierina covered a soft pillow with a towel and put it under her feet. Then she disinfected and bandaged Donna's feet, which were full of blisters, the skin broken and bleeding.

A kind-hearted woman with salt-and-pepper grey hair, Pierina was well aware of Donata's troubled life and understood the mistreatment she had endured from her stepmother. However, because she was still a minor, the police would inevitably be looking for her. Pierina let Donata rest for a few hours before she contacted her father. She requested to meet him privately at her home, without Zorka.

The following day, Pierina met with Andrija and proposed that Donna rent a room from her. Pierina lived on a widow's pension, so the extra income would come in handy, and Gina would help her get a job at the Ambassador Hotel, where she worked.

Andrija was grateful and readily consented. This was the best outcome for his daughter, and it would appease his wife, too. On his way home, Andrija stopped at the detention centre to inform the staff that Donata was safe and to stop looking for her. The old baker, Vitomir agreed not to pursue the matter of the allegedly stolen money with the police further. Since Donata was still a minor, she was never charged. Whenever Pierina informed Andrija about Donata's progress, she would return from the markets with a bag full of smoked sausages, sweet grapes, and a few bottles of Andrija's wine.

Living in Opatija changed Donata's life. She and Gina secured an apprenticeship at the Ambassador Hotel. Following the apprenticeship, they enrolled in a prestigious school to study for a Diploma in Tourism and Hospitality. Both girls did practical training during the summer school break at the Ambassador and Adriatic Hotels.

In the two and a half years that Donata rented a room from Pierina, she only visited her family twice, once during Easter and once during Christmas. Gina and Donata became extraordinarily close and saw each other as sisters. Working in five-star hotels, she earned good wages and tips from wealthy and generous holiday guests. Opatija, only a few hours' drive from Venice and a short drive for Italian tourists coming for a weekend away or longer. Hotel guests also came from various other European countries, significantly from the chilly Scandinavian nations, Germany and Switzerland.

The local girls were staunchly against alcohol consumption and looked down upon those who engaged in drug use. Instead, they chose to spend their money on the latest fashions, usually from Italian or French designers enjoying a popularity boom during the sixties. Once work was over, Donata and her friends would party until the early morning hours before taking their tired feet home, often stopping for a gelato or an espresso. Whenever Aida returned from Italy, she and Donata would reconnect, frequently making the most of their time together during long weekend breaks.

Since they lived in the heart of the fashion world, Donata and her closest friends adopted nicknames of the popular models of the time. Aida earned the nickname BB due to her striking resemblance to the sultry French model Brigitte Bardot. Miroslava's curly hair led her friends to affectionately call her Shirley Temple, while Gina took her name after the renowned Italian actress Gina Lollobrigida. Donata, in turn, was lovingly referred to as CC, inspired by the iconic Claudia Cardinale.

Her friendship circle widened, and she enjoyed socialising with others. Mariana was tall and slender. She enjoyed playing basketball with her boyfriend Ivan, who had a Harley Davidson and often took her to tournaments. However, when Mariana became pregnant at eighteen, her sports career ended suddenly, and they married just days before their son, Allan, was born.

Dubravka garnered attention for her good looks but had an inferiority complex, having contracted polio as a child, which resulted in her limping. This did not stop her from being active and never missing out on disco nights.

Rayna, named after a German river, moved to Australia, but the group lost touch with her.

The most peculiar among them was Ludmila, dubbed after the eccentric singer Janis Joplin. She was high most of the time, experimenting with hashish and LSD, copying her idol's behaviour.

The teenage girls would catch buses to attend big music

concerts, often held in the capital city of Zagreb or the industrial city of Rijeka. After the shows, the night came alive with disco dancing as they flocked to nightclubs, indulging in lively parties and sipping cocktails until their money ran out.

Donata and her friends enjoyed Elvis Presley's provocative dance moves and the intoxicating music of The Beatles, The Rolling Stones, The Doors, Creedence Clearwater Revival, the Bee Gees, The Beach Boys, and The Platters. The music resonated throughout the hotel's beer gardens, discos, and other late-night venues, and there was no shortage of delicious wine and food.

In the afternoon, Donata and her friends would head down 'Via Lungo Mare' for a stroll or to relax at the beach.

Locals and tourists would mingle in the hotel cafes, enjoying the flavours of percolated coffee, espresso, cappuccino, or caffè latte. Young and old indulged in delicious puff pastry delights or creamy chocolate cakes with friends.

In Opatija, Donata first experienced a teenage romance and fell in love. Her boyfriend Damir's parents owned The Ohrid Restaurant, which graced the promenade and was renowned among locals and foreign tourists for serving the finest seafood dishes in the region. Damir often took Donata and her friends to Trieste, Italy, a one-hour drive away, for shopping trips. He wanted everyone to know he had money, so he drove a French car – an olive-green Citroen nicknamed 'Frog' – and paid for the girls' meals and drinks.

Damir engaged in other romantic liaisons with Swedish women. When Donata challenged him, he dismissed them as mere summer flings, insignificant and purely physical. To Donata, this admission marked the end of their union.

Religious beliefs became a significant factor when Damir began pursuing Miroslava, Donata's school friend, who came from a Bosnian Orthodox background. Damir's family welcomed Miroslava, but this highlighted the religious prejudice that had plagued Donata's mother and continued to be passed down to the next generation. Deep down, Donata knew this relationship was doomed from the start.

Despite everything, she remained an ardent romantic, convinced she would eventually meet her ideal partner, guided by her guardian angel, her cherished dove.

ભ

When Gina visited her sister Linda and her husband, Slobodan, who worked in Heidelberg, Germany, Gina fell in love with Roger, and they were engaged during her stay. Gina promised that, as soon as Donata turned eighteen, she would apply for her working visa, and the two friends would be reunited again.

ભ

One bright Sunday morning, Donata heard a car horn honking loudly outside her apartment. When she looked out of the window, she saw that Aida was frantically pressing the horn of an Alfa Romeo convertible.

"Ciao, Bella! Hey, are you deaf? Hurry down; let's go for a joyride!" Aida called out, her voice filled with excitement.

Donata quickly grabbed her jeans, put them on, and hastily combed her long hair. She glanced at herself in the mirror, but there was no time for makeup. With a rush of anticipation, she hurried outside, ecstatic to see her best friend.

"Are you surprised to see me? Come on, don't just stand there. Hop in the back seat, and let's go for a drive! You won't believe how fast this Alfa Romeo can go on the Autostrada," Aida exclaimed, her smile beaming as she embraced her friend tightly.

"Oh! I didn't know you moved to Milan. When did that happen?" Donata asked.

"My Aunt Antonia stayed in Padova, but I moved to Milan to be closer to my boyfriend," Aida explained with affection.

Aida turned around, her wavy blonde hair cascading over her face as she leaned in to kiss her boyfriend again.

"This is my boyfriend, Giannico Santoro," Aida introduced him with pride, his face momentarily hidden by her flowing locks. She smooched Giannico, leaving lipstick marks all over his face. Smiling happily, she introduced her best friend by her short version name, Donna, meaning woman in Italian. "That is the perfect title for the best woman I have ever met in my life." Aida and Donna hugged, and couldn't stop chatting.

"Cara mia, amica, what do you think? This Alpha Romeo is amazing." Aida grinned as she adjusted her front seat for Donna to squeeze in the back.

"Your boyfriend must be rich," Donna said, impressed.

"Yes, but believe me, it is not his money. I would love him just the same if he were poor. Giannico owns the House of Villa-Vela, one of Milan's most affluent and influential families. We met on the catwalk in Milan and fell head over heels in love."

Aida kept on chatting, then said, "Donna, where do you work now?

"This is my last year of training at the Adriatic Hotel," Donna replied.

"Now listen, Donna, there's no time to waste. You must quit your job and move to Italy. I've already arranged a job for you. You'll be working for the Santoro family," Aida exclaimed.

Turning to Giannico, she spoke to him in Italian. Donna, who had a good grasp of the language from her school days, so understood their conversation. It was apparent Aida and

Giannico were indeed deeply in love.

"I want to go with you. It'll be just like the old times we had in the orphanage," Donna replied excitedly.

"Oh, please, Donna, don't mention the orphanage. I haven't told anyone, and we must keep it between us," Aida responded, embracing her friend tightly. Donna could see that Aida didn't want her wealthy boyfriend to know about their shared past and nodded.

"Alright, then, it's all sorted, start organising your passport. The Santoro family owns Villa Verla, and Giuseppe and his wife Philomena will sponsor your working visa. You will be a governess for their two children, but you can also work on the ground floor where the designers create their clothes," Aida explained keenly.

"We'll return next month to pick you up. I can't wait for you to come and live with me in Milan. We'll have so much fun. So, my friend, start packing ..." Aida smiled radiantly.

As planned, Donna resigned from her job. However, being a few months away from turning eighteen, she was still considered a minor and needed her father's permission to sign her passport and approve her move to Italy. First, Donna expressed her gratitude to Pierina, who had been like a mother to her, for her kindness and generosity.

Then, she went to the post office phone booth to inform her friend Gina about the change in plans. Gina understood, and the two friends wished each other luck. Their friendship remained unshakable, and nothing could ever come between them. Donna promised she would be present at Gina's wedding in Heidelberg, and Gina pledged they would spend their honeymoon in Italy.

A month later, as arranged, Donna received a telegram from Aida stating they would arrive in their Alfa Romeo on Saturday before noon and to wait for her at the market grounds.

That morning, Donna packed her belongings and sat on a wooden bench at the front of the market, prepared to leave everything and everyone behind. Aida and Donna had shared their past, even carving their initials on the back walls of the orphanage. This friendship reassured Donna that she had made the right choice. Nervously pacing up and down the market, she eagerly awaited Aida's arrival.

Right on the dot before noon, Aida honked the horn, signalling their arrival. The loud sound caught the attention of everyone in the market as Giannico parked his Alfa Romeo on the edge of the footpath.

This time, Donna dashed forward as if she had wings; she tossed her bag inside and hopped into the back seat. Without wasting a moment, Giannico accelerated, and the Alfa Romeo's tyres screeched as they sped away, almost as if they were about to take flight.

Sitting in the back of the convertible Alfa Romeo, Donna put on her dark sunglasses and leaned back in the comfortable leather seat. The warm mid-summer wind blew through her shoulder-length hair, and for the first time, Donna felt like a glamorous movie star from the early sixties.

Their final destination was Milan, the fashion capital of the world. Donna was thrilled to accompany Aida to renowned catwalks and couldn't wait to visit the iconic La Scala Opera House. As Giannico sped along the Autostrada freeway, Donna felt like they were competing in the Grand Prix of Monte Carlo. In the Alfa Romeo, they would reach Milan in no time. There would be plenty of time to dress up, go out for dinner, and even attend the famous opera.

Donna had never felt better. Her new name had significant meaning in every sense of the word. DONNA justified the

Italian translation of "woman." And she had indeed blossomed into a beautiful young woman. Sitting in the back of the Alfa Romeo, Donna closed her eyes and began daydreaming about the beautiful world she was about to embrace.

She was ready to embrace La Dolce Vita.

Chapter 10

The Fashion House of Villa Verla

The world was hopeful and prosperous when Donna arrived in Milan in the late sixties. Enthusiasm was in the air. The world stood still when the Apollo 11 mission landed on the moon in July 1969. Everyone tuned in to watch the live black-and-white images transmitted from the Moon to Earth. This unique, momentous event connected everyone on this beautiful blue planet. Australia played a crucial role in tracking and broadcasting the images around the globe. However, once the euphoria of the moon landing died down, Australia seemed so far away that it might as well be on the moon itself.

Watching that remarkable occasion on television was a special memory that remained engraved in Donna's mind. If man can land on the moon, everything else is possible. This was indeed one small step and a giant leap into an exciting future for her.

The Santoro family owned the Villa Verla Fashion House, which designed and produced the latest fashion with its exclusive label. Giuseppe and Philomena Santoro were responsible for production and marketing. The younger Santoro brother, Giannico, co-director of Villa Verla, was not interested in the day-to-day business operations.

As a young woman newly arrived in Milan, the world's fashion capital – her new home – Donna belonged to a group of young women who felt liberated and wanted to emulate glamorous film stars like Elizabeth Taylor or Italian icons such as Sophia Loren, Gina Lollobrigida, Claudia Cardinale and French sex kitten Brigitte Bardot. These women were admired for their voluptuous figures, full breasts, slim waists, and rounded bottoms; they were statuesque goddesses. During this fashion era, it became fashionable for women to forego shaving their legs, embracing a sense of natural beauty that defied societal norms.

The Italian fashion scene was experiencing a boom, with renowned models gracing European catwalks. Young women eagerly followed the latest trends, investing their hard-earned money into luxurious garments from esteemed fashion houses such as Christian Dior and Gucci and reputable French designers like Coco Chanel and Yves Saint Laurent.

The era showcased mini dresses that boldly teased the visibility of tiny bikini briefs beneath, complemented by high-heeled stiletto shoes. During the colder seasons, long maxi dresses and a black coat were typically paired with tight leather boots that extended over the knees. In the winter, snug jeans and a leather or fur coat were the height of fashion.

Young women who frequented discos or nightclubs spent hours before the mirror perfecting their appearance. Their faces had to be flawless, adorned with layers of makeup – powdered cheeks, rosy blush, and meticulously applied false eyelashes. Hairstyles changed with the prevailing trends, often pinned up intricately and sprayed to achieve a bird's nest effect.

With the emergence of the British model Twiggy, hair fashion changed significantly. Her long, stringy hair and slim physique set a new trend many embraced for a season or two. Aida had beautiful, long, curly blonde hair and was unhappy with its outdated style. Donna assisted in transforming Aida's hair by meticulously straightening it. They laid it out on an ironing board, covered it with linen or surgical gauze, and carefully used a hot iron to prevent burns to Aida's neck or face.

On the top floor of the esteemed Villa Verla fashion house, Aida was selected to present and showcase the new fashion designers' creations to clients who came to review and select their final garment purchases.

Donna initially served as a governess, attending to the owner's children. Her Italian improved significantly within the first six months, facilitating smoother communication. This boosted her confidence and self-esteem. In her spare time, she worked on the factory floor, sorting the imported silk and linen by grading and selecting wool and other fine materials.

The Santoro family liked Donna's easygoing, bubbly nature and welcomed her into their close-knit family.

As she gained more experience, she became a sales and marketing department member. She had a promising career and enjoyed working with designers and tailors on the ground floor, sewing on Singer sewing machines. Working for the fashion house of Villa Verla was her dream job. She lived on the Santoro estate, which offered secure and private accommodation for full-time workers. Donna often did overtime to make extra money and saved for her first car.

Donna and the rest of the Villa Verla House staff were offered discounted prices on imperfect clothes. Donna started attending lavish parties dressed in top fashions and was fully optimistic about her future.

Aida was hired to model for the House of Villa Verla on Milan's catwalks, and her modelling skills and appearance soon attracted the attention of other famous houses.

Donna, however, being of average height, with a curvy figure, dark brown curly hair with red streaks across her forehead, and hazel-brown eyes, preferred comfortable attire such as dresses, jeans, T-shirts, and sneakers. She felt much more at ease working behind the scenes. Sometimes, though, she would choose exclusive dresses and pair them with silk stockings and stilettos for special occasions, like cocktail parties. Accessorising with French shoulder bags, perfumes, makeup, and large earrings, she looked graceful and feminine but would promptly change into cozy tracksuits or flannel pyjamas upon returning home.

While Donna worked on the factory's ground floor, Aida advanced her career in modelling and began to travel for her modelling assignments, often accompanied by Santoro's younger brother, Giannico, and sometimes Donna as support staff. Behind the scenes, Donna mingled with famous fashion models. After the show, they would wine and dine at their favourite al-fresco restaurant. The following day, they would rise just before noon and then shop until they dropped before sitting at a corner café and enjoying a cappuccino or espresso. Then they would party all over again, attending cocktail parties dressed to impress. Aida tried to set her up with eligible men, but Donna wasn't interested.

Then, at a cocktail party after one of the catwalk shows, Donna met Mirvano, a football player. Everybody in Italy, young and old, attended football matches on the weekend. Supporting their local team was part of the Italian culture. The City of Milan came alive when football came to town, and staff at the Villa Verla fashion house were crazy about football.

Mirvano's football career was vital to him; he played left wing for Inter Milan and travelled with his club all over Europe for matches. He was away for weeks and Donna found out he had a girlfriend in every city. Women loved footballers, and Mirvano could choose anyone he wanted. Sick of competing for his affection and fed up with his empty promises and lies, Donna booted him out. She wanted a man who belonged only to her and believed true love would one day come her way, and she would get married for life and stay together until death.

Meanwhile, however, Giuseppe disapproved of Giannico's union with Aida. The Santoro family was devoted to the Catholic faith, whereas Aida belonged to the Orthodox faith, and mixed marriages were not welcome by conservative families.

Aida deeply resented the Santoro family. Having secured some independent modelling gigs, she aimed to break free from their contracts and display the latest trends to high-profile celebrities. She took up residence in Giannico's flat in a fashionable district of the Milanese suburbs.

Donna happily stayed single. She had many friends and enjoyed working in the fashion house. Sometimes, she accompanied the Santoro family on long weekends, day trips, and excursions. She adored Giuseppe, Philomena, and their two children.

Meanwhile, Aida busied herself with modelling. During the winter months, she and Giannico escaped the hustle and bustle of the fashion world and spent a few weeks in Giannico's villa in Tuscany or his apartment in Rome.

Aida's aim was to be on the front page of Vogue magazine. When she achieved that, she wanted even more. Giannico was not the marrying type, but when Aida fell pregnant, they married. Aida decided to have an abortion, tearfully saying to Giannico that she'd had a miscarriage. Obsessed with her body image, Aida determinedly avoided another pregnancy.

The happy couple packed up and drove to Tuscany, spending money like there was no tomorrow, attending exotic parties with the rich and famous, and spending a small fortune at the Monte Carlo Casino. When Giuseppe scolded him about his reckless lifestyle, the family feud became bitter, resulting in the brothers splitting the business.

Aida eliminated everything that would have been detrimental to her modelling career, and she had no interest in having children. Giannico became possessively jealous of her success; he turned up at her shows drunk and caused scenes; he verbally abused her and violently accosted her. She took out a restraining order against him, barring him from attending any fashion shows where she took part – image was everything in the fashion industry. Eventually, Giannico became an outcast among the fashion elite and inevitably, Aida and Giannico broke up. Their marriage was dissolved, and Aida's settlement enabled her to buy her own Alfa Romeo convertible, and an apartment in an exclusive area of Milan.

Giannico returned to his playboy ways, moved to his Tuscany villa to escape adverse publicity and, mixing with the rich and famous, began experimenting with drugs. He severed all ties with the house of Villa Verla, and the payout from his share of the business was enough to sustain his reckless and promiscuous lifestyle. When Giannico's homosexuality came to the surface, the Santoro family kept it hidden; when later diagnosed with AIDS, that was hushed up, too.

Aida opened a perfume shop at the fashionable arcade boutique, catering to a wealthy clientele. She stocked only trendy designs and fragrances from top fashion houses worldwide. Becoming highly ambitious and focused on building her image and accumulating wealth, the two best friends chose different paths in life and drifted apart, but they promised to keep in touch.

CB

Nearing Christmas, Donna received a telegram from her father inviting her to join them for the celebrations where she would meet her much older sister Mara, who was coming all the way from Australia. Donna had not seen her family for over two years and had no memories of Mara, who had emigrated when Donna was a small child.

At the height of the festive season, Donna packed her overnight bag and boarded the train to Rijeka. Sitting comfortably in a first-class cabin, she pressed her face against the cool window glass as the train sped through the majestic scenery, with snow blanketing the fields. Her thoughts turned to her relationship with her family. Now an independent young woman, she was no longer angry and bitter, and preferred to focus on the positives. Although her relationship with her family was almost non-existent, she excitedly waited to meet her sister.

She thought this would be a picture-perfect white Christmas and New Year, and looked forward to welcoming her sister and attending Midnight Mass and Carols by Candlelight.

When Donna arrived home, she immediately noted, and expected, Emil was not there as he spent every Christmas with his godparents, who owned a skiing chalet in the mountains.

The festivities soon turned joyful, and after a few mulled wines, Mara, who was sixteen years older than Donna, cried and embraced her baby sister, the bear hug so tight it left Donna breathless. Mara's brown eyes sparkled when she smiled. Although overweight, she looked proportionally built in the tightly fitted, green floral dress. *She must be rich,* Donna thought, *with all that gold dangling around her neck. She glitters like a Christmas tree.*

The Christmas luncheon included homemade products, the best Prosciutto, cheeses, delicious walnut apples, and cinnamon cakes. Donna felt honoured to taste Andrija's wine from the Verities Winery, which started to gain popularity. Mara enjoyed it too, and after a few glasses of the grappa-based pear liqueur, she blurted out, "Why don't you come with me to Australia!"

"No way, I don't want to go that far!" Donna scoffed, waving her hands with resistance. "Besides, I fear flying; I've never been on a plane before."

"Don't be silly, sissy. Qantas Airways is the safest plane in the world. Qantas planes carry our Australian emblem."

"What are you talking about?" Donna frowned.

"On the Qantas plane's tail sits our national emblem, a red kangaroo," Mara stated.

"It is safe because if the plane can't fly, it can hop its way there."

Everybody burst out laughing at Andrija's joke. "Come on, Mara, let's have another of my wines; last year's vintage was one of the best."

Andrija kept laughing, happy to have his children around him.

That week, as Donna and her older sister became friends, Mara kept up the pressure.

"Come on, little sister," Mara urged, determined to persuade her younger sister. "Come and live with me Down Under. Australia is the best country in the world, and I have no regrets. It is the best thing I have ever done."

But Donna always shook her head. "Why would I want to move? My career in sales and marketing at the Villa Verla has just begun. And I love my life. I love Milan and don't want to leave it. It's the centre of European fashion, music, and culture. Why on earth would I move to the bottom of the world, all the way to Australia?" Donna protested.

When all her prompting failed, Mara played her last card. "Listen, sissy," she said, "I have a proposal for you: You come to Australia. Stay for two years, and learn English. If you don't like Adelaide, I promise to cover your flight back to Italy."

Mara looked around for family support, and when their father, Andrija, applauded Mara's suggestion, Donna gave in, reasoning that, in those two years, she could learn English, which would give her an advantage as the house of Villa Verla purchased wool from many Australian sheep farms. With her marketing skills, when she returned to Italy, she could work in the export and import section, purchasing foreign materials, so she had nothing to lose but very much to gain.

After the festive celebrations, Donna returned to Italy to inform Santoro's family that she was leaving, which saddened them, but they wished her luck and gave her a gift.

"Donna, Cara Mia, you need good travel luggage," Philomena said.

"But Gucci luggage? That is expensive," Donna protested, feeling grateful yet humbled by such gifts.

"Don't worry. We want you to take a few of our best garments with you, and for that, you need good luggage."

Philomena smiled as she hugged Donna goodbye. "When you land in Australia, you must wear the latest winter garments from our showrooms. Most of our winter garments are made of pure Australian Merino wool. Please display and promote our label. We buy the best quality wool from Australia and New Zealand. You could help us build a profile in that part of the world." Then Philomena and Giuseppe spoke in one voice. "We will miss you so much."

Santoro's kids hugged her tightly, unwilling to let her go.

"Thank you for all these lovely gifts. I will write you a letter every week." Donna graciously accepted the latest fashion-designed garments and neatly packed her valuables in her Gucci suitcase. Her hand luggage, designed by Yves Saint Laurent, was full of expensive French perfumes and enough makeup to last her a lifetime.

Donna looked forward to displaying all her exclusive gifts as soon as she arrived in Adelaide. "Remember, Donna, if you ever want to return, your job is guaranteed," Giuseppe promised as he said his goodbyes. Donna needed that reassurance; the safety net eased her worries about immigrating to Australia.

The farewell party was full of joy and parting tears. Some of her work colleagues on the ground floor in the sewing and designing rooms believed she would never return.

"I don't think we will ever see you again. My brother left twenty years ago. We lost contact with him and don't know if he is alive anymore," one of her supervisors told her.

Donna heard so many similar stories, but her mind was made up. Saying goodbye to her friends and the Santoro family was painful. She loved them all, and they loved her. Everyone on the ground floor wished for Donna, "Buona Fortuna!"

Donna already had a passport, and after the medical test and vaccination, her immigration visa was approved. She boarded the flight in February, in the early seventies, while Europe was blanketed in snow.

As she boarded her first flight, she remembered her sister's words: "Qantas is the safest place on this earth", so she soon began to feel more at ease. The impeccably groomed flight attendants in their blue uniforms and tiny hats offered her a warm towel, food, and refreshments and were very polite.

Donna pressed her face against the small oval-shaped window and pondered the effortless flight of the enormous metal bird with its massive wings as it glided above the grey wintery clouds. She must have dozed off and, drifting into deeper sleep, she dreamed that her little dove was flying beneath the plane. Knowing that her little dove would never leave her gave her a sense of safety and assurance.

She must have slept for hours when she was awakened by the engine noise and felt the plane's vibration. Once again, the reassuring Captain's voice came through the plane's intercom, reminiscent of Captain Kirk from the starship Enterprise. Donna felt like she was in it, landing in an unknown world. This was not just one small step, but a giant leap into an unknown frontier, where she would explore the new world down under.

"Ladies and gentlemen, this is your captain speaking. Please adjust your seat to an upright position and fasten your seatbelt. We are about to land in Adelaide where the weather is sunny and hot; the expected temperature is 35 degrees.

"We hope you had an enjoyable flight and wish you a pleasant stay in Australia."

Part Two

Life Goes On

Chapter 11

Down Under

Donna sighed with relief as the plane began its descent towards Adelaide. The colossal steel bird landed on terra firma with a slight squeal of tyres. The moment the plane stopped, Donna started applying her makeup using a compact mirror, a mix of nerves and excitement making her want to make a positive first impression. She had purchased an exquisite French perfume as a gift for Mara, confident it would be well-received within the chic social circles of this vibrant metropolitan city.

The first thing she noticed was that the airport terminal was practically empty – hardly anyone around. *It must be because it's late Sunday afternoon,* she thought, looking around. Suddenly, her sister's loud voice echoed around the small airport, shouting at her husband. "Martin, come quick. Donna has arrived. Hurry, help her with the suitcases."

Turning, she spotted Mara in the small crowd.

Mara clutched her and squeezed her, tears of joy flowing as she asked, "How was your flight? You must be tired and hungry. Don't worry, sissy, we have lots of food."

"I can't wait for a cappuccino or a good espresso. The flight was long. Can we stop at a cafe on the way home?"

Before Mara could respond, Martin politely interrupted, "Let me help you with your luggage. Our home is only a short drive from the airport, and you must be tired after such a long journey."

Mara introduced her husband, Martin, a bald, short man with

an enormous beer belly. A talkative, friendly man, he looked much older than Mara.

When they exited the terminal, Donna was immediately struck by late February's sweltering, dry heat. She had travelled from the snow of Europe to a scorching summer. The heat was stifling, and the air was thick with flies. People frantically waved their hands in front of their faces while greeting each other.

Martin's car sat in open space in an almost empty car park. The rusty old Holden Monaro was his prized possession, even though its wheels were covered in red dust, and the windscreen was smudged and covered in dead flies. Donna gasped when he grabbed her expensive Gucci luggage and hurled it into the boot among his greasy old tools as if it was made from cheap cardboard. Before Donna sat in the back seat, Martin quickly wiped the vinyl covers with a greasy old cloth and threw it beside him, but by now, she was too hot to care. Relief came when the engine started and air-conditioning blew into her face. It was so refreshing.

Martin drove through the broad, empty streets of Adelaide as if he owned the road. The city centre had a few high-rise buildings and one or two churches from the colonial past. Donna noticed there were no alfresco dining restaurants and no cappuccino strip. There were a few green parks. She felt like she had just landed on the moon. The footpaths were empty as if people didn't live there. In contrast, Sunday afternoons in Europe were abuzz with life and crowds.

"Where are all the people hiding?" she asked.

"This summer has been exceptionally hot, so everyone is indoors next to their fans or air-conditioners. If not, they're in the pub or on the beach. Don't worry, sissy, this is a very hot day. Tomorrow, we will go for a drive and take you to see our lovely sandy beaches," Mara tried to reassure her sister.

Looking through the window as they drove through the

suburbs, Donna saw rows and rows of single-storey family dwellings built in a similar design, each with picket fencing and large front lawns. They drove past a few green parks, but mostly, the side of the road had dry bushland.

When they arrived home, Donna first noticed a large bowl of fresh fruit on the kitchen table. What a lovely surprise. She had just come from the cold European winter and stepped into a hot summer and abundant fruit. I've entered the Garden of Eden, she thought as she ate watermelon, grapes, apricots, peaches, and sweet rock melon. She was already falling in love with Australia. After the delicious culinary indulgence, Donna finally succumbed to jetlag and went to bed.

Mara opened all the bedroom windows, leaving the mesh screens closed. "They're flywire screens," Mara told her. They allow some breeze into the house and stop flies and mosquitoes."

For Donna, the heat became unbearable, so she had another cold shower, but by the time she reached her bedroom, she was too hot again; she wrapped herself in a damp towel and placed a smaller one on her forehead yet still struggled to find sleep in the oppressive heat. Then Mara brought in a portable water cooler, which only raised the room's stifling humidity. *This must be like living on Venus or Mars*, Donna thought. *How will I ever endure two years in this stifling heat?*

Suffering from jet lag and the anxiety as her future unfolded once again as an unwritten story, she tossed and turned all night.

The next day, Martin and Mara took Donna on a sightseeing tour of the suburbs and the beach, but Donna wasn't impressed. Only a few families gathered under the shade of the pine trees, enjoying their barbeque and several children played on the swings. Donna looked for more people, but Glenelg Beach, stretching for miles and miles, was dull and empty, with no fun activities.

"What a waste of such a beautiful sandy beach, but hardly anybody swimming. If this beach were in Europe, it would be noisy, full of umbrellas and people tanning their bodies until brown. There is no music, no fun activities. Where are the outdoor cafes to sit and sip espresso coffee, latte, cappuccino?"

"Most families stay home having barbeques or are at the pub watching a game of cricket on a big TV. This is cricket season."

"What is cricket?" Donna asked.

"It's a game where you hit a ball with a flat wooden stick. Just like the one we used in the village to bash our washing," Mara laughed.

"Look over there. That's a cricket bat the children are playing with," added Martin, pointing to a small group.

"Mara, can you tell me if the city has any nightlife? I want to go to nightclubs, discos, or street parties to meet people."

"Yes, we have drive-ins," Martin said. You sit in the car with an esky and a dozen cold stubbies, then hang a speaker on a window and watch a movie. We can go next week if you like."

"I have never seen that before. That should be fun, but what is stubby?"

"It's cold beer in a small bottle. Let's escape this heat and go to the pub to cool off and get lunch."

"Is there any dancing at the pub?" Donna asked keenly.

"There's no dancing, but sitting in the beer garden in the shade and having a BBQ is fun, too. Most people visit pubs to meet up with their mates, drink, and play two-up. So many people watch cricket or football on the big TV screens. Footy is very popular here," Martin explained.

"Great, I like football," Donna exclaimed, her eyes lighting up. "In Italy, we would watch live football matches at the weekend. I supported Inter Milan, where my ex-boyfriend Mirvano played. After the game, a group of us would party until the early morning, stop at a café and order freshly baked croissants, yummy cakes, and cappuccino. The streets were full of supporters, and the atmosphere was crazy. It was so much fun," Donna recounted.

"Oh, no, you don't understand. You have it all wrong," Martin said. "It's not the football you remember from Italy. Here, that is called soccer. However, only Wogs and Dings play that silly game; it is boring to watch, scoring one or two goals only. That game is for poofters, grown men hugging and kissing," Martin laughed. "Australia has a real football, Aussie Rules, but most people call it 'footy.' It's played with an egg-shaped ball, and the goal has four big poles. The players can score a hundred points in one night. We love Aussie Rules. It's huge here. You can take a six-pack of beer and have fun with your mates."

"What about women? What entertainment do they have?" Donna asked.

"Don't make me laugh, you silly girl. Women stay home. Footy is a bloke's game."

"What! I have never heard something so ridiculous as a woman staying home while a man goes to watch football that has no net," Donna snapped sarcastically.

After finishing a BBQ lunch at the local pub, Martin drove home as if he was competing in the Grand Prix. Drunk as a skunk, he swerved from one side of the empty road to the other. Donna had to open her window for fresh air.

Donna was relieved when Martin left with his mining partner, Ivan, for Coober Pedy. She wouldn't have to stress anymore while sitting in the back of his Monaro. The fridge would no longer be full of beer, and there would be no more drinking sessions with his mates. He would no longer shout at Mara or turn violent when drunk.

One evening, after Martin left, Donna and Mara were relaxing with a cask of wine on the back patio. "Do you need to work so hard?" Donna asked Mara.

"I have to work to earn money to support Martin. He needs new mining machinery and extra gelignite for his opal mine."

Mara never discussed the family history when Martin was around. Now he was gone, she was more relaxed, and after a few extra glasses of wine, the truth came out.

"Why have we never met before? What happened to our family?" Donna asked.

Mara shook her head. "Our family life was very complicated and sad. After our mother's tragic death, the whole family fell apart. I don't enjoy discussing it, as I may get upset and cry. Remembering the past is difficult."

"Please, Mara, don't stop," Donna pleaded. "I need to know."

"Our family fell apart, separated, and scattered all over Europe. Anka, our oldest sister, moved to France, where her four children had all finished schooling. Anka misses the village lifestyle, and I am sure that one day, she will return to our village. She loves the simple life."

"I miss Anka too. I enjoyed spending my school holidays there. It was so special, and we all had lots of fun. I will forever cherish those special summer days when Aunty Pavica told us so many unbelievable stories. Anka was like a mother to me, and my whole life turned upside down when Anka moved to France," Donna said with deep sadness. "How come you ended up in Australia?"

"When our mother died, our village had no prospect of a better future. I was seventeen years old when I moved to Germany, and Draga followed a year later. We worked in kitchen at one of the biggest hospitals in Hamburg and we lived in a staff accommodation on the hospital grounds. This gave us more independence and hospital food was good. Just look at me." Mara squeezed her fat belly, laughing.

"No, Mara, you look good. You are not that fat."

"Oh yeah? Who are you kidding? I eat when stressed, and food is my comfort. I gave up on dieting. What is the point? Besides, Martin likes me fat."

"Come on, stop, diverting. Tell me what happened in Hamburg," Donna asked impatiently.

"We had what we needed to survive: employment. Unfortunately for migrants, education was difficult. After the Second World War, nobody cared if you could read or write. You only had to sign your name to receive your wages. For migrants, especially girls, life was tough. I got stuck as a cleaner and have worked in kitchens ever since."

"How did you meet Martin?"

"Martin worked at a hospital's building site. He was kind, generous, and a fatherly figure. He spoiled me with gifts and took me to expensive restaurants. I was young and fell in love with the wrong man."

"Draga was fortunate; she married an older Swiss art dealer who helped her get educated and introduced her to affluent art circles. But her husband disapproved of her association with me, an uneducated peasant woman."

"Do you keep in touch?" Donna asked.

"I moved to Australia over ten years ago and haven't heard from her since. I miss her so much." Mara wiped away her tears.

"Our other sister, Vera, is seven or eight years older than you. Our mother had another miscarriage, then a stillbirth, and a few years later, you were born.

"I heard from distant relatives that Vera had a hard life as a teenager, sexually abused while she lived with her adoptive family. She had no one to turn to. But she was determined to survive and make a good life."

"Where is she now?"

"To escape her oppressive life, she married a man from

another village. Her husband inherited an old stone house in southern Croatia, and they opened a bed & breakfast for tourists.

"You were merely two years old when our mother passed away. I only encountered Zorka once; she was a harsh woman. How did you endure living with her under one roof? Our father was more interested in his vineyard than his daughters. How can you forgive him for sending you to the orphanage?" Mara inquired.

"To forgive is far more satisfying – resentment and hatred affects your inner peace. I've stopped perceiving myself as a victim. Feeling vulnerable is not an option for me. However, let's shift the focus from me. I'm curious about your life. Why do you stay with that old bastard?"

Mara nodded. "When Draga left for Switzerland, I met Martin, but I didn't know he was already married and had grown-up children. I was lonely and missed all the signs."

"So why did you move to Australia?"

"Eventually, I got sick of being caged like a bird. Martin kept me hidden as his mistress, so I ran away to Australia."

"And he found you?"

"I sent a postcard to my friend I worked with at the hospital; she may have told him. I wish that the old bastard had never found me, but he did. Martin drinks far too much, and when drunk, he is abusive and violent. The old bastard will outlive everybody. In our village, women used to say that God protects only children and drunks." Mara laughed.

"Why have you never had children of your own?" Donna wanted to know.

"Martin has four grown-up children and doesn't want any more kids. I was pregnant a few times, but he forced me to have an abortion." Mara then cried again.

"It's not too late. You can still have children," Donna said, trying to cheer her up; she poured another glass of wine.

"I'm approaching forty soon." Mara's voice trembled, and she wiped her tears, but she kept on talking. "I had so many abortions that I stopped counting. God will punish me the way he punished our mother. I am a sinner like our poor mother; I will burn in hell for eternity."

"Don't be so hard on yourself. I am sure our mother would have been very proud of her daughters. One day, we could get together to honour her. Our mother deserves to be remembered by all her daughters."

Mara embraced Donna. "That would be wonderful. I will hold you to that. But God will never forgive me for living with a married man," Mara said.

"Don't be silly, Mara. God loves you. You can change your life; it is never too late," Donna said softly.

"On, no, I can't. Martin threatened that if I ran away, he would kill me. Nobody can help me; I got used to living this crazy charade." She wiped away more tears.

"What charade? What are you talking about?"

"We never married; Martin never got divorced. His wife still thinks that one day he will come back home. We are living in sin. In our small migrant Catholic community in Adelaide, we have to pretend to be married.

"When we travelled to Europe last year, Martin stayed in Germany with his wife, children and grandchildren. On the way back, we met at the airport, like two strangers, and flew back to Adelaide together. All of our migrant friends in Coober Pedy believe we are happily married but not lucky enough to have kids."

Mara paused for a moment, wiping away her tears. She looked at Donna sternly. "Now, you listen to me, young lady, you must promise me to keep this between us."

"Of course, I won't say anything. But you don't have to stay with that drunk," Donna responded.

"There is no point complaining about my life. It is too late to change anything now. I made my bed, and now I must lie in it."

Managing a smile, Mara hugged her baby sister. "I feel so lucky now, having you living here with me. I finally have a family of my own." Mara calmed herself by finishing her glass of wine. "I think that is enough for tonight. It is getting late. I need to get up early for my cleaning shift. Let's talk some more tomorrow." Mara started yawning and headed for bed. "Good night, my child."

A week later, Donna decided to go around the neighbourhood and introduce herself to the neighbours in the hope of making new friends. However, she experienced another cultural shock. When she knocked on their doors, most people thought she was a religious caller offering spiritual magazines and selling Jesus Christ as their saviour. Donna was so disappointed when doors were slammed in her face. So she felt excited when Mara informed her they would attend a neighbourhood barbecue. She told Mara, "I told you it was a good idea that I went knocking on doors. Those neighbours want to be our friends.

"What should I wear, this blue or purple dress? Which one will suit me better?" Donna said excitedly, but Mara was busy baking a walnut cake in the kitchen and ignored her.

"We are invited to a barbeque, so why are you baking a cake now?"

"We have to bring a plate," Mara said, continuing to melt chocolate.

"Don't Aussies have plates?" Donna asked, frowning.

"Don't be silly," Mara burst out laughing. "It's not an empty plate; it means to bring some food. Aussies like Wog's and Ding's food. It's a big novelty for them," Mara laughed.

"What do you mean?"

"Well, you better get used to these words. Aussies don't mean any harm by calling us Wogs or Dings. It is a term of endearment. You need to get used to the Aussie sense of humour."

"It is strange to bring food. When invited out for a meal in European homes, bringing fresh flowers, a box of chocolate, or a bottle of wine for the host is polite. They would never bring sweets, meat, or salads. That would be too insulting. It makes little sense." Donna realised she still had much to learn about Aussie culture and customs.

Upon arriving at the barbecue, Donna instantly felt out of place. She'd overdressed in a lilac dress, hat, and black high heels, which made her stand out. Looking around the backyard, she noticed everyone else had opted for shorts, t-shirts, and thongs. Observing the social dynamics, Donna saw that the men and women mingled in separate groups. The men gathered around the grill, beer in hand, and talked about cricket and football.

Women stayed close to their children, who jumped into the above-ground pool and splashed around with the garden hose to cool off. They were absorbed with stories of their children's sports and swapped recipes. Most women drank shandies, a mix of beer and lemonade. Some gossiped about other neighbours, and others complained about all the foreigners coming to their country and stealing their jobs.

Mara warned Donna not to talk in their native language. It was not polite, and people would be offended. Still, with her limited English, Donna felt embarrassed because most women didn't understand her. But, when Donna approached a group of men at the barbecue and spoke in broken English, some wives gave her disapproving glances, which unsettled her. She couldn't understand why her behaviour was inappropriate. She had no intention of stealing their husbands; she only wanted more stimulating conversation, to talk about foreign affairs and sports and to learn more about Aussie football. She was not interested in exchanging recipes.

୭

As the weeks passed, Donna started feeling more isolated and depressed. She slept most of the day while her sister worked as a cleaner at a nearby hotel; she was lonely and incredibly bored, with nothing to do but watch TV shows she didn't understand, or sports like cricket that went on for days and never ended. Going to the pub could have been better. She attended once or twice, but usually, young people congregated in their little groups, drinking beer and telling jokes – those she didn't understand either. Some people she met ridiculed her fashion choice. Donna's mini or maxi dresses were famous all over Europe, and wearing a hat was fashionable. In Adelaide, women wore hats only to the beach and for fun activities such as the Melbourne Cup.

On Sundays, Donna had to accompany Mara to the Catholic church. They also socialised at the migrant's ethnic clubs, where Yugoslavs, Greeks, and Italians mingled. At the ethnic clubs, Donna was ridiculed, and women told her.

"Donna, you look silly in all that makeup. Don't waste money or time polishing your nails; you should start volunteering at migrant community clubs like us," one woman advised.

Another suggested, "Why don't you come with some of us as seasonal workers, picking grapes, apricots, oranges in the Riverland area? It is hard work, but the money is good. The faster you pick the fruit, the more money you can earn."

"Yeah, but you better cut your nails," someone else laughed.

However, Mara didn't want her sister to move away. She had

waited nearly twenty years to reconnect with her baby sister and was not letting her go. She had much better plans for them both.

Like most Croatian and Italian migrants, Mara was a devoted Catholic. The church was where migrant families congregated, participated in social gatherings, dressed well, and met newly arrived migrants. The women volunteered to bake and sell cakes for fundraising for some social clubs. Migrants kept to themselves, cooked traditional comfort foods and sang traditional songs. They hardly ever spoke English, leaving Donna little chance to learn. While living in Croatia and Italy, she had never met such an old-fashioned group of people as these, and she felt like a stranger in the migrant community.

She felt lost and insecure; she was a foreigner who couldn't speak or write English. Now, she understood how it felt to be deaf, mute or illiterate.

Donna looked at herself in the mirror and sighed. She looked tired and pointed a stern finger straight at her reflection. Snap out of all these nostalgic, romantic thoughts about the life you left behind. This is Adelaide, *not the fashion house of Villa Verla. If you intend to return to Milan, find a job. Pronto!*

Focus on the current reality. Thinking about the past is unproductive. Get your act together, and stop feeling sorry for yourself. In the past, you have encountered much harder circumstances and survived. Start looking for a job. Any job will do. Besides, you have plenty of experience cleaning blocked toilets in the orphanage. You are an expert in cleaning, washing dishes, or washing clothes in freezing water.

Luckily, Mara introduced her to a Macedonian woman. Svetlana worked in a large city cafeteria, and Donna got a job in the kitchen; it didn't require experience or education, and speaking English was optional.

On her first day at work, she was given an oversized plastic apron, giant gloves, and black rubber boots. Her job was to scrub large industrial pots, using a hydraulic pump to lower them into the correct position. Charred pots needed to be soaked in harsh chemicals overnight before washing early the following day.

Donna rolled up her sleeves. The kitchen had no air conditioning, and the heat was unbearable but she scrubbed the pots with a steel scourer as if her life depended on it. But she soon realised she would not learn English if she continued working in this kitchen. Most women who worked there were Greek, Yugoslav, Russian, or Italian, and they communicated in their own language.

However, at that early stage, her only dream was to work at the front counter, take orders, and work as a cashier at the register. Serving, clearing tables, and talking to customers was the only way to learn English and move forward.

One day, Donna gathered enough courage and, in her limited, broken English, she asked her supervisor, "Please, I like to work at the front counter to learn English?"

Her supervisor, Florence, put her back in her box. "Listen, Donna, kitchen work is good enough for all the other migrants. It should be good enough for you, too. If you don't like it, you can quit and go back to where you came from."

Donna went to the rooftop to join some women for a quick break, cool off and cry.

"Florence thinks she is better than we are. Just because she can speak English doesn't make her a better person. Don't get upset," Rose said.

"Big deal, none of us understand Florence's Pommie accent," Sofia burst out laughing.

While Sofia tried to comfort Donna, Olga was furious. She hugged Donna and said, "Don't let Florence crawl under your skin; ignore her, just like we do. Don't worry, you are still young. You will get to work at the front counter. Maybe not here, but it will happen."

So she quickly adjusted to kitchen work. Scrubbing pots and washing cafeteria floors was okay, but cleaning the men's toilets was the worst. She had to kneel to clean the filthy urinal with bleach and a wooden brush; it made her feel sick and reminded her of the orphanage.

The migrant women used to cheer her up and kept telling her, "We live in the best country in the world. In Australia, even if you don't work, the government gives you money, but you don't want to be called a dole-bludger. It is much better to earn your own money."

Laughing at themselves and others was always so much fun. The women enjoyed a laugh during a quick cigarette break on the rooftop.

At night, Donna soaked herself in the bath to eliminate the awful kitchen smell and put on an old tracksuit and thongs. She had no further use for her costly makeup and false eyelashes. Her hands became crinkled and her nails cracked, and she stopped caring about her appearance. Maintaining a hairstyle seemed pointless. In the sweltering heat, short hair proved practical and easier to manage.

Donna now had a master plan. Her only goal was to save enough money to buy a one-way ticket and go home. If she disciplined herself enough, in two years she would finally say goodbye to this nightmare.

Also at night, Donna enjoyed listening to familiar pop songs on her radio cassette player, and classical music she had brought from Italy. She found it easy to save money, as there were few boutiques or fancy make-up shops near where she lived. She found little entertainment, no discos, live shows, or music festivals. Her only expense was to help Mara pay the rent and do some shopping.

Determinedly, Donna focused on the bigger picture: keep working and save enough money for a one-way ticket home to the House of Villa Verla.

℘

Just when Donna had saved nearly half the money she needed to return to Italy, Mara announced they would move on to another adventure.

"I have purchased two bus tickets for us. Soon, we will join Martin in Coober Pedy. It is time to quit work and say goodbye to your friends at the cafeteria. We are leaving at the end of this month. Coober Pedy is a small mining town, just like the American Wild West cowboy movies you like. I am sure you will like it much better than Adelaide," Mara promised her.

"Now is the best time to travel, as the scorching desert heat has eased. I suggest you buy some cool summer dresses. Coober Pedy is always hot. It gets chilly at night so you can wear your designer clothes then."

Donna was now stuck Down Under, but hopefully not for long. Nothing would stop her quest to return to Villa Verla. Her little dancing dove, her guardian angel, would protect and guide her no matter what. Soon, Donna would fly back home to where she belonged.

But not yet …

Chapter 12

Bonanza – Little Joe's Country

Donna was so excited that she couldn't sleep properly. The previous night, she packed her best clothes in her Gucci suitcase. Since winter had arrived, she could finally wear her leather stiletto boots, hat, and stylish maxi coat, manicure her nails, and wear makeup again.

When Donna and Mara took a taxi to the bus station, Donna chose to sit behind the driver for the best views on the drive from Adelaide to Coober Pedy.

"I have packed some lunch and drinks for us in ice boxes. Let me know when you get hungry," Mara said to Donna.

"I am too excited to eat, as I cannot wait to explore the heart of Australia. Driving through the desert is a once-in-a-lifetime experience; I don't want to miss." Donna relaxed and rested her face against the large bus window.

After a while, she asked, "Mara, please tell me something about Coober Pedy."

"Well, do you remember telling me you enjoyed watching the American Cowboy movies and your favourite TV show 'Bonanza'?"

"I never missed that show. It was extremely popular in the mid- to late-sixties. I had a crush on Little Joe; he was so handsome. I wanted to marry him, but then all the girls in the orphanage wanted to marry him, too." Donna laughed.

"Then I am sure you will like Coober Pedy. It is a small Opal mining town where everybody knows one another. Just imagine Bonanza's TV show – the Cowboy Ranch, but without horses or trees. Instead, you can see kangaroos hopping around in the bush just outside our dugout before sunrise. You'll love it, I promise," Mara smiled.

Donna thought going to the middle of the red desert sounded fascinating. Bonanza was set in a small Virginia town with rich silver and iron-ore mines, while Coober Pedy was a town with opal mining. Searching for precious gemstones sounded exciting, just like in the gold rush era when the first settlers arrived. It all sounded so romantic.

Mara continued, "People live in dugouts to escape the heat, as it's hot most of the time; however, from July to October, it is cooler."

"What are dugouts?"

"Dugouts are underground buildings. Some homes are as nice as any apartment, with elaborate furniture and décor. Even the church was built underground to keep cool. Not surprisingly, the Aboriginal people named the place Coober Pedy, which literary means 'white man's hole'. It hardly ever rains. But you don't want a sudden downpour; the streets turn to mud, and cars get bogged. One year, it rained so heavily that the dirt road got soaked, and some trucks were bogged for a few days. That night at the Coober Pedy drive-in, all the cars were stuck in the mud. It was chilly that night. People covered themselves with blankets and slept in their cars. Rumours around the town are that many babies were conceived that weekend," Mara laughed.

"Believe me, Sissy, rain is only welcome to fill our water tank for drinking. Water gets delivered by large semi-trailers for everything else, but it is salty and not for drinking. During bad weather, most people stay in their dugouts."

"What do people do for fun?"

"In the town centre, there is a hotel, a post office that serves as a bank, grocery shops, a police station, and a small medical centre. The Italian and Greek clubs have a jukebox playing familiar songs. There is a pub in the hotel. Some music bands use Coober Pedy as a stopover to break the long journey to Alice Springs."

"I can't wait to get a better job where I can wear makeup, manicure my nails, and grow long hair again," Donna smiled.

Mara was delighted to see her sister's enthusiasm for moving to Coober Pedy. "This will be your new adventure, and who knows, you may even find a handsome Little Joe, just like in Bonanza, or even better, you may find a rich opal miner," Mara said, winking at her sister.

Soon after their first stop at Port Augusta, where they bought refreshments, the bus hit the dirt road, lurching as it hit a few potholes. So much red dust covered all the bus windows. It was surreal. Nothing was green, just a red, rocky, flat surface stretched to the horizon. Donna attempted to sleep on the bus, but the noise and jolting from hitting potholes on the gravel road kept her awake.

It seemed like hours had passed. Donna became impatient and looked at Mara. "Are we there yet? This is such a long trip. I could have travelled to half of Italy via the Autostrada in less time."

"Don't worry, it will take a while. Go back to sleep," Mara said, tapping her sister on the shoulder.

As morning stretched into afternoon, the bus stopped at Andamooka, a dusty old truck stop that sold petrol, cigarettes, Coca-Cola, greasy chips, and hamburgers to weary truck drivers. It was a place to use the toilets while beating off the flies, fill an extra jerry can with fuel and top up with water for the long distance through the deserts and dusty roads.

Every few hours, Donna asked Mara, "Are we there yet?"

"Not yet. Stop asking me. I will wake you up."

Now and then, the bus wheels screeched as the driver tried to avoid hitting another kangaroo.

Donna couldn't see anything through her window because everything was obscured by a vast cloud of fine red dust that billowed up around the bus like a dust storm. Even inside the bus, she could smell and taste it. She wondered if the bus would ever reach Coober Pedy, and slumped back into her seat and dejectedly commented:

"We left Adelaide before dawn and travelled almost all day. In Europe, this distance would have spanned two countries," Donna expressed her impatience.

Mara reminded her that, due to Australia's vast size, they were used to travelling long distances. "… and this is the best time to travel on desert roads. Bus drivers typically keep a safe distance from the semi-trailer to avoid the swirling dust that could obstruct their vision. During the rainy season, the roads become muddy and slippery, making driving difficult."

During the long bus journey, Donna lost track of time and repeatedly dozed off. Eventually, in the late afternoon, Mara tapped her on the shoulder.

"Come on, get ready! We're almost there. And I have a surprise for you … the Italian Club is organising a live music band at the end of this month. This is a rare event for Coober Pedy, but Martin has already secured a reservation for us. Luckily, your twenty-second birthday falls close to the festival date so we can celebrate it together."

"Oh, wow! That's excellent news," Donna said excitedly.

She took her makeup kit from her shoulder bag, examined her face in a pocket mirror, and realised her makeup needed more than just a touch-up. Despite the bus shaking, Donna carefully applied eyeliner and blended some eye shadow to highlight her brown eyes. She then outlined her lips with a lip liner, used a lip brush to apply lipstick, and finished with some blush to give her a healthy glow. After applying makeup, she felt pleased at how it had transformed her appearance back to the breathtaking young woman she used to be.

It was in the early seventies when Donna arrived in Coober Pedy, the world's opal capital. She stepped off the bus gracefully, wearing black glossy, over-the-knee boots and a black Greta Garbo brim hat. The first thing she noticed was that people covered in red dust slept on the footpath under the post office veranda to escape the sun. Some held wine flasks in brown paper bags; others lay on the ground, ignoring the flies on their faces. Donna had never seen Aboriginal people before but had heard snippets of their conversation in an unfamiliar foreign language. The dog sleeping among them lazily rose to its feet and barked at new arrivals.

Flies buzzed everywhere, especially around people's faces, and the air around her was hot and sticky. When Donna gasped for breath, a fly flew into her mouth; she panicked and tried to spit it out but to no avail. Then, a strong gust of scorching wind blew directly into her face, filling her eyes with red dust. She tried to clear her eyes with her knuckles and accidentally pulled off one of her fake eyelashes. As she stepped forward, the strong wind eddied around and blew off her wide-brimmed hat, swirling it and rolling it across the dusty ground. Instinctively, she dashed to grab it but almost got hit by a passing car.

"Watch where you are going, you silly cow," the driver of the old grey truck yelled. "I nearly ran over you." Driving wildly, he pulled his head back in the cab and accelerated, leaving a vast red dust storm behind him.

Recovering from her shock, Donna realised people were watching her. Standing further away and covered in dust-caked, worn-out clothes, some laughed and shouted encouragement.

When Donna finally retrieved her dusty hat an enormous cheer rose, followed by applause and more laughter.

Her face red with humiliation, she felt nauseous, realising that she now looked more like an overdressed drag queen from a movie rather than someone dressed in elegant Italian labels.

Grief-stricken, she struggled not to break down in tears. Then Mara's steady hand grabbed her and pulled her sideways, away from the laughing spectators. "Come on, Sissy, don't worry. Let's get away from these bastards."

Martin was walking towards them in a great hurry.

They collected their luggage and tiredly followed him back to his dugout. As Donna later found out, it was a desirable place to stay since no matter how hot the temperature outside was, inside the dugout, was always comfortable, both day and night, summer and winter.

However, at this precise moment as they neared the dugout entrance, Donna saw only a big hole in the ground, sloped with low ceilings that required careful steering to avoid hitting her head. Once inside, she gazed around at a big cavity encircled by rough, unfinished walls and a few sponge mattresses lying on the floor, evidently for their comfort. A small, rounded plastic table with four dusty chairs and a kerosene lamp dimly lit the dingy, miserable den.

Martin also had a caravan parked nearby, used as often as the temperatures outside allowed. His breath smelled of stale beer as he proudly unlocked the van and showed them inside. The place was full of fine dust and the foul smell of leftover food, but he seemed not to notice. Smiling, he wiped his greasy, unshaven chin into the elbow of his dirty shirt.

Outside the caravan was a 44-gallon drum used as a water tank. A makeshift shower positioned alongside the drum, covered in blue plastic sheeting, functioned as a shower curtain. In the middle, suspended by the rope, was a small galvanized bucket with salty water. Despite the additional challenge of using soap in salted water, the quick shower was refreshing, and the hair dried quickly in the heat.

A few metres away was a makeshift public toilet that everyone in the immediate vicinity used – an abandoned mining shaft with a deep enough hole to keep it from being infested with flies. Above the hole sat a shabby corrugated iron shack with an old rusty door. While sitting inside, the user could read the newspaper clippings of toilet paper pinned on a rusty nail with one hand while using the other hand to tightly hold a string that held the door shut. Otherwise, unpredictable gusts of wind could fling the door wide open and expose the sorry sight inside.

Donna looked from the top of the hill across the bare land where a few humps of dirt indicated neglected mineshafts. She could see why walking in the dark posed a danger and realised she would disappear forever if she fell into any one of them.

No one was around during the day, and she could hear the whooshing wind swirling dust around like a small twister. The eerie silence made Cooper Pedy seem like a ghost town. Some miners who had some money sought refuge in the air-conditioned pub, drinking beer, while others stayed hidden in their underground dugouts.

Martin's dugout was nothing more than a large hole into the ground, with a galvanized vent shaft sticking out of the earth near the caravan for ventilation. Instead of a traditional door, the entrance was covered with plastic sheeting to keep flies out, though a swirling cloud of dust and debris often foiled it.

Though feeling claustrophobic, Donna sought refuge underground to escape the unbearable heat. She did not cope well with the heat and dust, and she was bored and lonely. She alternated between sleeping on a dirty sponge mattress or sitting at the small plastic table. She wrote letters to her friends in Italy, saying that she would soon return to the house of Villa Verla.

After only hours in that wretched dugout reminiscent of a rat hole, Donna prayed she would soon escape the nightmare. Now and then, when the heat subsided, she slept in the dingy caravan, the flies hovering around dirty dishes in the sink and buzzing mosquitoes keeping her awake.

She became so isolated that her relationship with Mara deteriorated. She had nothing to do, and that drove her crazy; she desperately needed to escape or find something to do.

"What happens in hotels on the weekends? Is there any music or dancing?" she asked Mara one day.

"Coober Pedy has one hotel offering dining options in the lounge and a drinking hole at the public bar. Occasionally, bands en route to Alice Springs stop overnight and perform at the hotel, drawing in locals for a dance and party. Tourist buses make overnight stops to rejuvenate before proceeding to Alice Springs. Some visitors opt for a brief stay of just a few days to engage in casual noodling …."

"What's noodling?"

"Fossicking. They sift for small pieces of opal accidentally discarded by the miners. Some tourists get lucky and find beautiful opal pieces that help pay for the rest of their holidays. I think you should try your luck, too," Mara explained.

"No, thanks. I don't want to waste time searching for opals in the dirt. Opal hunting is addictive, like the gold rush. Just look at you and Martin. You have spent nearly ten years in this place and still have nothing.

"The only way to make money is to work and earn wages. I must get a job. Seeing cash in my hand is all that I want."

"Sissy, don't be concerned. Martin now has new partners and a promising new mining shaft. Last week, a gypsy woman read my palm and predicted that this year would bring us luck." Mara smiled.

Donna found it impossible to relax, and sleeping was equally tormenting. The noise coming from a generator nearby sounded extremely loud. Flies were everywhere during the day, and the mosquitoes took over at night; it was unbearable. Martin frequently drank excessively and was verbally abusive, and Donna's inability to change the circumstances of witnessing domestic violence made her furious. And she grew anxious about the money she had saved while working in Adelaide.

Coober Pedy was as bad as the lawless Wild West movies she had seen on TV. She knew she needed a job, and then she could open a bank savings account. However, in the meantime, she found a safe place – an ideal hiding spot for her money –behind the caravan amidst the pile of bricks that supported the rainwater tank.

One day, Donna snuck out of the caravan to get some money from her secret hiding place. She wanted to go to the store to buy shampoo and conditioner to ease her shower using salty water. But she couldn't find her money. Frantically, she checked all the bricks, but it wasn't there. She was devastated; all of her savings had disappeared. Donna felt a desperate urge to scream, to release the fury and bitterness that raged deep inside her.

Accusations, blame, denials, and criticism followed. Donna knew where her money had gone: Martin was always broke, so how could he afford a portable generator and a winch for his mining shaft? The rest of her money was spent on alcohol.

The conflict between the sisters escalated.

Highly disappointed knowing Mara had been complicit in the crime as she was the only one who knew where she hid her money, Donna realised that her sister had an alternative motive: Mara never wanted Donna to go back home, so she'd sabotaged her plans. In addition, Martin needed the new mining equipment to improve his chance of finding opals.

That was the straw that broke the camel's back. For Donna, that was something she could never forgive. She had to find alternative accommodation or leave that shit hole of a place for good.

While packing, her sister Mara shouted bitterly in her limited, broken English. "Go! I- not- like- you anymore. Go away, not-come back. You- want- go home- Buy one ticket, no come back."

After those few broken parting words, Donna packed her things, left the caravan, and walked down the hill to the hotel. And from that day forward, the two sisters hardly saw each other.

℣

Now Donna needed a job. Any job would do. She had to start from the beginning and save enough money to get back home. Her first stop was at the only downtown hotel, where she met with the hotel manager, Peppy Carmelo. He was a cheerful, short, chubby man from southern Italy. Peppy felt sorry for her and offered her a job in the kitchen and accommodation in the staff quarters. Donna was ecstatic; she finally had a proper toilet and a bathroom down the hall, which she shared with other staff. Upon receiving her first wages, she opened her first bank account at the Post Office agency Commonwealth Bank. Her money was now safe. She again prioritised saving money for a plane ticket home.

She enjoyed working in the kitchen. Speaking Italian was familiar, and the Italian cuisine was comforting. She felt less homesick, and her life in Coober Pedy became bearable.

Her spoken English improved, but much slower than she'd hoped, and her written English could have been better. So many English words, and when spelled differently they meant something else. It was so confusing. Donna always enjoyed reading, but she couldn't even read the newspaper. For the first time in her life, she felt totally illiterate.

While working at the hotel, she faced difficulties due to her limited knowledge of English, which sometimes resulted in funny incidents, such as when she assisted in the dining room, serving a busload of tourists with a set menu. Donna made a simple mistake: instead of asking how many of them wanted soup, she asked, "How much soup do you want?"

After the laughter died down, some rowdy customers at the back of the room yelled, "Fill it up, you fool!"

Another time, after another customer asked, "Can I have an entrée?" Donna innocently responded, "Yes, I always carry food on a tray." People clapped, and the atmosphere was joyful.

The kitchen was cheerful, and everybody liked their boss, Peppy. It was an open secret among the staff that Peppy tried to hide his homosexuality but with little success. Regrettably, some miners, when drunk, ridiculed Peppy, made fun of him and called him derogatory names, such as poofter or poof.

Peppy was a good boss and was adored by all the staff. He had an easygoing personality and a kind heart. He also missed Italy, which helped them develop a cordial friendship.

He tried to help Donna, patiently translating Italian to English. Tactfully and calmly, he told Donna to listen carefully to customers' orders.

"Cara Mia, no need to hurry; jot down everything and not be concerned about spelling.

Once, Peppy asked Donna to write a dinner menu on the outdoor blackboard displaying the menu of the day. Donna had to practice writing in English because the restaurant's unique menu changed daily.

She used chalk in multiple colours to advertise the pub's special of the day. While in the orphanage, she had learned calligraphy in art class, and was pleased to showcase her art now.

The menu of the day was 'Pee & Ham Soup, Roast Pork, and Apple Pie, all for $3.50.' Peppy praised her for making the display colourful, telling her that she only made one mistake: she wrote 'pee' rather than 'pea'. Peppy grinned as he told her, "The customers were so amused at the silly Wog who couldn't even write simple words." Lunch revenue increased that day, so Peppy kept the special 'Pee & Ham soup' on for the rest of the week.

Donna took it all in good stride. The customers' ridicule didn't bother her. She had a good sense of humour and could laugh at herself. Most of the time, customers were courteous, but occasionally she encountered a grumpy drunk who enjoyed being obnoxious and obscene.

One miner all the wait staff tried to avoid was Bruce, the Scottish ogre.

The large brute came in one evening and waved at Donna to place an order for his dinner. He spoke with a Scottish accent, which sounded more like Chinese than English. Still, Donna understood that he had ordered Pea and Ham soup with Roast Pork as the main course. She carefully wrote it down, hurried to the kitchen, placed the order on the kitchen bench, and rushed back. She served the Scottish Ogre his Pea and Ham soup and put a bread roll and butter on the side plate.

That night, the dining room was jam-packed with a busload of tourists just arriving. The exhausted staff was rushed off their feet, taking dinner orders from impatient, hardworking miners. By the time they ordered their meals, they were already half-drunk. The staff jokingly referred to such men as 'Hungry Banditos'.

Bruce eventually shouted in a deep, rough voice. "Oi! You! Come here! You bloody Wog! Where is my bloody dinner? I've waited for ages for my roast pork!"

Everyone in the dining room looked up as the comedy

unfolded. Embarrassed that she had forgotten to serve Bruce the main meal, she quickly apologised and returned to the kitchen to check his order. Peppy, however, regretfully told her they had just run out of Roast Pork. Could she go back and ask him if he would like something else? Donna's previous panic turned to despair. She was too scared to tell him the bad news. She begged, "Peppy, please, can you deal with the Scottish ogre? He will bite my head off."

Peppy waved both hands and hurriedly responded. "Can't you see I am too busy with a busload of people? Tell Bruce he can have beef fillet steak or something else. Don't worry, Donna, with your smile, I'm sure you'll be okay. But, listen, you better be nice to Bruce," he explained in Italian. "He is one of our regulars and is generous with tipping waiters."

Having no choice, Donna mustered all her courage and returned to face him. She politely said in her limited English, "Sorry, no more Roast Pork. You want steak or other hot cooked food?"

He looked at her in a wild rage, took a big breath, and, in disgust, said, "Get lost!"

Donna nervously turned around to check on the menu board to see exactly what he had just ordered. She didn't know what to do next. Roast pork, roast beef, beef pie. These sound identical. It must be another dish. But she couldn't see it on the menu board. Peppy will know.

So, Donna, with her most charming smile, politely said to Bruce, "I'll check with Peppy; he will cook a 'get lost' dish for you."

Bruce looked at her, and started laughing hysterically. Then he grumbled to no one in particular, "Either I've had too many pints, or this cheeky Wog is making fun of me." He looked surprised when Donna took the money from the table, charging him $3.50 for dinner. He glared at Donna speechless, his eyes bulging as if he was choking on something.

Encouraged by the lack of immediate response, Donna quickly wrote 'Get Lost' as a new order. Relieved, she promptly returned to the kitchen, pleased with herself for how well she'd resolved a customer complaint so professionally. She gave Peppy the order ticket.

Busy at the stove, Peppy could only turn his head and ask, "What has Bruce ordered?"

"I'm not sure because it wasn't on the menu. It sounded like Roast Pork," Donna explained, half in Italian and half in English.

Peppy stopped working and looked at her. "So, what is it?"

Donna checked her docket. "Well … he ordered 'Get Lost.' Can you cook that medium-rare because that's how he likes it? Peppy, please, hurry."

Everyone in the kitchen erupted in hysterics, and laughter rapidly spread to the other restaurant staff. Donna's face slowly smiled as she asked, "What?"

In the next moment, the Scottish ogre stormed into the kitchen like an enraged bull, swearing and yelling uncontrollably at Peppy, "Listen, you bloody poof, I don't know what kind of restaurant you're running here. I've been waiting for my Roast Pork all night. You shouldn't give the job to bloody Dings or Wogs who can't understand plain English. First, this girl with a bird brain forgot all about my dinner and when I told her to get lost for being so ignorant, she just smiled at me, took the money, and charged me for it."

Everyone in the kitchen stiffened for a second. But they soon exploded again into fits of laughter, even louder than before. The smile fell from Donna's face. Humiliated, Bruce stormed back out of the kitchen and went to Roofer's bar across the road.

By the following weekend, the incident was forgotten, and the Scottish ogre proved he was not that scary after all, and coached Donna to understand his difficult Scottish accent. He patiently tolerated Donna's lack of English, and always left a generous tip for her.

After this hilarious episode, Donna's confidence grew as she made fewer mistakes. She also found that most customers coming to the hotel were kind, patient, and tolerant. She enjoyed her work. Most customers were generous, particularly those who had found opal.

Coober Pedy was a multicultural place with many nationalities, and Donna no longer felt the odd one out. She was one of many people with limited English proficiency and diverse accents. The other migrants told Donna she needed to accept words such as Wogs and Dings, as they were just a part of everyday conversation and didn't bother anyone.

Donna was excited when she received letters from The House of Villa Verla. The Santoro Family encouraged her to give the unfamiliar country a chance. However, if Donna wasn't happy, they would love to have her back. That inspired her to work harder and save money; she would return home if things didn't work out.

ଔ

Donna's life improved when she met Sandra, who worked in the restaurant. Sandra, a few years Donna's senior, spoke fluent English, managed the staff work rosters and provided Donna with ample overtime. This led to a significant increase in Donna's savings. Subsequently, the two decided to share a room, which halved their accommodation expenses. In addition to working together, they shared many common interests, quickly becoming close friends. As a result, Donna's feelings of loneliness diminished.

Sandra was deeply in love with Fabricio, and fully dedicated herself to their relationship; they spent most of their time together in his cozy, well-furnished dugout. Fabricio's family was well-known and esteemed within the town's mining community, and owned a significant opal-mining field and extensive mining equipment. Fabricio's devout Catholic mother wanted her eldest son to marry a distant cousin from Calabria, so she never approved of Sandra, an agnostic.

However, the happy couple disregarded family disputes. After discovering a significant opal, Fabricio wanted to surprise Sandra with a gold engagement ring that featured a solid black opal encrusted with rubies. They planned to elope next summer and get married in Calabria.

Then, out of nowhere, Sandra's entire world turned upside down when, in a mining accident, Fabricio was crushed under a bulldozer that had faulty brakes. The Flying Doctor Service transported Frabicio to Alice Springs Hospital, but sadly, he died from internal injuries the following day. Only immediate family members were allowed to see him before he died, and she never received that engagement ring.

After Fabricio's fatal accident, his family sold the mining rights to another Italian family and permanently left the town, never to be heard of again; rumours spread around the city that Fabricio was buried in his village in Calabria.

Mining accidents were, unfortunately, a common occurrence in Coober Pedy. Driven by greed, miners often compromised on safety measures. The intense heat in which they worked all day made a cold beer a tempting way to quench their thirst. Unfortunately, many miners also used unsafe equipment such as explosives, ropes, picks, and shovels. The only legal requirement for mining was a registration, and nobody asked any questions beyond that. As a result, many young men tragically lost their lives.

Not coping well with her grief of losing Fabricio, Sandra left Cooper Pedy and moved to the Barossa Valley, where her aunt owned a small vineyard. Although her friend's departure saddened Donna, she understood Sandra had to move on from that tragic event. The friends promised to write and keep in touch.

ʘ

A month later, Sandra wrote in her letter that she had settled in Riverland; she worked on a fruit block owned by her cousin in a small town called Renmark. It was picking season, and Sandra wanted to make some fast money to visit Fabricio's grave and meet some of his distant relatives in his tiny village in Calabria, Italy.

Donna was familiar with Riverland seasonal fruit picking. The migrant women she encountered at the cafeteria in Adelaide disclosed they made a lot of money picking fruit in just one season. Seasonal workers were in high demand, picking grapes. They stayed for a few months, earned a good wage, bought a new car, or saved a deposit for a house.

In the meantime, Donna continued working at the Coober Pedy Hotel. In addition to her wages, she earned generous tips from wealthy Japanese and Hong Kong opal buyers and local miners who struck it rich. She grabbed the opportunity to do more shifts in the filthy public bar. It helped her get up in the morning to clean the public bar and vacuum the lounge room. She was finally on a winning streak. Her bank account grew, and the extra work helped her recoup all the stolen money.

As Donna's English improved, the hotel owner, rewarded her skills, hard work, and bubbly personality by offering her a supervisory role. Now with better working conditions, Donna upgraded her accommodation to the outside room with air conditioning and a private en-suite; she could now have a long shower twice a day and loved the soft toilet paper imported directly from Italy. Normality returned to her life.

No longer in a hurry to leave Coober Pedy, she felt relieved she was moving in the right direction. When she saved enough money, she would book the first flight back to Italy.

Within a year, she would return to the house of Villa Verla where she belonged.

Chapter 13

Opal and Pearl

Donna worked hard by taking all the overtime she could, cleaning, cooking, and working at a bar. Her savings grew steadily, and she saw she was getting closer to her goal. In a few more months, she would have enough money to fly back to Europe

On her rare day off, Peppy was in a state of panic. He couldn't secure a substitute for Gertrude's shift as nobody wanted to work in the Public Bar, where women and children were not allowed, and the only place the Aborigines were allowed to be served alcohol. Donna volunteered to take that shift, which paid overtime.

The bar was a rough place to work in, a haven for down-on-their-luck miners and the town's homeless men. At the end of the shift, the public bar stench was awful. The bar's cement floor had to be washed with a high-powered fire hose at night, the powerful blast of water helping to wake the few drunks who had fallen asleep on the floor. The water blast refreshed the room, removing all the food scraps, cigarette butts, and dried beer stains. After the tsunami of water cleaned the floor, the bar didn't smell so bad the following morning.

Donna disregarded the unpleasant surroundings; she was focused on earning more money and achieving her larger goals. Her motivation high, she knew every penny she earned contributed to her growing bank account, her ticket out of that desolate place.

Donna busily served drinks and brought food from the kitchen while opal miners gathered to discuss their luck. Most felt Lady Luck had turned her back on them. Like in a gold rush, the miners never lost hope that she would smile at them again tomorrow.

By lunchtime, the public bar was crowded. It was another scorching day outside, so the miners found relief in the bar. The first thing ordered was a cold beer to quench their thirst and wash the dust from their throats. Impatient, hungry miners gorged on chips and burgers made from kangaroo meat.

When the lunch rush subsided, Donna replaced the beer-soaked wet bar runners. She noticed one solitary figure standing at the end of the bar. Another out-of-luck miner in grey, limestone dust-caked overalls. His running sweat turned the dust into slush on his exposed skin and soaked his clothes. He looked like a sculpture moulded out of clay. Donna approached with a faint smile and a questioning look to take his order. She had a cool glass in her hand and was ready to pour another beer. When he lifted his downcast head, only his green eyes showed signs of life. In a rasping voice, he mumbled, "Double Scotch, please."

Donna paused. When he noticed Donna's hesitation and uncertainty, he tiredly pointed at the bottle of Johnny Walker on the display shelf behind her. Slightly blushing, Donna hurriedly took the bottle off the shelf and served him his drink.

Then, her curiosity rose at his odd behaviour; she backed away a little, never taking her eyes off him. As she kept busy pouring beers for thirsty patrons and serving hot chips with tomato sauce, now and then she glanced at the mystery opal miner at the end of the bar. He looked exhausted, disillusioned, ignoring his surroundings and staring at his glass. Then, he mechanically lifted the glass to his cracked lips and drank his whiskey in one gulp. He placed his empty glass on the bar, left the money on the bench, and silently walked back into the desert.

A few days passed, but he never came back. He disappeared from sight until one evening he walked into the hotel dining room, clean-shaven and better dressed. He chose a corner table and sat down on his own. Music played on the jukebox, and the restaurant's atmosphere was cozy. As soon as Donna saw him, she quickly went to his table.

"Good evening, sir," Donna said with the sweetest smile as she arrived to take his order. "I may have seen you before."

"Yeah, the other day … you served me a Scotch in the Public Bar," the mystery man responded.

"I didn't recognise you. What is your name?" Donna pretended not to remember him.

"Tom. My name is Tom. The extended version is Tomislav, after the last Croatian King. I like your smile; the other day in the Public Bar, you cheered me up," he said.

How appropriate, Donna thought. He has confidence, and the King's name suited him just fine.

"How come you ended up in Coober Pedy?" she asked out of interest.

"I arrived in Australia in 1969 to hunt crocodiles but ended up in Coober Pedy instead. I aimed to discover the mother lode of opals, get rich, buy a yacht, and sail into the sunset. Unfortunately, I had no luck in finding opals. However, I console myself with the thought that someone unlucky in material things may be lucky in love." He did not take his eyes off her.

Donna took his order and busied herself with other customers, stealing a few precious moments here and there to return to his table.

"I heard Martin and Mara threw you a big party for your

twenty-second birthday at the Italian Club," he said at one point.

Donna smiled. "It was fun. We partied until the early hours of the morning. Look at the bracelet my sister gave me." She leaned over and showed Tom the beautiful opal bracelet.

"That's nice, but it is triplets, not solid. A girl who is as beautiful as you should only wear solid opals, preferably black opals," Tom explained.

"What's the difference?" Donna asked, still smiling.

"Well, a solid opal is the genuine article. The polished stone and the vibrant colours of a good opal should catch your eye, just like I'm catching yours right now," Tom playfully teased.

She blushed and put her head down, trying to hide her embarrassment.

"What is your birthstone?" Tom asked. "My birthstone is pearl, but I prefer opal," she replied.

"Then you are in the right company. My birthstone is opal." Tom smiled.

Donna shyly put her head down and blushed again. So, she quickly asked, "How come you know so much about me?"

"Mara told everyone that her much younger sister Donna was coming to Coober Pedy. She told everybody that she is looking for a rich opal buyer for her sister, and that's not me," Tom stated, not taking his eyes off her.

"It is only fair that I ask you how old you are," Donna wanted to know.

"I am ten years older than you. Sadly, I'm too old for a young chick like you. I heard your party was grand, but I was not invited. Your sister didn't invite losers, like me. She is looking for a rich opal buyer for her baby sister," Tom repeated.

"The party was good; we danced all night. Unfortunately, my relationship with Mara and Martin broke down. I couldn't stand living in that small caravan, and Martin gets abusive and violent when drunk. I moved out and got a room in the staff quarters in the hotel." Wanting Tom to know that she was independent, Donna nervously continued. "Tom, you don't look older than me. Men's maturity is measured differently than women's."

"Yeah, it must be my good genes, but I've aged a lot since I arrived in Coober Pedy. This town can do that to you." He grinned cheekily.

"I heard old Jack calling you Ringo earlier. How come?"

"With such a name as Ringo, nobody bothers me much. I have to work underground with so many nationalities. The animosity between Muslims, Serbs and Croats runs deep, so I prefer to keep a low profile. I came to Australia to get rich, not to fight political battles."

"How come you chose that nickname?"

His grin widened. "I lived in London during the wild sixties when the Beatles were big. Ringo Starr is the best drummer in the world, so why not?"

She recognised the name but couldn't recall where she'd heard it. However, she didn't dwell on it. Instead, she admired Tom's good looks as he ran his fingers through his wavy, light brown hair, revealing his handsome, sunburned face and captivating emerald green eyes. They gazed at each other as if under a spell.

Donna immediately realised she had found her own Little Joe, and there he was – Tom – sitting right in front of her! She remembered how the Bonanza TV show's Ponderosa ranch resembled Coober Pedy and how the lead actor, handsome Michael Landon, had caught her eye. But Tom was even more strikingly attractive, his piercing green eyes stealing her heart. She had found her soulmate and vowed never to let him go, but Tom didn't know it yet.

Tom, too, was instantly mesmerised by Donna's beautiful eyes. They looked at him intently, and he almost felt their warm embrace. He thought, What a gorgeous young woman! He had recently seen a photo of her when Mara had brought it to the public bar, boasting of her beautiful sister coming to Coober Pedy.

Mara was looking for the highest bidder. Perched at the far end of the bar, waiting to be served, Tom was last in line to receive the photo. When the picture finally reached him, he was stunned by Donna's smiling eyes. For a second, he imagined how wonderful it would be to have this beautiful young woman in his life. Then he angrily stopped himself with a stern reprimand for being so utterly stupid, thinking that such beauty would want to be with a broke loser like him. He'd returned the photo and gave in to his emotions as he wallowed in self-pity.

Tom was usually broke, and had no time for romance. His dreams of owning a yacht were out of his reach; instead, he found himself below deck in the dark, rat-infested bowels of the ship, unable to see the blue skies, feel the soft sea breeze on his face or taste salt on his lips. As an opal miner, he had little hope of striking it rich or finding love. Fortunately, he found some opal, which he sold to a buyer from Hong Kong a few days ago. Otherwise, he would not have been here tonight.

Tom stopped dwelling on his self-pity when he saw Donna returning, serving him steak and salad,

She broke the silence, asking, "What would you like to drink?"

Tom smiled back and lifted his head, gazing at her with piercing green eyes. "Please bring me a packet of Camel cigarettes and a glass of Glenfiddich."

❦

The following night, Donna felt anxious as she couldn't find Tom in the packed restaurant. She began to worry that she might never see him again. But when he finally appeared in the dining room, she felt relieved and excited. Her heart raced as she hurried to his table to take his order.

Tom greeted her with a smile and again ordered a Glenfiddich whisky and a packet of Camel cigarettes. She wrote his order on a duplicate carbon order book and left the customer's copies on his table. She was busy that night and had no time to chat with Tom, but she couldn't stop thinking about him and admiring his handsome looks. She loved his emerald-green eyes, the most beautiful green eyes she had ever seen. He was well-dressed in a sky-blue shirt and jeans and appeared to be a polite and well-spoken man. *Quite unusual for Coober Pedy,* she thought. *And wow! This man knows his whisky, which shows sophistication. In this pub, nobody has ever heard of Glenfiddich whisky.*

When she served Tom his whisky, she watched him as he lit his Camel cigarette. They glanced at each other, and Donna smiled timidly. She suddenly became flushed and excused herself. After a few steps, she froze, turned around, and quickly returned to Tom's table. "Sorry, I forgot to ask what you want for dinner this evening," she said, slightly flustered.

Tom said he didn't want to order a meal as he had already had dinner. However, he didn't want Donna to know that he was broke and that he and his partner, Alexis, shared a can of tuna and some old crusty bread. They were living in a shabby dugout and were struggling financially. Tom only came to the restaurant to see her, arriving late, hoping that Donna wouldn't be too busy and that they could get to know each other.

Tom came to the dining room every night just before closing time the following week. Soon, they started seeing each other every night after Donna finished her restaurant duties. Donna fell in love with Tom – a dream fulfilled. She found her own 'Little Joe' in the Australian desert.

Tom also found it hard to believe that Donna could love

someone like him. He was perpetually broke and fearful of letting his emotions rule his heart. He couldn't offer Donna a bright future, but he held onto the hope that their shared love would carry them through the tough times.

ℝ

Tom's journey to this point had been long and arduous. He was born in Zagreb, the capital of Croatia, and named after King Tomislav, the first king of Croatia, who reigned in the tenth century.

His childhood days were carefree and joyous. His father had worked as a finance clerk at the central railway station. As a young boy, Tom would stop at his father's office every day after school, fascinated with the steam locomotives. To him, they were living, powerful beasts pulling long freight trains, always loaded to the brim. The engines were a glorious sight as they used all their strength to get moving, huffing and puffing, straining and groaning, letting out massive clouds of smoke and white steam.

The family lived in the central part of the city in a massive five-bedroom apartment that his friends called a 'football field'. It served as the Italian Consulate before the Second World War.

In autumn and winter, the city centre was quiet, with only a few cars on the streets. Horse buggies delivered fresh milk, cheese, and butter to their front door. Promenades lined with giant plane trees encircled the central park, where Tom spent most of his childhood playing with his friends and two younger siblings.

After bed, he often listened to the soft and barely audible honking of migrating wild geese flying over his house and wished to be among them, flying far, far away. Long after the geese were gone and silence descended on the quiet place again, he would gradually fall asleep, with the fading echo of wild geese blending with his dreams.

Tom's idyllic childhood soured when his parents' marriage deteriorated. He found solace in the library's silence to escape the incessant arguing, losing himself in history books for hours.

His chemistry studies at the university were put on hold when he was called up for two years of mandatory military service, a disruption he welcomed. He romanced a young graduate teacher who taught underprivileged kids during his service. They could see each other only when she was on school holidays or when he was on army leave. However, their connection faded when Tom was reassigned to complete his military duty in Montenegro.

After completing his military service, Tom learned that his parents were getting a divorce, so he started planning to relocate to Canada. He received an offer from his cherished uncle, Richard, to sponsor his visa. Affectionately called Ricky, he was a talented musician and saxophonist with a famous jazz band.

While touring Canada with his family, Ricky was involved in a catastrophic car accident. A large truck ran a stop sign and collided with their vehicle, the collision resulting in a heartbreaking loss: Ricky and his entire family perished instantly.

Tom was devastated, and his plans to emigrate to Canada were put on hold.

While Tom was studying at university, his mother married again. Tom's two younger siblings couldn't stand the new family dynamics and moved away. His brother Marko followed his German backpacker girlfriend to Munich. At the same time, Tom's younger sister Enda married Tom's best friend Tony and moved to Eastbourne a town in the southern part of England. When she secured a job at a beauty salon, she sponsored Tom, enabling him to move to England.

Tom settled in London, quickly taking to his new

surroundings. During the lively sixties, London was regarded as the capital of the world of rock and roll, hippies, drugs and liberated sex. However, after two years as a lab assistant at Imperial College, Tom became discontented with the low salary and scant prospects for advancement.

One day at the local pub, he encountered Derk from South Africa and Saburo from Osaka, Japan. After a night of revelry until dawn, Derk proposed one of the wildest ideas: "Let's head to Australia and hunt crocodiles for their skins. There's good money to be made," Derk said.

Tom readily agreed; he had a few girlfriends, which was all good fun. However, he was seeking an exit from his relationship with Patricia, who was persistently pressuring him to get married. Tom was not ready to settle down, and there were no sparks of love between them. So, the opportunity to move to Australia seemed like a godsend.

The newfound friends were all enticed by the prospect of quick riches. They resolved to begin their venture together in the New Year, mere months ahead. However, their unity soon dissolved: Derk turned to peddling drugs from Morocco to the London black market, and Tom, disapproving of Derk's illicit activities, severed ties with him. Meanwhile, Saburo, stricken with homesickness, returned to Osaka. Thus, once as close as the Three Musketeers, the trio went their separate ways.

This left Tom alone, and when his British work permit expired, he decided to move to Australia. The cost was minimal, only ten pounds for an Australian visa and a plane ticket, an offer he couldn't pass up. The sole stipulation was that he had to remain in Australia for at least two years.

Tom estimated that two years would be enough to acquire many crocodile skins and get rich. Departing London with just $84 Australian, he sought fortune in 'the land Down Under'. Arriving in Melbourne in late 1969, a taxi driver dropped him at a South Yarra motel, where he secured a room. Within a week, Tom had landed a position at Coates Brothers Ink laboratory.

Eager to get to the Northern Territory to start hunting crocodiles, he first needed money, and saving money with his paycheck was impossible. So he resigned from his job in the lab and sought a better salary at Mount Isa Mines.

At the pub, miners discussed heading to Coober Pedy to find opal. Tom weighed his options: continue his dream of hunting crocs or try his luck in the opal fields. Deciding that opal, his birthstone, maybe his safest bet, Tom set off for Coober Pedy.

There, Tom partnered with a Greek man, Alexis, who was supposedly very experienced. At the police station, they brought a mining licence for an abandoned opal mine in Olympia Fields, which had failed to produce opals for the previous owner. However, Alexis convinced him that opals were still there; they only needed to follow the seam further, which led them to a pocketful of beautiful rocks. Not knowledgeable enough about these matters, Tom agreed since everything else had failed so far.

Early in the morning, they left Coober Pedy in a dirty old car with equipment and two boxes of gelignite. They came to an old, disused mine shaft after driving on a barely recognisable rough road. All around was quiet, a grey, dreary land with sparse tussock grass, total wilderness with only termites, snakes and lizards. They unpacked the explosives, picks, shovels, a big container full of water, carbide lamps, rope, and a manual drill with a long wooden compacting stick to hammer the gelignite sticks into the drilled holes.

After lowering all the equipment, they grabbed the rope. Tom followed Alexis and slowly lowered himself down the twenty-four-metre-deep mineshaft, carefully watching for deadly snakes and spiders often trapped in there.

They collected their equipment and went deeper into the shaft. Tom kept wiping his sweaty face with his hand, although new rivulets would soon find their way back into his already sore eyes. Awkwardly dragging their equipment behind them, they crawled and crept on all fours through the gloomy tunnels until they found a circular arched mine-face with a promising opal seam. It was a thin, almost horizontal vein of glass 'potch' without colour, which would hopefully change its direction and descend into a pool. Unfortunately, the running courses of these seams were very unpredictable. Deciding how to place an explosive was crucial. It took knowledge and experience. Tom believed his partner Alexis had worked in Coober Pedy for many years. He should know what to do.

First, they had to drill nine holes underneath the seam. The aim was to remove one cubic metre of solid limestone underneath the opal seam. However, the most important thing was to drill only a short distance or all may be lost. The opal seam had to be protected from the destructive explosion by at least thirty centimeters of thick limestone slab.

Opal is a quartz-like form of hydrated silica, like glass. If shaken too much by the explosion, it would shatter to pieces. If the holes in the top row were drilled too low from the seam, it would mean more work with a pick and shovel to extract the opal embedded above after the blasting. Tom figured this could be the best option to avoid damaging the opal.

Alexis took the first turn and started drilling holes at the top, each a metre deep. Tom held the carbide miner's lamp above his head for good illumination and watched him drill. *Too close to the seam*, thought Tom. "We may be drilling too high," he said to his partner.

"No, it will be okay," Alexis responded annoyingly.

Tom needed more convincing. Sure, Alexis had more experience, but he was lazy and didn't want to work too hard to remove the remaining chunk of limestone under the seam.

"I'm sorry, but I still think we're too close to the seam. Why risk it? Let's drill a little lower, just to be safe."

"No. I know what I'm doing," Alexis snarled back.

After that, they both remained silent. Tom took his turn and drilled more holes. After an hour and a half, they were finished. Next, they inserted detonators into the gelignite sticks and then pushed them into the empty holes, detonator first. Once the holes were filled, they used a wooden stick to compact the explosives tight against the solid wall. All done, Alexis lit all nine fuses, and then they both ran as far from the blasting area as possible for safely, stumbling a few times over rocks and loose ground. They waited hidden in a crevice. Then they heard a loud explosion.

Looking at each other, they smiled. *This is it!*

Waiting for the thick dust and smoke to disperse, they walked back to inspect their handy work. Today was going to be a lucky day.

Slowly, they approached the face of the blasting area. Tom lifted the lamp high in the air, and they saw it. At the back of the blasted section was an entire, thick opal seam that gleamed like a rainbow with the most beautiful flashes of every spectrum colour.

Tom was greatly concerned when he saw that the front part of the limestone slab surrounding the opal had been partially blasted away—an indication that the holes had been drilled too near to the opal stream.

However, he kept his concern to himself, for the sight before them was awe-inspiring – a potential fortune right within their grasp. The allure of the treasure melted away their worries, and they allowed themselves to relax and get comfortable. Alexis leaned back, propping his feet up.

"Tom, let's take some time to appreciate this moment. You may never encounter something as beautiful as these magnificent rainbow colours."

They both dreamed of wonderful times ahead of them in silence. They were set for life; they would be rich and famous.

Tom decided to buy a luxury yacht and sail around the world, living like a promiscuous monarch. He murmured, "Monte Carlo, get ready. Tom is coming."

Suddenly, Alexis's voice pulled Tom back from his daydreaming. "Let's fill our bags and get out of this Aladdin's cave," he said, laughing.

"Yes, let's get rich," Tom agreed.

They slowly stood up and collected empty gelignite plastic bags to carry the rough opal. "We may need more bags, Tom said, and they laughed some more, and then set to work.

Tom let Alexis take charge and just held the carbide lamp for him. Alexis took a small pick and leaned closer to the rhapsody in lustrous colours. Then, instead of using a small tool, he touched it with his forefinger. As he felt it, the beautiful solid opal disintegrated into tiny grains, like sand on the beach, which seeped out of the cavity in a small stream resembling a sand clock.

Alexis pulled his finger back as if burned by a flame. He touched it again, not believing what was happening before him. The same horrific result occurred: the opal was smashed, shattered, pulverized, and destroyed.

So stunned, Tom was oblivious to the sweat dripping down his face. His hand holding the lamp trembled so much that it created moving shadows on the wall behind them. Alexis fixated on the unfolding scene; his breath caught in his throat. He quivered and convulsed, overwhelmed by the intensity of his emotions. Tom resisted the powerful urge to say, 'I warned you this could happen,' but kept his mouth tightly shut for fear that Alexis, who was powerfully built and suffering the loss of emotional control, may attack him. He could even kill him.

Finally, after what seemed like an eternity, Alexis regained control of himself and pressed his hands to his face. Lifting his head to face Tom, he drawled in a deep, hoarse voice, "I'm sorry."

Again, Tom said nothing. He lowered his hand with the lamp and lit a cigarette.

"Well, we still may get something out of it," Tom said, frowning.

They recovered some opal but only a tiny fraction of what they could've had, maybe just enough to keep them going for a few months if they cut back on their drinking.

They returned to Coober Pedy in a sombre mood, not trying to hide their disappointment. They split their findings and went their separate ways. Tom went to the hotel and found an opal buyer. After some haggling, they agreed on a price. Tom returned to his room at the single men's quarters with money in his pocket and cleaned himself up.

○3

After nearly two years of searching with very little success, Tom now had few spare dollars in his pocket. He wanted a nice dinner at the hotel, wondering if he would see that gorgeous new barmaid who had served him a drink the other day in the public bar. Would falling in love be his jackpot?

Tom was correct; fortune favoured him. Although he didn't discover opal, he found love instead. Before long, they devoted all their spare time to each other. Tom and Donna became a couple, deeply falling in love.

For two lovers, time stood still as they spent all their free time together; days turned into weeks. Eventually, Donna asked Peppy if Tom could move in with her, which would help them save more money.

Tom and Alexis continued working together, hoping that that old dark shaft might still have hidden opals. They started planning to buy mining equipment and try their luck together but they needed more money.

Donna found extra work at the Roofus Club across the road, a Greek restaurant where the miners came for a hamburger, chips, and drink until they couldn't stand. On the weekends, the Roofus Club stayed open until early morning. The club would bring in belly dancers, strippers, and musicians. Patrons had a great time, and it wasn't unusual to see local police officers joining in and partying with the locals. The police station was across the road, next to the post office and supermarket. It had only one lock-up cell which was almost always empty. Police turned a blind eye when opal miners drove home drunk. Only on some occasions, if there was violence or a brawl on the street, did the police lock-up serve a purpose. Infringements were rarely given, and warnings and promises of good behaviour served the town much better.

Those miners who had found opal threw money around like there was no tomorrow. Drunks often tipped the belly dancers with $20 notes. Instead of just giving them the money, they would drop a $20 note on the floor and tell them they could have it if they turned their backs to them while bending over to pick it up. Everyone was pleased: the dancers got their money, and the miners got a good look.

Those joyful Greek miners would always leave a good tip. The happier they were, the bigger the tip. Donna's job was to clear tables, gather empty glasses, and ensure the miners never had empty glasses. Her wit and good humour quickly endeared her to the miners, and to maintain her privacy, she always dressed in trousers or long outfits, shielding herself from prying eyes.

With her excellent humour came an abundance of tips. Many patrons advised her to take all the coins from the table, and she gladly complied. She deftly collected the loose change swiftly, depositing it into the large pockets she had thoughtfully sewn onto her apron for this purpose. After coming home and emptying her apron's pockets all over the bed, Tom and Donna couldn't believe how much there was, more than Donna was paid in wages for the entire day.

Tom needed a car for prospecting, so he bought one cheaply from a miner in a hurry to get away from the opal fields. It was a 1956 FJ Holden, which ran on more oil than fuel. Having a car opened more prospecting opportunities. The mining business was expensive, and more money was needed to buy explosives and equipment. Tom needed to buy a winch to lower himself into the shaft so that he may get lucky again.

The Post Office offered a variety of postal services. When the phone booth was in service, customers used the post office switchboard to call family within Australia. However, calling Europe was more complicated and often led to unreliable connections. Sending letters through the post office remained the safest, albeit slowest, method.

The post office also offered banking services. With her earnings from tips and cash at the Roofus bar and a collection of loose coins she found on the ground, Donna would gather all her coinage into a galvanised mop bucket and head to the bank in the morning. The two middle-aged women working there were not fond of counting coins, which took time and effort.

As Donna arrived with a bucket of small change, they both ducked behind the counter, dreading counting all those coins, which would take more than half a day.

"Ah, here she comes with her bloody bucket again. I think it's your turn today to sort out her coins."

The other woman just dropped her mouth in annoyance.

Placing the quarter-full bucket in front of them, Donna cheerfully said, "Good morning, girls, lovely to see you. Counting coins will keep you busy."

"Yeah, sure. Let's get on with it," said the unhappy woman whose turn it was to do the counting.

However, Donna was not deterred and kept chatting in her usual bubbly way, both women soon surrendering to her cheerful demeanor. Donna didn't need to wait for a receipt; in the small mining town during the early seventies, customers dealing with trustworthy service providers was a routine aspect of daily life.

When Tom returned home from his tiring job, Donna cheered him up by proudly displaying their earnings.

Collecting the small coins that Donna took to the post office every Monday had finally resulted in paper money. Tom wished to purchase a motor diesel-powered winch. This would have simplified the mining job significantly, as descending into a shaft on a rope and a folded metal ladder was arduous and unsafe.

One afternoon, when Tom arrived home, Donna surprised him. She had gathered all the money she had saved and spread one- and two-dollar bills over her bed. It covered the entire bed; she had hidden a few more pieces of paper money of higher value, five and ten dollars, beneath the pillow.

Tom stood in shock. "Where did you get all this money?"

"These are the coins I have been saving for months. These insignificant coins in time turn into paper." She smiled and kissed him, and then they both fell on the bed, started rolling among the paper money. One-dollar bills flew all over the room when Tom turned on the ceiling fan. Donna leapt off the bed, and both began grabbing money, laughing, kissing, and falling back onto the bed, then made passionate love as the money floated around the room like leaves blowing in the autumn wind.

Afterwards, when they started collecting the money, Tom asked, "Where will you hide all this money?"

"In my leather boots, of course. In such hot weather nobody in their sound mind will steal my boots."

The following week, Tom brought a motor winch, hoping that with this new equipment, he might uncover a few more solid opal stones hidden deep in the shaft.

Now, Tom and Donna had everything they wished for. What mattered to them the most was they loved each other, and belong solely to one another.

Chapter 14

The Outback Adventure

Donna prepared for a weekend trip to the desolate bushland by packing an icebox with food and several litres of water. Water, food, and fuel were crucial necessities when travelling in such arid regions. Tom was eager to take Donna to the Olympus mine site. The mining zone was noticeable from a distance, with countless mounds of earth excavated from the shafts on the dusty plains – a snapshot of the outback extending towards the far horizon.

After driving a few hundred miles towards Alice Springs, Tom took Donna to the approved camp. Next to the toilet's shaded area, Donna noticed a colossal sign warning tourists not to swim in the freshwater creek.

After unpacking, Tom and Donna trod carefully through the bush. The freshwater creek, much more expansive than anticipated, flowed steadily downstream. The oppressive heat of the dry desert made the sight of water in the outback a tantalising invitation to cool off. Mindful of the warning signs, Donna kept a vigilant watch for crocodiles, maintaining a safe distance from the water's edge.

Suddenly, Donna was startled when somebody shouted at her.

"Stop, you silly girl," yelled one of the Aboriginal women standing in a group under the shade. She walked down hastily and grabbed Donna by the hand as she pointed toward the muddy part of the creek further upstream.

"Can't you see the enormous crocodile sleeping under the tree? You don't want to wake up that hungry beast," the Aboriginal woman said.

Donna bent down, but she couldn't see anything.

"Crocodiles hide in mud. Keeps them cool, waiting for you to get in."

"Oh, no, I'm not going for a swim in a freshwater creek," Donna responded.

"But crocodiles are fast on the land, too. Silly tourists come here for a swim … crocodiles have a good feed. I've seen them crocs snatching a full-grown kangaroo from where you are standing."

Donna instantly ran to the higher ground.

"At this billabong, crocs prefer white people; they taste much better," another elderly woman said. All the children gathered around laughed, their white teeth gleaming.

Donna turned around and instinctively tried to hug the woman to thank her, but she moved away. The atmosphere became much more relaxed when Tom introduces Donna as his wife.

Another woman from the Aboriginal group said, "You come with us. We show you where it safe to swim."

Tom and Donna joined the Aboriginal group of women and their kids and safely walked around the billabong. In the distance, covered in red dust, hardly noticeable, two monstrous crocodiles slowly moved back to the water to cool from the scorching sun.

After walking further down the creek, the Aboriginal women allowed the children to jump in to cool off. Donna frowned.

"What about kids? Aren't you scared that a croc may get them?"

"No worries. Our men fish here, so it's safe. The creek water is clear, and there are no crocodiles. You can swim; white people are safe here, too. Crocs only like muddy water." She smiled.

However, Donna preferred to stay further away from the crocs, but she felt welcomed and secure. A few women remained beside the billabong looking after the children while other Aboriginal women started gathering bush tucker, warning them to be careful.

"I am so scared of snakes," Donna said.

The Aboriginal woman pointed towards the nearby bush. "Watch over there under bush. Two sleepy lizards are hiding. You will be safe when you see sleepy lizard; no snake around. Still, be careful and watch where you are going. Don't last long if step on snake out here."

After tasting some bush tucker, the small red berries tasting sweet, others tasting bitter, they stopped by their campsite, where elderly women sat by the open fire roasting some meat. Donna asked one of the Aboriginal women who spoke reasonable English why no men were around.

"Traditionally," she said, "Aboriginal woman's job is to protect and look after the children, search for bush tucker, and find remedies to treat health issues. Men fish and hunt.

"We have deep connection with the land. Our women and children spend much time in the bush. It is home to us. We like that white men have brought supermarkets to our community … we can buy food." She chuckled. "Aborigines can live in two different worlds, but white man cannot survive in the outback."

"What is that meat you are eating?" Donna asked.

"After swimming, kids get hungry. Kangaroo meat is tasty. Goanna tastes like chicken. You want taste some Witchetty grubs? Taste like sea snails."

Indeed, as they sampled the long white grubs, the bug snails, Donna immediately remembered her childhood when she ate sea snails with all the children in the village. Her childhood was as carefree and happy as the indigenous women and children she had just met.

It was getting late, and Tom and Donna thanked the women and kids for welcoming them and sharing their cultural knowledge with two unexpected white guests. They waved goodbye and returned to their campsite, a comfortable distance from the billabong, and sat under a large tree. Tom spread the blanket over the red dust so Donna could set up plates for a picnic lunch. After quenching their thirst, Donna spread the food out on the blanket; Tom gulped a cool beer in one go, smiled and said, "Initially, I came to Australia to hunt crocodiles. At least now, I have seen one from a distance. And I prefer it to stay that way. She is right. I certainly wouldn't be able to survive in the bush."

That day, Donna learned a valuable lesson: never take the environment for granted. She gained enormous respect for the Aboriginal people. They cherished family life, lived in harmony with the land, protected the environment, and took only what they needed from the land to survive.

"Tom, darling, I am so glad I met these lovely Aboriginal women and their children. From now on, I will never be prejudiced against Aboriginal miners who come to the public bar for a beer or two."

"I agree, my love. While in Coober Pedy, I have seen many injustices towards Aboriginals. It is difficult for them. They are just trying to adapt and survive in the white man's world," Tom said. Then he reached out and squeezed her hand. "I came to Coober Pedy to find opals but I found a diamond."

"Not quite," Donna smiled. "I am a rough diamond that needs polishing, but not here. I fear snakes, which could hide behind some of these bushes." Donna leant over and hugged Tom.

After gathering their picnic chairs, blankets, and dishes, they headed to the nearest motel to rest before their return drive to Coober Pedy.

Early the following day, Tom sat behind the wheel of his cherished FJ Holden, a birthday gift from Donna. With one hand on the steering wheel, he lit a cigarette, elbow propped on the open window. Donna leaned her head against his shoulder, absorbed in the radio tunes, as Johnny Cash's voice filled the car. The warm breeze wafted through the window, gently tousling her hair.

Chapter 15

Under the Southern Cross

Whenever Donna found time from work, she would pack a modest picnic, a bottle of wine, blankets, and two foldable chairs into the dusty trunk of Tom's FJ Holden. Tom, always prepared, would bring extra water and fuel, and they'd venture 20-50 km into the desert outback. There, they'd relish their late afternoon picnic, engage in light conversation, and wait for the sunset to start their stargazing. The desert nights were chilly, making their snuggles all the more special. After a few beers and a glass of wine, Tom's curiosity about Donna's love life piqued.

"Come on, Donna, tell me some of your secrets. Who did you love before me?"

"When I was seventeen, I experienced my first love, puppy love. However, the relationship didn't stand a chance from the beginning. My boyfriend's Orthodox family rejected me because of my Catholic background. It's disheartening that some people are firmly rooted in their religious beliefs even in this modern era.

"Nevertheless, he married my school friend. She is happy, and I am glad for her. I had another casual relationship when I worked for the house of Villa Verla. Nothing ever came out of that. Footballers can't stay faithful to one girlfriend. For him, it was just a fling, and for me, it was infatuation, nothing more.

"And here we are; I had to travel to the bottom of the world to find my true love. I believe in fate. It must have been written in the stars that I was to come to Australia to meet the man of my dreams, found my soul mate under the Southern Cross Star." Donna leaned over and kissed Tom.

"Come on, now it is your turn to spill all your secrets. Who did you love before me?" Donna grinned, teasing Tom.

"While in London, I have had a few girlfriends. That was crazy sixties, music, sex and rock-n-roll. Combine all these together in one group, and you get a perfect storm. During the sixties, life was rolling along at a very fast pace. It suited me just fine." Tom laughed.

"Have you ever been in love before? I am curious to know."

"Well, I had a few close calls. One Irish woman chased me, but I was not the marrying type so, when I moved jobs, that fizzled out. Patricia, the last girlfriend, was much more determined. She worked for the American Embassy in London, but when her term of employment was about to expire, she wanted to get married and move to Chicago, with me. Luckily, I escaped in the nick of time and moved to Australia to hunt crocodiles. That was a much safer option than getting married," Tom said, smiling.

"Did you have any girlfriends before you moved to London?" Donna kept probing

"I served in the army, based in Ljubljana. During my leave, my army mate Guido invited me to visit his family on the island. Despite the long train journey and unreliable ferry services, the trip was worth it. Guido introduced me to his sister. Maria was very attractive. She was one hot chick that got away."

"What happened?" Donna's curiosity spiked.

"We never really broke up. The last time we briefly met was when I was transferred to another army post. Maria had to accompany one of her sick students to the hospital that day, and we couldn't meet. After that, I moved to Montenegro to finish my army service. I never saw Maria again. When I moved to

London, that was that. Now you know the history of my love life," Tom concluded.

Donna gasped. She had to ask. "What is the island's name? Did Maria give you your nickname Ringo?"

Tom grew slightly agitated before responding. "What's all this nonsense? It feels like the Spanish Inquisition. Guido played in a local band, and his sister Maria nicknamed me Ringo after I attempted to play the drums. I liked the Beatles, so the nickname stuck. Why are you interested in my previous love life?"

Tom looked at Donna, who had covered her mouth with her hand, trying to regain her composure. She seemed surprised and confused, unable to believe what she had just heard. Maria, the subject of their conversation, had been Donna's arts and crafts instructor at the orphanage on the island of Cres.

"What is all this about?" Tom asked again, not amused.

"Tom, your girlfriend was my arts and crafts teacher. Maria wrote me a letter telling me she was heartbroken when her brother Guido told her that her boyfriend Ringo had moved abroad." She couldn't stop giggling.

"Now, you are not making any sense. You only had one glass?" Tom still couldn't grasp what he was hearing

"I was that young girl Maria escorted to the hospital. I was just fifteen years old then. Coincidentally, you were at the jetty when the ambulance came to transport me. Unintentionally, I disrupted your weekend with Maria, not knowing that one day we'd unexpectedly meet on the opposite side of the globe.

"A serendipity effect and that intrigues me?" Donna said.

Tom sat, shocked and in disbelief at the news. He found it hard to believe that they were so close to achieving their goal, yet still so far away. He was amazed by the coincidences that had brought them together, and how life had a way of surprising them in unexpected ways. It seemed that destiny had played a role in bringing them together in a distant world, under the glow of the brightest stars.

"I believe in faith," Donna said. "When I was fighting for my life with a perforated appendix, during my stay in the hospital, I was blessed with the presence of a guardian angel who watched over me. Every morning, a little dove would come to my window, tapping her beak, spinning around, and dancing to keep my spirits up. That little dove saved my life, and I believe it was a divine intervention that brought us together." Donna rested her head on Tom's shoulder, tears streaming down her face. He wrapped his arms around her, and gently kissed away her tears.

"Hey, why are there all these tears suddenly?" Tom inquired. "You should be smiling."

"When I recovered from the abdominal infection, doctors told me that I might never be able to have children. You might not want to stay with me now." Donna wept.

"That doesn't matter to me. I want you, and if we can't have children, that's okay. We don't need to have kids to be happy. It is you and me, love, that is all I desire."

Tom wiped Donna's tears, kissed her cheeks, and embraced her tightly; he then pointed towards the Southern Cross star to calm her down. "Observe this star," he said. "It's radiating with such intensity tonight, presenting a splendid spectacle. It's fortuitous that our paths crossed under the constellation of the Southern Stars. With this dazzling star as our guide, we could never stray."

As they witnessed a star streak across the sky, they held each other close. Making love beneath the stars on a warm night seemed to transport them to a celestial realm. Afterwards, as they lay hand in hand, they both dozed off.

On the drive back at a late hour, Donna stuck her head out the window, gazing up at the stars; it appeared the Southern

Cross was guiding their path forward.

Over the next six months, Tom and Donna's romance became stronger and more distinctive, like a rare solid opal found in the ground. They frequently went on late-night drives, parking their FJ Holden on the deserted dirt roads of the outback. They would bring along a bottle of wine and a battery-operated cassette radio on which to play classical music.

On a night with no moon, they parked their car far from the road, where the lights of the town could not be seen. It was a dark and tranquil place, a vast open space that was not empty but filled with a heavenly silence. The sky was clear, and billions of bright, shimmering stars covered it. They hugged each other tightly, and after sharing kisses, they lay down on the warm, red, dusty ground and made love.

Afterwards, while resting on a blanket and gazing up at the crystal-clear stars, Tom and Donna listened to the Vienna Philharmonic Orchestra directed by Karajan. The magical sounds of Mozart, Bach, Beethoven or a string quartet's Adagio in G Minor echoed throughout the desert lands of Coober Pedy. For a few hours, in total silence, their hearts beat as one and the happy couple felt in heaven.

Motionless and silent, they lay in awe of the universe's vastness, gazing at the sparkling stars above. It seemed as though the sky had orchestrated grand fireworks display just for them. Donna, unable to look away from the magical stars lighting up the expansive sky, held her soul mate close. She felt a deep sense of contentment and joy. Edging closer to Tom, she planted a soft kiss and whispered softly: "I am certain that our meeting beneath the Southern Cross was preordained by fate, written in the stars long before my birth."

Tom looked across at her, then rolled to his side and kissed her. "I love you, Donna, my love, and I've just decided something," he whispered. "We should get married. How would you like that?"

Donna eagerly responded, "Yes, I would love that!" She rolled on top of him and buried her head in his bare chest.

"I promise you that when I find opal and get rich, I will take you to Notre Dame de Paris, where Napoleon married his great love, Josephine," Tom said. He had read all the historical books, and Napoleon was his hero.

☙

Tom and Donna frequented the drive-in cinema in Coober Pedy, watching mostly cowboy movies. Although the sound from the little speaker attached to their car window was breaking up, most patrons didn't seem to mind. The food kiosk at the cinema sold burgers and beer, and at night, young lovers were more interested in each other than in the movies. Whenever the sky was clear, Tom and Donna drove twenty kilometres out of town to stargaze, talk about their wedding plans, and dream about finding opals. Tom envisioned sailing around the world on his big yacht for their honeymoon.

As they became more acquainted, they discovered that they shared many interests. They engaged in discussions about politics, world affairs, and governments and found that they held similar views on these topics. They even had lively debates about the rival football teams they supported. One night, while gazing up at the night sky, Donna joyfully announced something important.

"Tom, dear, I'm pregnant."

"This is an unexpected surprise," Tom said.

Donna thought it was impossible to get pregnant after her appendix infection. "Are you disappointed?" she asked Tom.

"Oh, no, love. I am speechless but thrilled. I was happy to

have you all to myself, but having a baby is the icing on the cake." Tom hugged her, wiped away her joyful and sad tears, and laughed.

"What's so funny, Tom?" Donna asked

"I am not surprised that you are pregnant. It was bound to happen after our making love under the clear sky and the Southern Cross star," Tom murmured before he kissed her.

"Well, we may never know exactly where we conceived," she replied with a smile. "However, my sister Mara did caution me that a lot of pregnancies occur at the drive-in theatre."

"Tom, remember the night at the drive-in when the massive screen vanished into a whirlwind of red dust during the storm? We huddled in the back seat, lost in love. And the time we slept in the car because the drive-in was submerged?"

Tom remembered. "The black clouds appeared out of nowhere. The window seals on my old car began leaking, and we both got soaking wet. My trusted FJ got bogged in the mud, and we had no choice but to spend overnight in the car.

"It was so cold and wet; we cuddled up, wrapped in a blanket. The following day, I had to dig the car out of the mud," Tom laughed.

"Well, my darling, I am now pregnant. I like to think that our love child was conceived beneath the Southern Cross constellations," Donna said, beaming with joy. She had never thought she would be blessed with children, yet it seemed the gods from the heavens above had bestowed their smile upon her. She had found the man of her dreams in a faraway place beneath the glistening stars. She now understood why immigrants called Australia 'the lucky country.'

Chapter 16

FJ Holden

Tom was filled with happiness and acted like a teenager in love. However, he also had another significant responsibility – he would be a father and would need to protect, care for, and support his pregnant girlfriend. So he started planning to get away from Coober Pedy. This mining town was for losers or dreamers who believed in getting rich fast. It was not the right place to start a family and raise a child.

One day, Tom grabbed Donna's hand and said, "Come on, babe, let's get out of this shit hole of a place. It would be better for you to be closer to a hospital in case of any complications," he declared firmly.

"Tom, we can't just leave. What about your dreams? You came to find opals, get rich, buy a yacht, and sail around the world," Donna retorted.

"I am already wealthy. With you by my side, what more could a man ask for? I have found something even more precious than opal – a rough diamond that needs polishing. This is it. We are leaving Coober Pedy. We are done here. I want my son to be born in a city hospital."

"What if it is a girl?" Donna asked.

"No way! The firstborn will be a son." Tom looked at her, smiling cheekily.

Donna turned around without a word, thinking nothing had changed. Men would always be men. Her own father desired only sons. Girls still had a long way to go to be as desirable as sons. But she still had a few more questions for Tom.

"But what about buying a yacht and sailing around the world? Giving up your dream puts a lot of pressure on me," she said.

"Well, we just have to come up with another dream. Having you with me is a pretty good start." Tom smiled and hugged her then gently patted her tummy. "We now have to plan and dream for three. Having a family of my own has always been one of my secret dreams. But I was too scared to think that something as good as this would come my way."

That reassured Donna that Tom really loved her. "But, Tom, what will happen to your mining rights? You are part owner of that claim and deserve to get something for all your hard work?"

"Yes, but who cares? Alexis blew all our riches to smithereens with the extra gelignite. So let's just get away from here and start fresh."

"But, Tom, don't just walk away empty-handed. Alexis may want to buy your mining stake."

"I don't care! I want to leave and forget this nightmare. I wasn't meant to get rich with money, but I am rich because I found you."

Donna gave him one of her cheeky looks. "Getting something out of the man who robbed you of your dreams will give you some closure. Money helps to keep the fire of passion burning, so don't give up," Donna said.

Tom frowned. "What are you thinking?"

"Did you tell Alexis I'm pregnant? I hope not. He doesn't need to know how desperate we are to leave Coober Pedy."

"No, I said nothing to him."

"Fine, then don't. Let's see if we can extract some compensation from the fool who dashed your hopes of owning a yacht and sailing the globe. Had he heeded your advice, you might now be a millionaire. He obliterated not just the opal but your aspirations as well. At the very least, he ought to pay you a few hundred dollars for your portion of the mining rights. After all, receiving any offer is better than walking away with nothing."

"Okay, what should we do?"

"You should ask Alexis to buy your share, or you will sell it to somebody else. He won't like that," Donna reasoned.

Tom smiled and nodded. "Donna, you are one tough cookie. Let's talk business tomorrow with Alexis."

"I will come with you to help negotiate the best deal."

The following day, Alexis met them as arranged, offering unsold opals in exchange for Tom's mining rights, as he was broke. He arrived with a bag of unsold opals – triplets, doublets, black and solid pieces of opals. Although these opals weren't perfect, Donna convinced Tom to accept the deal since it was the only option available, and Tom agreed.

After Tom received his package of opals, he went with Donna to the police station to complete the transfer of mining rights. On their way back, Donna expressed her hope that one day she might sell the parcel for a few thousand dollars.

"Listen to me, Donna. What we got from Alexis is not worth much, but it may attract thieves, so we had better hide it. When miners become desperate, they will steal from their own mothers. Stealing in Coober Pedy is common," Tom warned her.

"Tom, I know where I can hide them."

"Surprise me," Tom laughed.

"My black leather boots. Coober Pedy is so hot, who would want to steal my winter boots?" Donna reminded him, smiling.

A few days later, Tom sold a dozen of the best pieces of black opal that the Japanese buyers loved and a few more solid opal pieces to a buyer from Hong Kong. The buyers were not interested in buying triplets or doublets and didn't even want them at a discounted price.

"What did you get?" Donna asked.

"The best I could get for selling the best black opals was three hundred and fifty dollars. That will be enough money to get away from here."

Tom, please show me the money. This is the most cash I've ever seen. It's more than I've earned in months, including tips.

Tom unzipped his money belt and pulled out the cash, throwing it up in the air. The money landed on the bed and the floor, the cooling fan blowing it all over the room.

Tom looked at her and opened a little purple velvet box; it contained an engagement ring.

"Oh, what a beautiful ring," Donna gushed, her heart skipping a beat. She leapt into Tom's embrace, and he squeezed her so tight that she could hardly breathe. They fell onto the bed and made passionate love as the fan blew dollars around like confetti.

Afterwards, Donna stashed the cash with the rest of the opals in her boots. She hid her boots under the bed among all the other dusty shoes she had never worn.

Donna couldn't take her eyes off her beautiful ring.

"Tom, how much did you spend on this ring?"

"I got it from the tourist souvenir shop, so there was little choice. Tourists come and go. This ring is a rip-off, but I want to give you the engagement ring that I bought in Coober Pedy.

"But I love it. How much was it?"

Then Tom pointed out, "Listen, don't expect diamonds, not for fifty bucks, maybe zirconia or something like that," Tom tried to explain.

Still, she was pleased. Tom put the ring on her finger; it fitted perfectly. The blue and green lustrous opal in the ring seemed to smile at her.

Donna kissed him. "This ring will remind me of Coober Pedy. I found my cowboy in the desert and fell head over heels in love with him. These memories will be engraved in my heart forever."

"One day, I will buy you a genuine diamond ring, but I already have a diamond right now in you."

ೞ

The following day, Donna informed Peppy she was leaving, and all the kitchen staff wished them good luck in their new life. They collected money and gifted the happy couple first-grade Merino woollen blankets and two feather pillows.

Donna finished packing, squashing everything in her Gucci suitcases. She asked Tom to wait in the bar so she could walk up the hill and say goodbye to Mara. Fortunately, Martin was not around, so the two sisters embraced. Mara cried and wished her sister the best. Donna promised to invite her to the christening when her child was born. Both sisters had regrets, but they were happy that all the bad feelings were forgotten and forgiven.

Pleased with that, Donna ran down the hill. Singing with joy, she climbed into their old FJ Holden.

"This will be a long journey," Tom said. "We have enough water, and Peppy packed us enough food to last until we arrive in Adelaide."

Tom put his foot down, and they left Coober Pedy in a cloud of red dust, never to return.

Tom wound the windows down, and the car radio blasted Johnny Cash's favourite hits as they headed towards Adelaide along roads full of potholes after the last rain. The tiresome journey to Riverland would be over a thousand kilometres. Donna had squeezed her winter boots into her hand luggage, which she held tightly.

Before departing, Donna stopped by the post office. As a farewell gift, she'd received a complimentary phone connection to call her best friend, Sandra, who now resided in Renmark, a rural town in South Australia's Riverland region. Sandra had sent Donna one hundred dollars, which was one month's pay, and she assured Donna that accommodation would be ready upon her arrival, and that there was an abundance of fruit picking and packing jobs available.

Tom and Donna looked forward to gaining seasonal work. Employment was one of the first priorities that would cushion them financially, and they planned to get married before the birth of their first child.

Tom put his elbow out the window, puffed on cigarettes and held on to the steering wheel while Donna tenderly leaned against him. Thrilled and excited, they discussed their future while driving.

After travelling 250 kilometres on a rough, dusty road, they arrived at Glendambo Roadhouse near Kingoonya, then kept driving south, praying their car would last the distance without breaking down or going kaput in the middle of nowhere.

The FJ Holden was overheating, and the temperature gauge was in the red zone. Tom noticed the burning smell and reduced his speed, hoping that staying below 60 kilometres per hour would allow the old car to make it through the journey.

After leaving Glendambo Roadhouse, the car muffler fell off. Donna worried, but Tom reassured her that, besides the loud noise, which sounded like a Formula-1 racing car, the FJ would keep going without any problem. There was nothing to worry about.

Weary, famished, and parched, they arrived at Pimba, a construction camp for the Trans-Australian Railway that had evolved into a township in the 1960s. Feeling somewhat rejuvenated and rested, they were eager for the next leg of the journey and were content with the knowledge that the most challenging part was behind them. With only another 125 kilometres to Port Augusta, marking the end of the rugged, incomplete road, they anticipated a smooth journey ahead.

But, not long after, the good, reliable FJ Holden refused to go any further. Worried, Tom lifted the bonnet. Steam hissed out of the radiator, and the smell of burning oil rose from the red-hot engine.

After allowing the car to cool down, he attempted every possible method to restart it, but his cherished FJ Holden, worn out from use, was irreparable.

Tom and Donna had sufficient water to sustain them for a few hours. Traffic on the dirt roads was almost non-existent, with the road primarily serving large trucks carrying water, petrol, and groceries to Coober Pedy. The empty trucks heading back to Adelaide would race down the dusty road as though they were in the Finke Desert Rally.

The only other traffic was buses and a few brave tourists towing caravans. Donna and Tom waited by the roadside, hoping to stop any vehicle travelling past for help.

Standing by the roadside in the desert on a scorching day, time dragged on. Tom flagged down a four-wheel-drive, hardly visible within the red dust.

Donna playfully suggested, "Shall I flash my leg to stop the car?"

Tom gave her a mischievous look. "Watch yourself, 'ma belle me'."

Donna jumped up and down as the car drew closer, waving her hands frantically. The car slowed down and stopped. A familiar head appeared out of the car window.

"What's the problem?" the man asked.

Tom leapt with joy as he recognised the local opal miner.

"Peter, you old rascal, I'm so glad to see you, mate. We are in trouble. Our car broke down and won't start."

Peter slid out of the driver's seat and, reeking of beer, said hello as he walked past her to the open car bonnet. He pulled out the dipstick and noticed the oil was not dark but light grey. He shook his head. "Tom, you have a cracked engine block. It looks like your car overheated because the radiator was leaking. As you can see here, it's still dripping. You must've lost a lot of water since you left Coober Pedy."

Returning to his car, Peter opened the boot, and returned with two bottles of cold beer from his icebox.

Tom swallowed his first gulp and thought that beer never tasted better. "Oh boy, this feels good; nothing ever beats this. What can we do?" Tom asked.

"Well, I can take you to Port Augusta where there's a mechanic at an auto repair shop. I have a strong mining shaft rope in the boot of my car. What do you say?"

"Peter, you saved us," said Tom. "Let's get hooked up."

Peter fetched the rope and grabbed two more beers. While he was under the bonnet of the car, trying to secure the rope, Tom embraced Donna and quietly explained, "Listen, love, we don't have enough water to keep re-filling the leaking radiator. We have no choice. There isn't a bus passing by here until next week, and with the rainy season approaching, traffic has slowed down. If we don't do this, we could be stuck here for days. It will be much safer for you to sit in the back of Peter's car." He hugged her quickly and rushed to help Peter secure the rope.

Donna opened her water bottle and was about to sip when a thunderous road train came from behind at high speed, leaving behind an enormous cloud of dust. Then, another road train roared past right behind the first, bringing more swirling dust.

Coughing and cursing, Peter and Tom escaped the car to catch a breath then resumed connecting the two cars when the dust settled. Hastily finishing his beer, Tom checked that Donna was settled in Peter's car, then both drivers slid into their cars, Tom nervous as he knew being towed on the rough road full of potholes would be difficult and potentially dangerous.

Peter fired up his car, shifted into gear, and hit the dirt track. The FJ Holden lurched forward as the tow rope tightened between the vehicles. The dust kicked up by Peter's car posed a visibility issue. Unperturbed, Peter leant back in his robust vehicle, propped his elbow out the window for extra ease, and quickly caught up with the two road trains he had seen earlier. Shouting, "Get out of the way, you slowpokes, you're holding us up!" he flashed a two-finger salute while clutching a beer can. Flooring the accelerator, Peter veered to the right side of the road to pass them.

Suddenly, they were enveloped in a dense cloud of dust stirred up by the trucks, which obscured the road ahead. Regardless, Peter continued to drive without faltering. Compounding the danger, the increased speed caused the worn tyres of the FJ Holden to slip on the rugged dirt track. The car swayed and skidded from side to side, nearly colliding with an oncoming road train. A single misstep to the left would send them tumbling beneath the massive wheels, leaving nothing but wreckage.

As Tom careered past one of the trucks, a big rock was hurled by one of the truck's wheels and rock smashed through Tom's windscreen, showering him with sharp glass shards all over his face and body. He lost visibility of the road ahead. Quickly recovering, Tom punched out the shattered windscreen with his fist so that he could see. However, Peter oblivious to the dilemma behind him, kept driving with one hand and drinking cold beer with the other.

As the windscreen shattered, a scorching gust of wind blew even more dust into the car. Tom frantically attempted to clear his eyesight, but the dust and tears made it difficult. He felt like a helpless man, drowning with no chance of survival.

Donna's lungs also filled with dust, causing her to cough continuously. A worried expression crossed her face as she glanced at Peter, who nonchalantly tossed empty beer cans out the window. Overwhelmed by fear and feeling powerless in her situation, she realised that only divine intervention could help now. With a silent prayer, she hoped her guardian angel, even with its broken wing, would safeguard her unborn child.

Then, as if God had answered Donna's prayers, they came out of the dust cloud and into clear, bright daylight. Driving on the correct side of the road had never felt better.

With the two road trains now far behind them, Tom felt like laughing and crying at the same time. Did they just come out of Dante's Inferno?

Without a windscreen, the hot wind blew into Tom's face. He accepted it as a minor inconvenience and settled down to a steady and more relaxed ride. An hour later, they were driving on a sealed road. When they arrived at Port Augusta, Peter took them to an affordable car repair shop where he knew a mechanic. As soon as Peter's car disappeared from view, the mechanic spoke with Tom.

"Listen, mate, it will take a day or two to fix this car, possibly by Friday lunchtime. It'll cost more than a hundred dollars to fix the basic problems, and it's hard to get parts for a FJ Holden these days. It needs a new radiator, a new muffler, a new windscreen, new tyres, and an engine swap to be roadworthy again," the mechanic explained.

Tom said, "We can't afford to change the engine. Can you fix what you can so we can drive to Renmark?"

"Okay, I'll do my best, but I recommend adding a sealing agent to the vehicle's cooling system. With a new radiator, you will get there, but eventually, this car needs a new engine."

"Alternatively, I can buy this car from you for a few hundred bucks and drive you to the bus station. That will guarantee you get to Renmark, which will be much cheaper."

"Thanks, but I am attached to my FJ. This old bomb and I have been through a lot together. I can't part with this car," Tom responded.

Donna and Tom had two days to rest, so they leisurely walked to a cheap motel. Exhausted and blessed to be alive, they ordered room service and relaxed.

"Can we sell our opal parcel you got from Alexis?" Donna asked.

"We could try it, but most jewellers want rough opal so they can polish and set it. What we have is worth around a thousand dollars, which would be very handy. But, Donna, I have a small secret that I couldn't tell you while in Coober Pedy."

"What are you talking about?" Donna said, frowning.

"Recall when Alexis travelled to Alice Springs to see his son in the hospital? He was convinced that a large opal was concealed in that shaft, and always worried someone might snatch it. While he was away, he entrusted me with guarding the mine. I camped out in a sleeping bag next to the shaft overnight, safeguarding our claim against any midnight cowboys who might try to grab the remaining opals," Tom said, watching Donna closely to gauge her reaction.

"So, what have you done?" Donna asked warily.

"I descended the 25-metre shaft using only a rope. With my pick and shovel, I continued to dig, searching for any opals we might have overlooked. The moonlight bathed the field so brightly that night, I had to be exceedingly silent to avoid waking the other miners guarding their finds. Had Alexis discovered me, he surely would have ended my life and discarded me down a shaft."

"Oh, Tom, I remember now when you had that big cut above your eye. Why did you have to take such risks?" Donna asked.

"Yes, on my way up, the pick got caught on the shaft, which nearly poked my eye out. When Alexis returned, I lied to him and told him that I had been in a fight at a public bar. It was not unusual for me to get into fights, so he believed me. However, look at what I found."

Tom took out of his pocket a magnificent opal shell. "Discovering a crystallised shell is a crowning achievement for any opal miner. I was lucky enough to find one. As I continued to dig, I unearthed several more solid opals, though they weren't of the highest quality – only this shell stood out. It's a rare jackpot that few miners ever encounter."

"You kept that secret until now? Where have you hidden it?"

"In my work boot, of course," Tom smiled.

"Wow, Alexis blew away a good trace of opal and missed a small fortune. Justice has prevailed." Donna hugged Tom, happy they had such a valuable opal to sell. That would give them a real boost to start their new life.

◌

During the two-day stay at the motel, Tom and Donna visited many opal jewellers, offering to sell the opal parcel they got from Alexis, but they had no luck. The next day, Tom caught a taxi to see his old friend Jimmy, an Irish opal cutter formerly of Coober Pedy. Upon seeing Tom's opal shell, Jimmy proposed to purchase it. Tom declined. Instead, he requested that Jimmy polish and form the opal shell into a heart. Needing additional funds to adorn the gold necklace with the opal heart, Tom compensated Jimmy with some rough opals he had unearthed. His intention was to surprise Donna with this gesture.

Two days later, when the FJ Holden was roadworthy again, Tom stopped at Jimmy's store and asked Donna to wait in the car.

Returning and sitting beside her, Tom held out the heart-shaped opal. "Donna, this gift belongs to you. Consider it a wedding gift." Tom said before kissing her.

"But, Tom, we are broke," Donna said.

"I could have sold this shell to Jimmy for three thousand dollars, but I refused because it belongs to you."

"Wow, it is beautiful and worth a small fortune," Donna said, excited to get such a magnificent and expensive gift.

"Money comes and goes. We still have the parcel we got from Alexis hidden in the boots. We may sell it one day," Tom said, continuing to tell her his story.

"Darling, please behold this magnificent opal shell. It has endured a million years at the sea's bottom, awaiting its transformation into perfection. It's astounding that it found its way to this sandy desert, patiently waiting for eons to meet its destined owner. This shell was meant for you," Tom said.

"Donna, you must promise me that you will never sell it, no matter what happens. This precious shell must be preserved for the next generation. When we get old, if we have a grand-daughter, you can pass it down to her," Tom insisted.

Tom leaned over and hooked the gold necklace with its opal heart around Donna's neck.

Donna took Tom's hand and placed it on her pregnant tummy. "Oh, Tom, I promise never to part with it, no matter what?" she said.

He smiled, then told her to open the car window. "Now, put your arm outside and feel the refreshing breeze."

The FJ Holden no longer rattled but purred as they continued their journey. Donna pushed a radio cassette into the player, and they listened to Elvis Presley's 'Love Me Tender' as they drove towards Riverland.

Donna leant her head on Tom's shoulder and, clutching the opal shell heart next to her beating heart, whispered, "Tom, I will never let go of your heart."

Chapter 17

Riverland

Tom and Donna arrived in Riverland late in the afternoon and met Sandra in the Renmark Hotel's beer garden. She was renting a room in the fruit pickers' area. Unfortunately, the fruit-picking season was in full swing, and there was never enough accommodation. She lent them two hundred dollars, which was very helpful, and told them that all the chalets were full of seasonal pickers, but she had reserved an old caravan that had been vacant for a while. They could have it for at least the first few months if they didn't mind a neglected and untidy interior. They took it immediately, happy they didn't have to spend the night in their car.

However, when they saw the old caravan, their hearts sank. It was dilapidated and leaning to one side. Donna had déjà vu. "Considering the caravan at Coober Pedy, this one is not such an enormous shock." They both laughed. The inside was not much better. Covered in dust, it smelled musty and mouldy. The wobbly table, worn-out mattress, and old blankets weren't inviting. As they walked inside, the caravan rocked, leaving Donna feeling nauseous.

The caravan park was clean and full of trees, so it was at least nice and cool. Tom looked at Donna and said, "Don't worry, darling. We will find a better home when the picking season ends," Tom encouraged. "Stay positive, it will all work out."

Tom started working at a fruit juice factory and earned a

weekly wage of $39 dollars after taxes. Meanwhile, Donna worked in a cannery, sorting fruits on a conveyor belt. Her basic weekly wage was $35 dollars. She had no choice but to work on the machines to earn extra money.

However, pregnant women were not able to operate machinery; it was deemed unsafe, so Donna hid her pregnancy by wearing loose clothing and carefully wrapping an apron around her growing belly. When she started working on the pear-peeling machine, she was the slowest of the migrant women. Twelve machines stood in a row, and these women were so fast they put ten pears into the machine cups for automatic peeling and were paid for how many crates of pears were peeled each day.

Determined to work faster and earn special bonuses, Donna developed a proper technique and soon became her shift's fastest 'peeler'. Her colleagues were envious because she processed the pear cases faster and earned more money. Donna felt overjoyed with her achievement.

On weekends, she began working on a fruit block. While it was comforting to work with migrant women, cutting apricots by hand was tiring. Donna earned twenty cents for a tray of cut apricots to dry in the sun. At first, she managed about twenty trays a day, which was tough on her hands, feet, and back. But with time, she caught up to other migrant women, who cut twice as many trays.

Sitting in their dingy caravan at night, Tom and Donna counted their earnings and discussed wedding plans. One night, while fast asleep, a storm came through early in the morning. Donna jumped up, alarmed.

"Tom, get up. The caravan roof is leaking. We are getting drenched." Tom lifted his head, confused. "Look, it is dripping onto our bed."

Now fully awake, Tom jumped out of bed and stood beside

her. Looking up, he saw the rain pouring through a crack above the mattress.

"Unbelievable. Quickly, move the blankets onto the floor."

Donna quickly placed a bucket on the bed under the leaking roof. Then, they both sat at the table.

"We need to find another place," Tom said with a frown. "We can't stay here, and we are paying six dollars fifty per week for this. No, we will start looking for something cheaper with a roof that doesn't leak. This is ridiculous."

Donna remained silent but nodded.

"Darling, I'll ask around at work tomorrow. There must be something to rent, I'm sure."

When dawn came, they were still in the same position, hugging each other and keeping warm. Soon, the alarm clock went off. Donna made strong coffee while Tom dressed for work, putting on stained white overalls and waterproof rubber boots. They were both miserable but determined.

Over the next few days, Tom and Donna spent all their free time looking for alternative accommodation, which they finally found through Christine and Carl, who they had met a few weeks earlier. They owned a sizeable wine-growing block bordering a large orchard that the Stamullius family owned. The old asbestos house with a tin roof was built for the seasonal fruit pickers. It was currently empty.

After getting directions, they drove to the Fruit Block and their new rental home. When they arrived, they saw it, even though it was half-hidden from the road by an immense vineyard and some trees close to the Murray River. They cautiously approached the house. It was a crumbling, miserable dwelling. Above the entrance hall, part of the roof was missing. Its remaining naked rafters protruded above the doorway. Tom forced the front door open, and the weathered, rotting piece of wood held by rusty hinges creaked. Tom turned to Donna.

"Well, we'd better go in. Let's find out about the rest of this place."

Donna looked sad and miserable. She was with child and had hoped for something better. She looked at Tom in dismay. "Oh, Tom, this is no good. How can anyone live here?"

Inside, it was dirty, the walls blackened by soot. It had a wood stove, an old table with two rickety chairs, and a cracked window. The bathroom door was made of uneven, ill-fitting wooden vertical boards.

Tom's hopes for privacy quickly dashed, and the bed sagged almost to the floor in the bedroom, but the roof above the bed was intact. Tom sighed and looked back over his shoulder. "Well, my darling, what do you think? We can buy a new mattress, and after a good cleanup, it will be better than the leaky caravan. It's only until we find something better."

Mr Stamullius told Tom and Donna that the weekly rent would be $8.50.

Donna struggled with her emotions but finally responded, 'Tom, we don't have a choice. It's either this shabby home or back to the leaky caravan. As long as you're with me, I'll be safe. We won't stay here for long. Okay, let's take it."

After making the decision, their friends helped clean up the place. They bought new mattresses, bed linens, towels, and the cheapest kitchen utensils. After all the hard work was done, Donna and Tom moved in. The picker's home was a slight improvement from the leaking caravan and was now semi-livable. There were, however, several issues, the most significant one being that the only available toilet was a run-down, rusty tin shed located outside. This unpleasant reminder brought back memories of Coober Pedy. The toilet was a deep hole with a shabby wooden seat and a tin door that could not be closed. Terrified of snakes, Donna would carry a toilet roll in one hand and a long stick in the other to keep snakes away, continually thumping the surrounding ground.

When Tom asked about the outdoor toilet, Mr Stamullius gave him the option to build one inside if he didn't like it. Although Tom was angry, he didn't want the situation to worsen because Mr Stamullius had promised to contact the telephone company and install a landline on their rented property. Living on an isolated fruit orchard, having a landline phone was an absolute must.

Within a few weeks of moving in, Tom and his new friends helped to build a toilet inside the house, despite being short of money. It took Tom only five days to dig the septic hole and install the toilet seat. They now had a toilet, a hot shower, and a wood stove. Somehow, that rugged old cottage became their first home together.

One day, Donna suggested brightening the kitchen with a fresh coat of paint. Tom agreed and, wishing to spend only a little, bought a brush and a small tin of light-blue paint, hoping it would be enough.

After covering two walls, Tom ran out of paint. The room looked striking: half painted in light blue and the rest remaining a filthy brown-black.

Donna had such a good laugh that tears flowed when she saw it. With a mischievous grin, Tom glanced upwards. Then, he couldn't help but burst out laughing as well at how closely their pitiful state mirrored their current situation.

Therefore, they left it as it was. Mr Stamullius could finish the painting if it bothered him, which was very unlikely. The miserable old miser wouldn't even build a proper toilet in his house for his seasonal workers.

One morning, after Tom went to work, Donna lay in bed, resting with her pregnancy. She noticed a giant hairy spider descending from the ceiling toward her stomach. She scrambled out of bed and ran screaming from the room. When Tom came home he sprayed the room and eradicated many spiders, some as big as Donna's hand.

In the kitchen and laundry, mice scurried searching for food scraps. Sometimes, out of boredom, Tom and Donna sat motionless to give the mice a false sense of security. When the emboldened mice slowly crept out of their small holes, looking for food, Tom and Donna would leap up and scare them. The mice would quickly scamper back towards their small burrows' safety, and that's when the show would start. Two scared mice running together into the hole simultaneously would get caught, with their heads stuck inside, squeaking. Their two little bums would stick out, wiggling in desperation with their hind legs pedalling in overdrive. Tom and Donna laughed and laughed. Eventually, the more energetic mouse would win and disappear, with the second one close behind.

Weeks passed when Donna unexpectedly came home from the cannery. Tom, who had finished his night shift, swung out of the jumped from the bed in alarm and embraced her.

"Darling, what's happened?" Tom said, concerned that she was crying.

"I was made redundant, being pregnant and visibly showing. The Cannery management told me that their safety regulations wouldn't allow pregnant women to work on the slippery surfaces at the cannery. I was told to pick up my lunch box and go home immediately.

"Fortunately, I can work on weekends and continue cutting apricots, but that is not much. Tom, what are we now going to do for money? Your pay won't be enough for our wedding."

Tom drew Donna onto his chest and softly kissed the top of her head. "My love, we'll manage. We always have." Then, seeing Donna's beautiful hazel eyes, he suddenly decided, "Let's get married immediately. We have saved some money, and we have waited long enough."

Tom's younger sister, Enda, and her husband, Tony, had kept on promising to attend the wedding, but travelling from England was difficult, and the airline tickets were expensive. Nobody was coming.

"We could get married next weekend – just the two of us. We don't need anybody else. What do you think, love?" Tom suggested.

When Donna's sad face quickly broke into a smile, Tom held her in his arms. "Listen, it is just us. It will always be just us. Soon, we will have a family of our own."

"I agree. There's no need to wait for anyone now. It's disappointing that my sisters, Mara and Martin don't want to come," Donna said, her sadness evident.

Tom stopped for a moment, holding Donna's hands. "I can understand why Martin can't leave Coober Pedy right now. He told me he had just pegged a new mining shaft, and he is worried about leaving it as it has a good trace of opal. He will camp on-site guarding his claim with a gun and his new German shepherd dog. So we have no reason to wait any longer. Let's get married next week. I don't want my son to be born out of wedlock." Tom spoke firmly, bringing Donna close and kissing her.

"Oh, Tom, I love you, but we might have a baby girl" They kissed tenderly and spent all evening planning their wedding day.

"Tom, I have nothing to wear for our wedding."

"Don't worry, my sweet. You will find something, but don't spend too much; we can't afford it."

The following day, Tom and Donna went shopping. Donna spotted a lovely maternity dress with a ladybird design and a red hat with a white bow. Tom rented a jacket, bow tie and well-ironed brown pants. They visited the Registry Office and completed the paperwork for their upcoming marriage. The date and time for the ceremony were now set.

The next task was to schedule a meeting with the Renmark Hotel manager to plan a small wedding reception. The Manager welcomed them warmly and asked, "How may I assist you?"

Donna responded quickly when Tom hesitated and requested a wedding reception booking for next Saturday.

His eyes lit up. Most Greek or Italian wedding receptions in Riverland catered to three hundred to five hundred guests. They typically involved a stretch limo, wedding flowers, bridal bouquets, an elaborate wedding cake, wedding photography, and a live band that made an excellent profit for the hotel. "I'd be happy to help you with that," he said keenly. "How many guests do you expect?"

"Six, possibly eight," Donna replied.

"Wow, that's great!" said the manager excitedly. He then hurriedly rose and walked to the reception desk. After a few minutes, he returned and informed them they could cater for six hundred people. However, he mentioned they were fully booked with a busload of tourists next weekend, so arranging such a big wedding reception would require more time. He then asked what kind of customised wedding package they had in mind for those six hundred guests."

Feeling uncomfortable, Tom and Donna glanced at each other. "Our apologies for any confusion, sir; we need a booking for only six people, eight counting us," Donna explained coyly.

The manager looked confused. "Yeah, we can cater for sixty or eighty."

"No, no, you got it wrong. We only have six people, maybe eight," Donna said, using her hands and showing the manager eight fingers.

Initially, the hotel manager seemed surprised but quickly composed himself and began shuffling through a stack of brochures he had brought from the front desk. "Alright, so there are only eight of you. We can arrange something for you.

Don't worry. We will take good care of you."

On Saturday afternoon, they drove to the Registry Office and exchanged wedding vows before the magistrate.

Donna looked radiant and elegant in her mini-dress, enhanced further by the opal shell she wore round her neck. Tom took her into his arms and warmly drew her to him. The moment was perfect.

As the formalities ended, Donna whispered to her husband, "Darling, I was so nervous I couldn't understand any of the words from our vows."

"Don't worry —" He smiled. "I'll explain it later."

Tom kissed his bride.

The few guests attending the wedding ceremony showered them with confetti while offering heartfelt congratulations, and after the ceremony, they enjoyed a glass of champagne with Sandra and Anton, Christine and Carl, Greta and Greg then took group photos together in a garden across the river.

The wedding reception at the Renmark Hotel was a big hit. The hotel manager had arranged a luxurious party with a lavishly decorated table for eight, adorned with flowers and two crystal candleholders. Donna had brought the wedding cake to the banquet hall's centre beforehand. Everything looked perfect, and the small wedding party was the centre of attention that evening.

The spacious dining area was filled with tourists who had arrived by bus. Saturday night was a special occasion for locals to dress up and enjoy dancing. The band was getting ready to perform. When the romantic tunes started playing, the hotel manager approached Tom and Donna's table, inviting them to lead the first dance.

Tom stood up, bowed gracefully to his wife, and kissed her

hand before asking her to dance. She accepted with a nod, and together, they made their way to the dance floor. All the guests watched in admiration, clapping as the newlyweds danced. They danced joyfully, twirling around the floor before sharing a tender kiss while holding each other close.

Donna whispered softly, pressing her face against his. "Darling, how many people are here for our wedding celebration?" After sharing a quiet giggle, she whispered again, "Tom, just look around, there must be at least two hundred people clapping as we danced. These tourists and local guests are here for our wedding. However, we'll only have to pay for eight people – how lucky is that?"

"Thankfully, everything worked better than expected. The Hotel management probably felt sorry for us." Tom smiled.

Donna glowed with happiness, and whispered to Tom, "Listen, my love, today, on our wedding day, I promise we will never be poor again. I am determined that one day, we will become rich."

Tom softly squeezed Donna and whispered, "I have already told you … I'm already a millionaire, dancing with my wife and holding you in my arms. It's all I desire."

The exhausted newlyweds arrived home late. Tom said to his pregnant wife, "Darling, the two of you are heavy, but let me carry you over the threshold."

Donna giggled and affectionately placed her arms around Tom's neck. He gently lifted her and stopped at the battered front door, holding Donna tight against him. When he tried to open the door, it only opened slightly. Despite Tom's efforts, the rusty door hinges remained stuck and immovable. Exhausted from his uncomfortable stance, he regained his balance, raised his leg, and forcefully kicked the door. The rusted door hinges gave way, causing the door to crash loudly onto the concrete floor.

As they both burst into laughter, Tom struggled to hold her; she was getting heavier by the second. Staggering unsteadily over the wobbly old planks, he carried her inside and into the bedroom. Gently placing her on the rickety bed, Tom collapsed beside her, still overcome with raucous laughter.

After calming down, Tom said, "Well, darling, wasn't that special for my exceptional lady? It's something to remember to tell our grandchildren. That will be special."

Tom and Donna diligently transformed the picker's shed into a cozy home. They refurbished it with second-hand furniture and laid down loose carpets. Carl, Tom's friend from a juice factory, installed a hot water system and helped set up the furniture. Anton, the carpenter, replaced several worn doors, and Tom completed the painting. Once finished, Carl's wife and several migrant women assisted in cleaning the space.

Whenever Donna needed help, her friends Sandra and Greta were always there for her. Greta, who had two children, generously gifted Donna with baby clothes, bedding, and toys that her daughters had outgrown; Donna wasn't too concerned about the colour of the blankets as she knew they would still keep her baby warm.

Donna received everything a new mother needed, a cot and a pram, as a generous gift from new friends she met while working at a fruit-packing cannery. She started to appreciate Aussies for their unique sense of humour and kindness.

As her due date approached, everything appeared to be on track. Despite having had an appendectomy, her doctor had reassured her that the baby's position in her womb was only slightly off-centre, and everything else was progressing normally. Donna had already packed her hospital bag and prepared for the upcoming delivery.

Tom and Donna enjoyed watching Bellbird and Coronation Street soap operas on black-and-white TV. On the day, the news broadcast political instability in Canberra in 1975 when the Governor General dismissed Gough Whitlam, the Prime Minister of Australia, Donna asked how the Queen's Representative in England could dismiss the Prime Minister elected by the people.

"I agree with you entirely, but Australia is a member of the Commonwealth, and its head of state is the Queen of England. However, my biggest concern is that Mr Stamullius hasn't installed a phone line yet. The baby is due in a few weeks, and we need a phone so I can help you get to the hospital on time. Despite his promises, nothing is done. I will speak with him tomorrow and find out what is happening," Tom said.

"Don't worry. Last week, when Mr Stamullius came to collect the rent, he said the phone company would come in a few days. I am sure he will keep his promise," Donna said as she continued packing Tom's snacks for his afternoon shift. She then kissed him before he left for work.

That afternoon, there was nothing to watch on TV except political discussions and the uproar about Whitlam's dismissal. Donna went outside and hung out the washing. After completing some household chores, she took a nap. On waking a few hours later, she realised her bed was wet. Initially, she thought her water had broken, but to her horror, she found that the bed sheets were soaked with blood. She was stranded in an isolated orchard in a rented picker's house with only basic amenities and no phone connection to call Tom at work.

Fear rose within her and she felt helpless. There was no time to waste; she knew she was in significant trouble. To safeguard her unborn child, she had to act promptly, and so she set out to walk down to Mr Stamullius's property. Quickly, she threw on her robe, went to the bathroom, grabbed some hand towels to stop the bleeding. She took a shortcut through an orchard filled with oranges and apricots to reach Mr Stamullius's house faster, shielding her face from low-hanging branches laden with fruit. Shrubs scratched her legs as she hurried in panic, all the while thinking:

What if I don't make it to the house on time? Will anyone ever find me in this remote location? What if I bleed to death like my mother, who died when her pregnancy went wrong? Thoughts of her mother's untimely passing consumed her, and she increased her speed, ignoring the warm blood that continued to flow, filling her slippers.

When she reached the house, Mrs Stamullius rushed her to the hospital emergency ward, where she received a blood transfusion. The doctor on duty concluded that the baby was now in a breach position and a c-section was needed. Unfortunately, the town surgeon was in Adelaide for a golf tournament, and it would be a few hours before another doctor could come from a nearby town. Until then, the nurses would monitor the baby's vital signs.

Donna felt cold, thinking, *What will happen if my baby is born dead? What if my baby has experienced oxygen deprivation? What then? What will happen to my baby? What if I die as my mother did? Who will take care of my baby?* Donna prayed for God's intervention to protect her baby, her thoughts dwelling on her childhood when her mother died during a pregnancy that went wrong. Nevertheless, she kept dozing off, dreaming of her mother and seeing her image as an angel descending from heaven in a snow-white gown. Her wings stretched out, but one of them was broken. She tried to fly but could not.

Donna awoke with a sudden rush of panic. Peering out the window, she found nothing but darkness. Through her prayers, she sought blessings for a positive outcome.

The nurse came to check Donna's vital signs and listened to the baby's heart. She reassured Donna that the baby's heart was beating.

"This baby has a strong heart and is determined to be born. What are you hoping for, a boy or a girl?" the nurse asked.

"My sole wish is for a healthy baby. Tom wants a son as his first child."

"Yes," the nurse said, smiling. "That's a typical man. My husband also wanted to have sons, but we have two beautiful daughters, and he loves them just the same."

"My friends Greta and Christine had baby girls, and they gave me all I needed for the baby. Everything is pink, including the baby's highchair, pram, blankets, and a bag full of pink baby clothes." The nurse laughed, too.

"Well, if you have a boy, he will look pretty in pink." The nurse checked Donna's intravenous blood transfusion. "Now, don't worry. The surgeon is expected to be here in a few hours; I will give you something to help you relax."

Donna's next memory was staring at the light in the operating room. When she awoke in the early morning, the friendly nurse placed her newborn baby boy neatly wrapped in a pink blanket in her arms.

"You have a beautiful baby boy. I told you he would look good in pink, and I was right. Your husband was here, but we sent him home to get some sleep. He will return later."

In the morning, while Donna breastfed her baby boy, she gazed out the window at the vast garden. She noticed a most beautiful dove sitting on the bottom branch of a eucalyptus tree close to her window. She couldn't take her eyes off it and was surprised that one of the dove's wings was slightly damaged and shorter. Donna wondered if this was her little dancing dove. She recalled her dreams from the night before as she gazed at the bird, wondering if that dove was her guardian angel who intervened in protecting her and her child. She embraced her baby boy and watched as the dove fluttered her wings, ascending and vanishing into the clouds.

Tom came to the hospital in the afternoon with many flowers and a beautiful card and was overjoyed at having a son. Donna, delighted and proud, thanked God for fulfilling her wish. When Tom left the hospital, she watched him through the window as he ran towards the car park, jumping over the footpath down the grassy slope and hopping around the hedge with ease as if he had wings. After reaching his car, he stopped, turned around, and gave her a victory salute in triumphant jubilation.

Tom named his son Richard after his uncle, the name soon shortened to Ricky. Tom now had everything that he had always wanted. His son, the apple of his eye, Ricky, carried his name. He would be his legacy. Doctors informed Donna that the pregnancy complications were due to damaged nerve tissue and weakened muscles from her appendectomy. She was advised against having any more children. It would be unsafe for both the mother and the child.

Ricky was, therefore, Tom and Donna's only child. After a traumatic hospital stay, the new parents settled down, sharing the sleepless nights. Tom was a hands-on father, changing nappies and bottle-feeding his son.

When Greta moved to the Goldfields at the end of the year, their friend Sandra bought a ticket for the Indian Pacific train a few months later and followed her to Kalgoorlie in Western Australia.

Tom and Donna wished that one day they would do the same. Tom continued to work shifts while Donna took on two jobs: working at a pub at night and cutting apricots during the day. She couldn't spend quality time with her infant son because of her busy work schedule, and Tom's night shifts left him exhausted. They had to rely on private family care because no daycare centres were available in their town.

Despite their efforts, they could not make ends meet and had to watch every penny. They bought the cheapest cuts of meat from the supermarket and drank cheap cask wine. Their lives became stagnant, and no matter how hard they tried to make ends meet, saving money was difficult.

After a year like this, Tom and Donna's lives took another direction; they received a letter from Greta and a copy of her husband's pay slip showing their earnings. The pay slip was all the evidence they needed. Tom and Donna immediately began preparing for the move. Kalgoorlie was the ideal location for earning a good income, as there were still plentiful opportunities to make a fortune.

However, before leaving Riverland, Tom and Donna decided to take Australian citizenship. Dressed in their finest attire for the formal ceremony, their toddler Ricky excitedly clapped his hands. In front of dignitaries and two friends who acted as witnesses, Tom and Donna pledged their allegiance to the Australian flag, which featured the Southern Cross star.

Upon reaching home, Tom uncorked an inexpensive bottle of bubbly and poured it into plastic cups. His voice filled with excitement as he said, "Donna, now we are True Blue Aussies. We live in a lucky country where everything is possible."

"Tom, darling, do you recall," Donna said, embracing her husband, "we met under the Southern Cross constellation. That is a good omen. This is a great beginning, and soon, we will earn enough money to buy quality champagne served in crystal glasses."

Donna smiled as she embraced her husband. Ricky ran towards them, and the family hugged each other tightly.

Chapter 18

Goldfields

In 1977, Tom reluctantly let go of his beloved FJ Holden, which he sold to a car repair shop for two hundred dollars. He then had to take out a bigger loan from the bank to buy a second-hand car, a Valiant, a dependable family car. He built a wooden barrier at the back seat for Ricky's safety in case he had to brake suddenly to avoid hitting kangaroos or other roaming animals.

After selling all their furniture and belongings, Donna packed everything into the boot and they were ready to embark on a new adventure.

Before starting the long journey, a thousand-plus kilometres to Kalgoorlie, Donna phoned Mara from the post office.

"Guess what, Tom? Mara is now in Adelaide for few weeks; we could stop in Adelaide, say our goodbyes and let her know we are moving to WA."

"No way, babe. It is out of our way, and besides, your sister doesn't like me. She wanted you to marry a rich man. I am certainly not rich," Tom said.

"But that is all in the past. I owed Mara my gratitude that she sponsored me to come to Australia. Without her pushing and bribing, I would have never met you. Because of her, my life is perfect; I am married to the man of my dreams; we have a son, and live in the best country in the world."

"In that respect, I am thankful to her too. But we don't have time. Sadly, your sister is stuck there, but our life is moving in a different direction," Tom said, smiling.

ଓଃ

Tom and Donna left at dawn the following morning. The journey to Western Australia began, and Ricky slept to the soft sounds of the car's engine. Tom smiled as he put his foot down, speeding the family onwards to their new adventure.

"Western Australia, here we come. I promise you, sweetheart, our life will never be the same. It will only get better. Isn't it strange that I went looking for opals, and now we are going to the Goldfields looking for gold?" Tom said.

Donna had a master plan, too. Australia is a lucky country; she was determined to make more money and get rich. That was her goal, and she would not deviate from that plan. She clutched the precious opal shell heart that Tom had given her, keeping it close to her heart while praying and wishing for a safe trip. Driving into the unknown distant state promised to bring them a much brighter future.

ଓଃ

Driving for long hours west across the Nullarbor Plain was challenging. Having experienced a disastrous drive with the FJ Holden on a dirt road, Tom was now much better prepared. He'd packed all the essentials, including food and water, spare tyres, necessary tools, and extra blankets as the desert nights could get chilly.

The arduous journey across the barren Nullarbor Plain was monotonous, an infinite expanse of treeless land, with nothing but red dust and long empty planes stretching into the horizon. Kangaroos hopped in the distance, and many more were dead beside the road, hit by trucks. Wild animals and flies feasted on the carcasses. It was no small wonder that the Nullarbor Plain literally meant 'a land without trees'.

They drove for hours admiring the Great Australian Bight, stopping overnight at the roadhouse in Balladonia, one of the most remote spots on earth.

Truck drivers often stopped to refuel and devour the local specialty, kangaroo or buffalo pies, with soggy chips. The motel had basic amenities. The sun warmed the pipes, providing enough warm water for a shower, and the bed linen was clean. Ricky quickly wolfed down his chips and fell asleep while Donna and Tom ate stale pies and washed them down with cold beers.

When it was time to leave the following morning, Tom filled an extra can of fuel, refilled the water bottles, and washed dead moths and flies from the car's windscreen. Luckily, he had sealed the boot before leaving, so at least some of the fine dust stayed out. Apart from more red dust across the endless landscape, the scenery changed slightly to more hardy shrubs that had adapted to survive and thrive in the harsh environment, and hardy trees, where kangaroos lazed, cooling down from the hot sun.

The straight road stretched to infinity; nothing else could be seen.

ʘʀ

As they approached the Goldfields, the national radio signal became more precise, and they heard the devastating news that Elvis Presley, the king of rock and roll, had died. The Country ABC radio played all of Elvis's hits, paying tribute to the legend of rock and roll.

They arrived in Kalgoorlie in the late afternoon, just as the sun set on a dusty red town. They were not surprised; it looked like another typical mining town, and reminded them of Coober

Pedy with its iron-shed houses, tin roofs, asbestos fencing, and ubiquitous red dust everywhere.

Greta and Sandra once again came to their rescue by arranging suitable accommodation. The house was built in an old colonial style during the gold rush. It had basic amenities with a shower and toilet inside. Modestly furnished, it wasn't flash, but anything was better than the pickers' shed in Riverland.

Greta's husband, Greg, helped Tom get a mining job underground. Sandra worked at the Palace Hotel, so Donna got a job there too, working split shifts, rushing home for a few hours to cook and clean then returning to work. She and Tom would exchange quick kisses in the hallway, but often kept missing each other as she worked until late at night. Thankfully, a kind, elderly woman babysat Ricky while Tom worked the afternoon shift.

The new neighbourhood was safe. Nobody ever locked their doors. Tom and Donna started attending typical Aussie barbeques, where everybody brought a plate of food. Ricky settled down well, too. His bedroom was filled with toys generously donated by friendly Aussie neighbours.

⋖

Within the first six weeks, Tom felt exhausted; using the heavy jumbo drills, he lost weight. Donna wanted him to work above ground; it was the safest option, and Tom hoped to find employment in a laboratory.

For Tom and Donna, however, life in Kalgoorlie was a considerable improvement. They had spare money to spend on themselves, like going out for dinners with old and new friends, and Donna regularly visited the hair salon. It was all a pleasant novelty, but they never took their good fortunes for granted.

While working underground, Tom met Warren Ross, a chief geologist at the mining site. Recognising Tom's background in mineral chemistry, Warren offered him a job in a laboratory. While the wages weren't as good, working on the surface was safer, and held better career prospects in the long term. Tom's previous chemical background helped when he enrolled at the Western Australia School of Mines in Kalgoorlie to upgrade his university degree, the advanced qualifications increasing his wages.

On the weekends, Tom and Donna joined friends prospecting with metal detectors and found everything from old rusty nails, tins and coins, but alas, no gold. The only other entertainment was going to the pub at the weekend, drinking a cold beer, playing darts or Two-up.

Whatever money they had left after Two-up, many miners visited the Hay Street red-light district, which the police turned a blind eye to because it kept the single miners happy. As darkness fell, the red-light district radiated with various colours.

Tom and Donna's newly rented home was across the road, and the noise prevented them from sleeping until early morning. They were amused while sitting on their verandah, watching stylish, sexy women inviting prospective customers into their nest.

Donna planned to eventually move away from the Goldfields, and every step she took moved them in that direction. So many miners became addicted to striking it rich; she didn't want Tom caught in the golden spider web with no way out; gold fever was an addiction Tom didn't need.

Believing hard work was the best way to move forward, she diligently saved every cent earned, and the bank interest gave her more money. She feared being poor again, and was determined never to experience the poverty they had left behind in Riverland. That nightmare kept her awake at night.

℣

When Sandra met Ian, a firefighter at the airport, she was ready to move on. Ian helped heal Sandra's broken heart, and when he was transferred to Perth Airport, the happy couple married and bought a house in Fremantle.

Once again, Donna stepped into the supervisor's role that Sandra left behind and worked tirelessly days, nights, and weekends. Tom's upgraded qualifications opened doors to a better job in the laboratory and advanced his career in the booming mining industry.

Meanwhile, Ricky spent his early childhood with babysitters and learned how to cope with loneliness. He struggled to mix with children his age, preferring to sit in the corner alone and not interact with others. Local doctors hinted that he might have some cognitive or hearing problems. That was the first sign that something might be wrong with their only son.

Doctors advised Donna to take Ricky to a specialist in Perth for further assessment. Perth was only seven hours on the Prospector train. Arriving at Ian and Sandra's spacious double-storey home in East Fremantle, she arranged for Ricky to undergo intensive testing with various specialists. His hearing was good, and speech therapy was not required. Doctors diagnosed Ricky as a hypoactive child with an exceptional memory; therefore, his cognitive assessment was also good. Pediatricians reassured Donna his social interaction would improve with age and that there was no need to worry. They suggested enrolling Ricky in some team sports that would bring him out of his shell.

However, back then, doctors knew nothing about ADHD or autism spectrum disorder, mental health illnesses dismissed as something individuals could overcome with a little effort and determination – mental illness wrongly perceived as laziness. A doctor informed Donna that some parents used ADHD as a justification for their kids' misbehaviours when what every child needed was strict parenting, not pills or wasting money on visits to psychologists.

During her stay in Fremantle, Sandra drove her everywhere and she instantly fell in love with Fremantle, a small fishing seaside town south of Perth; the place stole her heart. Sandra spoiled Ricky with gifts, and during the first week, they took him to Perth Zoo and other fun adventures.

The following week, while Sandra looked after Ricky, Donna went on a quest to sell the opal parcels that, for a long time, had been hidden in her boots. She visited many jewellers and wholesalers, selling a few pieces here and there. Her motto was never to give up, so before the end of the week, she attended the recently opened Burswood Casino. She knew that wealthy visitors from China and Japan had a strong affinity for gambling and opals.

The casino that weekend was full of tourists from Hong Kong, so she didn't have to hustle too much to get the best price. The jeweller's shop purchased all the opals she had left. Donna completed the sale, and the money she earned was enough for a house deposit. She couldn't wait to tell Tom about her plans to move to Fremantle and surprise him with a bag full of cash.

Tom waited for them at the train station. On arriving home, she was so happy to see a beautiful bunch of flowers in the middle of the dining table. That afternoon, Tom and Ricky assembled a giant train set, complete with a beeping locomotive and many carriages. Ricky played with it for hours and, when he fell asleep next to his new toys, Tom lifted him gently and put him to bed.

After dinner, Donna told Tom the good news about Ricky's health issues.

"The specialists assessed Ricky and told me he is developing like other children. There is no issue with him. I must be an overprotective mother," she said.

"I could have told you that. You should stop babying him; he is still a child, and as he grows up, he will mature, just like the rest of us," Tom responded.

Donna wanted to celebrate her successful sale of the opal parcel and told Tom to wait outside the bedroom. Upending her handbag, she tipped the cash all over the bed the covered it with the bedspread.

"Tom, darling, close your eyes, come see my surprise," she called.

When Tom walked in and closed the door, she led him to the bed. "Keep your eyes closed and take off the bedspread." He did and stood for a moment, covering his mouth, unable to utter a word. He just stared. When he could speak, he almost spluttered. "What is this? Did you win the lotto or rob a bank?"

Donna retrieved her large boots and vigorously shook them, but nothing came out.

"No way. You couldn't. I can't believe it – you sold all the opals."

"Believe it, my love." She went to him and kissed him.

"How much money is here?" Tom said, shocked.

"Three and half thousand dollars in paper money and some coins, too. I couldn't fit it into my boots, so I put it in my luggage. We now have enough deposit to buy our first home." Donna smiled, waiting for Tom's reaction.

"What can I say; I was looking for opal and came to Kalgoorlie looking for gold. I was blind not to see 'lady luck' standing before me." Tom pushed his wife onto the bed, and they started rolling among all the cash, igniting their desire for each other.

Exhausted, Tom fell asleep among the money. However, Donna stayed awake, thinking about moving to Fremantle. She had grown tired of the Goldfields. Being near the beach had such an inviting atmosphere. To convince Tom, though, she decided to take their next holiday in Perth and visit her friends in Fremantle.

ʘ

On their next trip to Fremantle, Tom didn't need convincing; his mind was made up. They imagined what life might look like for them one day. Fremantle resembled the Italian lifestyle she had left behind. It rejuvenated their hope for a better future yet to come.

The port city of Fremantle bustled with migrants from across the globe, particularly Italians, which led to its endearing nickname, 'Little Italy'. Tourists filled the small cafes and drank café lattes and cappuccinos sitting outdoors and sampling aromatic dishes alfresco.

Donna and Tom spent hours in Fremantle shopping or seated at a café. Freo', as it was affectionately called, offered breathtaking views of the Indian Ocean that perfectly represented the local culture. In the late afternoon, the gentle summer breeze known as the "Fremantle Doctor" wafted the rich scents of cappuccino and espresso across the garden terrace. They felt completely relaxed after a couple of glasses of Australia's finest wines, captivated by the breathtaking sunsets that lit up the aqua-blue sky in a brilliant blaze, which gradually dipped below the horizon into the vast Indian Ocean.

They took Ricky to the beach, where they relished the feeling of the sun-warmed sand between their toes and the gentle waves lapping at their feet. As they sat on the sandy dunes watching Ricky build a sandcastle, they marvelled at the miles of pristine sandy beach.

Spending time with their friends in Fremantle felt like they were back in Europe. They devoured oven-baked pizza, spaghetti marinara, cannelloni, and mushroom gnocchi; they indulged in tiramisu made with creamy biscotti soaked in Italian coffee liqueur to satisfy their sweet cravings. Every corner café reminded her of the days she'd spent living in Milan while working in the House of Villa Verla. Donna had finally found a place she could truly feel at home.

Tom enjoyed fishing with Ian. They dropped wooden lobster pots and came home with two giant fresh crayfish. Tom looked happy and dreamed of owning a boat and a stylish home like their friends.

Sadly, Sandra and Ian were not blessed to have children of their own, but they would have been the best parents in the world. Sandra adored Ricky and volunteered to look after him while Tom and Donna drove to the Margaret River wine region.

Experiencing the stunning array of natural flora and fauna, Tom and Donna were left speechless by the magnificent adventure. On their way back, they stopped in a small southern sea-side town – Mandurah – where city dwellers spend weekends camping, or staying in caravan parks, and fishing.

ରେ

Tom and Donna enjoyed a whole afternoon in Rockingham, their final destination before Fremantle. They swam in the safe, clear, pristine beaches sheltered by Garden Island, and watched dolphins swimming and splashing around a short way off shore. The sandy beaches extended endlessly to Fremantle. They sat under the shady canopy of pine trees, unwrapped newspaper coverings and feasted on fish and chips, all the while amused by seagulls snatching up tossed left-over chips. Later, during low tide, they walked across the dunes to Penguin Island. Sitting on the rocks, soaking their feet in the sea, they observed from a safe distance huge seals lounging in the sun and penguins safeguarding their eggs from seagulls.

"Tom, let's move to South Fremantle and buy our first home. That would be a significant investment."

"Okay, I agree. That is your reward for selling the opal parcel."

Days later, back in Fremantle, they paid the deposit on a block of land in South Fremantle, a perfect spot within walking distance of the majestic beach and nearby school.

Donna tingled with excitement. "We must move as soon as possible," she told Tom, "… so Ricky can start the new school year after the summer holidays. We move to Fremantle as soon as possible, and embrace the new chapter in our lives."

"When I return to Kalgoorlie, I will apply for a transfer. But I may not get it," he warned her.

"Don't worry, my love. We are so lucky that we moved to Western Australia. It has offered so many opportunities. The mining industry is booming, and you have great analytical skills in mineral science. It is time to take a few risks, so let's bite the bullet and move, regardless."

However, there was no need to be concerned. The mining company valued Tom's skills in chemical analytical processes and approved his transfer to the Alcoa Alumina Refinery south of Perth.

"Darling, I feel good about this move, and with you at my side, how can we ever go wrong? I can't wait to build the house of my dreams. This will be our new beginning. The future looks bright," Tom said, hugging his wife.

Chapter 19

Home Sweet Home

When Donna and Tom settled in Fremantle, they knew it was the perfect spot to raise a family. Fremantle was still an undiscovered jewel in the crown, with its diverse, unspoiled flora and fauna and miles of pristine white sand beaches where dolphins came to play. First on the list was to build their first home.

Donna wanted a small three-bedroom house, but Tom objected, protesting, "Building a small home is not what I hoped for when we moved to Fremantle. Why can't we build a double-storey home with ocean views like Ian and Sandra? What's the point of working if we can't enjoy our money?" Tom complained.

"Building a small home means a small mortgage. We can save more money that way," Donna said.

"But it will take years to get what I want."

Even though Tom sounded unhappy, Donna dismissed any idea of wasting money on an enormous home. "Tom, you must be patient, learn to be humble, take small steps. Rome wasn't built in a day, and even God needed seven days to create the earth. All good things take time. Trust me," Donna tried to explain.

Tom gave in to appease his wife – she was right. They had a big deposit, and borrowing money was simple. When their first modest home was completed, fitted with furniture and an established garden, they moved in. Donna said, "Tom, my love, I will name our first family home 'Hilton One.'"

"Why couldn't you pick another name, such as Home Sweet Home?"

"Well, sweetheart, compared to Riverland and all the places we have lived in, our new home feels like we have moved into a five-star resort. So, the name fits."

"But why Hilton Number One?" Tom asked.

"Hilton hotels are all over the world. This being our first home, Hilton One is a good start. For the next house, we will call it Hilton Two, and so on ..."

"How do you intend to do that? Getting my signature won't be as easy for you next time. If we can't enjoy life in style, what's the purpose of pursuing money?" Tom complained.

"But, listen, Tom, the only way to make money is to earn, save, and invest it into properties or shares. We live in a lucky country where everything is possible. My dear husband, you must have patience and not lose sight of a long-term dream. That is essential to securing our financial future," Donna tried to convince him.

A few months later, their modest residence was completed and adorned with stylish Deco furniture that perfectly captured the essence of that period. Tom found joy in purchasing a colour TV and a video recording machine. That was a big novelty.

In time, he came to terms with his new home. He constructed a spacious pergola and planted hanging baskets, the flowers bloomed in many colours, and native plants and shrubs attracted birds to build their nests.

The house's exterior blended into the natural surroundings of an enormous park, with a natural lake that served as a watering hole for many birds. Before sunrise, possums and kangaroos hopped into the garden, grazing on green grass where native plants grew. On the other side of the park was a playground where cockatoos played among the olive trees. The noisy parrots worked in groups, shaking branches, frantically, feasting on the ripe olives and skillfully spitting out the pips.

At the new primary school, Ricky made new friends. He became a member of both swimming and judo clubs, and while walking to school, he ran along the footpath, scaring off the loud parrots. Like all of his school friends, he was obsessed with Star Wars movies; he collected figurines and played sabre games with his friends. Ricky was an introverted child and, after school, preferred to stay in his room watching Sesame Street and playing games on electronic gadgets, such as the Commodore 64.

The neighbourhood was an excellent environment for children to grow up in. Families enjoyed picnics on the beach. Children used their hands to eat fish and chips wrapped in newspaper, feeding the seagulls the leftovers. Most weekends, family and friends gathered around the barbecue and played cricket on the beach.

Tom and Donna started entertaining again at home, making many new friends. Old and new friends constantly visited that tiny house. "Bring a plate" eventually made sense to Donna as it allowed for serving different international dishes.

Their new home had a large backyard. Guest gathered around the barbecue fueled with distinctively scented dry jarrah wood. The aroma of freshly caught prawns, crayfish, and seafood wafted around the garden. The pergola Tom had built was full of lush greenery and the decorative hanging baskets.

Donna praised her husband. "You built the best outdoor pergola on the street. That is why we have a great party atmosphere. Our modest cottage-style home will one day pass to our son Ricky. He will inherit this beautiful home. I don't want our son to struggle like we did."

"Yeah, I agree." Tom nodded. "We will never sell our first home. Our first house should be called "Home Sweet Home." Tom looked at his wife, his eyes glowing with joy.

"Yeah, okay. That sounds perfect." She was so happy to see Tom content that her heart sang with joy.

☙

Tom's career at Alcoa refinery progressed well. He enjoyed working in the laboratory and took great pride in his job. His analytical process was highly accurate and Tom gained enviable respect from his work colleagues. In his spare time, he enjoyed reading history books and enrolled in university to study history externally.

The pair were happily married, and the future looked bright. They enjoyed going out for dinners with their friends. At night, the Fremantle foreshore buzzed with life; restaurants and cafés were full of people. In the early morning, before dawn, the fishing fleet was ready to catch the best fish to sell in Fremantle markets. Cicarellos Fish and Chips restaurant was always packed with locals and tourists.

☙

Donna continued to work relentlessly. Fremantle had many restaurants, and she had two jobs. She balanced her home life and busy working schedule well and continued to obsessively save money. Her priority became reducing her mortgage and buying a second block of land.

Her energy was boundless, and she handled motherhood efficiently. She took Ricky swimming, to other children's activities, attended school assemblies, and listened to him read and assisted him with his homework. At night, she told him stories that her Aunty Pavia had told her during her childhood.

It was important to pass on stories to the second generation. And remembering people she loved kept their spirit alive.

Spending time in the orphanage had made her resilient, but taking care of her own survival had made her less intuitive to other people's feelings. Prioritising her own survival diminished her ability to empathise with others. Hence, she had overlooked Ricky's early childhood development and failed to notice that Ricky struggled to interact with his peers. When she had time to sit down and take a break, she convinced herself that it was all part of growing pains. Ricky had plenty of love and toys, which should be enough. She expected Ricky would find his own way in life as he grew older.

However, in time, a few cracks appeared at home, which affected their family harmony. Tom struggled to adapt to modern parenting styles. Raising Ricky with no experience in parenting, Tom was a discipline-driven father; he was the boss of the house. Tom learned his parenting role from his father, an autocratic ruler of his children. Hence, Tom did the same.

Donna disapproved of his rigid parenting; she compensated by taking Ricky to outdoor play activities, refusing to see that Ricky longed for his father's love and approval. She pleaded with Tom, but he stubbornly refused to change, and that was that.

Although they loved each other, seeing Ricky's unhappiness filled Donna's heart with sadness, and eventually, that issue encroached into their harmonious lifestyle.

Chapter 20

C&C Travel Agency

Donna worked in the hospitality industry for years, often working late nights and weekends. She was exhausted from this schedule and wanted to focus more on herself. With Ricky about to start high school, she felt it was the right time to make this change.

After finishing a travel course with Ansett Airlines, Donna joined the C&C Travel Agency. Carol and Camilla, two elderly sisters, ran a business that offered guided tours to Asia and Europe, specifically catering to women aged fifty-five and older.

Despite their golden age, Carol and Camille managed their business effectively and professionally

Before computers became necessary, electronic ticketing technology was still in its infancy. Previously, airline tickets were processed manually, with prices calculated based on the distance travelled, including any stopovers. Travel documents were printed on carbon copy paper, and travel agents relied on the TIM (Travel Information Manual) as their indispensable reference. Travel staff had to know different countries' airport codes, time zones, and currency exchange rates and keep track of arrival and departure times across different time zones. The travel industry was very demanding and did not tolerate mistakes. Donna had to adapt fast, or she would lose her job.

Within the travel community, Carol and Camille were commonly referred to as 'two hot sisters", but it was never openly acknowledged. The topic of lesbians or homosexuals was taboo, hidden, and perceived as shameful.

Carol and Camille, despite their age, behaved as if they were much younger. In their spare time, they enjoyed hosting sexy lingerie parties at home, laughing over a glass of wine or exotic cocktails. Women who attended the lingerie parties were loyal clients and frequently joined travelling groups, benefiting the C&C Travel Agency.

Carol and Camille's house had a spacious layout perfect for entertaining guests. The family room boasted a well-stocked bar with duty-free beverages from all over the world. The upstairs bedroom had classy antique furniture and a queen-sized waterbed. Once, when Donna attempted to lie on it, she felt nauseous from the intense wobbling.

ʘ

As time passed, Carol and Camille began accompanying more groups on longer trips, and Donna's responsibilities increased. On one such occasion, Carol asked Donna to take care of a few things when she and Camille were away on their extended European tour.

She gave Donna the key to their house and requested that she water the lawn and feed their cat. In addition, Carol asked her to pick up four nuns from St Andrew's College and drive them to the airport using Camille's station wagon, which would accommodate the nuns' heavy luggage of books and bibles. Carol reminded Donna that the nuns brought them a lot of good business, so taking good care of them was essential.

"I've recorded all the details in my diary," Donna assured them. "Now you two go and have a splendid holiday."

ʘ

Three weeks passed in a flash, and when Donna picked up Carol and Camille from the airport, she received duty-free gifts, perfume, and a nice bottle of whisky for Tom.

"Hi, ladies, how was your trip?" Donna inquired as she helped them with their luggage.

Carol seemed tired but responded by smiling. "There's nothing like the feeling of returning home. The cruise from Singapore to Thailand was an exhilarating experience, and everyone had a great time.

"How did you go with the nuns? Did they have to pay extra for the luggage?"

"Oh, no problem with luggage. I sorted that out, and they checked in on time. But don't expect them to return soon," Donna remarked while exiting the car park.

"Why? Did you do something to offend them? They are frequent patrons and bring us significant income!"

Donna cleared her throat and proceeded to tell them about driving Theresa, Mother Superior, and three nuns to the airport.

"Mother Superior is as big as an elephant, so I had to adjust her front seat. The three nuns squeezed into the back seat. On the way, Mother Superior started sneezing and asked if we had any tissues, so I told her to open the glove box. Well, …"

"Come on, don't stop," Camilla said from the back seat.

Donna hesitated shortly and started to giggle. "Well … Mother Theresa reached in for a tissue, but instead of tissues, she grabbed a large, grotesque, purple vibrator and panicked. And in shock, it fell into her lap."

Camille and Carol burst out in hysterical laughter.

"Mother Theresa looked disgusted. She tossed that huge, rippled rubber object back and forth as if it were a scorching hot coal from the fire. The nuns in the back seat never uttered one word."

"Look what you have done, you silly girl. I told you never to keep these sex toys in the glove box. When exposed, it's not a pleasant sight." But Carol couldn't help but laugh as she scolded her 'sister'.

"Yeah, I meant to take it with us on our tour. The oldies would have had such a good chuckle, but I forgot."

"Come on, Donna, tell us what happened next," Camille wanted to know.

"Well, Mother Therese chucked that monstrous dick out of the window; it landed amongst the tools in a toolbox in some rugged old Ute that was passing by. The poor bricklayer didn't know what was happening, but he gave us the two-finger gesture. When he saw Sister Theresa sitting on the front seat, he sped off."

Camille was rolling around in stitches in the back seat "Can you believe the poor bugger when he got to his building site; instead of picking up the screwdriver, he'd be picking up the rubber dick …"

"I bet you his mates at work had a good laugh too," Carol said.

"I bet you Mother Theresa never had so much excitement in her life and the younger nuns probably have some fun too. After all, these nuns are human and have the same feelings as us," Camille said, laughing at her own joke. She reassured Carol not to worry, saying, "They'll be back next year. Attending Christian seminars must be boring, but mingling with sexy priests is something they won't want to miss out on."

CR

Donna enjoyed working at C&C Travel Agency despite its busy nature. The job was lively and exciting, and something new happened daily.

Another significant time was when Carol and Camille planned to take a group of retired women to Spain and Italy.

Many women had already signed up for the trip. Betsy, an elderly widow living in a retirement village, had terminal cancer. She had always dreamed of visiting Spain and Italy. However, Betsy needed more money to pay for the tour; this was her last chance before she died to experience the trip of her dreams. Betsy hoped to sell her rented two-bedroom apartment and use the proceeds for this special trip, but the sale did not happen in time.

Carol asked Donna to help find potential buyers for Betsy's apartment in South Fremantle. She suggested Donna contact some of her acquaintances from diverse backgrounds who could afford the property.

After seeing Betsy's home, Donna noticed that the gardens, lawns, and shrubs were overgrown, dry, and needed pruning. It was one of the worst gardens in the street. The apartment required interior and exterior renovations. However, the major asset was that it was only a few streets from the beach; when renovated, it would bring good rental incomes. Betsy also owned the block of land next door, which could be a perfect building site for another house.

However, despite trying hard to help find a buyer, Donna ran out of time and could not find any takers. After exploring all options, Carol suggested Donna buy Betsy's place herself, saying it would be a tremendous investment.

On her way home, Donna thought seriously about buying Betsy's place and the land, but only if she could get it at a reasonable price. The City of Fremantle had increased in popularity.

However, persuading Tom proved complicated. As expected, he wanted to avoid being stuck with renovating.

"But why don't we wait longer?" he said.

"The longer we delay, the more it will cost ... much more. Fremantle is a popular town and property close to the beach will become much more expensive."

"But that will be a big financial commitment," Tom said, worried about borrowing more money.

"I had a conversation with Sandra at the bank. She offered us a great deal to refinance our mortgage at a low interest rate. I believe that renovating this apartment is a smart investment that will pay off.

At first, Tom wasn't interested, but Donna intended to convince him, so she had another strategy in mind. She knew Tom was not happy living under the same roof as his son, so he would definitely agree to Ricky moving out.

"Betsy's place is close to the university. When Ricky finishes high school, he can move in and gain his independence. It would give him freedom and lift up his self-worth."

That sealed the deal.

That same day, Donna presented Betsy with an offer she couldn't refuse. Carol appointed her friend, who worked as a settlement officer, to prepare the documentation and formalise the sale.

When Tom arrived home from work, he was surprised and delighted to see Donna nicely dressed, with a candlelight dinner waiting for him.

After dinner and a glass of port, Tom asked warily, "Come on, what's up? You are up to something bad. I can see it in your face." He laughed.

Donna smiled and relayed cheekily how she'd bought Betsy's place at a very reasonable price. She put a duplicate offer of acceptance on the kitchen table for Tom to sign.

"Why do I have to sign so many copies?" he asked.

Donna needed to come up with a quick solution. "The settlement office photocopying machine is out of order, so we signed duplicate carbon copies for both the buyer and the vendor. Tomorrow morning, I need to return the documents to the settlement office as Betsy is in a hurry to get her money and travel to Europe. I don't want to miss out on a great deal," Donna explained.

Everything happened as Donna had planned. She'd deceived her trusting husband, who never read the fine print of the documents he signed. He did not realise that Donna had given him two different offers: one for the duplex and one for the piece of land. The next day, both offers were accepted, and the settlement went smoothly.

Despite this, Donna felt guilty, but when she eventually explained her reasons – that Tom could now build his dream two-storey home – she trusted that he would forgive her.

However, when Tom did find out the deception, Tom fumed. "Oh, Donna, why are you so devious and manipulative? You are such a control freak. When will you stop with your crazy investments?"

"Tom, you got it all wrong," Donna tried to explain. "I don't consider myself manipulative or controlling. When I was ten, I learned to rely on myself and be resourceful while living in an orphanage. I learned to take advantage of opportunities and create my luck. Everything I do is for our benefit. Western Australia is growing, and mining is becoming more prosperous. This is a crucial moment; we cannot afford to miss this opportunity." She promised that would be her last investment, her last deceitful purchasing incident, and the argument was forgotten.

Poor Tom worked many weekends on the renovations and completed the basic work.

The sale worked out to be a win-win situation for all parties. Betsy went on her dream trip to Europe, and Donna earned a travel commission and bought a great investment property too. Tom was happy because Ricky moved from the family nest and into Betsy's apartment.

Donna was an excellent travel salesperson for C&C Travel Agency, consistently generating lucrative sales. In return for her hard work, Camille and Carol compensated her generously by offering her discounted airline fares and luxurious accommodations at five-star resorts from the hotel wholesalers.

As a result, Tom became accustomed to travelling in luxury. During their trips to Asia and Europe, they had a great time flying in business or first class and indulging in luxurious five-star hotels.

On one such brief holiday to Phuket in Thailand, Donna and Tom got a fantastic deal on a five-star resort. One evening, they enjoyed cocktails at a glamorous rooftop bar while a band played music. As the night progressed, they spontaneously began to dance. Donna turned to Tom and said, "My love, do you remember this song? We danced to it on our wedding day. I promised you that day that I would make you a millionaire."

"I remember it well. And as I said, I am already a millionaire. I got you, babe; holding you in my arms makes me feel like the wealthiest man in the world." As they walked towards the elevator slightly intoxicated, Tom held Donna's hand, the other hand clutching a bottle of champagne. Once they returned to the clubroom suite, Donna jumped onto a king-sized bed, and Tom poured champagne. They kissed, Donna surrounded by his love.

Chapter 21

A Journey Down Memory Lane

Donna returned home, brimming with exciting travel news. She shared the exclusive flight deals to Europe with Tom. Annually, the airline provided special upgrade offers to loyal Travel Agencies, and C & C Travel Agency extended this privilege to Donna, granting her a first-class upgrade.

"Tom, darling, we must get this deal. This is a once-in-a-lifetime experience. I want to make a booking for Easter. After all these years, I have found all my sisters, and we will meet at our village during the Easter Holidays."

"In that case, please start making the travel arrangements. I will write to my brother and sister so that we can all gather. I am eager to introduce you to my family."

Tom, too, began making plans.

Donna's background in the tourism sector endowed her with the skills and knowledge to recognise that the upgrade to first class was exceptional. She desired to dazzle her husband with luxuries that only a fortunate few ever encountered.

As soon as they boarded the plane and settled into their comfortable Boeing 747 First-Class seats, they were served Dom Pérignon champagne. Canapés followed; these followed by a lobster and caviar salad served on spacious tables covered in white cloth with a red carnation in a tall vase. Their champagne glasses were refilled whenever they got low.

The journey began with a stop in Germany so Donna could

spend a few days in Heidelberg with her friend Gina and her husband, Roger. The two old friends reminisced about their school days and fun times as teenagers and valued their long-term friendships throughout their lives.

Heidelberg was a picturesque city teeming with history, home to ancient castles and prestigious universities. The river cruise offered unparalleled views of quaint towns and breathtaking landscapes, complemented by typical German cuisine and oversized beers.

Tom wished to travel to Zagreb by train, as spring was the best time to witness the majestic scenery, with snow melting from the mountains and the farmland bursting into vibrant spring colours.

Arriving in Zagreb, Tom was thrilled; it was his first time returning home, and he was eager to introduce his wife to his family.

Tom's mother, Dinka, an attractive, elegantly dressed woman with perfectly groomed hair and makeup, resembled a classic movie star; she greeted her son and his wife with tears of joy.

The first thing Dinka wanted to know: "How come Ricky didn't come with you?"

"Ricky decided not to come. He had swimming commitments. He had to attend extra training to qualify for the state championship. He is old enough to stay home on his own," Tom explained.

Tom's younger brother Marko lived in Germany, and his sister Enda with her husband Tony arrived from England a week earlier than expected.

After years of separation, Dinka was overjoyed to have her three adult children together under the same roof. The apartment, which once served as the Italian Consulate, was spacious enough to accommodate all family members.

After a week, Donna wanted to meet Tom's father, Ivan. However, her mother-in-law vehemently opposed any interaction with her ex-husband. She strongly resented her ex-husband and was jealous of Ivan's blissful second marriage in contrast with her own unhappy one. She criticised her oldest son's decision to marry a woman raised in an orphanage, disparagingly referring to Donna as a 'village girl'.

Feeling insulted, Donna resolved to visit her father-in-law and informed Tom that he was welcome to accompany her if he chose. If not, she would go on her own, and Tom resentfully agreed. Fortunately, Donna's interactions with Tom's father, Ivan, and his wife were much better.

Donna wanted her husband to stand by her side, but he kept silent. He didn't want to upset his mother, so Tom kept telling Donna to be tolerant of her.

Donna remembered Tom telling her a story about his childhood family's camping trips during the summer school holidays. He felt sorry for his poor mother because she had to walk to the market while on holiday to buy fresh produce from the village women. Only when her chores were done could she join them for a swim.

Tom, a city boy, could never understand poor villagers who didn't have the luxury of taking holidays. During summer, the village women slept on the market floor with their children. One of those village women could have been Donna's mother.

Donna recalled her Auntie Pavica's words: "A well-fed man can never truly understand the hunger of another."

Following the family dinner, Marko initiated a conversation about religion. He proudly recounted his pilgrimage to Jerusalem and Bethlehem, the birthplace of Jesus, and urged them to start reading the Bible. Tom expressed his preference for history books instead. His sister Edna and her husband Tony disclosed that they did not believe in God and identified as Atheists.

However, after a few more drinks, the atmosphere turned sour when Tom mentioned that Donna's mother had an Orthodox background. Marko reacted vehemently, declaring mixed marriages sinful and aimed rude and offensive remarks directly at Donna.

Afterwards, Donna said to Tom, "Your brother's God-worshipping is hypocritical. Marko had no moral values, which are essential for any decent person. And your sister and her husband sat there laughing as Marko was spitting his vicious abuses towards me."

Donna didn't feel welcomed by her mother-in-law, and Tom's siblings had shown her no respect. She couldn't wait to leave. Before they all departed for their respective countries of residence, Tom suggested his siblings visit Australia.

Marko immediately scoffed at the idea, exclaiming that Australia was a vast, scorching desert full of spiders and snakes and that swimming in the ocean with sharks was not a holiday he desired.

Fed up with Marko's arrogance and ignorance, Donna decided to shut him up in front of the whole family.

"Australia is a modern and prosperous country with diverse natural beauty. Sunshine is available all year round, and sandy beaches are safe for surfing and swimming. Australia's natural beauty is not yet widely recognised. Still, it is best to keep that a secret to prevent it from becoming the most sought-after tourist destination. Besides, ignorant tourists like you are not welcome, anyway."

Donna had a last laugh. Tom's younger sister Enda and her husband Tony, who lived in southern England, explained that they couldn't travel to Australia because of business commitments.

Enda owned a beauty salon in Eastbourne, a popular

destination for wealthy celebrities whose clients depended on her services. She told Tom that she had a fear of flying and travelling to Australia by ship would be excessively time-consuming. They preferred brief holidays driving across the UK and Europe and had no desire to travel to another continent. Australia was not on their travel bucket lists.

Tom was disappointed. "It's a shame my brother and sister have such a narrow view of the world. They do not know what they are missing. Australia is a hidden gem with amazing, unspoiled scenery."

"I'm sorry to say that your siblings disappointed me. They didn't want to know much about Ricky, which was shameful. I am so glad we live in Australia; staying away from them is a blessing," Donna said.

"Now you know why people say, 'You can choose your friends, but you are stuck with your family'," Tom said as they packed to leave.

∞

The following day, Tom and Donna left Zagreb and boarded a train to visit her family in Opatija. Andrija met them at the train station. He looked old and frail, and his eyes didn't smile anymore. When Donna hugged her father; he put his head on her shoulder and cried.

When she arrived at the house where she'd spent part of her early childhood, it seemed empty; everything looked so strange, different; the interior renovations that her father had undertaken had made a tremendous improvement.

The first thing Donna noticed as she looked through the kitchen window was that her cherry tree still stood tall. It reminded her of her mischievous childhood memories. She remembered climbing to the top, hiding from Emil as she picked the crunchiest dark-red cherries, and amused herself by seeing how far she could spit the pips. However, she couldn't hide from her dog, Lucky, who barked below, wanting her to climb down and play.

Donna hugged her father and thanked him for not cutting down the cherry tree.

"I'll never cut down this old tree. In springtime, it blooms, attracting bees and birds. Its deep roots keep it firm against the wind and storms. It reminds me of you. I hope you will become as strong as this tree," he said.

Donna had never heard her father speak of that tree with such love and affection. His words moved her.

Donna's stepmother prepared a hardy winter meal. Zorka smitten with Tom, labelled him Mr Perfect, and couldn't believe Tom, a handsome man, albeit slightly older, would want to marry someone like Donna. She warned Tom about Donna's disobedience, saying she might not change her ways, and cautioned him that a leopard can't change its spots.

Donna ignored her stepmother's insults. She was used to it. Arguing with her stepmother was not good; it would upset her father. She was only here for a few days, so why spoil the last memories?

Donna joined her father and Tom in the cellar to taste some of the best red wines, and while there, Andrija explained that Zorka couldn't come to terms with her only son Emil, who, after finishing his apprenticeship in the city's biggest ship yard, chose to work as a machinist on foreign ships. Emil had no interest in staying home and inheriting Veritas Winery.

"The entire hard work in establishing my vineyard was for my son to take over from me, but now my dreams are gone too," Andrija said, his eyes filled with tears.

Donna encouraged him to be hopeful, that one day Emil would return. However, she knew that Emil chose to be in charge of his own destiny, just as his father did all those years ago.

Donna hugged her father. Seeing him as a broken, frail, old man made her feel sad. His obsession with his son's legacy to fulfill his dreams was his downfall. Sadly, Andrija never saw his five daughters as equals or viable options.

As they were leaving, Donna's father said, "Listen, my child, when I was young, I made mistakes, and one day God will judge me. Follow God's commandments, be true to yourself, love your husband, and take good care of your son.

"I was lucky to marry your mother; she was my true love. Please light a candle for her so her spirit will stay alive. I'm glad you have found love in a faraway land. True love is rare, like winning the lottery. Tom is your jackpot."

Her father tearfully bid her farewell as they knew this was the last time they would see each other.

❧

Tom and Donna departed on a Hovercraft speedboat. After two hours, they arrived in Zadar, in the southern part of Croatia. The old city had much historical significance from the ancient Roman Empire. After sightseeing, they hopped on the bus to Donna's little village where she was born.

Arriving in her little village after so many decades, Donna noted nothing much had changed. Her beloved Aunt Pavica was now a frail older woman, but when she spoke it was obvious her spirit and zest for life was still strong.

Donna asked Aunt Pavica if she still entertained children with her incredible stories in her courtyard and whether the doves still built their nests in the tree.

They sat beneath a giant fig tree and reminisced about the good old days, the memorable summer school holidays that Donna spent in her village.

"I am older than this fig tree. I remember when your father

planted that tree, but we don't have many sweet figs nowadays. That must be why the doves are not nesting here anymore. During the summer, few children come to the village anymore and my grandchildren, too, prefer to stay in the city with their friends. Nowadays, everything has slowed down, and it is so quiet," Pavica said.

Talking about the past awakened Pavica's painful memories of her love and loss. After all these years, she still missed Josip, who'd died at the end of the Second World War. That was when her world fell apart; she became a young widow and had to raise her twin girls on her measly war pension, but cleaning the church helped her to educate her girls.

Pavica's hard work had rewarded her, and she told Donna that her daughters now had prosperous careers, teaching in a secondary school as science and math teachers. They lived in the city with their families, and village life was not for them anymore.

However, Pavica was connected to the land, to the village where she was born. She told Donna that when her time came, she wanted to be buried next to her beloved Josip.

❧

Donna's trip held great significance for her. She had spent years searching for her much older sisters, which had been challenging. She had written letters to many European cities, talked on the phone, and searched for lost documents. Finally, after so many decades apart, all five of Smiljana's daughters, including Mara, who had arrived from Adelaide, gathered for the first time to commemorate their late mother.

The opportunity to connect with her elder sisters, their adult children, and adolescent grandchildren proved a rewarding experience. Donna took great pride in her lineage, and she finally grasped the meaning behind her mother Smiljana's words: 'My daughters are as strong as steel and as gentle as feathers.'

Donna's sisters and their family members had arrived a few weeks earlier and enjoyed swimming on the beach. They preferred to stay in a modern bed & breakfast accommodation close to the beach that catered to occasional tourists travelling from the city and nearby islands for good spot of fishing and sailing on the calm Adriatic Sea. However, Donna and Tom preferred to stay in the home her father had built. Anka, now a widow, had returned from France, and after much dusting and cleaning, modest renovating and furnishing, had turned the neglected abode into a cozy and comfortable place to stay. Donna chose to sleep on Pavica's rugged blanket which she used to sleep on as a child.

In the afternoon, all the family members gathered and the old courtyard came alive and buzzed with activities. After indulging in food and wine, everyone gathered around Pavica and sat beneath the ancient, towering fig tree, chatting and reminiscing about the good old days.

Donna's older sisters agreed that their mother deserved the best spot for her memorial. Sadly, there was no grave for Smiljana, who died as a persona non grata and had never had an identifiable burial ground. The sisters chose the perfect memorial site, on top of the hill next to the old church. The iron gate led to the cemetery. In the middle, under the shade of an aged olive tree stood a commemorative mausoleum for fallen soldiers. The family agreed that was the perfect resting place and began planning to celebrate Easter together as they had all these years ago.

☙

The old church entrance was still inviting, guarded by the Angel with a broken wing that stood majestically. However, the church roof, battered by the salty wind, desperately needed repairs.

When Donna first requested a special mass to honour their mother, the village priest refused to perform a commemorative service. However, when Donna offered to pay for church roof repairs, the old priest quickly changed his mind.

On Easter Sunday, Donna and her older sisters walked together to the top of the hill and joined other villagers for a special mass.

Aunty Pavica, who had difficulty walking, was driven to the top of the mountain in a Fiat car. Apart from electricity and tap water, the village remained unchanged, with no other noticeable modern developments.

Finally, Donna's dream came true, and their mother got a beautiful memorial with a silver engraved plaque bearing her name. The plaque stood right at the entrance of the small crematorium for all to see. The cycle of life and death was completed, and their mother could finally rest in peace.

Smiljana, their mother, would never be forgotten.

As they started to leave, Donna stood for a moment in front of the church entrance observing the statuette of an Angel that still guarded the church entrance. Suddenly a little dove landed and perched on one of the angel's fractured wings. Donna approached the little bird and softly caressed its soft, warm, silky feathers. The little dove remained motionless as if to greet her, and then she began to flap her wings and flew away into the clear spring blue sky.

Donna was convinced this dove was hers; it had followed her since childhood and was destined to be with her forever. Her faithful dove would always be there no matter how far she travelled.

◦◦

The festivities continued all week until late at night, and the entire village helped celebrate that epic occasion. The highlight came when they all celebrated Anka's jubilee birthday. Donna looked up to her older sister. When their mother passed away, Donna was just a baby, and Anka had become her substitute mother, taking care of her for two years. As the family's matriarch, Anka had to marry at a young age. Despite having only a few years of schooling, she'd helped establish a folk dancing group and travelled all over Europe to perform cultural dances, entertaining presidents and royalties. To Donna, her sister Anka was a role model and a source of inspiration.

Donna learned that all of Smiljana's daughters turned out to be resilient, independent women who live productive, self-reliant lifestyles. Donna was proud of her heritage and strong genes.

Spending two weeks in her village was so special for Donna. Before leaving her village, Tom and Donna set up a scholarship for one of Donna's nieces to complete her university studies. Donna was hopeful that some of the younger members of her family might come to Australia for a visit. She looked forward to a brighter future and a good life ahead.

When the time came to depart, Donna tearfully said goodbye to her Aunty Pavica, knowing they would never meet again. Pavica smiled, holding onto Donna's hand. She said, "Your mother, Smiljana, was an exceptional woman. She used to say that her daughters were strong as steel yet soft as feathers. I can see her words were true now that I have met you. As a grown woman, you embody her spirit. Please promise me that you will continue to tell stories to your son. Passing on stories to the next generation is crucial to keeping the spirit alive. Know that I will always be with you in spirit to protect you and your family."

Donna embraced her aunt and smiled, thinking that one day,

when Aunt Pavica departed from this earthy life, she would entertain the angels in heaven with her fascinating, earthly stories.

When the time came to say farewell, Donna promised to keep in touch with her sisters. They had all shared memorable experiences, fun activities, and celebrations. It was time to move on from past tragedies, rejuvenate to live in the present, and cherish those special moments forever.

"The following day, in the late afternoon, Donna was saddened to leave her little village behind. She knew she would never see her Aunt Pavica again, but a sense of relief came from knowing Aunt Pavica's spirit would follow her to Australia.

❧

While seated at the back of the bus heading back to the city, listening to the monotonous sounds of the bus wheels, Donna closed her eyes and leaned her head on Tom's shoulder; it felt so soothing. She had a powerful feeling of déjà vu relating to her in-laws, whom she met for the first time in Zagreb. It had similarities to her mother's life. Smiljana had also endured verbal abuse from her mother-in-law and family that was devoted to the Catholic Church. She tried to appease them, but she never met their expectations. Tragically, Smiljana passed away before winning her mother-in-law's approval. Unfortunately, her mother lived during the era of the Second World War; trapped in poverty with no way out. Thankfully, Donna, her youngest daughter was blessed to live in Australia, in the modern world where women had many more choices.

❧

That same evening, Tom and Donna boarded an overnight ferry from Zadar to Brindisi on the Italian coast. In her last letter, Donna had promised to return to Milan to visit the fashion House of Villa Verla and introduce Tom to the management and staff. Giannico and Philomena, the owners of Maglificio Villa Verla, greeted Donna with open arms, happy to see that she had found love in Australia. That evening, some of the household staff Donna knew served them a sumptuous dinner, which Tom thoroughly enjoyed. The following day, Philomena took them on a behind-the-scenes tour; Donna was thrilled to reunite with former colleagues she had worked with.

"The fashion house's team has expanded with more designers and tailors working hard to meet deadlines and compete with renowned fashion houses. Our new fashion trends are displayed on runways in Italy and abroad. Our son, Gianni, is learning about fashion trends and will eventually take over the business, and our daughter, Natalia, sells our garments in Milan's fashion district."

"Do you still import Merino wool from Australia?" Donna asked.

"Villa Verla thrives on loyal suppliers and high-quality Merino wool from Tasmania. Our new fashion garments are exported to Asia, and we are selling in elegant boutiques in America, too," Philomena proudly told of their success.

Philomena then invited Donna to the viewing room to choose any dress style from the factory floor. She selected a high-quality sports suit with a timeless design in soft graphite grey made from the best-grade Merino wool. The suit had pure silk lining and silver buttons, and was easy to maintain; it became Donna's pride and joy as it reminded her of her youth at the Villa Verla fashion house.

When Donna parted with the Santoro family, she invited them to visit Australia and explore the natural beauty of diverse and unique landscapes. Visit Tasmania farms, the source of Villa Verla's Merino wool imports. "I would love you to visit us in

Fremantle, a city renowned for its excellent coffee culture, influenced by Italian migrant customs."

◌

Donna's next task was to reconnect with her friend Aida. The two friends had first met at the orphanage, and despite the distance between them, they had always kept in touch. Aida owned a perfume shop in a trendy shopping district of Milan and often travelled to Paris and Monte Carlo to select premium perfumes. However, that week, she had stayed home to spend time with Donna. First, they sat in a cozy tavern and enjoyed delicious Italian specialties. Tom ordered a Prosciutto Pizza, and Donna treated herself to a serving of strawberry gelato. Later, Tom returned to the hotel for his afternoon nap while Donna and Aida explored some of Milan's most fashionable boutiques.

They shopped for hours until they couldn't shop anymore. Completely exhausted, the two friends sat in the cafeteria to rest and chat. Donna was curious why Aida had not married again.

"I don't have time for romance. Marriage is demanding, and I cherish my independence. I own a dog that I need to feed; he is so fussy; he wants cooked meals. My tomcat roams the streets, prowling around town all night long, then slip back home silently in the early morning.

"That's a fair representation of men, wouldn't you agree?" Aida chuckled as she filled their glasses with more Lambrusco wine. Meanwhile, Donna was still savouring the last bites of her Chocolate Cassata, whereas Aida avoided ordering desserts. She adhered to strict dietary rules to maintain her slender figure.

"You haven't changed at all. You looked the same as the fashion model you used to be. It was so lovely to reconnect with you after all these years.

"I hope you will come to Australia for a holiday so we can

237

spend more quality time together?" Donna said.

"I find it hard to stay away from my business for a long time. But if I could find a man like your husband, I would move to Australia immediately. I wish to have what you have – a handsome, caring husband and a son, too." Aida said tearfully, promising that someday, when she retired, she would come and visit her friend in Australia and stay for good."

Donna, however, knew Aida would remain married to her business.

Early in the morning the following day, Aida arranged and paid a chauffeur to transport them from Milan to Rome airport in a luxurious Mercedes limousine. Tom and Donna felt relieved when the boarding announcement echoed through the airport speakers. As they settled into the first-class cabin, each holding a glass of Bollinger champagne, Tom turned to his wife with a loving gaze and whispered, "Sitting next to you, my queen, I feel like a king. Now I know how royalty lives. I could easily get accustomed to this luxury lifestyle."

"And I consider myself fortunate to be employed by C&C. I hope to receive an additional bonus next year, as we have many destinations to explore."

As the aircraft ascended, Donna pressed her cheek against the window, observing Rome's silhouette fading into the dense mist of grey clouds. She knew that her previous existence was now behind her. Recollections overwhelmed her of when she first departed from Villa Verla on her inaugural journey; she had been apprehensive and scared about starting her new life in Australia.

She turned and gazed at Tom with love. Instantly, she filled with immense happiness, realising that all she had ever wanted was right there with her. The joy of returning home was overwhelming, and she eagerly expected Ricky's news about possibly being chosen for the state swim championship.

Donna squeezed Tom's hand and whispered, "I can't wait to get back to Australia. This is where we truly belong."

"Me too, love." Tom smiled back.

Part Three

A New Era Begins

Chapter 22

End of One Era - Beginning of Another

A pivotal change occurred with the closure of the C&C Travel Agency, which resulted in Donna losing her job and travel bonuses. Computers and electronic ticketing systems had revolutionised the travel sector, rendering traditional businesses like the C&C Travel Agency redundant.

Carol and Camille had worked for over thirty years in the Travel industry and had no choice but to retire. Feeling out of place in an ever-changing world, their skills, and expertise had become obsolete and irrelevant. They did, however, quickly adapt to an alternative lifestyle by expanding the lingerie parties, using their sales expertise to market seductive merchandise to women of all ages – golden-age lesbians teaching married women how to explore erotic toys and teach their husbands new tricks.

Donna held Carol and Camille in high regard for their adventurous spirits. She warmly remembered when Camille imparted some wisdom to Donna, saying, "Listen to me, young lady. Despite your youth, you may not realise that some of us oldies still feel young. Age is just a number; after all, it is completely normal to look for happiness with a partner of your choosing. Falling in love is a natural experience at any age, with a person of any gender. Love is essential for everyone, whether young or old, gay or straight. Unfortunately, society often imposes artificial moral standards upon us. We do not see ourselves as old; however, younger individuals frequently do until they become acquainted with us, at which point their perceptions often change."

Donna agreed with Camille wholeheartedly.

After the C&C Travel Agency shut down, Donna resolved not to seek employment with another agency. C&C had become her second family, and electronic ticketing felt too impersonal. Donna cherished direct interactions with customers.

She, therefore, decided it was time to advance and set out on a new adventure. Ricky had embarked on his university journey and was thrilled to rent Betsy's residence for a nominal fee. The location was perfect: near the beach and a brief walk from the swimming sports centre where he attended intensive training regimen.

Donna would wake up early to take him to his training sessions, acting as a timekeeper and preparing morning tea for the famished and exhausted swimmers.

Tom bought Ricky his first car, which helped him travel with friends to swimming competitions and social gatherings. Tom hoped that this would give his son the freedom to meet young women and have greater independence.

The relationship between father and son was never good, and Tom compensated for the lack of affection with generous gifts. However, Ricky still longed for his father's approval, but it was never given freely; it always had conditions attached.

Donna wanted to expand her travel career and work in the vocational sector as a teacher. However, she was ill-prepared during her first interview with a Registered Training Provider and lacked the skills to work in that sector.

She continued working evenings, managing a small restaurant to finance her studies. Her greatest asset was never giving up, staying positive, being motivated and enthusiastic about learning, and she upgraded her qualifications.

Eventually, Tom built his dream home. They searched for

months for suitable designs, Tom making sure every single detail was perfect.

When the house was fully completed, Donna sold Betsy's apartment, which had increased threefold in value. After the America's Cup fever died down, Fremantle gained global recognition as the most sought-after tourist destination, causing property values to surge. Donna was grateful to Carol for talking her into buying Betsy's apartment. It was the best investment she'd ever made.

Ricky happily returned to the family home, where he had many happy childhood memories, and where his dog, Bluey, had a big, fully fenced, safe garden to play in. When Tom suggested transferring the family house deeds to Ricky, Donna instinctively rejected that proposal, stating:

"Tom, dear, the safest action is to keep the house deeds in our name. Ricky is so naïve; if he meets a girlfriend who may exploit his vulnerabilities, he may lose the house and end up sleeping under the bridge."

୧

After completing her studies, Donna faced challenges in finding a new career path in the vocational sector. Despite her extensive experience in tourism and hospitality, transitioning to a role in vocational training was not straightforward. She decided to conduct some research during her next holiday in Queensland. While visiting Cairns and Harvey Bay, she met with several registered providers and gained valuable insights; she observed the students' work experiences and gained an understanding of how vocational materials and eco-tourism courses were delivered.

Collecting all the materials, books, and resources that she needed, on returning home, she spent considerable time and effort adapting and changing training modules.

Donna aimed to deliver environmental interpretive tourism. She focused on preparing training focused on Western Australia's environment, including indigenous land content and a wide variety of flora and fauna.

After creating her first training module, Donna attended another interview, and this time, she landed a job in the Vacation Education Training Sector. Initially, she offered a short course to disadvantaged teenagers, some of who came from dysfunctional families. Donna related to these teenagers as she had experienced abandonment and a lack of self-esteem in her adolescence. With the support of the local community, she facilitated the employment of many students in the hospitality and tourism industry.

Eventually, to advance her career in eco-tourism, Donna transitioned to offering courses in Interpretive Eco-Tourism. She gained the respect of her students and colleagues.

Both Tom and Donna focused on advancing their careers and overlooked the most vulnerable stage in their son's development. As Ricky's parents, they were blind to his unhappiness. He never complained or explained, and kept his emotional pain from them. Ricky was a good student, active in extracurricular activities, particularly excelling in swimming, arts, and music; hence, his parents were not concerned. However, Donna's motherly instinct told her that all was not good. She often felt guilty for neglecting her son's emotional development, but then pushed it aside. As Tom would say, "It is all part of growing up."

℞

Tom and Donna loved their new home and their new lifestyle. They enjoyed entertaining old and new friends by holding cocktail parties and barbeques. Their house, situated in a perfect location, faced a natural lake filled with blossoming water lilies, native plants, and lively animals. Ducks nested, pelicans visited, and sometimes, black swans landed on the lake.

After work, sitting on their balcony, Donna and Tom chatted about their day and enjoyed the stunning sunsets above the Indian Ocean. On one such perfect day, they celebrated their wedding anniversary with a bottle of champagne chilled in an ice bucket poured into two crystal glasses.

"Tom, my dear, do you remember our time in Riverland when we lived in a fruit picker's shack infested with rats, and we used to drink cheap wine from plastic cups? It has taken us over two decades of hard work and struggle to achieve the Australian dream of owning our dream home, and Ricky has his home too, so he never has to struggle as hard as we did. How lucky is that?" She looked at her husband, beaming with pride.

Tom turned his head, smiling. "It is not just good luck; it is entirely because of your hard work and perseverance. I was lucky you came into my life." Tom leaned towards her and tenderly kissed her.

Donna raised her champagne glass and toasted her husband. "You are the reason for all my achievements. Your love and support encouraged me to grow and pursue my dreams. You made me shine brighter than any star in heaven," Donna said, caressing Tom's silver hair.

He lifted his glass of champagne. "Well, my dear wife, we did it the hard way, but look at us now. We are the dream team, babe …"

Chapter 23

Saving Ricky

One night, a phone call turned their world upside down. Donna had always feared this moment; for years, she had lived with the constant dread of receiving the news that broke their hearts.

"Hello, Donna, this is Anne from the church social group. I'm sorry to tell you that Ricky was involved in a car accident. My husband Laurie drove him to the hospital, and he is not in critical condition. We didn't report the accident to the police because Ricky had been drinking. We thought avoiding trouble and stress at such a difficult time would serve you better."

Donna started shaking and sobbing. She had to sit down to settle herself before speaking. Tom was up already, so she put the phone on speaker so he could hear what Anne had to say.

Anne described how Ricky endangered his life with his careless driving. She said a witness from the opposite house saw him smash into their ancient gum tree, which snapped from the force. He was lucky to hit the tree, otherwise, he would have hit the brick wall and that could have killed him."

"Oh my God, what am I going to do? Anne, how can I ever thank you?" Donna said, her voice trembling.

"Go to church and thank God for saving your son's life."

Donna and Tom hurried to the hospital. The doctors informed them that Ricky was in intensive care and recovering. One of his knees had been severely crushed, and needed reconstruction with surgical screws but, with physiotherapy, it would get better.

The following day, Donna left flowers at Anne's front door. Seeing the smashed-up car, Donna knew that her Guardian Angel with a broken wing had saved Ricky's life. The car was totally smashed; it had to be towed to the scrap yard.

Throughout Ricky's rehabilitation and prolonged physical therapy, Donna supported her son's recovery, fearing at times that he would never fully recover. But eventually, he started to improve. Ricky, however, felt crushed physically and emotionally.

03

After visiting him in the hospital, Donna drove to his home to feed Bluey, the puppy they had bought him a few years ago for company when they had moved into their new house, leaving him to live independently to boost his confidence and self-reliance.

When Donna started cleaning Ricky's place, seeing the pigsty this beautiful family home had become made her cry. Empty pizza boxes, fast food wrappers, and beer bottles were scattered on the kitchen bench. An empty bottle of vodka sat among the dirty dishes.

Donna opened all the windows to remove the overwhelming stench of beer and stale food scraps. She rolled up her sleeves, put on her gloves, and cleaned his house.

While dusting the Jarrah display cabinet, she stole a moment to admire the family portrait with Ricky smiling, the photo taken when Ricky enrolled at the WA University. It made her reflect on how handsome he once was. Ricky, a former champion swimmer, had a physique that only Michelangelo could have sculpted. She gazed at her son lovingly, wishing that all of this was nothing more than a bad dream.

Tired from cleaning Ricky's house, she rested on a chair under the backyard patio that Tom had built. The garden was a chaotic tangle of neglected plants and overgrown shrubs. Donna was saddened as she remembered her family's happy time in that once beautiful home.

She watched Bluey as he dropped a tennis ball at her feet, wanting to play. Bluey sensed Donna's pain and jumped into her lap; she hugged him and started to cry. When Bluey licked her tears, she remembered her dog from her childhood and how Lucky had licked her tears when she was sad; it always made her feel better.

Donna rested in the garden while thinking about Anne's call. She wasn't surprised by it, as it had happened before. The previous year, she had to pick up Ricky from the police station after they caught him driving dangerously. They had used a spike strip to stop his car and prevent a fatal accident. On that same day, Donna drove Ricky to the hospital because he had alcohol poisoning. Afterwards, Ricky later told her that he wanted to end his life. He'd filled up Bluey's food and water bowls, took the car keys, got drunk, and went for a joy ride in a car.

☙

Donna supported her son during his hospital therapy. Eventually, with extensive physiotherapy, Ricky regained mobility but his leg would never be the same.

When he was released from the hospital, Donna visited him regularly. She cooked him homemade meals, cleaned his home, and took Bluey for a walk. She did not indulge in self-pity; feeling vulnerable would not help her make positive decisions. She had to face the ongoing problems head-on.

Most days after coming home, Donna was emotionally drained. She went straight to bed, but sleep eluded her, her mind buzzing with memories. She remembered Ricky's early childhood when they were a happy family. Ricky's primary school mirrored any typical child; he was playful, innocent, and naïve. They raised their son following traditional family values passed down for generations.

When Ricky was at primary school, his performance fell behind his peers. At a parents' meeting, his teacher suggested seeking professional advice to assess his mental development. Donna had left the room in tears, devastated by the news, but Tom would hear nothing of it. There was nothing wrong with his son! After all, Ricky had his genes. Tom decided to tutor Ricky in every subject.

"I will help Ricky with tutorials, and he will excel in learning. I'll show teachers how wrong they are," Tom fumed, scoffing at the teacher's arrogance.

True to his word, he immediately began tutoring Ricky in each subject. With Tom's efforts, Ricky's school reports improved. His teacher confessed that her initial assessment might have been wrong; she even recommended Ricky for the school achievement award for the most improved student of the year.

When Ricky started high school, it was more tumultuous than expected. In his adolescent years, Ricky felt like an outsider, he was bullied and called a nerd. Ricky focused on his studies to win his father's approval. However, Tom kept shifting the goalposts, making it impossible for Ricky to meet his expectations. Donna knew there was no point arguing with him. Tom was stubborn; he believed education was necessary for prosperity and a happy life.

Donna often felt guilty because they had focused on advancing their own careers but had overlooked the most vulnerable stage in their son's development. They'd been blind during that time because Ricky was excelling in extracurricular activities, particularly swimming, arts, and music. Although blessed with his father's good looks, Ricky was awkward with girls. When he was chosen to perform in a lead role in Grease in local theatre productions, many young girls wanted to be around such a handsome man.

As a healthy heterosexual male, Ricky wanted to experience love with girls. But he was self-conscious and shied away, too scared to attempt a relationship, constantly worrying about being rejected. Unfortunately, he lacked a meaningful connection with his peers, and always remained an outsider, and couldn't form long-term friendships. However, Ricky had an excellent memory, and memorised stories he'd read, and he was good with numbers and timetables at an early age. Later, he excelled in math and remembered all the chemical elements and symbols. He memorised homework practical tests and passed all his school exams with excellence.

Unfortunately, at that time, medical science had little understanding of the autism spectrum. Doctors reassured Donna that Ricky was going through adolescent pain, and as he got older, all the problems would disappear.

Ricky completed high school with top grades and enrolled in university to study mineral science to appease his father, but the following year, he switched to social and art studies.

Tom, regarding education as a top priority, was highly disappointed, and the divide between father and son grew wider. And, when Ricky dropped out of university for good, the relationship between the father and his son deteriorated even more; they avoided each other altogether.

Devastated, Tom's greatest fear came to life: his only son, who he hoped would carry on his legacy, dropped out of university and became dependent on social security. Tom became depressed and retreated into his study room. Burying himself in his books was his only reprieve.

It saddened Donna to witness that Tom's love for his son always had conditions attached, that he set expectations that his son struggled to attain, and when he did, Tom lifted the bar higher. Although she idolised Tom and depended on him for her happiness, she pleaded with him to put more effort into helping Ricky. She believed that showing more love would bring the son and father closer together and cure all the wounds.

However, Tom wouldn't be swayed. He'd learned his parenting style from his own father and, despite frequently complaining about his father's inflexible and dictatorial manner, Tom inherited some of his father's negative parenting traits.

Donna pleaded with Tom, but he hated discussing issues about his parenting skills. His answers were always the same. "All this nonsense about mental illness and Autism is a good excuse not to finish his studies. Ricky needs to stand on his feet and sort out his problems."

Tom often said to Donna, "Stop obsessing about Ricky and focus on our marriage; we deserve to be happy, too."

On the surface, Donna and Tom's life was picture perfect; however, hidden beneath their blissful life were signs of difficult times ahead of them. Donna started to resent Tom, and stress crept into their relationship. She grew angry with him, but he was unwilling to reach out and extend a supportive hand to his son.

Donna neglected her husband's needs. Growing tired of attending social gatherings and smiling as though her life was perfect, she buried her feelings and carried the burden alone. As a mother, she suffered in silence, hiding her pain.

Donna hopelessly watched Ricky tumble down the rabbit hole, but she was determined to get him out of the rut. His mental illness affected his self-esteem, and he retreated further into himself, compensating for his emptiness with food, and binging to satisfy his cravings. His bulimia and depression slipped under the radar for the longest time. He spent a week inside his house, sitting in front of a television screen, eating away his feelings. Ricky's sole reasons for getting out of bed were Bluey and the company of alcohol and food. He lived in isolation for more than ten years and became a morbidly obese, lonely man. Then he numbed that emotional pain with excessive food and alcohol consumption.

Donna tried many things to help him to no avail. More psychiatrist trips left him with more labels than answers – clinical depression, anxiety, ADHD, personality disorder –but despite the professional opinions, Tom was still dismissive. He wanted nothing to do with Ricky's 'condition'.

☙

Usually at night, Donna couldn't push these destructive thoughts away. She was alone, carrying a burden that only a mother would know. Falling asleep proved challenging and she kept having the same dream over and over: she was clinging to a rope and pulling with all her might, attempting to save Ricky from sinking into quicksand, but Ricky held on tightly, causing both of them to fall into the mire.

Donna needed a good night's sleep to bring her more clarity. To cope with her insomnia, she relied on sleeping pills but ended up tossing and turning for hours and having another night of terrifying, dream-filled sleep. In the new dream, Donna was in a raging river, struggling to rescue her infant son from drowning in the wild, frothy water that swept them downstream. She gasped for air, choking and suffocating. The swift current slammed her into submerged rocks, her hands scraping the rough surface, desperately searching for her son.

She finally caught him by his little shirt, but the powerful water dragged her under the murky water, the swirling rapids tossing her on the rocks. She thrashed around, looking for her child, her legs slashed by the short shrubs and fallen branches at the bottom of the river, the cuts so deep the water turned red with her blood. She couldn't free herself from the fast rapids that pulled her along the sand or the muddy water that engulfed her. She saw another shape through the dirty water – small arms reaching out, but she couldn't reach him. He was always just beyond her grasp. She tried to scream, but water filled her lungs.

Donna woke with a silent scream in her throat, the bed sheets soaked with sweat as a testament to the horror she had experienced while trapped in her nightmare.

In the morning, with the dream still fresh in her mind, she knew what she had to do with certainty. Donna told herself not to feel vulnerable; she had to motivate herself to stay positive and strong. She thought about something that inspired her: When you don't see the light at the end of the tunnel, walk through the darkness and light it up yourself. Then, you will see and find your way out of it. That was it! Donna had to save herself first, and then she could save her son.

❧

She had spent more than ten years looking for the answers and trying to get professional help for Ricky. Ricky finally received a diagnosis of personality disorder, anxiety, eating disorder, and depression, which made him drink too much alcohol to cope. Most doctors didn't know much about the autism spectrum and how it worsened Ricky's mental health.

Regardless of the lack of progress, Donna stubbornly kept on trying. Saving her son was a mother's duty, so she made that her number one priority and disregarded everything else.

She persuaded her son to enrol in courses for personal growth and attend anger management classes. However, the effects of these courses were always short-lived and did not bring any significant change. He soon quit going to therapy and flushed his pills down the drain.

Ricky's dog, Bluey, was his only faithful friend; he cherished him more than his own life. Bluey motivated him to handle lonely nights, to wake up and feed him, and take him to the beach for a dip. Donna grasped at straws, hoping Bluey would continue to encourage Ricky to get out of bed and take him for a walk.

Ricky's physical injuries from his disability hastened his mental illness, which had a devastating impact on his parents. After trying all the available treatments, Ricky ended up on a permanent disability pension.

When that happened, Donna felt like her life was crumbling down. She preferred to stay at work until late; finishing administrative duties kept her mind busy. However, due to lack of sleep, she felt drained and exhausted, often while driving home, and Donna's emotions were so intense she could not hold them back. She felt like a pressure cooker about to burst. To avoid falling asleep at the wheel and causing a car accident, she would pull over, roll down the window, and cry uncontrollably, howling like a wounded animal in pain.

Often, she cried on her way to work, too, feeling depressed and overwhelmed; when tears blurred her vision she had to pull over to calm down. She would then touch up her make-up to hide the dark circles under her eyes and put on her professional mask.

Donna's job was demanding, but it helped her cope and stay sane. She excelled in her career and would not let her personal issues affect her work. She was always professional and consistent, never making excuses or complaints. However, she struggled to maintain her home life, which slowly fell apart. She barely managed to keep her head above water at home.

◦◦

One day when Donna cleaned her home, she wiped the fingerprints off the glass display cabinet that spanned one entire side wall of the family room. She stopped and looked at the framed family photos with nostalgia, but it seemed that this was in another lifetime. She also cherished her extensive collection of porcelain clowns, which she had been collecting for years. Many friends wondered what drew Donna to the porcelain Pagliacci Clown figurines. She had more than two dozen in the glass cabinet, each with a unique facial expression.

Donna often made jokes to amuse her friends and colleagues, seeming carefree and happy-go-lucky. By putting on different masks, she could pretend to be someone else, as if she had a split personality. She changed her mask as needed. She showed a cheerful and carefree persona to others, while hiding her sadness inside. Donna felt like the Pagliacci clown, who smiled on the outside but cried on the inside. She suppressed the pain that lingered in her soul.

At night, Donna cried silently, hiding her unhappiness, pain, and loneliness from everyone she knew. Tom stopped caring, too, and spent hours studying, just reading books. Both chose to ignore the another's pain. Heartbroken, Donna pleaded with Tom to help, but he would not or could not.

In time, Tom and Donna drifted apart, pretending that everything was as it should be. They suffered in silence, unable to comfort one another. Days passed without words spoken between them; the house became a dark vacuum of tension and resentment. Eventually, their relationship became so bad they started sleeping in separate rooms.

Donna acknowledged her helplessness and asked God to watch over her son. She had nothing else to offer; her only hope was to entrust Ricky to God's care. She felt trapped in her suffering, but found comfort in church. There, she felt God's presence and knew she was not alone. Church was her refuge, where she could find some peace.

When Ricky survived the car accident, Donna had thanked her guardian angel for saving her son. She realised it was a sign that God had a plan for Ricky and would open new doors for his well-being and happiness.

One Sunday, when the mass ended at the local Catholic Church, Donna ran into one of Ricky's long-term friends from primary school. Dean was now married to Beverley, and on that same day, they had baptized their newborn daughter, Louise.

Donna and Beverley quickly bonded as best friends. After Beverly's mother died, Beverley grieved for her loss but also felt comforted and helped by Donna, who had acted like a second mother to her for a while.

Ricky and Dean, two old friends, reminisced about their school days for hours after Beverley invited them to a barbeque. Ricky felt his heart melt when Beverley handed him baby Louise, who smiled at him sweetly. Donna saw a spark in Ricky's eye that was new to her. She realised that Ricky secretly wished for a family and a beautiful baby like Louise.

Her thoughts raced at full speed. However, before Ricky could start a family, she must find him a girlfriend.

Donna was already considering matchmaking, and she wanted to discuss that with Beverley. Believing in fate, she knew it was no accident that she'd crossed paths with Beverley at church. Her guardian angel with the broken wing had orchestrated this special friendship to show her the way.

Donna appreciated and respected Beverley's viewpoints. As they sipped coffee by the beach, Donna felt comfortable speaking her mind.

"Suppose I could find Ricky a girlfriend. This might motivate him to transform his lifestyle and miraculously resolve all our issues."

"I'd talk that over with Tom first," Beverley advised.

"When I have a goal in mind, Tom knows I won't give up until I accomplish it," Donna admitted, her mind zooming ahead. "My Aunt Pavica was a matchmaker for my parents, and they had a happy marriage. In addition, you and Dean have shown that online dating can work and you are a happy couple. Perhaps one day Ricky will meet his ideal partner, get married, and have children like you and Dean.

"Donna, trust me when I say finding love online is difficult. I was lucky because Dean is a dependable provider, a devoted husband, and a good father. Please be careful because online dating has so many unforeseen risks," Beverley warned her about the pitfalls.

When Donna reached home, she brought the idea up with Tom, but he was not interested; in fact, he glared at her with disapproval.

"You are playing with fire, but don't ask me for support when things go wrong. Online dating will make things worse than they already are. I know your ideas are noble, but don't forget that the path to hell starts with good intentions."

Donna didn't want to argue with Tom; instead, she walked to the beach to clear her mind. Walking barefoot on a sandy beach was therapeutic and rejuvenated her physically and emotionally. Salt and sea breeze were the medicine she needed to recharge her empty emotional batteries. Here, she decided to stop feeling sorry for herself and fight instead of cry. There was no point in her asking, God why me? Instead, she should ask, why not me?

Donna remembered attending a luncheon at Fremantle Yacht Club. On the wall, she read a sailing slogan that inspired her to keep on fighting.

THE PESSIMIST COMPLAINS ABOUT BAD WEATHER WHILE THE OPTIMIST ADJUSTS THE SAILS TO GO THROUGH THE ROUGH WEATHER AND SAIL INTO CALMER WATERS.

Donna, being the eternal optimist, decided to adjust her sails too, to navigate through the torrential stormy weather, and sail into calmer waters.

She remembered the words from her favourite famous movie 'Gone with the Wind' when Scarlet O'Hara said, "As God is my witness, I will never go hungry again."

Donna rephrased that quote for herself and said, "As God is my witness, I will never be helpless again."

Chapter 24

Obsession

Russian girls

Donna brought Ricky a computer the following week and encouraged him to play games or write stories. However, the primary purpose was to prompt her son to browse online dating sites.

"Listen, Ricky, give it a go. What do you have to lose? You should start searching for a girlfriend online. Just see how happy Dean and Beverly are. They met on an online dating site, married, and now they have a beautiful baby daughter Louise. I can help you create an online profile and you can put up a photo."

Within a few weeks, Donna noticed a significant change in Ricky. Since he began using the Internet to search for a girlfriend, he exhibited enthusiasm and a new zest for living. He started to take better care of himself by joining a health club to lose weight, and he attempted to keep his house clean. He became cheerful and full of energy – all he had ever wanted was to find love and start a family – a hopeless romantic at heart.

As expected, Ricky quickly became addicted and spent the entire night in front of the screen, eagerly waiting to reconnect with the attractive Russian girls who'd shown interest in him. Donna had to step in and warn Ricky.

"Exercise caution, Ricky. Don't be too naïve."

When the Russian girls started asking for money, Ricky became suspicious and changed to another dating site. After browsing several online dating sites without success, Donna noticed a twinkle in his eyes, confirming her belief that finding the right girl was the only way to save her son. She assured Ricky that she might find good old-fashioned girls with similar moral values at her church, and Ricky agreed, hoping his mother might find a girl to start a friendship with and potentially develop a romantic relationship.

Donna knew that in today's modern world, finding a golden girl would be as hard as looking for a needle in a haystack. At home, she maintained a poker face, only informing Tom of what was essential for him to know.

No one or nothing could deter Donna from achieving her goals. She was on a mission to find Ricky a woman who would love him and share his bed with tenderness and care.

Remembering the matchmaking story her Aunty Pavica had told her when she first introduced Donna's father and mother, and their happy marriage, Pavica had played a crucial role in saving her father. He'd been lost and unhappy but, when he found the love of his life, his destiny changed. Her parents' happy marriage motivated her to play matchmaker for Ricky. That was the only way she could save her son. She had a strong intuition that an unseen power was linking everything together, and that she must follow that path. She knew that help would come from her guardian Angel with the broken wing who had already saved her son twice already. Indeed, Ricky's destiny had yet to be fulfilled.

She immediately put her plan into action, and put together a small photo album highlighting Ricky's best pictures and the beautiful interior and exterior of their home.

Any girl would be thrilled to live in 'Hilton Number One', a spacious house near the beach, complete with a dog and a charming, kind-hearted young man.

Donna envisioned the perfect situation to make her ploy seem believable. She truly believed that, when Ricky met the perfect girl, they would fall in love, and would accomplish anything. She would never give up to achieve this; she was back in her element, once more taking control; being in control allowed her to function optimally, bringing her a glimmer of hope.

The first girl Donna encountered was at her tennis club. Virginia, one of the players, celebrated her fiftieth birthday, and introduced Donna to her daughter Lisa. Lisa had just moved back home after ending her relationship with her boyfriend, who was cheating on her.

Donna aimed to connect Lisa, a thirty-two-year-old, with Ricky, a trustworthy and loyal man who could mend her broken heart. After persuasion and a few white lies, Lisa agreed to chat online with Ricky. After a few weeks of chatting online, they met at McDonald's. Donna hoped that this friendship might last.

A month later, Donna found out that Lisa had returned to Queensland, telling Ricky that she still loved her ex-boyfriend Greg, who had promised to change. Ricky had driven her to the airport, knowing he would never hear from her again.

Ricky felt let down, but Donna advised him to keep going.

Not long after, once more on a mission, Donna bumped into Natasha in a gift store.

"Hello, Donna, it's been such a long time. I can tell it's you because you still wear matching hats with your dress," Natasha remarked.

Donna recalled Natasha, who had attended the same high school as Ricky. They'd belonged to the drama studies group. Also, they were cast to play the lead role in a musical production of Grease at the local amateur theatre. Donna had fond memories of when she'd helped backstage during the long rehearsals, and accompanied the production through different theatres. During that time, she'd witnessed Natasha flirting with Ricky, and he'd reciprocated her feelings. However, the production manager forbade any romantic interaction between the cast to maintain a smooth show production.

"How long have you been working here?" Donna wanted to know.

"I started a job at a gift shop after my divorce. What is Ricky currently up to?" Natasha inquired.

"He is currently unemployed, but he will start working soon," she replied.

Donna came to that gift shop frequently. She bought gifts for her friends and stocked up on Christmas and birthday presents. Befriending Natasha, she finally persuaded her to meet Ricky at the local pub.

Ricky told his mother that during the production of Grease, he'd had dreams and aspirations, but now he was a different person altogether. He worried that she wouldn't have anything to do with him now that he'd gained weight and struggled to walk. Nevertheless, Donna encouraged Ricky to meet Natasha, a divorced, lonely woman. After not hearing from him for a few weeks, she visited him to check how he was doing.

The moment she walked into his house she knew Natasha had rejected him. Ricky was in a terrible mood. Empty beer bottles were scattered around the kitchen bench, and the sink was full of dirty dishes, with ants feasting on scraps of smelly food.

After doing the dishes, she drove home, crying buckets of tears. As soon as she arrived home, she headed straight to bed. Tom was curious about what was happening but Donna didn't want to explain anything to her husband, who always lectured her. She didn't want to hear the words "I told you so."

Donna had many matchmaking failures, so, she decided to lower her standards. She began searching for a girl who came from a disadvantaged background and didn't possess Natasha's beauty.

Next on her list was her cleaner. Mariana and her family had escaped from Lebanon when her husband died fighting the opposition in the civil war. Donna invited Ricky over and they seemed to like each other, but soon after, Mariana moved to Melbourne to marry a Lebanese boyfriend that her parents had arranged for her.

Tom was furious, and after that, Ricky avoided visiting his parents. He didn't come for Christmas or birthdays either.

Donna was ashamed to admit to her husband about her latest matchmaking fiascos. Saying nothing to Tom eliminated unnecessary explanations and additional stress that she really didn't need. Tom was unhappy, and shut himself off from the world. The only thing Tom longed for was to have his wife back, but Donna was lost, she couldn't find any happiness.

As Tom became more distant and withdrawn, Donna tried hard to save her marriage; she tried to reconnect with him, but he ignored her. Overwhelmed by his emotional turmoil, he sank into a 'dark hole' that he could not escape from. Donna wanted to rescue their relationship, but Tom's isolation became stronger. He seemed unable to manage his emotions or the surrounding situations, and Donna felt helpless again.

But she loved Tom and had to find a way to get him back. Donna assured him that from then on she intended to focus more on their marriage, so when Tom proposed his grand plan of travelling to Europe, Donna agreed. Their love was strong and both of them deserved to be happy again.

Tom was overjoyed to have a few weeks with his wife, finally unburdened by the issues that had plagued them for years.

A Goddess of Love – Greek Aphrodite

Donna and Tom took that holiday to the Greek island of Corfu. They were excited to visit old friends from Australia, Vasilia and Stavros, who inherited an old stone house they converted into a fashionable modern B&B and a terrace restaurant with amazing views of the crystal-clear blue of the Ionian Sea.

When Donna and Tom arrived, Vasilia and Stavros welcomed them with a table full of cured meats, olives, and fresh produce from the nearby villages. The delectable smell of honey, spinach, cheese dough, and garlic-infused seafood tempted the hungry guests to try the scrumptious local dishes. Tom and Donna were enchanted by the olive tree-filled land and fragrant Mediterranean greenery. Stavros kept refilling their glasses with ouzo, which further enhanced their cheerful mood.

After a few days lazing around, Tom and Donna sailed around Corfu's crystal-clear turquoise waters on Stavros' yacht; unable to resist the temptation, they jumped in together, and after a refreshing swim, continued sailing around Santorini Island. The coastal scenery resembles an oil painting, with a hidden village tucked between majestic cliffs and vibrant pine forests. Stavros anchored his yacht below the secluded village and was greeted by a handful of old farmers at the wooden jetty. They were there to sell him fresh fish and farm produce to take back to his restaurant.

Tom and Donna found that coming to Corfu revived their love. It was the perfect opportunity for them to take a break and concentrate on their struggling marriage. They enjoyed dining under the stars, with candlelight setting the mood. Tom couldn't help but gaze at his wife lovingly. He had almost forgotten how stunning she was. Donna had an oval face framed by shoulder-length black hair. Her sensual mouth had a touch of rose lipstick, complementing her beautiful skin tone. A delicate application of eye shadow highlighted her dark-brown eyes. They now felt like they had rediscovered paradise and rekindled the love in their hearts.

After returning from their fishing trip, Stavros busily prepared his outdoor restaurant for the upcoming weekend rush of tourists. The whole place was a hive of activity. Before long, traditional Greek music filled the air. Several locals stepped up and danced the conventional Greek dance Masahiko, and formed a line facing the guests. Tom and Donna couldn't resist the sounds of Zorbas, and other guests joined in. Placing their hands on others' shoulders, they moved with the music, alternating from a slow to a faster pace, wiggling between the tables, and clapping hands.

During a restaurant outing, Donna spotted an attractive staff member, Monica, a waitress. Her aqua blue uniform matched her eyes. The white apron fitted snugly enough to enhance her body curves. Her sun-tanned limbs moved with grace and fluency. Immediately, Donna started plotting and strategising for her next matchmaking venture. She had brought a pocket album of Ricky's photos, just in case she needed it.

Donna swiftly established a bond with Monica, who worked in the restaurant during the summer. In winter, she spent time with her family in an impoverished village in Albania. Excited about her new matchmaking challenge, Donna explained to Tom that Monica could be a perfect candidate for Ricky.

"Is it possible that a beautiful girl such as Monica could fall in love with Ricky?"

"Sorry, but that's only a fantasy, my dear. Besides, I thought this holiday was just for us. Your obsession will split us apart." Tom rose and disappeared behind the bar to watch football on the enormous TV screen.

But Donna's unstoppable determination to find Ricky a wife

did not stop her. After most of the guests had left, Donna remained behind to converse with Monica, who spoke some English. Tom decided to go for a swim to avoid any further embarrassment.

Donna gained valuable insights into Monica's cycle of poverty. Her family lived in a small Albanian village, a sheep farmer with no hope of a brighter tomorrow. However, Monica said she was moving to Dubai after this summer's job as a domestic servant for a wealthy family. That was her way of getting out of chronic poverty.

The next day Tom and Stavros went fishing early in the morning. After serving breakfast, Monica was free and met Donna at a local cafe where they enjoyed a cappuccino and sweet baklava made with walnuts and sugar syrup. They had developed a friendship and were having a great time together, laughing and joking.

The following day, Donna accompanied Monica to the market. Seated at a corner cafe, they savoured fresh lemonade accompanied by lemon sorbet. During their conversation, Donna took out her pocket portfolio of photos, casually displaying photos of Ricky's cottage house with lush green gardens and a walking path to magnificent sandy beaches. Last, the pocket photo album contained a few of Ricky's best photos.

Donna noticed Monica's interest in Ricky's photo; he looked like a film star. In the picture, he had a bronze triangular shape showing a six-pack, which he had from his younger days as a swimmer. He had an athlete's body, strong cheekbones, sharp, piercing brown eyes, and dark, wavy hair that young women couldn't resist. Then Donna's eyes saddened as she looked at Ricky's older photos when he was such a handsome man, yet today he was not that man any more.

Monica was captivated by Donna's story about the stunning sandy beaches of Australia, kangaroos hopping around in the bush, and koalas sleeping in gum trees. She suggested Monica should think about relocating to Australia rather than Dubai, because of the uncertainty in employment and the possibility of exploitation. Donna even offered to assist her in finding a job at a nearby restaurant and suggested covering her flight expenses to Australia.

Monica promised to visit Perth over the summer. She always wanted to visit Australia for a holiday, but it was too far and therefore too expensive. Donna recommended she go on a backpacking trip with Ricky; she would be safe. Monica thought it was a fantastic idea, and she gave Donna a two-page handwritten letter for Ricky and enclosed her own photo.

Donna wanted Monica to believe that if she came to Australia, she would step into Aladdin's Cave, blessed with unlimited wealth and good fortune. As a goodwill gesture, she gave Monica a few hundred dollars for her trip to Australia, and promised to handle her airfare expenses and arrange a tourist visa.

Monica promised to write, and they parted on a happy note.

Back home in Australia, Donna handed Ricky the letter and a photo of the beautiful girl. Ricky was so happy, and he promptly sent a reply to Monica.

Deciding to prioritise his health and well-being, he also agreed with Donna's suggestion and attended counselling to address his mental health issues. After visiting his GP, Ricky began taking prescribed medication to ease his depression, paranoia, and anxiety.

Donna was thrilled, and even Tom began to believe that maybe Donna was right after all. Ricky's quick and significant transformation confirmed Donna's belief that her obsession was valid. Monica might be a divine gift to rescue Ricky from his self-destructive actions.

Unfortunately, Donna's high expectations were shattered

after months of false hope. Monica never replied to Ricky's letters. When he discovered it was a complete hoax, he was completely devastated. Monica was just as bad as the Russian woman on the dating site who attempted to scam him for money. Furious with his mother for giving him false hope by being involved in the deceitful game, Ricky considered she deserved to be scammed. He didn't want any further contact with his mother and returned to his old self, excessively drinking, eating, and suffering depression, and isolation.

Later, Vasilia informed Donna that Monica had quit her job and moved to Dubai as a domestic worker. Her betrayal was disgraceful; she not only took the money but also failed to send a postcard or thank-you card to Donna.

Donna learned a valuable lesson. In the future, she would approach any matchmaking attempts with much more caution.

Tango dancing with a girl from Chile

After the Monica fiasco, Donna's relentless determination in her matchmaking efforts remained buried, with no possibility of resurrection. However, while catching up with her friend Maria for coffee at the Fremantle Boardwalk Cafe, Maria mentioned that her niece was staying with her. Pamela had arrived from Chile on a tourist visa and would soon return home.

Divorced and with no other family, Maria hoped Pamela would stay with her permanently. She suggested a meeting between Pamela and Ricky.

Donna felt apprehensive, but Maria convinced her not to miss such an opportunity. *An excellent chance, but I must get it right this time. It won't be easy to convince Ricky, but he knows Maria is a family friend, so he may be interested.* But Ricky had reverted to his old lifestyle of staying home, giving in to his depression, and gorging himself on food and beer.

A few weeks later, Donna invited Maria and her niece for lunch, suppressing her guilt for not telling Tom of her motives. She remembered what Tom had said to her last time, that the path to hell was paved with good intentions.

Donna invited Ricky, casually mentioning Pamela, a beautiful young woman looking forward to meeting him to start a pen-pal friendship. Donna pleaded with Ricky to shave and wash to remove his foul body odour as it was repugnant. It broke her heart to witness her son's transformation, this once handsome young man who had metamorphosed into a massive, tremulous body, an uneven mass of floppy flesh.

She fumed when Tom had compared Ricky to Jabba the Hutt from Star Wars. She needed Tom's support in this, but he became more and more distant from her. Tom repeatedly expressed his disapproval of her manipulative tactics and opposed bringing 'girls as if for sale' into their house. He was embarrassed about this entire business, and Donna could see it.

Rather than joining them for lunch, Tom chose to go to a beachfront café for a hamburger, which set up Donna's resentment towards him. But she kept her pain deep inside her core, the hole in her heart unable to be healed.

But there was no turning back. She was on a mission once again.

ʘ

When Maria and Pamela arrived, they looked elegant in high heels and flawless make-up. Donna arranged a dining table setting with plates and polished silver cutlery, and the glasses sparkled as if preparing for a royal visit.

Donna felt increasingly nervous, especially since Ricky was running so late they began their lunch without him. Donna was about to serve coffee when Ricky finally arrived. He had shaved his head and resembled a bald old man. Even ill-fitting clothes couldn't perk up the image. Instead of sitting on the dining chair, he moved to the couch, as it was more comfortable.

They all moved to the lounge room and joined him, sipping coffee, chatting about nothing much. Ricky tried to smile, but his puffed-up, sweaty face never made it passed a twisted grin. The setting resembled a film studio where they were filming "Beauty and the Beast".

Besides everything else, Ricky promptly drank five cans of beer, as if he were at a pub during happy hour, causing him to become even more talkative. However, his speech became slurred from alcohol. Sadly, his drinking made things much worse.

Donna's heart sank. Holding back her emotions, she wondered if Ricky would ever revert to the person he used to be – a handsome young man – as her son now was hardly recognisable anymore.

Pamela fidgeted with her coffee cup, wishing she could disappear while Maria, somewhat tipsy, topped up her glass with more champagne. As Maria and Pamela prepared to leave, Ricky, by now well drunk and with unbounded confidence, pathetically tried to appear cool like the tough man he should have been, and thinking he was God's gift to women.

He stumbled to the car and returned minutes later with a Koala Bear toy with a dangling colourful love heart tag, which he ceremoniously gave to Pamela as a parting gift –something to remember him by; they exchanged addresses to write to each other.

Donna didn't know if she should laugh or cry. She found this whole matchmaking spectacle tragic but also immensely comical. She knew it was all her fault, but put a brave face on yet another failed attempt at the matchmaking saga. Instead, while her heart cried with pain, hiding her emotions was something Donna could do with ease.

When her guests left, Donna told Ricky to sleep in the spare room and drive home tomorrow when he sobered up. While washing the dishes, Donna started to cry as she recalled the doctors warning Ricky that he must stop binge drinking. His blood tests confirmed the symptoms of alcoholic liver disease, causing his liver to deteriorate. Sadly, Ricky had stopped caring about his well-being a long time ago. Seeing her only son's self-destructive lifestyle that would undoubtedly send him to an early grave caused her much pain and anguish.

When Tom returned home, he didn't inquire about the matchmaking outcome; he could tell from the expression on Donna's face that it didn't go well. The dining room still reeked of alcohol, which showed that Ricky was drunk again.

Seeking solitude, Tom retreated to his study and closed the door, wanting to avoid his son. The following morning, he went to work without kissing his wife goodbye.

Donna, however, was used to dealing with disappointments. Despite feeling a significant loss, she found comfort in her job. Her professional life was well managed and regulated, even though her personal life was filled with disorder and chaos.

A few months later, Maria invited Donna for tea and scones. Maria told Donna that Pamela had started work at the Norwegian ocean cruise company, and she had met a well-off young man from America.

Donna felt disappointed and dejected. Once again, she experienced a letdown. Pamela found her dream man, but Ricky was not that lucky.

Unfortunately, Donna had lost yet another fish. But there were many more fish in the ocean. With some luck, next time, she might catch a beautiful mermaid.

Indian Delights

Tom and Donna attended a wedding reception for an Indian family. They were seated next to Mr and Mrs Rajah during the reception dinner. While Tom enjoyed a variety of spicy Indian dishes from the buffet, Donna conversed with Mrs Rajah and some of the serving staff.

After the wedding guests dispersed, Donna and Tom sat in the dining room sipping tea with some of Mr Rajah's family and their two daughters. The Rajah family were Sikhs from the Punjab region somewhere in India and were waiting for their working visa to be upgraded to permanent residency.

Tom and Donna occasionally went for dinner at that Indian restaurant where Mr Rajah worked as a chef, and his whole family worked in the kitchen. Immediately, Tom suspected Donna's motive as she visited the restaurant frequently despite not liking spicy food.

"Why do we always go to the Indian restaurant? Can't we try Thai or Vietnamese food for a change?" Tom asked.

"Sure, we can try those cuisines sometimes. I'm planning my next trip to Thailand, where we can try many dishes."

Donna thought that if Indian matchmaking didn't work out for Ricky, she would have to plan more trips to Asia, as Ricky's chances of finding a Caucasian girl were slim. White girls had so many more choices; Ricky would remain at the bottom of their list. Therefore, Ricky would have to lower his expectations, too. *Finding true love has many twists and turns.*

At that Indian restaurant, Donna met Mr Rajah's two daughters again. The elder, prettiest daughter was engaged, but the younger one, Shania, was still single.

Donna recalled the story her Aunt Pavica had told her about how her parents were matched. Her father met two sisters and desired an elder, pretty girl with a pleasant smile. However, the elder daughter was already engaged, so Andrija chose his second preference and married the younger sister, Smiljana, instead.

Andrija and Smiljana had five daughters. Donna was the youngest. They lived happily ever after until death parted them. That recollection ignited Donna's determination to attempt another matchmaking.

While dining at the Indian restaurant, Donna approached Mrs Rajah, who supported the matchmaking arrangement because it could help them get permanent residency. Donna invited her family to her home for some genuine Australian hospitality. Feeling proud, Donna told Tom about her matchmaking skills.

After finishing his curry chicken and spicy rice, Tom nearly choked on his food. Coughing uncontrollably, he put his cutlery down and stared at her amazed, yet scornful. "Oh no, not again, oh ... for Christ's sake, you can't be serious."

"Yep, I am, but this will be the last time," Donna said defiantly.

Tom pushed his plate away and stopped eating altogether, but Donna continued, undeterred. "I worked it all out. You have nothing to worry about. Trust me, darling."

"I'm worried when you say 'trust me'. You will never succeed and only embarrass yourself and me. When will you stop."

"Maybe you're right, but I'll keep trying until it kills me," Donna said determinedly.

Tom shook his head in disgust.

"My mother and father's arranged marriage was successful, so why not give it ago. Please, Tom, let me try this one more time." Donna envisioned an elaborate Indian wedding with all her friends in attendance.

A day later, she visited Ricky's house and invited him to a barbecue the following Sunday. She described Shania as an attractive young woman with long black hair, dark brown eyes, and thick eyelashes, casually mentioning a girl from India. However, Ricky immediately declined the invitation.

"Mum, I don't want an Indian girl. I want to find a nice Aussie girl."

"Yes, look where that got you. The last girl you met, Norma, had two kids with two different fathers and was addicted to drugs. When you refused to grow marihuana in your backyard, she wanted nothing to do with you. Face it, son, your chances are limited; you don't work, and you live on a disability pension. Good Aussie girls want financial stability, so stop being so fussy."

Her frustration evident, and after a mentally exhausting tug-of-war with stubborn Ricky, he finally agreed to come. Donna advised him to respect their culture, avoid saying anything that might offend them, and drink in moderation.

☙

On the Sunday when The Family Rajah was coming for lunch Donna spent hours tidying up outdoors, setting the table among the hibiscus plants in the garden. The garden, patio plants, and roses were in full bloom, and the flowerbeds were neat and tidy. Everything looked perfect, like in a show home.

Despite Tom's disapproval, he helped tidy up outdoors; he removed a naked statue of a woman's torso from the garden pond and locked it up in the shed so as not to offend the conservative family.

Donna prepared finger foods, including hot and cold hors d'oeuvres, appetisers, peanut butter, spring rolls, and sweet pies. She was mindful that Mr Rajah and his family didn't drink alcohol, so she provided a refreshing fruit punch instead. Donna planned everything down to the minute details. Nothing could go wrong."

Tom walked into the kitchen and asked, "Who will eat all

these beef and mushroom puff pastry wraps? It serves you bloody right to stuff this up."

Donna had paid attention to every detail; she knew Indian people considered cows sacred; she had taught cultural awareness to her students! How could she have missed that? Donna panicked. When she pleaded with Tom to go to Red Rooster and buy two roast chickens, he gave her one of his dirty looks to let her know he was not pleased. However, he still hurried to the shop to rescue his wife's embarrassment for such a culinary mishap.

Everything was done on time: the outdoor setting table was decorated with fresh garden flowers and green and gold napkins, Donna wanting to present herself as a down-to-earth Aussie. They still spoke with a foreign accent, which helped ease their tension and made their guests feel comfortable.

Donna wanted to highlight Australia as a welcoming and multicultural country that embraced people from all over the world. After a quick cold shower, Donna dressed in an elegant sari, representing Indian culture and tradition. She had bought the pure silk apricot-coloured sari laced with silver threads during one of her trips to Brunei with Tom. The sari was eight metres long and covered their king-size bed. By wearing this magnificent silk sari, she hoped to make her new Indian friends feel more welcome and bridge the cultural differences. Besides, she hoped to look stunning for Tom, who had never seen her wear it.

Donna gazed at herself in the mirror and delicately pinned pink and white hibiscus flowers in her hair. She felt content with her appearance and looked like an Indian princess. Tom wore a floral shirt he had bought on his trip to Bali, and looked ready for a leading role in a Bollywood movie.

Ricky arrived on time, looking cheerful and smiling, which was unusual because he was usually moody, argumentative, and miserable. Donna's outlook on life improved immediately. He helped himself to a beer, which soon became a few more. Nevertheless, he remained in high spirits and a party mood.

Then, the doorbell rang, and the Rajah family arrived, dressed in casual Western clothes; Donna suddenly felt uncomfortable and overdressed. *Oh, my ... did I make a mistake with my sari?*

Mr Rajah shook Tom's hand and said, "G'day, mate!"

Tom froze with surprise and embarrassment.

After a brief introduction and many smiling faces, everyone took their seats. However, some tension was still in the air, which made Ricky uncomfortable. Mr Rajah, a large, turbaned man with a firm but friendly face, started a conversation with Tom. Mrs Rajah, the plump middle-aged woman, wore so many golden bracelets that she jingled at every turn.

Donna hurriedly went to the kitchen for hot appetisers and cold hors d'oeuvres. The sari pleats were so tight to her body that she walked awkwardly. Instead of looking like an Indian princess, Donna walked in small steps as if she were a Japanese Geisha. She no longer felt elegant or beautiful in her sari but rather uncomfortable with her tummy, cleavage, and back exposed.

When the second course was about to be served, Mrs Rajah offered to help in the kitchen and talk privately with Donna about the matchmaking business. She bluntly said, "In our culture, we expect money to be offered as dowry. Our younger daughter Shania should fetch a very good price; any man would be lucky to have such a pretty girl. You are a rich family; our daughter will make your son a good wife; she will give him many sons."

Donna, stunned by the unexpected and straightforward request for money, immediately became aware that Mrs Rajah was under the impression she and Tom were wealthy and wanted to have a piece of that pie too. She recalled what Aunt Pavica had told her: Smiljana's father, Iljia, sold his daughter to Andrija for one Prosciutto. *Not much has changed since the end of World War II.* In modern times, Mrs Rajah was trying to sell her younger daughter to the highest bidder, too.

When Donna said that this was not an appropriate discussion, Mrs Rajah sat beside her husband, finished her lunch, and remained silent. The matchmaking debate was over and would not be talked about any more.

For Donna, her humiliation deteriorated when she realised Ricky was already drunk, oblivious to their guests and not participating in any conversation. He sat motionless in the lounge room, watching football and drinking beer.

He rose unsteadily and approached his mother in the kitchen, where she prepared desserts. Donna looked up at him with distaste, but he stooped over her shoulder, and whispered through the stench of his beer breath, "Mum, just look at you. You look ridiculous in that sari; both you and Dad look like you are going to the Sydney Mardi Gras parade. You would win a first prize at a fancy dress party." He laughed. "You must be blind not to see that these curry-eating Indians are using their daughter to get an Australian visa. The next thing will be to sponsor a dozen of their family members and support all of them. Mum, you've lost the plot. I want to go home, get away from here." He grabbed another beer from the fridge and walked out without saying goodbye to their guest.

Donna didn't say a word, but her disappointment rose at his stereotyped racist remarks. She'd brought her son up to respect all cultures and religions. Donna put her head down, ashamed of herself.

After serving apple pie with fresh cream and the best Indian-flavoured tea with lemon and ginger, the party ended. The Rajah family thanked them for their hospitality, politely said their goodbyes, and drove back to their restaurant.

Sometime later, Mr Rajah's family moved to Sydney. Donna heard from one of the staff at that Indian restaurant that Mr Rajah could not secure sponsorship from his employers and their application for a permanent Australian visa was rejected. Mr Rajah and his family returned to India; his two daughters had to obey their father's wishes and had no choice but to accept the arranged marriage from the highest bidder.

The Orchid Cruise to Thailand

Ricky informed Donna that he had re-connected with his friend from high school. Mick had asked Ricky to come to his place for a few drinks and introduced his wife, Mary, a Thai woman he'd married the previous year while on holiday in Thailand.

It wasn't until a few weeks later that Donna and Mary could meet for coffee and catch up. Donna told Mary about Ricky's desire to meet a loyal and kind Thai woman, and requested that the arrangement remain private, as both Ricky and Tom would object to her meddling.

A week later, Mary informed Donna that she had arranged a meeting with a peasant Thai girl from her village. Donna then hatched the plan to go on holiday to Thailand.

She booked a luxury cruise that started in Singapore and ended in Bangkok. Tom felt relieved: they could finally focus on themselves with no distractions. Donna reassured him that their brief stay in Bangkok for two nights was purely for shopping and relaxing. To make him happy, she booked into the luxurious five-star Dusit Resort. The clubroom facilities close to the outdoor pool gave Tom and Donna a delightful experience. The rooftop bar offered a lovely ambience to savour cocktails under the starry sky.

The following morning, Donna did some shopping. Tom preferred to stay by the pool with a beer and a good book. Upon returning, Donna playfully joined her mischievous husband for a swim in the pool, openly admitting that she intended to meet a girl from the village, a rendezvous that her new friend Mary had pre-arranged.

Despite his dislike for the situation, Tom reluctantly agreed to go to the hotel lobby with his wife.

As Tom and Donna entered the lobby, the hotel concierge promptly approached them and gestured towards the two girls, patiently sitting and waiting. He informed Tom that the Dusit Hotel had strong security measures, emphasising that visitors from outside had to be registered before being granted access to the garden restaurant and bar area.

Tom complied with the request but immediately felt uneasy when he noticed the hotel reception staff laughing as he guided Donna and two Thai girls to the bar.

Tom ordered finger food snacks, cocktails for the girls, and a beer for himself and sat back comfortably in the garden bar.

Donna was surprised as Nanta was nothing like the photo Mary had shown her. Nanta and her friend Minty wore short dresses that barely concealed their underpants, and the stiletto shoes gave the impression of being taller than their height. Immediately she knew these two girls didn't come from the village. Seeing their long, false polished nails and well-groomed hands, these two girls had never worked a day in the rice fields. Most likely, they were call girls, probably working in some sleazy nightclub, pole dancing half-naked; they probably enticed lonely old men to spend some money and get some cheap sex.

Tom couldn't help smirking. He couldn't take his eyes off both girls with the overly-exposed, pumped-up breasts and provocatively 'dressed to impress' outfits. He found the entire matchmaking scenario pathetic, ridiculous, yet humorous.

After a few more cocktails, Nanta became more talkative. She addressed Donna with respect. "Madam, why didn't your son Ricky come with you to Thailand? I want to marry him."

"Sorry, but he couldn't get the time off work," Donna responded quickly, waiting for Tom to comment, but he wasn't listening, his eyes glue to the girls.

The other girl, Minty, sculled her cocktail, ordered another, and soon got tipsy. Giggling, she asked, "Donna, do you know any other single man for me? I don't care if he is old. I will look after him well." Her voice echoed around the bar.

Donna tried to hush these two cheap call girls to avoid further embarrassment, telling them to keep quiet. As Minty and Nanta, who were already slightly intoxicated, continued to giggle, the hotel security discreetly approached their table and whispered to Tom, "I'm sorry, sir, but our hotel is known for its excellent reputation. We don't allow prostitutes on our premises. However, if you and your wife wish to have a good time with girls, I can recommend a hotel down the road."

The hotel manager asked the girls to leave immediately. Tom was never more embarrassed than on that occasion. Apologising, he made an instant decision: "Sorry, sir. We meant no disrespect. Can you organise transportation to take the girls to the train station?"

It was clear to both girls that Tom and Donna were uncomfortable and didn't want hotel security involved. Nanta spoke first. With a nonchalant smile, she casually told Tom they had nowhere to stay. Minty wanted to extort some money, suggesting that her uncle had no money to purchase train tickets to return them to a province outside Bangkok.

Tom impatiently waited in the lobby for the car to arrive, eager to escape the embarrassing situation. To ease his discomfort, he quickly grabbed his wallet and generously handed $100.00 to each girl. Some hotel guests standing nearby waiting for taxi service were curious about how much Tom paid for the two cheap-looking escorts.

When the hotel car service arrived, Tom rewarded the driver with a tip and instructed him to drive the girls as far away from Dusit Resort as they could go.

Tom couldn't hide his amusement. Smirking, he leaned over Donna's shoulder and whispered, "Hey, love, it's possible that girl's uncle is their pimp working in the nightlife scene in downtown Bangkok."

Tom clutched Donna's hand and retreated to the pool terrace to soothe their bruised reputations. After enjoying a revitalising swim, they became more relaxed and started laughing at the embarrassing situation they had ended up in.

Tom and Donna remained in the pool to avoid the scorching tropical heat, chuckling often when reminiscing about the rumours among the hotel employees.

"I bet you, Donna, that the manager thought we were planning a threesome with these two sluts" Tom said.

Donna smiled. "Tom, dear, you make a lousy pimp," she laughed. "You don't know how to be discreet … everybody in reception witnessed you giving money to girls. The staff were probably saying that it was you who wanted to satisfy your own sexual fantasies with two sexy call girls," Donna teased him.

"Don't be silly," he smirked. "After all these years of marriage, I only have fantasies about you." Tom swam towards his wife and planted an oversized smack on her lips.

"Let's cancel our candlelight dinner at the restaurant. I am too embarrassed to be seen by the hotel staff right now. They probably gossip that you must be some sex maniac who enjoys having sex orgies. We should order room service instead," Donna suggested.

"It doesn't matter what the hotel staff thinks; we won't return to this hotel again. The nighttime view from the restaurant and rooftop bar, however, is breathtaking.

"However, if you insist, we can order room service and a bottle of champagne. It is just you and me, babe, so let's have some fun," Tom said playfully, hugging her.

Fortunately, Tom and Donna left early in the morning for their flights back home, sparing themselves any additional embarrassment from the hotel staff. And that was the end of that crazy affair. Donna decided that pursuing Asian girls would not lead to anything beneficial.

Upon her return, Tom suggested she should seek professional help. Donna, however, preferred to talk with her long-time friend Greta, who was also a counsellor. Greta offered a shoulder to cry on, and with her counselling skills, Donna learnt how to handle her anxiety. She confessed that her obsession was negatively affecting her emotional well-being and if she didn't stop, her marriage would be over.

Bible Studies

Donna's worst fears became a reality when Ricky's beloved dog, Bluey, passed away. For sixteen years he had been Ricky's steadfast and devoted companion, and Donna's solace, knowing that Ricky would survive as long as Bluey was there. Bluey had been both therapy for Ricky and Donna's only source of security for many years, but now that he was gone, Donna's fears kept her awake at night.

Losing Bluey left Ricky utterly devastated, overwhelmed with grief, and emotionally shattered. He isolated himself from the outside world for several weeks. Donna regularly visited his house, always bringing comforting food for her grieving son. One day, with a strong sense of anxiety, she repeatedly knocked on the door, hoping for a response from Ricky, but he didn't reply. She now faced her deepest fears, and constantly worried that Ricky would sink into a deep, black hole of depression.

Ricky used to have some resilience while Bluey was alive, but now that had vanished, leading him to contemplate suicide. Amid his darkest mood, Ricky disclosed to his mother his intention to hang himself on the patio constructed by his father. One of the wooden beams was strong enough to support his body; he searched for a rope in the shed to hang himself but couldn't find it, so he got drunk and fell asleep.

Because of her personal anxieties and fears, Donna kept her son in the dark about throwing the rope in the rubbish bin. Whenever she became emotional, she would confide her inner concerns to her friends, Greta and Sandra. Throughout the years, their friendship remained as solid as a rock. With Tom dealing with his own depression, Donna had to turn to her friends for support and a shoulder to cry on.

Donna cried so many times that she became desperate due to not hearing from Ricky. After work, she drove to his house, taking with her some comfort food. When he did not answer the door, she climbed over the fence and bushes and peered through the window, hoping to glimpse any signs of life. She had also become friends with the neighbour, Margaret, a kind-hearted, classy 'English Rose', as Donna often called her. A widow, Margaret kept a concerned eye on Ricky and often informed her about any unusual happenings next door.

During conversation on night, Tom advised Donna to stop being an excessively protective mother, to be more realistic and disregard the idea that she had the power to influence Ricky to change his destructive lifestyle. Only Ricky could do that.

Maureen, one of her tennis club friends, recommended that Donna explore other social groups or clubs that promoted strong moral values. Maureen became a member of a recently established church, and invited Donna to attend. Motivated by her desperation, Donna found refuge in the local church, a newly formed community church that embraced all individuals.

The preacher delivered the Sunday sermon on the stage. The congregation swayed back and forth, lifting their hands above their heads with closed eyes, as if in a trance, while praising the Lord. A band of young church members performed on stage, and the audience sang songs dedicated to Jesus and their saviour. Donna sang, too, usually out-of-tune; she even attended Bible studies with Maureen.

Deciding that her new challenge was protecting Ricky from sliding into the dark side of life, Donna planned for Ricky to join the church band at the New Born Christian Church. She intended to connect Ricky with the church's social club, become part of the church band, and establish a sense of belonging.

The church had a music band and required a new guitarist. One Sunday after mass, Ricky went with Donna to see if he could join the church band. He was a moderately talented guitarist, but with a few more practice sessions, he improved and was offered a spot to play with the band for the church Sunday service. Occasionally, Ricky joined the bible studies at his home, too.

Worried that somebody from the Catholic congregation might see her, Donna kept a low profile. Although she preferred to attend her Catholic church, she joined The New Born Christian Church only to get Ricky involved. And she worried that Father Michael would not forgive her sins and so avoided going to confession – moving away from the Catholic faith was blasphemy.

Feeling desperate, she begged God for forgiveness for the many lies she had told to fulfil her selfish desires. She would accept whatever punishment God deemed appropriate for her dishonesty and manipulation, and hoped God would forgive her sins and lead her to salvation.

Tom made fun of Donna's newfound religious beliefs. Her actions mystified him, and he stated his case categorically. "Don't even think that you will drag me to come along to the bible studies. You've lost all your marbles; your behaviour is outrageous. I never expected that you would betray your faith and beliefs. Your obsession has no boundaries and resorting to such extreme measures is crazy. I think you need to have your head examined," Tom fumed.

"Tom, don't be so harsh. While there is only one God, many diverse religions are protected under a common umbrella that covers all of us." Donna believed she was guided by an invisible source that compelled her to keep searching and moving forward. Despite her search, she remained uncertain about the divine plan that God had planned for her life.

"I decided to stop looking for Ricky's girlfriend; I failed in that department miserably. However, I still want Ricky to meet other young people and join a church band," Donna reassured her husband

"Okay," Tom sighed with relief. "I was worried that you were up to your old tricks. Playing in the church band will allow Ricky to engage socially with people of good moral values. I can see your point. The church will give him alternative options. But I would advise you to hide better. When Father Michael finds out you have abandoned the Catholic Church, you will be perceived as a traitor." Tom laughed.

"Oh, no, this is only temporary; I'll quit when Ricky settles down in the church band. I don't want to hang around and cloud his independence."

"Now you are making some sense." Tom hugged her.

Donna was delighted to see Ricky's transformation. He continued playing in the band and made some friends; it gave him mental stability and helped him find inner peace through spiritual growth.

A few months later, her mission accomplished, Donna quit attending the New Born Church. However, she secretly hoped Ricky might find a lovely, God-abiding girl. Church girls were friendly and not judgmental.

☙

Ricky joined the Bible studies group after playing at the church on Sunday. During a social gathering, he met Belinda who was in her early thirties. She dressed modestly, wearing mostly old-fashioned second-hand clothes. She also suffered from epilepsy and had a slight tongue-tied disorder, a mild speech impairment caused by decreased tongue mobility. Despite her imperfections, Ricky was unfazed and offered her his friendship. They hit it off and started playing pool together with her brother at the local pub once a week. Ricky would also invite them to his house to watch the latest movies on his incredible wall-to-wall screen. The sound from the Bose speakers that Tom had gifted him for his birthday was simply amazing.

When it was Ricky's turn to host Bible studies, Donna spent hours cleaning his house and baking cookies to make a good impression on Belinda and her tight-knit Bible study group. Ricky even contemplated being christened again, accepted into the church congregation, and starting a fresh journey as a born-again Christian.

Over time, the church embraced Ricky and welcomed him into their community.

As a result, Ricky abstained from alcohol and improved his health significantly. Donna felt pleased with how things were progressing. Because of their friendship, Ricky began to suspect that Belinda had feelings for him. Time went on in monotonous and repetitive cycles, with nothing noteworthy happening.

Ricky asked Belinda on a movie date during a congregation

gathering at the tearoom. She responded with a mixture of confusion and amusement. In her stuttering, slurred voice, she told Ricky that she had no romantic feelings for him and that he was not her type.

Ricky was shell-shocked, mortified. He felt pain in the bottom of his gut, was unable to move or speak, and wished the ground would swallow him up. Belinda, who had little hope of ever finding a boyfriend, had rejected him, ultimately destroying his self-esteem. So embarrassed, Ricky withdrew from the church band and never returned to the church.

He told his mother, "Mum, if a girl like Belinda won't go out with me, what chance do I have with anyone else? No girl will ever pick a loser like me. I've hit my breaking point. I don't need your help anymore. I am not interested in finding a girlfriend. This is the end of the line for me."

Despite Ricky's irritation, Donna remained composed and focused as he expressed his grievances.

"Mum, you are to blame for giving me false hope to believe in God. Now, we both know that love can't be found in church. Even God has abandoned losers like me. I am not worth saving; I am nobody, just a bum trying to survive one day at a time. Mum, I want you to forget about me, leave me alone, and stay out of my life."

Sewer Rats

Shortly after leaving the church, Ricky began to feel incredibly lonely and fell into a deep depression. It came as no surprise that he lacked self-control and soon fell back into his old habits of overeating and excessive drinking. His mental health demons resurfaced, bringing chaos and turmoil back into his life.

Eventually, he grew sick of staying home alone and couldn't handle the isolation; his self-esteem plummeted to rock bottom, but he desperately needed to be accepted. The only solution was to join some of his high school dropouts, a low-class circle comprising the unemployed, alcoholics, or drug addicts. The group met on the weekend at Andrew's dilapidated, asbestos-built beach house.

Andy and Ricky had attended high school together, but they'd never really mixed. Andy was a school dropout, pre-destined to become a petty thief and a drug dealer. However, Andy was the boss this time and welcomed Ricky into his dark world.

Andy had a tight-knit group of friends, all involved in drugs; he was a petty crook selling marijuana. Andy's job as a middleman for bikie drug lords was to distribute ice and heroin to satisfy the growing local demand. Secrecy was vital. Drug transactions had to be paid in cash. Local drug users were kept in the dark as to where the supplies came from.

When the druggy group partied, Ricky had to bring a bottle of vodka to get a free weekend pass. Donna feared his life would spiral out of control, mixing with such a crowd of lowlife alcoholics and addicts.

The 'Sewer Rats', as Tom called them, would be a game changer, a steep slope bound to end tragically.

Broken, devastated and utterly disillusioned, Donna admitted defeat; she had failed to rescue her son from his sewer rat druggy friends. Nothing was left but a sea of infinite misery and pain, a powerful tsunami of pain and grief. Completely drained of energy, she hit rock bottom and allowed depression to creep back into her life. She even doubted that her beloved husband still loved her.

All her hopes and aspirations vanished when Ricky joined the Sewer Rats. At this crucial moment, only her faith in God kept her sane. She held on to slim hope that her guardian angel, her dove with a broken wing, would come to her son's rescue and save him from eternal damnation.

At night, choking back tears, Donna reminisced about those distant, happy days when she and Tom were young and hopeful about their sweet future. Unfortunately, the present turbulent time was a roller coaster of persistent and prolonged sadness, intense anger, and self-blame.

Donna felt guilty that her workaholic life had obstructed her view of Ricky's mental illness at the earliest age. With proper medical treatment she could have made some difference. How it hurt now to think about it.

Sadly, Tom lacked the motivation to have anything to do with Ricky. He almost hated his son, and was unwilling or unable to prevent him from falling into the bottomless pit, though Tom knew he himself was heading the same way because of it.

To compound their already immense weight, the traumatic event of their son falling victim to the drug-infested criminals was a profoundly distressing experience.

Now Donna had much bigger problems on her hands. Ricky's neighbour, Margaret, informed Donna about the parties, loud music, and cheap call girls. Ricky was already an alcoholic, and if he got addicted to drugs as well, his life would end tragically. This eliminated any chances of Ricky getting married and having his own family.

Since arriving in Australia so many decades ago, Tom and Donna had always dreamed of having grandchildren. They wished to be remembered for the time they had spent on this magnificent blue planet.

Sadly, now, this elusive dream was out of their reach.

Donna sank into that black hole of quicksand, which choked her. She couldn't see the light at the end of the tunnel, she was lost in the darkness of that tunnel of misery, trying to find a way to light up the fire and find a way out. Memories of her days in the orphanage filled her thoughts. By facing challenging life lessons, she had gained the skills to survive. Indeed, she had always found the strength to overcome all obstacles. In her current situation, she knew she had to dig deep to find the resilience buried in her inner core. That was the only way to protect her mental health and aid Tom in his battle with depression.

Chapter 25

The Seminar with Fringe Benefits

Donna had exhausted all avenues in her search for potential girlfriends for Ricky, which had so far proven to be a total disaster. She'd encountered many obstacles, learned from her mistakes, and accepted defeat. She recognised that such a matchmaking task was beyond her human capabilities, so she put her faith in God.

At her work, Donna put her name down to attend a two-day professional development course with some senior staff members from her department, to be held at the University campus. The Ambulance Service for Mental Health course was to help those dealing with mental health issues and create an understanding of underlying psychological disorders they might encounter with their students, and provide advice as to where they could seek professional help within their community. It gave educators additional tools for dealing with students suffering from drug or alcohol use and showed lecturers how to recognise those underpinning issues that affected students' performances and how to preserve their psychological well-being and safety when involved with such individuals.

However, because of unexpected work commitments, Donna could not attend that first planned professional development session with her work colleagues.

However, while on holiday during summer break, Donna saw an advertisement in the local paper for the same course.

She wanted to enroll for a very personal reason and learn how to help Ricky so he could move forward. The course was attended primarily by mature women.

On the course-opening day, the facilitator started a group discussion where participants shared their individual concerns. Donna saw a woman in her early sixties who looked unsure of herself. Her name was Francesca but she preferred to be called Francis.

At first, Francis seemed shy and quiet, her soft voice and strong Italian accent made it hard for her to express herself in English. She fidgeted with her hands, which was an obvious sign she felt uncomfortable. Francis wore blazing-red high-heeled shoes and a short flame-orange floral dress imprinted with daffodils and daisies. Her slender shoulders and deep décolletage exposed her ample breasts. She looked as if she was going out to a nightclub rather than attending a seminar.

Donna's first impression of the woman lowered further, as her dress style was not appropriate for such an occasion, was far too provocative for Donna's taste, and suggest simple sophistication. Giving her second glance, she noticed her intense dark shade of nickel mascara, stone grey eye shadow, and fire engine red lipstick, all applied haphazardly. Further, her excessive flamingo pink cheeks made her look like a cheap call girl.

Francis shared her story with the group, looking down to avoid their gaze. She had come to the seminar to support her youngest daughter, Lucy, a single mother who had gone through a traumatic break-up with her partner who had physically abused her. Lucy was still battling depression and had cut off contact with her mother for a long time. Francis hoped to learn how to communicate better with Lucy, who remained silent and distant. Towards the end of her speech, upset and on the verge of tears, and her voice shaking Francis said her daughter had brought her nothing but pain and disappointment.

Donna immediately assessed that poor Francis had an inferiority complex. She was embarrassed and self-conscious about her Sicilian background, yet she desperately wanted to fit in and belong.

When Donna's turn came to speak, she was careful not to overexpose her issues and only admitted to having minor problems with Ricky. However, she was there only because she had missed the professional development course last time. This time, she decided not to disclose anything too soon.

Donna's mind drifted; she couldn't concentrate on the facilitator's voice. The only thing on her mind was Francis' youngest daughter, Lucy, who was unattached and single. Instantly, she knew Lucy was her next target. She had been looking for the right girl for over two decades. This time, she was adamant that she would cage this bird and keep the key. She will not allow Lucy to flee from her grasp.

Donna had to act quickly, as the window of opportunity to bring Ricky and Lucy into the relationship was slightly ajar.

During the afternoon coffee break, Donna befriended Francis – Donna always found it easy to make new friends. Her optimism and easygoing personality were a magnet that drew people to her, which was why Frances felt comfortable chatting with her.

Two newly formed friends sat alone in the outdoor cafe in the University gardens.

"We have a lot in common, speaking with accents. It has been years since I spoke Italian, so I forgot many words." Donna smiled, wanting to make Francis feel less self-conscious.

"Don't worry, Cara Mia. I will help you. Soon, you will remember what you have forgotten," Francis said.

Donna smiled again. Speaking in Italian, she quickly established a friendly rapport. Then Francis started telling

Donna about her new puppy, Daisy.

Being careful not to spook Francis, which could jeopardise her fast-evolving plan, Donna did not disclose anything – her private life was not up for discussion. She had to be patient, so she played along – puppy talk was harmless.

"I always wanted to get a little puppy, but my husband didn't want a dog because it shed hair." Donna thought the only interest she had to show was buying a puppy; if she really wanted to buy a poodle, she would.

"Cara Mia, poodles don't shed hair," Francis explained.

"Wow, how can I get such a puppy?" Donna replied enthusiastically.

"My oldest daughter, Pauline, works at the veterinary surgery. She could get you a poodle," Francis said. "I can ask my daughter to save one puppy for you, but poodles are expensive."

"I don't care. I always wanted a puppy. I want to surprise Tom for our wedding anniversary," Donna responded casually.

"Come to my home for an espresso after the course if you like. Meet my puppy, Daisy. After that, you can decide. Puppies are just like small children and demand lots of attention."

When Donna came home later that afternoon, Tom immediately noticed her high spirits and gave her an inquiring look. "Donna, what is that smirk on your face? You look like you struck gold?"

"Tom, you are right. I met Francesca … Frances …, a lovely Italian woman who will help me buy a puppy. I always wanted a puppy. Poodles don't shed hair."

"Where did this come from? We don't need a dog. I am retired now, and we plan to travel more," Tom said, surprised by his wife's sudden decision to own a dog.

"Besides, when I buy a puppy's love, I will get another love for free," Donna said, bouncing around like a wind-up doll, confusing poor Tom even further.

She decided not to say much to Tom; he would only disapprove. Instead, she'd keep him in the dark until the matchmaking deed was done.

Befriending Francis was important, but she knew she would never choose her as her friend. Donna had to play her cards right; the charade had to go on. But this time, she was an expert. She'd learned from so many previous mistakes. Donna read a quote by an intelligent business executive who once said, "You learn much more from your failures than successes." Donna had had many failed attempts. She'd weathered many storms and dealt with embarrassing failures, which had taught her a valuable life lesson.

❧

The following week, Donna visited Francis's home. She brought her a bunch of flowers and a box of chocolates, as was customary when visiting an Italian home for the first time.

Francis' modest home was tastefully decorated and immaculately clean. Her little, black curly-haired puppy was a bundle of joy and energy, jumping around excitedly and chasing a ball around the family room.

"I love your puppy. She is so cuddly, but I would prefer a white poodle," Donna said.

"My Daisy was the odd one out. She looked like a black sheep. My daughters think I am the odd one out, too." Francis smiled. "But don't worry, I've phoned Pauline, and she will reserve a white poodle just for you."

"Oh, that would be great. I spoke with my husband and told him I have a special surprise for our upcoming anniversary," Donna chirped.

Francis put coffee cups on the table and some homemade chocolate biscuits on a silver plate; the aroma of freshly made espresso coffee was inviting. Donna and Francis started chatting in Italian again. They established a friendly rapport, and Donna soon learned they belonged to St Patrick's Church and lived in a nearby Fremantle suburb.

"How come you call yourself Francis? Donna asked.

"Francesca is my birth name, but Francis sounds more English," she said.

"What happened to your husband?" Donna guided the conversation.

Francis fidgeted, yet kept chatting, opening up about her life. "We divorced when my youngest daughter Lucy was a teenager, and my two oldest girls were at university. Giuseppe married again and had two kids. He died five years later; it serves him bloody right to marry a younger woman. No wonder that he died from a heart attack."

Francis paused, then said. "Lucy was very close to her father and blames me for the family breakdown. She blames me for everything that went wrong in her life. Lucy gave me so much heartache."

"Don't be so hard on yourself. Every mother wants the best for her kids, but it's not easy. Divorce can be hard on them," Donna empathised.

"It is hard for me, and kids don't understand, especially when both sides tell different stories," Francis said, her voice trembling.

Donna tried to comfort her, but Francis became agitated, so Donna remained quiet; she listened patiently, encouraging Francis to continue talking without many interruptions.

"Come here, Cara Mia," Francis said casually and, pointing to her display cabinet, showed Donna photos of her daughters and grandchildren.

"You have such lovely daughters. You must be so proud."

Frances took out Lucy's photo from the display cabinet and handed it to Donna. Seeing Lucy's picture, she thought, Wow! What a beautiful young woman, and her daughter Emma, such a pretty girl. Donna held on to Lucy's photo admiring her oval-shaped face with its peach complexion, shoulder-length curly brown hair, and hazelnut eyes. Lucy's sensual pink lips resembled the best rose in her garden, and her high cheekbone enhanced her smile and pearly teeth.

Although slightly overweight, Lucy had a proportionally-built, curvy body, and Donna was spellbound. She looks like a love goddess.

This was it. Donna instantly knew that she had found that jewel in the crown that she was seeking. Her mind wandered as she imagined what Ricky would say when he saw Lucy's photo – he would instantly fall head over and heels in love with her.

Francis poured another cup of coffee and started talking again. "Lucy was twenty-two when Emma was born. Johnny, Emma's father, was such a bastard … violent and abusive. When such a relationship is broken, it can't be mended again. Johnny is associated with a notorious bike group, and he introduced Lucy to marijuana. But when they separated, I helped Lucy quit drugs. She has been clean ever since.

"My motto in life has always been. When somebody does you harm, you never see that person again, no matter what. You cut them out of your life permanently as if they have never existed. I never visited Giuseppe's grave and forbade my daughters to meet their half-sisters. That is a Sicilian way," Francis stated firmly.

"Does Emma's father see his daughter?" Donna wanted to know.

"Parental rights gives Johnny access to Emma every second weekend, but I wish I could keep my granddaughter away from him forever. Thank God he lives in Coolup – the further away from Lucy, the better."

"That is such a long drive. Who drives Emma to Coolup?" Donna asked.

"Well, if he wants to see his daughter, Johnny will have to put up with driving." Francis smirked; she walked to the kitchen to brew some more fresh coffee and left Donna to continue browsing the family photos.

After finishing another coffee, Donna didn't want to overstay her welcome on her first visit and promised that next Sunday, after church, she would revisit her and bring some cake to complement her espresso coffee.

"I have to rush home and tell Tom the great news that we will soon become happy parents to a new puppy. I am excited to get a pretty puppy like your lovely Daisy," Donna said and hurried to her car.

✿

The following weekend, after Sunday mass, Donna brought a walnut cake and revisited Francis. When Francesca refilled cups of coffee and finished another slice of walnut cake, she said to Donna, "You said last time that your son Ricky is single now. He may like to meet Lucy," Francis said.

"Oh, I don't know. I don't like to meddle in his life. Ricky recently split up with his long-term girlfriend. He is still heartbroken," Donna said casually, hiding her desperation.

"Come on, tell me some more," Frances prompted.

"Ricky met Belinda while playing in the church band; he is a talented guitar player who enjoys gospel music. Belinda, a God-abiding girl, cheated on him with one of the band members." Donna sighed. "Thank God, this is over. I was never happy that Belinda lured Ricky away from the Catholic Church." Donna felt pleased that she sounded so convincing, knowing nothing could be further from the truth. She thought, *Gotcha ya!*

She knew Francis would approve; being Sicilian, the Catholic religion and customs were a significant part of her life.

"Cara Mia, the best way to treat a broken heart is to find another love. I wish Lucy would one day meet a decent man who would treat her well. Poor Lucy escaped from that violent partner and now is untrusting. But she deserves to be happy." Francis kept staring at her coffee cup, wiping her teary eyes.

Donna came closer to Francis and hugged her. "I agree with you wholeheartedly. You want what is best for your daughter and your granddaughter. As a mother, I also feel so sorry for poor Ricky; he got involved with the wrong girl, too. He deserves better," Donna said mournfully, evoking some sympathy from Frances.

Frances nodded in agreement and in a sympathetic tone, hastened to reassure Donna of the better times ahead.

"Cara Mia, Lucy and Emma deserve to belong to a wonderful family like yours."

Donna played it cool yet feared losing the opportunity for Ricky to meet Lucy. She had to stay patient until her task was completed and not lose sight of the bigger picture. Thank you, Guardian Angel with a broken wing, *for bringing me to Francis's home.*

To woo Francis even deeper into her spider web so she had no chance of escape, Donna knew she must not be seen as the chaser. Francis was doing an excellent job of crawling and spilling all her secrets, so there was no need to rush her.

"Here, Donna, take this photo of Lucy and show it to your son. However, please don't say I gave it to you. Lucy would be furious if I tried to set her up for a blind date. Let us keep that between us. I don't want to have any more arguments with my daughter."

"Okay, there is no point in rushing things. Ricky is very independent, and it is best that I don't meddle in his life," Donna said, as if not interested, but her heart missed a beat, and she had to take a deep breath to regain her composure.

After the weekend, Donna invited Francis to the beach boardwalk for lunch and a glass of wine. Donna drove so she didn't want to drink, but Francis could drink as much as she wanted. *Alcohol untangles stiff tongues.* Soon, Francis spilled more secrets. After ordering desserts, Francis had another glass of wine, and Donna casually asked her, "What happened after you got divorced from Giuseppe?"

"Two years after my divorce, I married again. Ken was a few years younger; it was my turn to be happy. However, Lucy disapproved of my new husband; she hated Ken. When she turned eighteen, Lucy packed her bags and moved out."

"Why did Lucy hate your new husband?" Donna asked, knowing that listening was superior to talking if she was to learn more about Lucy.

"Lucy had no justification for resenting my new husband; Ken always treated her kindly. I was devastated when Lucy began spreading false accusations, claiming to her two older sisters that Ken had made advances on her. I confronted Lucy and told her to stop flirting with him and dressing inappropriately. How could a man resist looking at an attractive young woman? It was only a natural reaction. Lucy exaggerated the whole situation. All Ken did was steal a kiss or two, and he meant no harm," Francis explained.

However, Donna suspected something inappropriate had happened to poor Lucy under her mother's roof. She nodded in support, careful not to rock the boat, and stayed silent.

"I shouldn't have ever married that bastard. Ken married me only because of my house. I got suspicious when he started taking solo holidays to Thailand. Eventually, Ken stayed in

Phuket for six months, got his new girlfriend pregnant, and we divorced." Francis grew teary; she was still bitter about her unfaithful and deceitful second husband, and she continued talking.

"The only good thing I got from that bastard was his surname. Now, I have a proper English name. Everybody in the Yacht Club knows me as Francis Smith. Francesca's name was old-fashioned, used by peasants and Sicilian families."

Donna was torn between pitying Francis and judging her foolishness, her negligence for failing to protect her teenage daughter from the sexual predator. She poured more wine and urged her to continue her story."

"Unfortunately, Ken had a lot of gambling debts. I had no choice but to sell our big two-storey home my first husband had built on the beachfront.

"My daughters never forgave me for selling their childhood home. I was left with only enough money to buy my current house," Francis said, lowering her head in shame.

"But it is a gracious home, and your garden roses are so beautiful. You must have green fingers," Donna said, trying to cheer her up.

"It is hard work to prune all the roses and the bushes. I hurt my back when I worked at Royal Children's Hospital and now I live on disability pension; the medicine helps to numb my pain. I shouldn't drink much; I want to finish this glass of wine."

"At our age, we have to look after our health, but you're still young and should enjoy your life," Donna said sympathetically.

"Oh, yeah, I do. A few months ago at the Yacht club, I met Stuart; he has a yacht, so we went sailing together. He is married, but I don't care. He makes me happy. Besides, I never want to get married again," Francis said, tipsy and now more cheerful.

"Let me drive you home and we can catch up next time. You must visit our home next time," Donna said, smiling.

"I am lucky to have met such a lovely woman like you. I trust you as if I've known you all my life." Francis looked at Donna to get her approval.

"I am so sorry to hear that you had such misfortune. I hope you will find some happiness you rightfully deserve with Stuart," Donna said compassionately while smiling politely. She was pleased that she had fooled Francis but didn't care about Francis's love interest. All she cared for was to get to know Lucy. Francis was only a vehicle to achieve that aim.

ʘ

The following week Donna invited Francis for lunch and drove her to nice beachfront restaurant. They again chatted about their problematic children. Halfway through bottle of wine, Francis became more talkative.

"What happened to Lucy, and where does she live now?" Donna asked.

"Lucy lives one street from the beach, in the old duplex that her father's building partner used as holiday home. Lucy and Emma lived in that shabby place for eight years, but the rent was cheap, and she liked her independence. The place is an absolute pig sty. I offered to come and clean it, but she refused. Lucy is depressed and has no energy to do anything with her daughter. She only sleeps, eats, watches TV and puts on a lot of weight. She has no computer, internet, or mobile phone, only a landline. She never answers the phone, not to talk to me or anybody else."

Donna touched Francis's hand as a sign of comfort and she off-handedly mentioned Ricky, her only son, telling her new friend, "My son Ricky is lonely too; he was heartbroken when Belinda left him. He is very depressed. I hope Ricky will find the 'right girl,' get married, and have Bambini one day."

Donna put her head down, eagerly awaiting Francis's response. When Francis suddenly became fully attentive and wanted to know more, Donna continued with her story. Telling her less, however, in this case, was more, and she thought no harm could come of bending and stretching the truth. She felt no shame in telling a few more white lies. After all, her motivation was to save her son in any way she could. *God will forgive me for some of my deceitfulness.*

"Is your son Ricky working?" Francesca wanted to know.

"When Ricky enrolled in the university to study mineral science, just like his father, he quit his studies and worked in the mines. He was earning good money, but now he is not working.

"Sadly, a few years ago, he had a terrible accident. It was not his fault when some drunk, speeding through the stop sign, crashed head-on right into his car. Thankfully, Ricky survived and recovered but could not return to the mining site. I hope that soon he will get another job. He is very responsible with his money and drinks only for social occasions but has never used drugs," Donna lied through her teeth to get Francis's sympathy. Although one thing was true, Ricky never used drugs; he was a hypochondriac, and sharing needles put him off drugs, but binge drinking alcohol was just as bad.

"Where does he live? Francesca asked.

"Ricky lives in our first family home, where he spent his childhood. It is only a ten-minute drive, and a lovely home opposite a beautiful park and not far from the beach. We decided to give Ricky his early inheritance; no point waiting until we dropped dead." Donna forced a laugh, impressed by her own ability to lie.

Now Francis was offering Donna another glass of wine.

"No thanks," Donna declined, saying." I am visiting a friend in the hospital this afternoon and can't drink and drive." Of course, that was another lie, as Donna wanted to stay in charge of the conversation.

"I never used to drink much, when I take or pick up Emma to school. But I haven't seen her for more than a year. I feel sorry for the poor kid. She has no friends, misses school, and often stays home. Sadly, Lucy doesn't want to talk with me. Now you know the reasons I attended that seminar. I wanted to learn how to resolve conflicts and get close to Lucy and Emma again.

"Lucy deserves to be happy. Cara Mia, Lucy is a good girl; she is overly protective of her daughter Emma." Francis looked up at Donna, expecting a response, but Donna kept a poker face, empathising with Lucy's decision to cut off ties with her mother. Lucy wanted to protect her daughter from meeting another of her mother's random boyfriends.

Instinctively, Donna felt sorry for Lucy, knowing she was the right girl for Ricky. *Searching for the right girl is like finding a needle in a haystack. Lucy is that girl; two lonely hearts who live like hermits will be a perfect match.*

Lucy is still young and can give Ricky the child he longs for. We may even have a grandchild. However, that dream was still beyond Donna's wildest expectations; it would need a miracle to pull it off.

☙

Every time after meeting with Francis, Donna felt she was close to achieving her goal. When Donna came home elated one day, she kissed Tom quickly and ran upstairs to change, taking two steps at a time. She had never felt as alive; she had zest in her steps and enjoyed every moment.

In retrospect, she found it rather intriguing how the circumstances had led to what happened. *Serendipity.* Donna felt that, if she had gone to the first session with her work colleagues as scheduled, she would not have met Francis. She wondered if that was a mere coincidence or if it was fated by a powerful force that caused everything to occur without a plan. It had happened unplanned and for a reason – just like many other things in people's lives.

Donna truly believed that meeting Francesca was predestined. She thought this was her fate, not just sheer luck – a chance meeting that changed their lives forever. She struggled to find adequate words for it – to clarify it – wondering if it was a miracle. How else could she explain the bit in her rational mind about the events that led to that fateful day when her path crossed with Francesca?

That unforeseen meeting changed history completely.

Excited, Donna's mind raced as she was on the verge of finding a precious gem she had been searching for so long. She had secretly prayed that her guardian Angel with the broken wing would point her in the right direction. Now, here she was.

Suddenly, Donna was playing the matchmaker again, feeling excited again; her zest for life was rekindled.

However, Donna now faced the biggest challenge. She had to become a master manipulator to gain Francis's total trust. Donna enjoyed playing chess, and was good at it. She would sacrifice all her pawns to get to the queen – Lucy. She would do everything to win that engaging chess game. But to do it, she must stay calm, keep a poker face, and use the right strategy. She knew she was getting closer to executing 'Checkmate.'

When Donna invited Francis to her home, she had prepared some snacks and wine, and they sat on the balcony overlooking the natural lake and distant sea views. It was a lovely, breezy afternoon. A flock of white parrots flew around on and off the trees, making chuckling noises, and performing acrobatics on the tree branches.

Francis relaxed, and drank her first glass in two gulps, which didn't surprise Donna. She immediately refilled her glass, ensuring she did not notice. While serving salmon club sandwiches with tangy hollandaise sauce, Donna again refilled Francis's glass. *The more she drinks, the more she talks and she mentions Lucy.*

Francis wanted to know more about Donna and Tom's lifestyle. Donna told her Tom's retirement didn't stop her from enjoying working full-time; she valued her career.

Francesca admired their two-storey house, luxurious leather furniture, paintings, library with thousands of books, modern kitchen, and lush green outdoor barbecue area. Francis was envious of their wealth and opulence; she was also impressed with Tom, who knew how to treat a woman. Tom was a charmer and a harmless flirt. Many of Donna's friends envied her for marrying such a handsome, well-educated, intelligent man.

Donna was always modest and hated showing off, but she allowed Tom to exaggerate their wealth this time. Donna talked about the good and prosperous life she shared with her husband, and Tom told Francis how much they enjoyed travelling to Europe and Asia in style. Tom had expensive taste, flying business class, where Dom Pérignon or Bollinger champagne was served as a welcoming drink, followed by hors d'oeuvres, caviar, truffles, French pâtés, delicacies made from goose liver. Tom kept telling Francis that such a grand lifestyle ensured they had a honeymoon experience and rejuvenated their romance and passion for one another.

When Francis asked to go to the toilet, she walked by the master bedroom and luxury bathroom fitted with the best Italian marble tiles. Donna quietly reprimanded Tom.

"Tom, please stop showing off and don't flirt with the woman. Francis has basic needs and is unfamiliar with champagne, wine, and deluxe foods. Francis, uses a cheap cask of wine in a plastic bladder and pasta dishes – as good as they may be, but that is all she knows. She seems slightly intimidated or very impressed by you." But that was precisely as Donna wished.

Tom didn't care. He appeared amused and found the whole affair humorous, but he didn't want to participate in Donna's scheming and withdrew to his study.

"Cara Mia, to Sei Ricco," Francis said in Italian.

Bingo! Francis believes we are rich. Having lured Francis into her web of greed and desire for opulence, Donna smiled and said, "Yes, we worked hard all our lives, made wise investments, and now are reaping the rewards. But money can't buy happiness," Donna said modestly.

"Oh, Donna ... but money can ease the pain," Francis giggled, happily tipsy.

About this time, Donna encouraged Francis to visit her daughter and re-establish contact with her granddaughter, Emma. "That will please Lucy, and she may reconcile with you."

Pleased with herself, and sensing Francis's hidden greed, which stemmed from envy and a longing for luxury and wealth she could probably never have, Donna played her last Ace. Her scheming, lies and Tom's exaggeration of their wealth had enticed Francis like a bee to honey. She knew Francis's greed had blinded her clear thinking. That would ultimately give Donna what she sought: a pot of gold, the ultimate Jackpot.

So impressed and enchanted by the splendour she could only dream of ever reaching, Francis was hooked. Donna's master plan had worked. If her daughter married Ricky, Francis would reap the rewards. She would finally have what she always wanted – wealth and the respect she thought she deserved.

Francis phoned Donna a week later. "I got some good news to share with you. A few days ago, I visited Lucy to give Emma a present, and Lucy invited me in," she said happily.

"That's a good start. Don't give up on your daughter." For a moment or two, Donna genuinely felt sorry for Francis, who appeared vulnerable, but this only lasted for a moment. "Now take her some flowers and chocolates. Your relationship with Lucy will improve with time. We love our children from the day they are born until we die."

Donna was pleased that Francis took advice and continued seeing her daughter.

When Francis brought a box of chocolates and some flowers for her daughter's birthday, Lucy finally started to trust her mother and allowed her back into her life. Eventually, Francis encouraged Lucy to agree to a blind date. She gave Lucy Ricky's photo and told her that Ricky hated drugs and lived a healthy lifestyle.

Lucy decided she had already wasted eight years, and it was time to change. She wanted to meet that man, who may be the right person to heal her broken heart. She agreed to meet Ricky and wrote her phone number on a small piece of paper.

That same afternoon, Francis visited Donna and gave her blessing and Lucy's phone number.

Donna hugged Francis and said, "Bella Signora, God willing, we will soon become relatives."

The two mothers embraced, happy that they had accomplished their matchmaking goals.

Donna felt overjoyed. She had been searching for a suitable match for her son for over ten years. Her quest was finally over. She had discovered Lucy, a girl who could save Ricky. No matter what difficulties they encountered, their love would give them the strength to overcome them. Love was the best remedy for sorrow and pain, and it could mend their wounded hearts.

Both mothers had justifiable reasons for this matchmaking venture, expecting a win-win selfish outcome – Francis, blinded by greed for opulence, and Donna delusional in believing she could control her son's destiny.

However, Donna, ever the eternal optimist let her heart fill with joy. She held onto that small piece of paper containing Lucy's phone number and drove straight to Ricky's home.

Chapter 26

The Fateful Encounter

Donna held on tightly to Lucy's phone number as if her life depended on it. Surely, Ricky would be over the moon when he saw Lucy's photo, that beautiful goddess from heaven.

Donna breathed a sigh of relief as the last piece of the jigsaw puzzle fell into place, completing the orchestrated picture that had finally taken shape.

She had to calm herself down as she drove and reminisced about the years she had spent searching and the many uncertainties and false hopes she had faced. The Angel with the broken wing had guided her in the right direction, and now she had finally found that elusive jewel in the crown.

Donna believed that having Lucy and her daughter Emma would give Ricky an instant family and save her son. She knew what it had taken to get Lucy's permission to give Ricky her phone number. At first, Lucy had been reluctant, but her mother had persuaded her that Ricky was a good man and nothing like her previous partner, Emma's father.

This was Donna's last chance; she had to convince Ricky that this was his last chance too. Of course, Lucy had mental health issues, too, but Donna would help both of them. Besides, love would enable them to grow stronger together. *Everybody deserves a second chance to be happy.*

Donna's life looked much rosier, and the sun smiled affectionately at her. She looked forward to meeting Lucy and her ten-year-old daughter. She would welcome them into their family with open arms, and Ricky and Lucy would live happily ever after.

ﻌﻌ

When Donna reached Ricky's home, the reality shook her up. However, she was used to handling this situation and somehow managed her stress to not cloud her reasoning. She forcefully collected herself and calmed down.

Taking a deep breath, she pressed the doorbell.

Nothing happened.

Then she pushed it again.

Nothing.

Moving closer to the door, she banged on it several times with her fist. There was still no sound of movement inside the house, and her mind immediately switched into panic mode: *Is he okay? Is he drunk or dead?* Dread washed over her.

Just as she was about to climb the side gate, the front door slowly opened.

The house was pitch dark and quiet; Ricky stood unsteadily before her like a monster from the Frankenstein movie. He looked awful. His scruffy beard and messy, bushy hair revealed his swollen red face with bloodshot eyes caused by heavy drinking. He smelled of alcohol, sweat, and vomit. And he was in one of his dark moods, made worse by a terrible hangover.

Donna felt sick to her stomach: Ricky looked worse than ever. She tried to sound kind and asked if she could come in because she had something important to tell him. For a moment, Ricky remained motionless, gawking and looking stunned. Then, lazily, he turned around, and, without a word, limping on one side, he dragged his feet back into the house with a great effort.

Donna quickly followed, closing the door behind her. It

looked like she'd be up against another battle with someone who wished to die. The inside of the house was in the same dreadful condition as he was. The foul air hung heavy in dark rooms, and the dog's hair glued all over the fabric of his couch. Dirty old clothes were strewn on the dirty floor. The kitchen resembled a foul rubbish tip: dirty dishes and old food scraps, some already turning green with mould.

Donna quickly moved into action. She prepared a strong cup of coffee and placed it before him. Then she sat down and watched him silently across the table. Ricky slowly picked up the big mug, unsure what to do with it. Then, at a snail's pace, he made a piteous move and took a couple of sips from an unsteady mug, his hands trembling and clumsy. Beads of sweat hung on his forehead. A few of them streaked down his swollen cheeks. He seemed unaware of it or didn't care. After a few gulps, he settled back in his chair and, for the first time, looked straight at his mother as if he had finally realised her presence and recognised who she was.

"Okay, Mum, what do you want?" Ricky mumbled in a deep, rasping voice.

"Ricky, I have good news," Donna said, desperately trying to lift the solemn atmosphere. "I found you a beautiful girl from a good Italian family. Her name is Luciana … Lucy. Here is her phone number; she wants to meet you, so please call her. A beautiful girl as Lucy will not wait long."

Ricky's first response was a tired, cynical smirk. Then he said, "Mum, stop tormenting me; go home and leave me alone."

Prepared for such a reply, she ignored him and opened her handbag and placed Lucy photo on the table. Next to it, she put that tiny, precious piece of paper with Lucy's phone number on it.

Ricky remained defiant and refused to look at the items on the table, but his curiosity improved. Holding his head in the same position as if still not looking, his eyes shifted slowly, but only enough to sneak a quick look at the photo.

After a much better second look, his shoulders sagged visibly, and his broken voice was full of the bitterness and despondency of another defeat. "Mum, thanks a lot ... but look at me. Nobody on this earth would want to be with me. Stop dreaming, Mum. Please stop doing this to me. I can't take it anymore. I'm done with girls!"

Donna refused to surrender and continued her providential encouragement because she knew that if she failed now, her whole family would be condemned to an eternity of misery and pain.

"This is your best chance," Donna again pleaded with him. "Please, Ricky, don't blow it. You may never have another opportunity like this again. Poor Lucy has low self-esteem; she is lonely, just like you. She lives alone in a dingy rental duplex with her ten-year-old daughter. You always wanted to have kids – this is an instant family, which would be good for you. You don't need to be lovers, but first, start establishing a friendship. It would be much better than mixing with that despicable company of yours, the no-hopers, and the dregs of our society. The low life of this group and being with them will only take you deeper into alcohol abuse, liver disease, and premature death. So, give it a chance … please, son, give it a chance!"

However, Ricky was still unmoved.

"Mum, no girl would ever want to be with me. Just look at me; I am a total mess. I look grotesque and incapable of having a normal relationship with anyone. Even the lowlife – the 'sewer rats', as Dad calls them – won't have much to do with me. They will only let me be with them if I bring them a bottle of bourbon.

"The only mate that I have in that group is Andy. We know each other from high school, and he understands me, but all his mates hate me. As soon as the bottle of vodka was empty, they throw me out of the house to get another bottle of Cougar.

"Most of the group doesn't want me around, and they all make fun of me. Because I don't use drugs, they believe that I will snitch on them. But I am lucky to have Andy as my friend; he is in charge and trusts me so that I can stay.

"Mum, please, go home, leave me alone. There is no hope for me." Ricky stood and walked to his bedroom, slamming the door behind him.

That afternoon, Donna drove home broken, defeated, and utterly lost. Luckily, Tom was not at home to see her in such a depressed state. She was emotionally and physically exhausted and at the lowest emotional point in her life.

Dragging herself upstairs to have a shower, her pain was piercing so deep inside that she curled up in a ball under the running hot water. She felt totally wrecked, squatting in a heap, wanting to scream, desperate to cry. But there were no tears to soothe the pain. She could not find tears when she needed them the most, so she howled like a wounded wolf. The warm and cozy shower was the only relief for her aching body.

The following Sunday, she went to church. After the mass, she stayed back, a few tears gently streaming down her cheeks. She asked, "Dear God, what more do you want from me? Jesus' mother suffered much more. She witnessed her son crucified."

Indeed, Donna hoped that Jesus' mother, Mary, could see her pain and hear her prayers.

Donna believed that Lucy and Ricky belonged together; meeting was their destiny. She instinctively hoped that maybe her guardian Angel with the broken wing would intervene, and help bring these two lost souls together.

When church mass ended, Donna stood for a moment under the statue of the Virgin Mary, thinking that she must return to Ricky's house to try again. With God's help, she might influence her son to change his mind about contacting Lucy.

As soon as he opened the door, Donna asked him, "Have you reconsidered giving Lucy a call?"

"No, Mum, I did not. Besides, it is too late. I have thrown away Lucy's phone number. That small piece of paper has gone into the rubbish bin. That's it! The rubbish truck came and emptied the bin. Lucy is out of my league; how could you believe a beautiful girl like Lucy would ever want to be with me? I can't take any more rejections. Go home, Mum, and forget about me like my dad did."

At first, Donna was speechless. She'd worked so hard, sacrificing her dignity to get that phone number. Then she got angry; her blood boiled with fury, and all her bottled-up anger erupted like a sleeping volcano. When she started yelling at Ricky, she lost her composure altogether.

Ricky hadn't seen his mother that angry, ever. He stood shocked. After she'd finished her outburst, they stood silently for quite a while, just wildly staring at each other. Then Ricky spoke.

"Mum, what must I do to convince you that it is all lost? Come outside. I'll show you the bin if you don't believe me. It's been emptied on Friday. Now calm down or you will have a heart attack. Come and have a look."

Taking his mother's unresponsive hand, he led her outside. Donna followed, only because she had no strength to resist. When they came to the bin, he lifted the lid and tilted it open towards her.

"It's empty. Look ... there is nothing here, no phone number." Ricky then froze mid-sentence as he spoke and indifferently glanced inside the empty green bin. He looked astonished.

Suddenly recovered, Donna also gave a quick look inside. That small scrunched-up piece of paper with Lucy's phone number was stuck to the gluey starch of beer at the bottom of the stinky rubbish bin.

They both looked at each other in utter amazement, then burst out laughing with a delicious sense of sudden jubilation.

Donna could breathe again, and Ricky seemed genuinely relieved. She didn't waste time and told him this was God's intervention.

"Ricky, this is your destiny. This phone number here is to give you a second chance at a better life. Please, son, give Lucy a call. Both of you deserve to grab a slice of happiness. Please reconsider. I went to church and prayed for you. God has answered my prayers."

Ricky then turned around, gave his mother an affectionate hug, and promised he would give Lucy a call. If Lucy wanted him, he would change his life completely. Ricky would do anything to be loved and to love. That night, Donna thanked her guardian Angel with the broken wing and slept soundly, which she hadn't done in a very long time.

That evening, Ricky called Lucy, and new chapters of their life began.

&

Lucy had waited patiently for over a week and had finally lost hope that Ricky would ever call. Then, one evening, unexpectedly, the phone buzzed. Lucy lazily reached for the handset, and then froze, undecided. She wasn't sure if she wanted to talk to anyone, but then changed her mind.

After timidly whispering "Yes," someone at the other end said, "Hi, I'm Ricky."

The first chat they had that evening lasted almost two hours. The following night, the conversations continued even longer. The phone calls kept coming. Lucy would ring Ricky late at night when Emma was sleeping, and they chatted on their landline phone until the early morning hours.

Lucy and Ricky were scared and worried about rejection, unable to overcome the difficulty of committing to another person or a relationship. They talked, chattering about everything and nothing, too scared to stop and too nervous to start something real. Lucy desired more. She wanted a man in her life; she deserved another chance to find true love.

These phone-calling romances extended into over two months of daily, hours-long talks without wishing to see each other. During that period, Ricky hoped this friendship could become a romance. He kept his house clean and tidied the gardens. He took great care in his personal appearance, just in case Lucy decided to visit him – he wanted to impress her. Most of all, he stopped going to see his druggy friends and stopped binge drinking and eating. Ricky started to believe that maybe his mother was right; Lucy was his best and only chance of happiness.

However, meeting in person was scary. She had to consider her daughter Emma; protecting Emma was her first obligation. What if they met and they didn't like each other? Their phone connection was their safety blanket that might be lost forever.

Lucy felt ecstatic that she had finally found someone with so much in common. Ricky understood her mental illness, as he was in the same boat. She looked forward to the phone ringing, and every fortnight when Emma went to her father's cattle farm in Coolup, Lucy told Ricky about her personal issues. Lucy was glad she had found somebody who would never physically or emotionally abuse her, as she suffered from Johnny. She felt safe and comfortable, and Ricky reassured her he was not like her previous partner, telling her he would protect and cherish her and her daughter Emma.

Their two-way communication progressively evolved into friendship and then love. Lucy believed Ricky was honest and slightly gullible. She found that endearing, so she started asking more probing questions. She wanted to know if he owned the house, how much money he had, and how he would support her and her daughter. Lucy was cautious and reluctant about meeting Ricky too soon. She wanted to be sure that Emma would be safe to meet a new man in her life.

She didn't have to worry about that: Ricky was old-fashioned. He looked forward to stepping into new shoes as Emma's stepdad. He liked the idea that he would have an instant daughter. His dream of searching and having an instant family was finally over.

Lucy learned from her mother that having money and the security it can buy is essential to love, so she casually started quizzing Ricky about his financial status. Ricky earnestly spilled his beans about everything without fully realising what he was saying. He told her about his problems and boasted about his parents' successful careers, financial achievements, investments, and good community standing.

This torrent of information stirred Lucy's imagination. She got hooked on the prospect of a new and better life for her and her daughter. Lucy liked the idea of Ricky's tightly knitted family background and wanted to be part of such a respectable and prominent family. She sought a family that would love her for who she was all her life. She had never received unconditional love. Now was her time to be loved and cared for. Besides, Ricky sounded so different from anyone she had known.

Lucy was pleased that Ricky had never used drugs. She'd split up from Johnny who had introduced her to cannabis. However, ever since she'd left Johnny, she had been clean. She'd quit smoking pot and never wanted to go that way again. That part of her life was over – out of her life forever. She had been on her own for nearly eight years and desperately wanted a fresh start, to have a safe life for herself and her daughter.

Ricky convinced Lucy that he was brought up in a family with strong ethical and moral values, but he didn't pretend to be perfect – just like Lucy, he was a damaged person with many faults, too. They both suffered from an eating disorder and sometimes liked to drink alcohol to a euphoric high. Lucy didn't see any harm in social drinking and didn't condemn Ricky when he told her he drank too often.

They loved music and movies, so boredom should never encroach on them and their relationship. They both had mental health issues, so they may help each other deal with them. Ricky sounded intelligent and educated and treated her with kindness and respect that she had never experienced from anyone before. The longer they spoke on the phone, the more Lucy liked this kind, well-spoken man.

Lucy felt she could easily fall in love with Ricky. She was so impressed with his honesty that he seemed kind and spoke like a genuine person. She accepted all his faults and was excited that somebody would love her for who she was, not who she must be.

Ricky, too, fell head over heels in love with Lucy. His lonely, miserable days were over; he had new hope for the future, and happiness had knocked on his door …

Gradually, Lucy realised that she needed Ricky's love; she was desperate to be loved. Ricky was the right man for her. Besides, he seemed a good catch – someone she could proudly show off to her mother, her well-to-do sisters, and their families. Emma will be so happy to belong to such a lovely family; it reassured her that Ricky would be a good 'male role model' in Emma's life. Lucy believed when her mother Francesca told her, "This is a miracle in making a new life filled with hope and prosperity for you and Emma."

Lucy couldn't believe her lucky stars. Just as she had lost all hope of finding love, out of nowhere happiness had come her way. She was convinced that her destiny was now intertwined with Ricky. He told her that, kindred spirit would bond them forever. This would be a new path for Lucy. Hope and happiness were coming her way, and she would never let them go.

Growing impatient, as Lucy was unwilling to meet him face to face Ricky thought that she might never come … He grew desperate, thinking, *what will it take for Lucy to finally meet me?*" He'd nearly touched the stars, and happiness was within his grasp. He'd had so many disappointments and could not face another failure. He was so scared that he may not be what she was looking for … and confided his fears to his school friend Dean.

When Ricky told his friend Dean about this unusual, well over two months long, preliminary introduction, his friend only shrugged his shoulders and unceremoniously remarked, "Mate, just give her time. Don't pressure her too much, or she may get scared. My wife Beverly said that women crave financial stability, home, and love, all in that order. Now that we have a baby girl, Beverly is extremely protective of Louise. Now you can see why women want that security to protect kids. That's what mothers do. So, relax, mate; don't blame Lucy. All she wants is security for her daughter, too. Besides, you are lucky to find a decent woman at your age. Only a few blokes have such an opportunity, so don't rush her. Make sure everything runs smoothly. Be patient."

After over two months on the phone, Ricky was ecstatic and happy when Lucy told him she would visit him the next fortnight while Emma was away at her father's farm.

Lucy finally got the courage; she was brave enough to make the first move.

Ricky spent days vacuuming up the last traces of Bluey's hair and cleaning his house and the outdoor garden area. He shaved, put on lotion and deodorant, and brought some lovely t-shirts. The place resembled what it once was: a beautiful, welcoming home. He brought snacks, low-alcoholic beers, and lemon, lime and bitters that Lucy might like.

When Emma went to her father's place, Lucy, nervous and scared, faced the situation and visited Ricky's house. When she rang the bell, Ricky opened the front door. They saw each other for the first time, but the encounter caused no rapture. Instead, they both became very uncomfortable at first sight and could not say much.

Ricky gazed at Lucy, wondering why she was dressed in an oversized black cardigan and a long skirt, thinking she was probably conscious of being overweight. As he gazed into her brown eyes, he noticed her beautiful oval face, strong cheekbones, and the bundle of curly hair extending past her shoulders. She was incredibly beautiful, and Ricky hoped she would like him too.

Lucy gave Ricky a brief look with a rather blank expression. He wasn't as tall as she had imagined, but he was still youthful and good-looking, although quite overweight. Ricky was well-dressed and clean-shaven. She liked his smile; it was genuine, and his eyes smiled at her, too.

Ricky tried to offer timid Lucy a welcoming grin but was so nervous that he could only manage a polite grimace. He invited her into the lounge and offered her a comfortable seat.

They both sat down, still struggling to find words. Their previous two-month-long, cheerful phone conversations were now ancient history.

Ricky offered her a drink to ease the tension, took his guitar, and started playing soothing tunes. Lucy relaxed, softly smiling, then cast her eyes downward submissively, showing Ricky that she was interested in him. After a few more drinks, they soon felt comfortable in their company.

Ricky had a growing sense that his life had taken a new turn – a promise of a fresh start and a new beginning.

Lucy was intrigued and charmed by Ricky. Unlike her last partner, Emma's father, Ricky was polite and treated her like a real woman. She fell in love with him and felt reassured that Emma would be safe. She was looking for security, a home for herself and her daughter, away from that filthy, little, dark duplex.

Lucy wished that one day she would move in with Ricky into his spacious, clean house with a lovely garden and fresh breeze from the ocean. She hoped that her life was about to change for the better and that she'd found the man of her dreams.

A few months later, Lucy and her ten-year-old daughter Emma moved in with Ricky. However, Lucy kept the old rental unit as her permanent residency as a security blanket. Ricky wondered why she continued paying rent for that dingy old place when his house was big enough for his new family; it was well furnished, close to the beach and in the heart of Fremantle close to the shops and famous Cappuccino Strip. However, Lucy nimbly skirted around the question and had yet to offer a straight answer. Ricky, confused, let it drop to avoid an argument – it was too early for that in their growing relationship. Instead, he remained patient – just as his friend had advised.

Ricky remained uncomplaining because he sincerely hoped for a long-term relationship like his parents had; he longed for a lasting bond based on love and respect with his life partner. He would not rush Lucy.

Tom and Donna waited patiently, not willing to encroach on their privacy. They would come around when they were ready. When Emma's birthday came along, Donna suggested she make dinner and a birthday cake, which broke the ice. When Donna suggested inviting Francis, Lucy bluntly refused to have anything to do with her mother.

Emma's tenth birthday turned out to be a good icebreaker. After blowing out her ten candles on the cake, Emma watched a movie while the rest of the family chatted together. After a few drinks, both of them relaxed. Lucy was overjoyed and talkative; Ricky sat next to her, holding her hand, lovingly gazing at her.

Donna's heart sang with joy and, as a mother, seeing her son happy was a special feeling she had not experienced in decades. She was overjoyed to see these two lovebirds who could not take their hands off each other; these two lost souls were in love and connected. The afternoon they spent together reassured Donna to expect a bright and promising future for the whole family …

When Ricky and his new family went home, Donna looked at Tom, beaming with enthusiasm that Tom hadn't seen in years.

"Darling, for nearly two decades, I was searching to find the right girl. It was written in the stars for these two lonely hearts to meet. Lucy's love will save Ricky." She clapped her hands, proud of her achievements.

"Don't count your chickens yet." Tom smiled.

"Oh, Tom, stop being so negative. You can see that Lucy and Ricky are in love," Donna protested.

"This is still the honeymoon stage. Let us hope it will last. But don't get too excited."

"Tom, dear, you must have faith. My Aunt Pavica helped with the matchmaking of my own parents. My father always said that his beloved wife was the love of his life, his soul mate. I hope Ricky and Lucy will become soul mates, just like you and me."

Tom turned towards her and said softly, "I do hope that God will grant you that wish. He blessed me when I found you. So, there could be hope for Ricky and Lucy too."

Donna kissed her husband. "I don't have to worry anymore; I've passed the buck to Lucy. It will be up to them to make their own future, just as we did."

"I am so relieved that your endless search has ended. Now we can start travelling again." Tom hugged his wife, so happy to have her back in his life.

Chapter 27

Free at last ...

Donna's heart swelled with happiness as she witnessed her son's joy. When Lucy and Ricky came over for dinner, they were in a state of blissful happiness. Lucy always had a smile and was in a happy-go-lucky mood. When Emma spent her school holidays with her relatives or with her father, Johnny, at the Coolup farm, Ricky and Lucy cherished their valuable alone time to nurture and strengthen their relationship.

Donna achieved her outcome. Lucy told her that Ricky was her soul mate, which reassured her that Lucy was a perfect partner for her son. She could concentrate on her own relationship and reignite their stagnant marriage.

Donna looked at Tom eagerly. "I'm due for long service leave soon. Now that all our worries are over, we could go on an extended holiday. We are free at last!"

"That's exactly what I've been thinking. We've been stagnant for so long, now it's our time to relish some joy," Tom said. His enthusiasm was palpable. He leapt from his chair and hurried over to kiss her.

છ્ર

Donna kept in touch with the local travel agency, and her extensive experience in the tourism sector allowed her to secure outstanding deals. She delighted Tom with an unexpected upgrade from economy to business class. Upon boarding the aircraft, they were welcomed with chilled Moët Chandon champagne. Throughout the flight, canapés were offered initially, followed by various dishes served on refined trays covered with white linen. Their champagne flutes were refilled whenever they neared emptiness.

Donna looked at Tom. His green eyes shone with adoration, and it felt like they were on their second honeymoon. She was thrilled to see him so relaxed. It had been ages since she had seen him like this. Their love was rekindled. After over four decades together, they still flirted and interacted with playful affection, like love-struck teenagers.

In the blink of an eye, flying time vanished when a sudden announcement startled Donna, alerting them of the impending landing. With a smile, Tom affectionately greeted her with, "Good morning, my darling."

Vienna had long been a favoured holiday spot for them. Upon arrival, they were chauffeured directly to the Palace Hotel, where they savoured Viennese schnitzel with fries and a massive beer for dinner. Afterwards, they spent the evening in the bar, enjoying cocktails, the gentle strains of classical music, and dancing until late at night.

The following day, they spent a relaxed morning exploring Vienna's Old Town, taking in the sights of palaces, buildings, historical monuments, hidden alleys, and traditional cafés. They indulged in the local specialty – apple strudel – and a delightful blend of coffee and milk reminiscent of a café latte.

They explored the grandeur of the Gothic St Stephen's Cathedral, where Donna silently expressed her gratitude to God for their blessings and offered prayers for Ricky and Lucy's relationship. Later that evening, they were captivated by the splendid acoustics of the Baroque St Anne's Church, enjoying pieces by Mozart, Schubert, and Beethoven. The next day, their experience was enriched by a concert from the Vienna Philharmonic Orchestra, adding a memorable touch to their stay in Vienna.

On the last day, they visited the nearby Habsburg Palace. Tom, a history enthusiast, excitedly informed Donna that this palace was the residence of the Habsburg emperors and was among the world's largest palace complexes.

As their palace tour neared, they ascended a staircase to one of the imperial apartments. Spacious and grand, it boasted large windows and elegant curtains embroidered with gold. It was set against walls adorned with Flemish art and gilded mouldings, all aglow under the brilliant light of baroque crystal chandeliers. The grand ballroom lay deserted, a silent expanse devoid of tourists. Overcome with awe, Tom and Donna exchanged a glance, wordlessly extended their arms, and began to waltz. They danced to the silent strains of Johann Strauss's 'The Blue Danube,' their movements elegantly smooth as they glided over the polished parquet. Smiles blossomed into ecstatic joy as they transitioned from the waltz's stately opening to the spirited whirl of the Viennese waltz, spinning faster and faster as if swept into the opulent world of nineteenth-century Vienna.

Once they finished dancing, they headed back to the Old Town's Town Hall Square, Rathausplatz, to relax and enjoy themselves in the late afternoon. Their indulgence in local specialties, beer, and music persisted. The square was filled with various colourful kiosks and food stalls representing different European countries.

Vendors in traditional clothing sold their distinctive products, while some entertained with singing and dancing. A massive movie screen adorned the town hall's facade, with garden chairs neatly arrayed before it. Holding bratwurst in buns and large beer glasses, they found front seats and prepared to enjoy the show.

As dusk fell over the square, the screen illuminated, featuring Herbert von Karajan's most memorable performances: the distinguished Austrian conductor and principal conductor of the Berlin Philharmonic Orchestra. The audience hushed as Karajan conducted classical pieces by Vivaldi Four Seasons, Bach's Badinerie, Mozart's Menuetto, and Tchaikovsky's Swan Lake and The Nutcracker.

With Tom beside her, Donna delighted in the harmonious melodies. As her favourite classical piece, Albinoni/Giazotto's Adagio, began to play, the town hall's facade sparkled with decorative lights, creating an illusion of merging seamlessly with the stars above. Donna closed her eyes, letting the blissful sounds of the violins resonate with her innermost being.

The evening music extravaganza ended with Strauss's famous waltz, 'Blauen Danau'. The sound engulfed the enormous square and the crowd erupted, stamping their feet and clapping with the waltz's rhythm. Some couples started dancing among the tables, swirling around as if dancing in the famous castle. It was a truly magical evening.

They chose to take a bus tour to Venice via picture-perfect scenery through the Austrian Alps and green pastoral lands in full summer bloom. Tom and Donna arrived in Venice in the early afternoon and strolled hand-in-hand through the streets, pausing at Piazza San Marco for cappuccinos and gelatos. Seeking refuge from the afternoon sun, they found solace in the shaded gardens of a restaurant, refreshed by the breeze of fans. As they indulged in pizza, fried calamari, and seafood risotto, the sound of church bells filled the air, affirming their presence in the fabled land of angels.

After a scrumptious lunch, they walked along the tiny, cobbled streets. Tom and Donna found a shop selling colourful Pagliacci clowns, moulded from Murano glass. Tom became animated and curious about why Donna was not buying her favourite souvenirs. "Would you like me to purchase one of these clowns for you? Murano glass is renowned worldwide," Tom inquired.

Donna hesitated, looking at other miniature angel statuettes, leaving Tom confused. She then caressed his face tenderly.

Seeing his wife smile again brought great joy to him.

"Darling, since Ricky's life has transformed, the once unhappy void in my heart has healed. I've decided to collect angels, not clowns. The Pagliacci clown's smile is a mask to hide his sorrow and pain. I no longer need Pagliacci's fake laughter to hide my tears."

Donna knew that her journey to recovery lay ahead, and she was determined to keep smiling forever. She brought a selection of charming Murano angels and miniature figurines. But when a tiny smiling clown caught her eye, she couldn't help but buy it for its cuteness.

Tom and Donna relished their romantic evening gondola ride. The breeze ruffled their hair, and the Venice lights reflecting in the canals made it a perfect evening.

Time was a valuable commodity, so even though they could have stayed in Venice longer, they had much more to explore and experience. Tom and Donna boarded the fast hovercraft from Venice, and in less than an hour, they arrived in Opatija: Donna's hometown and her favourite spot in Croatia.

During a week's stay in Opatija, Donna rekindled some of the happy memories of her teenage years. The tourist season was in full swing, and the city buzzed with life. Opatija became the centre of Croatian tourism, where the rich and famous docked their yachts. People walked along the promenade, enchanted by views of the stunning Adriatic coast.

Tom and Donna chose to stay at the Hotel Kvarner. During her youthful school days, Donna worked in that hotel, serving rich and famous movie stars. This old hotel, perched on the

Adriatic Sea's edge, was an idyllic, sophisticated spot often chosen to produce Italian films in which Donna and her fellow students had once been extras. The grand ballroom, adorned with sparkling crystal chandeliers, was known as the Crystal Room and annually hosted a major music festival.

Donna felt like pinching herself, not believing that now she found herself as one of these wealthy tourists that she used to envy. As was his custom, Tom ordered a seafood platter and purchased the best regional wine. The couple wined and danced under the stars late into the night.

For Donna, however, that visit home was bittersweet. With her father's passing, she felt she had nothing left there. Andrija died a bitter and unfulfilled man, leaving his Veritas Vineyard in ruins when his only son Emil was killed in mysterious circumstances. Pirates attacked foreign ships near the Cape of Good Hope, and many sailors fell, swallowed by the sea. Emil was among those unfortunate souls, and his body was never recovered. In the wake of this tragedy, his mother, Zorka, died of a broken heart, followed shortly by Andrija's death. The house now belonged to distant unknown relatives and the glorious cherry tree had been cut down severing all her cherished memories.

Paying tribute to Tom's parents involved a swift train journey to Zagreb to light candles and lay fresh flowers at their graves. Tom's mother had passed away unexpectedly. Overwhelmed by her second husband's betrayal, alcoholism, and gambling, she met a sorrowful end. Deeply affected, Dinka succumbed to complications from self-inflicted wounds in the hospital. She was interred next to her first husband, Ivan, Tom's father, and her one true love.

After Dinka's death, her second husband, Vlado, liquidated their apartment to clear his gambling debts. A year later, Vlado died from alcohol poisoning.

Regrettably, animosity persisted among Tom's family members throughout their lives, leaving numerous disputes unsettled. Tom's siblings harboured lingering bitterness due to their parent's divorce. This division of loyalties caused the unresolved issues to deepen. As time passed, geographical separation and hectic lifestyles made the siblings estranged.

During her visit to Croatia, Donna had a brief layover in her village, where she was born. Sadly, her beloved Aunt Pavica had passed away, leaving the common courtyard quiet and silent. Standing under the old, dried fig tree, Donna looked up at the branches; no sweet figs hung there, and the dove's nest was no longer visible. She was pleased her sister Anka had returned to the family house and made modest improvements and converted the Tower to a fashionable bed & breakfast; sister Vera still lived on a nearby island.

℣

While in Rtina, Donna encountered many relatives previously unknown to her, including Anka, the backbone of the family; she listened to their stories and realised that nothing much had changed since her mother's tragic death. Smiljana faced discrimination because of her religious background, and the perpetuating cycle of religious flames of animosity between Catholic Croats and Orthodox Serbs still caused distress for many mixed marriages. This persistent hatred kept brewing, resulting in the inevitable outcome when the civil war erupted between the Serbs and Croats in 1990.

That reignited the bitter fight that festered for centuries. This conflict had a devastating impact on many families who lost their loved ones in that war. Donna's beloved Aunty Pavica lost her grandson; her uncle Mirko's son became a victim of a landmine. Donna's maternal aunty grieved the loss of her only son who fought for the Serbian side. Many of Donna's school friends from Serbs, Croats and Muslims died defending their religious and cultural rights. Countless lives were lost, leaving many young men to content with enduring life-long physical and psychological scars.

Although the civil war ended in 1995 with the Dayton Agreement, the deep-seated animosity continued into the new generation. Donna pondered that even today, in their modern world, people remained divided by religious beliefs. She questioned when humanity would acknowledge that war was not a solution. Indeed, there had to be a more constructive way to resolve territorial, cultural, or religious conflicts.

Thankfully, she felt blessed by fate's intervention and was grateful that her guardian angels led her to move Down Under, where she truly belonged. Australia, a multicultural nation where people from diverse cultural and religious backgrounds coexisted peacefully, was indeed a lucky country and one of the safest places on Earth.

✿

Donna and Tom looked forward to reuniting with their Australian friends in Split, which allowed them to showcase ancient references to Diocletian's Palace from the Roman Empire era. Their travels took them to a national park and through several untouched villages, where time seemed to stand still. They journeyed along rivers and were captivated by the breathtaking scenery. Immersing in local traditions, they savoured village delicacies, wines, and homemade liqueurs made from walnuts and pears. As they bid farewell to their Australian friends, Tom shared their plans to purchase an apartment on the island of Brac, and invited their friends to visit. When Donna retired, they would divide their time between Australia and Croatia.

A layover in Dubrovnik reignited Tom's desire to buy a yacht, the allure of navigating the Adriatic coast of Croatia with its thousand islands, mooring in small villages around the coast with plentiful sunshine still strong. Croatia provided perfect sailing conditions in the summer, owing to its breathtaking coastline, clear waters, tranquil, pristine beaches, and private yacht moorings. Owning a yacht would be the ultimate indulgence.

Tom's smile broadened with the realisation. However, getting a skipper's licence was the first step. Donna's expression was restrained with triumph. "Don't fret, darling. I've got everything under control. I'll enrol you in the Recreational Skippers Ticket course at Hillary's Boat Harbour," she declared, her voice brimming with excitement.

ʘ

As their Croatian journey concluded, Tom and Donna savoured a delightful dinner atop an ancient castle, where the view beneath sparkled with myriad lights along the Adriatic coast. Gentle guitar melodies filled the air. Tom drew her near and tenderly kissed her neck, Donna felt the warmth of his chest and gently caressed his silver hair. For a moment, Tom appeared lost in contemplation.

Turning to Donna, he declared, "We've devoted our lives to our careers, and now it's time to relish the rewards. We are truly lucky to have the best of both worlds. We can appreciate the greatest country on earth, and revel in perpetual summer – six months in Australia and six months in Croatia. This is the life I've envisioned for us."

Donna nodded in agreement and gazed across the terrace; on the city's far side, a burst of shimmering colours lit up the skyline. She pointed to the distant lights sparkling in the sky. "Look at the fireworks. Let's go up the stairs for the best view," she suggested.

As the display concluded, Donna turned to face her husband. "Nothing tops the Perth fireworks. Remember when we stayed at the Hyatt and enjoyed the prime views of Riverside Drive? The Australia Day fireworks were spectacular," she reminisced.

"True, but let's keep that our secret," Tom smiled. "We wouldn't want a flood of tourists crowding Perth's shores and spoiling its untouched beauty."

Donna placed her finger on Tom's lips to silence his words. "Let's cherish this moment. I'm overjoyed: all my dreams have been realised, my love. Now, Ricky has his own family; he is happy and content. What more could any mother want for her son? I agree that we've earned the right to enjoy our golden age."

Pleased by her words, Tom embraced her tightly. She felt the heat of his breath as he whispered, "At last, my love, after decades your obsession is finally over. You are mine once more. At last, we are liberated, truly free ..." he said, smiling broadly.

Chapter 28

The Sicilian Connection

Following their Croatian adventure, Tom and Donna embarked on an overnight voyage from Split to Brindisi, Italy, followed by a brief train journey to Rome to begin their reserved Italian/Sicilian tour. Both were fond of Rome, albeit for distinct reasons: Tom was enamoured with its historical richness, while Donna revelled in its lively, carnival atmosphere. Hand in hand, they wandered among the city's ancient ruins and historical landmarks, exchanging kisses and basking in their love.

They meandered without purpose, nearing the city's heart. Arriving at a grand piazza, they noticed a majestic church in the distance. Upon checking the city map, they learnt it was the Basilica di Santa Maria Maggiore.

Venturing inside, they were captivated by the mosaics dating back to the 4th century. Sometime later, Tom leaned in towards Donna and murmured, "In such a place, piety seems almost inevitable."

After exploring the church, Donna wanted to see a priest for confession. Meanwhile, Tom waited outside, growing impatient at an endless wait. When Donna emerged, Tom greeted her with a smile and a playful tease. "Took you forever; must have been quite the confession."

"The church is enormous, and it is easy to get lost inside, with several confessional booths providing services in various languages. I was looking for one booth in English, and guess what? ... The priest I spoke with spoke with an Australian accent, and we started a conversation. Father Stefano came from East Fremantle; we might have been neighbours, and he was acquainted with our local Irish priest. Father Stefano was homesick; he enquired about how the West Coast Eagles were doing. I couldn't offer much insight since my knowledge of football is limited, but we had a pleasant chat." Donna laughed.

"The world seems to get smaller," Tom replied, only half-listening. "So, did you confess your sins?" he wanted to know.

"I confessed I neglected my marriage because of being consumed by Ricky's problems and matchmaking endeavours. Father Stefano promised to keep us all in his prayers, which made me happy."

Tom teased her, grinning. "You're so easy to please, but what penance did the priest give you?"

"Father Stefano said that the wife's first duty is to her husband. I was given a penance of five Hail Marys." Donna smiled.

"Wow, he's my kind of priest. You should take his advice," Tom chuckled, pulling Donna into a tight hug. Seeing the gelato stand across from the church, Donna's face lit up.

"Tom, how about we get some gelato? I can't resist the Tutti Frutti sorbet – it's my favorite."

"Sure, I'd be up for another one. I've already had two while you were chatting with Father Stefano, but when in Rome, do as the Romans do." Tom smiled and took Donna's hand and they walked blissfully down the Spanish Steps before slowly disappearing among the crowd in the piazza.

CB

Two days after arriving in Rome, Tom and Donna joined a guided tour to Sicily. Donna was quick to introduce herself to the other passengers on the bus and joined in with the group's lively atmosphere. The majority of the group consisted of American tourists who were exploring their ancestral roots. Some tourists teased Donna about her foreign accent, the Americans playfully remarking that she couldn't be a true-blue Aussie. However, this didn't deter Donna from advocating for Australia as the world's premier tourist destination.

Seizing the microphone, Donna enthusiastically described Australia's natural wonders to everyone on the bus, and before long, her fellow passengers vowed to put it on their wish list.

Pompeii was their first destination, where Tom immersed himself in his love for Roman history. Their bus journey featured stops at charming villages where they indulged in the local cuisine and wine and tasted the robust regional grappa – a fragrant grape-based brandy and Limoncello, a sweet lemon liqueur. Adding to the joyful atmosphere, the bus driver played lively tarantella music, a traditional genre known for its fast tempo.

After several stops and more Limoncello, back on the bus, Donna started singing the Australian bush ballad "Waltzing Matilda." The other bus passengers, however, began to sing along, mimicking the lyrics and clapping. Only Tom abstained, indifferent to Donna's performance. He preferred to be engrossed in the passing landscape to hide his embarrassment.

The bus tour group crossed the Mediterranean Sea by ferry, heading to Sicily. During the Sicilian tour, they stopped in the wine region to sample local wine and indulge in culinary specialties. One of their first visits was to a picturesque village winery passed down through Sergio's family for generations.

Sergio proudly told the group, "Vino-Rosso is my pride and joy. The older the grapevines, the more resilient and robust they become – just like most of us, we mature with age, just like fine wine."

One tour group member asked, "Why did you plant rose

bushes in front of the vines?"

"The roses play a vital role. Bees gather pollen from these flowers, aiding in pollinating our fruit trees. More importantly, the bees defend grape vines against pests and birds; birds leave the grapevines undisturbed when bees are present. Yet, these fragile roses are deceptive, akin to a beautiful woman, attracting men and bees alike, only to surprise them with a sting." Sergio chuckled, gesturing towards the vineyard. "Come autumn, when the roses are in full bloom, our vineyard transforms into a vibrant tapestry of colours," Sergio added.

Another traveller asked, "What colours do the bees prefer?"

"Bees are attracted to vivid colours, yet they favour the shade of crimson. Our sunflowers are flourishing; their brilliant yellow petals and dark brown centre resembling chocolate are cherished by bees and birds. The sunflowers indicate changes in the weather, turning to follow the sun, capturing that final burst of energy indicating that grapes are ripened for harvesting, culminating in producing great wines," Sergio described.

"Come on, but be careful. In Sicily, bees will sting to protect their territory. It's time to head to the wine cellar and sample some of our honey and finest wines from recent years," Sergio invited, and the travellers followed him into the wine caller.

Following the Vino Rosso tour, many American travellers purchased honey and wine. Frankie, an 85-year-old man from Chicago, slightly tipsy, distinguished himself as mischievous and endearing. He shared a story of his family's emigration to America post-World War II. He fled because his father could not settle a debt with a local Mafioso who had threatened severe retribution.

Frankie longed to visit Alfico, his birthplace, but the village lacked tourist appeal and wasn't part of the tour plan itinerary. Yet, the bus passengers unanimously urged the bus driver for a detour. Rose and Jerry, New Yorkers on a pilgrimage to pay tribute to forebears who left Palermo during the California Gold Rush, proposed pooling tips for the driver to reward the detour.

Alfico, a village nestled among wild terrain, olive groves, verdant fields, and sheep, was a cherished home from Frankie's younger days. The old Trattoria still served El-Forno pizza, baked in a wood-fired oven. The proprietor, Gabriel, offered the travellers a welcome drink. The garden area provided much needed shade under the canopy of grape vines. The cozy Trattoria also offered an assortment of local wines and fruit-based spirits.

After enjoying several glasses of local wine, the tourists gathered around an accordion player and a singer performing traditional Sicilian folk songs. Despite the lyrics being challenging to comprehend, the melody was delightful. The audience tapped their hands and feet in sync with the rhythm. Following the performance, the musicians collected spare change in their hats, with contributions from all.

Frankie, keen to delve into the past, probed Gabriel with questions about the village's history. Gabriel, recognising he had an attentive audience, grew lively as he shared tales of youthful days. Frankie was pleased to serve as a translator; he was fluent in the local Sicilian dialect, which left the Italian-only speakers bemused, unable to comprehend a single word.

Tom and Donna followed Gabriel through the quaint village, its narrow cobblestone streets lined with stone houses featuring Baroque facades. Frankie went to the church to light a candle for his ancestors. Next to the church, in front of the iron-gated entrance to the cemetery, stood a statue of an angel, one hand holding a bowl of water and the other a bowl of birdseed.

Donna stopped, transfixed for a moment. Clutching Tom's hand, she exclaimed, "This is the same village from a picture I saw in Francis's house. It's where her grandparents are buried."

"Don't be silly. Every village we have seen so far in Italy had a statue of angels or saints in front of the church or cemetery." Tom waved a hand, dismissing Donna's silly statement.

But Donna was sure she had seen the photo before. "Tom, I can't believe my eyes. We stopped in this small village to assist Frankie in rediscovering his roots, and here we are at Francis's birthplace. This was unplanned; it must be divine intervention," Donna declared.

Tom laughed. "You must have sunstroke or had too many glasses of grappa."

However, Donna wondered if this coincidence or fate drove them to Alfico. She remembered precisely seeing the same grave inscription in the photo displayed in Francis's house. She dragged Tom by his arm and excitedly cried out.

Tom dismissed the possibility. "You can't be serious."

"Francis showed me some photographs that she kept in her china cabinet. The photos were taken when Francis was eighteen, just before her family's immigration journey on a ship from Naples to Fremantle. In one photo, she stood in front of the church of St Veronica next to the cemetery entrance, where her grandparents are buried. Francis told me the villagers had placed an angel statue at the entrance to keep the church steps free from bird droppings. Ironically, the church steps remained clean, but the statue became a target for the birds. Francis laughed as she showed me the photo of her smiling beside the angel statue adorned with bird droppings.

"Tom, surely that can't be a coincidence. This is St Veronica's church, and the same angel is covered with bird droppings.

"Tom, please take some pictures of me standing in the same spot. Right here on the church steps."

In a swift move, Donna positioned herself beside the angel statue, anticipating Tom's click. Suddenly, a thirsty dove perched on the statue, leaving Donna in awe. Her thoughts wandered to her little dove and how it might have guided her to this village.

Tom remained silent while taking multiple pictures from various angles, yet the dove appeared undisturbed. Tom managed to photograph her against the backdrop of the church.

Upon their return to the pizzeria, Donna asked Gabriel if he could recall Frances. According to Gabriel, Francesca Bevanetti lived in this village, as she was called back then. She had a secret love affair with Alfonzo, the son of a Mafia boss.

"What happened? Can you tell us the story of Francesca and Alfonzo?" Donna asked.

"I remember Francesca. She was very pretty. At that time, I worked as a driver for Don Giovanni Giallombardo, and messing with girls who worked for him was not allowed, but it is best not to talk about the past."

However, Rose pleaded with Gabriel to disclose every detail. With her Italian/Sicilian fluency, she translated things for clarity. Gabriel, emboldened by another glass of wine, started his tale.

"It's a well-known secret among the villagers, but it is best to remain that way," Gabriel warned, yet Rose persisted, eager for the secret disclosures.

"Francesca came from an impoverished family. They resided on a sheep farm on the outskirts of the village. Life was hard back then, but the villagers offered their support. In Alfico, the townsfolk held their leader, Al Capo, a Mafioso boss, Don Giovanni Giallombardo, in high esteem.

"The villagers' traditional way of life gave them a sense of security, albeit one rooted in fear. Most individuals employed by Don Giallombardo – Cosa Nostra – found themselves ensnared in debts that bound them to the Mafia for life.

"Luigi, Francesca's father, refused to accept any favours

from Don Giallombardo. He was afraid that accepting any favours could enslave him and his family in a trap, just like it happened to his brother Fabricio. Luigi promised Don Giallombardo that he would repay his older brother's debt, which was left unpaid when Fabrizio Bevanetti fled to Australia.

"Luigi and Maria were an honest and hardworking couple with two daughters. Their elder daughter, Philomena, was already married and lived in Perugia. His younger daughter, eighteen-year-old Francesca, took on a job as a house-cleaning at Don Giallombardo's residence."

Leaning back in his chair, Gabriel refilled his glass of wine before continuing.

"Francesca was thrilled about an upcoming job opportunity to help her escape the poverty and monotony of her daily life. Her mother, Maria, accompanied her on her first day and warned her daughter not to bring shame to the family name.

"Francesca was handed a large bucket of soapy water and a mop to begin cleaning the downstairs toilets. She continued a monotonous regime of cleaning, washing, and scrubbing. Francesca was captivated by the Giallombardo family's opulence. She was awestruck when they entered two large bedrooms with wooden floors and a luxurious white marble bathroom with twin basins and a double shower.

"Then, one day, as she was on her knees washing the marble floor in the hallway, she unexpectedly felt someone standing above her. She looked up and saw a young man dressed in fashionable clothes smiling at her. Alfonzo, a son of Don-Giallombardo, was instantly smitten by a beautiful peasant girl.

"The next day at work, Francesca arrived with a ribbon in her hair and wore a skin-tight sleeveless blouse that highlighted her curves. Alfonso, handsome in his crisp white trousers and navy-blue linen blazer, followed Francisca to the upper floor bathroom.

"The story goes that she initially resisted him but soon gave in to his advances. Afterwards, she pushed him away and threatened to tell his mother about his inappropriate behaviour.

"These little games continued for another week until Francisca let Alfonzo fondle her breasts and kiss her. When it happened, she held Alfonso close to her body for a long time. They knew it was so wrong, but it just felt so right. That is what love does to you." Gabriel smiled.

"I chauffeured Francesca and Alfonzo in secret. In the village, gossip among women swirled as young men sought romantic liaisons with village girls. Hence, they began meeting in the vineyards in the late afternoon, seeking secluded spots away from prying eyes. Francesca's beauty and sex appeal captivated him, and Alfonzo fell deeply in love for the first time. Francisca was in love with Alfonzo and wished to indulge in the opulent lifestyle, which was like scenes she'd only encountered in films. Nothing else mattered to her. Having never witnessed such affluence cemented Francesca's resolve and clarity about what she aspired to achieve."

He heaved a deep sigh then went on. "Their mutual desire could no longer be contained, and the lovers decided to reveal their relationship to the world. The people in the village were surprised when they saw Francisca and Alfonso joyriding in his father's car. The two of them were brimming with joy, their speech animated and overflowing with affection for one another. It was clear to all the villagers that these young lovers were deeply in love. Older village members shook their heads, not disapprovingly, but in surprise. They knew that such a union would never be allowed by either Signora or Don-Giallombardo. Marriage was definitely out of the question."

"When Don Giallombardo heard of the scandal, he called his son into his office and gave him a good scolding. 'Our family comes first!' he told him angrily. 'What is expected of you is to marry a nice girl from a prominent business family in Palermo, not a peasant floozy? If you intend to take over the family business, you must learn not to draw attention to yourself because, in this family's business, you must learn to be a shadow, not the spotlight.'

"Alfonso only cringed and looked at his mother for help, but the support wasn't forthcoming because, this time, his mother was in total agreement with her husband. That was the end.

"Upon hearing about Francesca's relationship with Alfonzo, her father was appalled and promptly confronted her. He firmly opposed the idea of his daughter marrying the son of a Mafioso, regardless of any romantic feelings involved.

"When Don Giallombardo disapproved of his son Alfonso's dealings with Francesca, he sought a favour that Luigi couldn't refuse – to defy a request from the Cosa Nostra's capo was unthinkable. Don Giallombardo vowed to clear the Fabrizio debt forever, but in exchange, Luigi and his family had to move and never return. Grasping the situation's severity, Luigi saw no alternative but to agree.

"The Bevanetti family's esteemed reputation in the village was Luigi's most valued treasure. He rebuked his daughter, declaring, 'Any dog will chase a tail-wagging bitch', blaming and cursing her for bringing shame and ruining the family's reputation. Luigi was determined to preserve the family's honour and to escape the family scandal, the Bevanetti family moved to Australia.

"Francesca was heartbroken. Not only had she lost the person she loved, but her dreams of a bright future had also sunk into the abyss of broken hopes and dreams. She blamed her parents for ruining her relationship with Alfonzo, yet her father remained unmoved."

Gabriel mentioned that the Bevanetti family was soon forgotten. He himself continued in Don Giallombardo's service until the Mafioso boss moved his family to Palermo. Gabriel put his finger on his lips, telling them he has so many more secrets, but he must take them to his grave.

The tour bus driver arrived and informed the passengers that they had spent too much time in the small village, which he deemed insignificant. He honked the horn impatiently, urging everyone to hurry. The tour was now seriously behind schedule. To make up for lost time, they would have to skip the following two villages, but all of the passengers on the bus seemed okay with that. Alfico was Frankie's ancestral village, and Frankie's happy face was every bit worth it.

Tom and Donna were the last to board the waiting bus. In next to no time, they were on the road again, everyone tired and tipsy from all the Limoncello, and the voices in the bus gradually subsided.

Soon, the engine's monotonous sound was all that remained. Tom rested his sleepy eyes on a lovely sunset, but Donna couldn't relax; her mind swelled with Francesca's sorrowful story. Donna remembered Francis telling her a brief story about her life before she migrated to Australia.

Francesca had told her that her father had immigrated to Western Australia where his brother Fabrizio owned a three-hectare vegetable market garden in Spearwood, near Fremantle. It was a family business, and Luigi and his family worked on the farm, too.

For Francisca, the new life bore no solace for her heartache. She treasured a single photograph of herself and Alfonzo, arms entwined, at the church's entrance by the Angel statue, a haven for famished and parched birds.

One year after settling in Australia, Francesca married Giuseppe, an arranged agreement between two Sicilian families. They wed and moved to Perth's northern suburbs of Wanneroo, where Giuseppe's family ran a modest vegetable garden. Cultivating lettuce, tomatoes, potatoes, and herbs was demanding labour. Over the next decade, Francisca bore three children. Giuseppe yearned for a son, yet Francesca delivered another girl, Luciana, affectionately nicknamed Lucy.

Francesca never desired the dual role of motherhood and farm work. She deeply regretted missing the opportunity to marry Alfonzo and resented her parents for spoiling her chance to wed a wealthy man. She also harboured resentment towards Giuseppe for not providing the wealth she believed she had been deprived of. The marriage was not a happy union, and when her girls finished school, Francesca and Giuseppe divorced. A few years later, she married Ken.

Tom's gentle voice brought the curtain up on Donna's musing. "Darling, we're almost at our next destination. Have you been dozing?"

"Yes, a little. It was so dreamlike," Donna said, returning to the present moment.

"I couldn't stop thinking about Francis."

Tom showed his indifference by shrugging. He believed that Francis hadn't changed since her younger days, and she still envied people with wealth. Despite agreeing to participate in a matchmaking deal for her daughter to meet Ricky, Tom warned Donna not to be fooled because Francis was captivated by the allure of wealth.

"Oh, Tom, stop being so negative. Francis had so much misfortune in her life."

Cynically, Tom responded, "Yeah, after our trip to Sicily, I can understand why Francis and Lucy don't get along. All this talk about the Sicilian vendetta of keeping secrets and never forgetting or forgiving until death is crazy. I wonder if Lucy would have agreed to meet Ricky if he were as poor as a church mouse," Tom considered.

"Oh, Tom, don't spoil this moment. Love keeps the world

spinning around. Ricky and Lucy seemed blissfully happy together.”

“Oh, yeah? On what planet do you live? Don’t tell me you haven’t told Francis a few white lies so Lucy and Ricky could meet.” Tom smirked.

“Ricky has nothing to offer, so I told Francis that Ricky owned his house. That was what sealed the matchmaking deal.”

“Okay, that proves my point. I rest my case. Lucy learned from Francis that seeing the dollar signs is hard to resist. Remember the saying, ‘The apple doesn’t fall far from the tree’. Lucy and her mother are alike. You wait and see when Lucy finds out Ricky has nothing to offer. The shit will hit the fan,” Tom said firmly.

“You must have faith. Love is blind. You had no money when I met you, but I fell in love with you anyway,” Donna said, smiling.

“Oh, please stop dreaming; this is some crazy romantic nonsense. Not all love is the same. Our love is unique like a chiselled piece of iron turned into steel. It has helped us navigate difficult times that only a few could endure and survive,” Tom said with conviction in his voice.

“But we must have hope. Right now, things look great. Lucy told me she has found her soul mate, and Emma completed the family dream, which is a blessing for Ricky. We must appreciate the present moment; that’s why it is called a present,” Donna reminded her husband.

Tom smiled. “What would I do without your positive thinking?”

Donna turned around and squeezed his hand to move him away from his negative thoughts. “Tom, dear, I believe God has answered my prayers.”

“Well, my dear, let us hope that the God you cherish so much has heard your words,” Tom concluded.

Chapter 29

Paper Rings

Tom and Donna concluded their tour of Sicily, said goodbye to their American companions, and looked forward to some quality time together. They were excited to spend five days discovering the romantic allure of Paris before their return flight to Australia.

They arrived at the Hotel Napoleon near the Arc de Triomphe, a monument commemorating Napoleon's victories. They made pit stops at local patisseries to indulge in tasty croissants and unwind at cafes. They explored renowned tourist attractions the following day, including the Army Museum, Napoleon's Tomb at the Esplanade des Invalides, the Eiffel Tower, and the Louvre.

On the last day of their holiday, Tom and Donna enjoyed wine with cassis liqueur aboard a barge anchored on the River Seine. Visiting Notre Dame Cathedral was of paramount importance. Donna fondly recalled the Phantom of the Opera production they had recently seen, a love story in which a masked man who played the organ held Christine captive until she returned his affections.

Tom and Donna strolled by the River Seine, going to Notre Dame, Quasimodo's ancient cathedral. Donna capered down the path in high spirits, channelling the alluring Esmeralda, beckoning Tom. "Come, Quasimodo, my love. Escort me to your bell tower." Tom, embracing the role, hobbled along, mimicking the hunchback, teasing her, "Where's your goat? Esmeralda is seldom seen without her goat." Their laughter mingled in the air, echoing the joy of their shared jest.

They stopped fooling around as they made their way to the Notre Dame. In line at the main entrance, Tom asked Donna if she wanted to hear a story about Notre Dame.

Smiling, Donna replied, "I bet it's got something to do with your hero, Napoleon."

A grin spread across Tom's face. "I'll tell you the fascinating story of how Josephine outsmarted Napoleon at his coronation."

Donna stopped and flashed a cheerful smile at Tom. "Hmm, this could potentially be intriguing."

Despite Donna's teasing, Tom was entirely in tune with historical facts. He continued eagerly, "Napoleon and Josephine were only married in a civil ceremony. When Napoleon brought Pope Pius VII to Paris for his coronation, Josephine told the Pope that they were not married before God, living in sin because she and Napoleon never had a church wedding. That unwarranted disclosure made Napoleon furious.

"He realised Josephine had outsmarted him because, to be crowned Emperor; he must first make their marriage legitimate in the eyes of the Catholic Church. They were married in the Cathedral of Notre Dame de Paris at the Pope's insistence in December 1804. Napoleon crowned himself at his coronation ceremony the following day, and Pope Pius VII consecrated the act. Then Napoleon, now the Emperor, performed Josephine's coronation by putting the crown on Josephine's head and proclaiming her Empress.

Despite her desire to moderate Tom's meticulous attention to historical details, Donna couldn't resist laughing, yet she felt compelled to comment.

"Resourceful Josephine – that's my kind of woman. If Napoleon had listened to his wife, he would have never invaded Russia where most of his army froze to death. Napoleon's ego was too large to take advice from a woman's practical wisdom. Unfortunately, men often chose war over love; Napoleon lost both the war and Josephine. I think Napoleon was neither brilliant nor much of a hero."

Tom stayed quiet, not uttering another word.

Donna had bought two entrance tickets. As they entered, the magnificent French Gothic architecture left them in awe. While Tom was engrossed in examining the artistry, from the stone carvings to the detailed mosaic work, Donna became restless. She reminisced about Tom's vow to wed her at Notre Dame, which Tom promised her in Coober Pedy beneath the enchanting stars. Subconsciously, she started to fidget with the tickets in her pocket, inadvertently folding them into the shape of two tiny rings.

Then, a brilliant idea dawned on her. Equally resourceful and intelligent as Josephine, she chose this moment to affirm her marriage to Tom in the Catholic Church by renewing their vows at Notre Dame today, witnessed by a priest.

Having decided that, Donna stealthily distanced herself from Tom to find a priest. Her eyes swept over the expansive cathedral until she noticed a solitary priest in a diminutive side chapel, seemingly at the end of his prayers, still beside the altar. Hastily, Donna returned to retrieve Tom, who was engrossed in the cathedral's stained-glass windows, particularly one from the 13th century. Seizing the moment, she clutched his arm and murmured, "Tom, there's something you must see. Hurry ... it's astonishing."

Surprised, Tom followed her into the small side chapel where the priest was sitting in quiet meditation. As Tom and Donna materialised abruptly before him, the priest, caught off guard, was unaware of what was happening around him. Donna took the initiative and politely made a request.

"Father, our marriage was not consecrated in the Church. We wish to transform our civil union into a sacramental one by renewing our vows. Could you assist us with this, Father?" Donna's hands clasped in pleading.

The priest listened politely, looking at them, speechless and puzzled. Since he didn't speak English, Donna rephrased her request in Italian.

"Father, please, can you give us the Nuptial Blessing?" Donna pleaded again.

An uncomfortable silence quickly ensued, but Donna was undeterred. She faced Tom and instructed, "Repeat after me: I celebrate my love for you," to which Tom immediately complied. In a rush, yet with precision, Donna retrieved the paper rings from her pocket, handing one to Tom as she whispered, "Let's exchange rings."

With Tom's response lagging, Donna promptly seized his left hand and slid her paper ring onto his ring finger. In a fluid motion, she extended her hand for Tom to place his paper ring on her finger, which he did. Then Donna made the sign of the cross, gently prompting Tom with her elbow to follow suit, and he mirrored the gesture.

Suddenly, the priest displayed understanding. He rose from his chair, took two steps forward, and blessed Tom and Donna with dignity, invoking divine grace. With smiles, Donna expressed her gratitude to the priest and, taking Tom's hand, they left the small chapel. A few steps down the cathedral's aisle, Donna paused and turned to face Tom, their hands still clasped.

"Darling, your promise to marry me at Notre Dame has finally been fulfilled. We are now joined in matrimony, just like Napoleon and Josephine – well, in a manner of speaking, though not with the same grandeur," Donna said, glowing with happiness as Tom held her tenderly and kissed his bride.

Their afternoon unfolded with a stroll along the Seine River, where they immersed themselves in the cultural and historical Paris sites lining its banks. As evening fell, Tom and Donna, basking in their 'newlywed' bliss, dined at the Eiffel Tower's Le Jules Verne restaurant, revelling in the stunning city lights.

❧

The following morning, it was time to depart. While packing and sorting out all the shopping Donna had bought, she happily pointed at her packages.

"Tom, look what I bought: lovely gold earrings and a matching bracelet for Lucy; for Emma, I found trendy clothes, sneakers, and a T-shirt for Ricky. I can't wait to give them their presents." Donna smiled.

Before long, they arrived at Charles de Gaulle Airport. "I'm overjoyed that we're finally returning to Australia. I feel homesick and eager to reunite with Ricky and Lucy. I hope they've resolved their early issues during our absence. I'm confident that everything will be alright. After all, love is all they need," Donna expressed.

Tom embraced her as they cleared security and settled in the business lounge with a glass of champagne and light refreshments.

"Let's wait to celebrate. When we get home, things may not be as you want." Tom wanted to continue but was interrupted by an announcement over the intercom.

When the announcement came that passengers for Perth were ready for boarding, Donna jumped up, but Tom pulled her back.

"What's the hurry, darling? Give me a few more moments to savour my champagne in peace. Let's relax; we can let the crowd pass. Entering last is the true luxury of flying in style," Tom remarked, grinning.

Chapter 30

Lucy's Grave Liaison with Mr Pot

After their extended holiday, Donna and Tom resumed their busy lives. Donna had to deal with a backlog of administrative work at her workplace while Tom was occupied with caring for his beloved roses and tending to the gardens. On weekends, they would catch up with friends, attend dinners or barbeques, enjoy wine and dine at the Fremantle cappuccino strip, and attend theatre performances and concerts. They also enjoyed taking trips to Rockingham and Mandurah for some seaside fun and casual picnics on the beach.

Tom and Donna were thrilled to see Ricky and Lucy as a happy couple. Emma had become a part of their instant family; she settled well into school, and their family life seemed peaceful and contented.

Tom and Donna respected Ricky and Lucy's need for privacy and space to nurture their relationship. They occasionally invited the couple over for dinner or barbecues. During these gatherings, Ricky and Lucy exhibited a solid devotion to each other as if they were still in the honeymoon phase of their relationship.

Donna welcomed Lucy and Emma with open arms and they soon became good friends.

Lucy confided in Donna that she separated from Emma's father and moved to Fremantle to escape the violent relationship. She had been single for eight years, renting a dismal duplex and gradually isolating herself from everyone. However, Lucy's life changed on her 34th birthday when her mother visited her, bringing her chocolates and flowers. Lucy's relationship with her mother had always been volatile, but when she offered peace and wished to reconcile, Lucy agreed to have a fresh start.

Her mother had encouraged her to give another relationship a chance; she had shown her Ricky's photo and Lucy agreed. Francis had emphasised that Ricky came from an affluent family with old-fashioned moral values.

They had developed a strong friendship, which eventually blossomed into love. Lucy was thrilled to have found a partner who truly understood and loved her for who she was, and Ricky became a positive role model and stepfather and felt grateful to have an instant family. Together, they found joy and happiness.

Although Lucy spent most of her time at Ricky's house with her daughter Emma, she continued paying rent for her small duplex to maintain a sense of security. But Ricky gave her space; he did not rush her to make an uncomfortable decision.

Every second fortnight weekend when Emma stayed at her father's farm, they spent time on the beach, happily playing among the waves. Before going home, they would order fish and chips and drink a few beers. They would walk home from the beach, holding hands, in love with each other and without a care in the world.

ʘʀ

At home, Ricky's loud snoring often kept Lucy from falling asleep, so she would sometimes go to the spare room to sleep. One night, after having a few extra drinks, Lucy lay in bed motionless, her mind flooded with memories that she tried to forget, but couldn't.

Lucy remembered her turbulent teenage years as if it was yesterday. Her mother had a quick temper and would often throw cups or plates at her husband during her fits of anger. This created a volatile environment that isolated the children, causing them frequently to hide in their rooms. Francis and Giuseppe eventually divorced.

After completing school, Lucy's two oldest sisters moved out and married. Lucy, the youngest daughter, still in high school, had no option but to stay with her mother. She struggled to make friends at school, and she felt insignificant. To cope with her loneliness and to fill her emotional void, she resorted to overeating, which only made her feel worse.

When her father Giuseppe remarried and had two more daughters, Frances' resentment towards him prevented her daughters from ever encountering their two half-siblings. Adhering to the old Sicilian tradition, never to forget or forgive, Francis's animosity was etched in stone forever. In an act of defiance, she married a much younger man. When Ken, in his drunken state, entered Lucy's room, she complained to her mother, but her grievances were ignored.

When Lucy turned eighteen, she moved out of her mother's place and started smoking pot with her first teenage boyfriend. When she couldn't get any weed, she replaced one boyfriend with another. Soon, pot became her best friend and her only love. She lovingly referred to it as 'Mr Pot'.

Lucy developed a dependency on cannabis, which she relied on to maintain her mental well-being. This led to her losing interest in forming deep and meaningful relationships. Eventually, her only source of love and desire, Mr Pot, left her because she could no longer afford to purchase his affection.

Lucy's life remained in the doldrums; she isolated herself from everybody until someone knocked on her front door. An old friend from work invited Lucy to her birthday party on the weekend. Before the party, Lucy went to the hairdresser, spent hours applying makeup, and chose a sexy long black dress that made her feel womanly. She looked and felt sexy again and wanted desperately to make a good impression. Arriving at the party, Lucy noticed the familiar musky scent of marijuana in the air. She moved around the crowd, following the sweet smell of cannabis, until she came across a man sitting alone, smoking weed. The smell of the smoke drifted towards her and drew her closer to him.

Lucy realised that by meeting that stranger, she would be reunited with her dear friend, Mr Pot.

"Hi, I'm Lucy. Can I sit here?" she asked.

"Of course you can. By the way, I'm Johnny." His face broke into a welcoming smile. He looked rugged, with a sunburned face, and was dressed in biker leather boots and a leather jacket with a Harley Davidson emblem. His long hair was tied into a ponytail, and he had a dark beard with a few grey streaks, making him look even more attractive.

Lucy drew closer to him and was instantly overwhelmed by the scent of cannabis. Johnny couldn't resist Lucy's imploring eyes and offered her a joint. She instantly knew that Johnny was her type. She would never lose Mr Pot again. Ignoring the rest of the party, they spent the rest of the evening together and left holding hands.

Johnny fell in love with Lucy at first sight. He was captivated by her beautiful dark hair that rested on her shoulders, piercing dark eyes, and curvy figure. Her radiant smile, charm, and good looks mesmerised him. Within a few weeks, Lucy had moved into Johnny's rented home. Considering Johnny's infatuation, Lucy was smitten with him too. Falling in love with Johnny was easy; she knew she would always be around Mr Pot, which was reassuring.

Johnny was twelve years older and worried the age gap might come between them, but it didn't. As long as he came home with Mr Pot, Lucy was happy.

Johnny lived in the city and worked as a motorbike mechanic. Once a month, he drove to visit his parents' farm in Coolup and spent the weekend with his boys. Sometimes, he would take Lucy for a ride on his Harley-Davidson to his parents' farm. It always made her feel alive – a mix of joy, fear, and freedom.

Johnny was known for his ability to repair and restore old motorbikes. He primarily worked at a bike shop that catered to the local bikie gang members, so he was well-connected, and there was never any shortage of cannabis to purchase. Johnny took great pride in introducing Lucy to his friends and bragged about how lucky he was to find such a beautiful girl. Some of his friends were envious and didn't hesitate to express it.

Most weekends, after the evening meal, they enjoyed listening to music and smoking a few joints together, which often led to lovemaking. Relaxing after their blissful union, Johnny once said with a half-scornful smile, "I think you love Mr Pot more than me." But Lucy smiled and wrapped her hands around him and said in a husky, sexy voice, "I love you both the same."

When Johnny brought some marijuana seeds and planted them in their backyard, she was overjoyed. She nurtured the garden as if it were her baby. She watered the seeds daily and waited impatiently for Mr Pot's first shoots to grow into a mature plant. For Lucy, mornings were the best part of the day; they were so peaceful. She would sit in the garden for hours, sipping her coffee, smoking, meditating, and talking to the plants. "Hurry, Mr Pot, you silly dope, why can't you grow faster."

Johnny had work commitments and schedules to keep so he couldn't afford to be stoned during the week. However, he enjoyed smoking pot with Lucy on weekends, but Lucy's appetite for cannabis grew stronger and became insatiable. She wanted to smoke every day. When Johnny came home without weed, she would rage and throw household items and scream abuse and insults at him.

"Next time, if you come home without Mr Pot, you won't find me home," she'd yell.

Johnny loved Lucy and wanted her to be happy, so he kept supplying her. She couldn't function without it. Even though it threatened their relationship, Lucy was adamant that Mr Pot was there to stay or it was all over between them.

After two years together, they discussed starting a family. Johnny wanted to settle and move into his parents' farmhouse; he wanted to get married and have a home so his boys could come and visit them on the farm, and they would be one happy family. That was Johnny's only dream.

Then, one beautiful morning, when Lucy nervously announced, "I'm pregnant," Johnny leapt with joy. Seeing him so happy, Lucy suggested, "Let's celebrate this special occasion with a joint."

"No, Lucy! You've got to stop smoking weed while you're pregnant; this is not good for the baby."

Lucy felt overwhelmed and distressed at the lack of marijuana. She'd spend her whole day in bed, depressed and miserable.

"Please bring me some weed, Johnny. Mr Pot eases my morning sickness," she implored, her voice escalating into a yell before she succumbed to tearful sobbing.

Eventually, Johnny gave in, and with Mr Pot back in her life, Lucy's mood improved dramatically, and she retreated into her spaced-out world once more.

The day after the new millennium, they welcomed their baby daughter, Emma. Lucy's only regret was that her beloved father, Giuseppe, passed away a few months before Emma was born.

The new parents quickly learned that having a child was a big life-changer. Lucy smoked every day. Mr Pot kept her calm. Once a month, they would drive a few hours south to his parents' farm and enjoy family time.

Johnny's boys enjoyed playing with baby Emma, and his parents, Lynn and Ian, enjoyed having Lucy around. She was polite and seemed happy and contented. Johnny's parents were pleased with their son's choice of a lovely partner, who bore him a beautiful daughter.

Upon his return to the city, Johnny imagined a farm surrounded by trees, gardens, and animals grazing in the paddocks as a serene sanctuary for Lucy and the perfect environment to raise their daughter. He saw this idyllic setting as the ultimate lure for her to move to the farm. Eagerly, Johnny shared his vision with Lucy. However, Lucy declared that the rural lifestyle did not suit her.

While in the city, though, Lucy struggled with the exhausting routine of household chores and caring for her baby. She was all alone and overwhelmed. Johnny worked long hours, and they never went anywhere. Most weekends, they went to the farm; his father was sick and his mother needed help with farm duties.

Lucy hated the farm and preferred to stay home. When Johnny came home from work, he often found Lucy in bed, craving her cannabis relief. Meanwhile, little Emma spent the day neglected in her bassinet, distressed, unchanged and hungry. Reluctantly, Johnny began to supply Lucy with marijuana again, hoping it would soothe her depression.

When Johnny was away on the farm, helping his parents, if Lucy ran out of cannabis, she ended up drinking Jack Daniels and gorging herself on takeaway foods. She gained weight. Looking at herself in the mirror, she saw a stranger staring back, triggering feelings of self-hatred and negativity. That was when she started cutting herself.

One day, Johnny caught Lucy puffing marijuana smoke close to Emma. Beside himself with worry and despair, he threatened Lucy that he would take Emma to his parents' farm permanently. Lucy retaliated, threatening Johnny that she would call the Tax Department and report him for not paying his taxes. She went ballistic, shouting, yelling, and screaming, demanding that he bring her marihuana.

"Okay, I'll get your weed," Johnny said, trying to quieten her down. He didn't want the neighbours to call the police for domestic violence.

After Lucy's emotional outburst, she informed Johnny that her mother was coming to meet her granddaughter and stay for a few days. Although Johnny disliked Frances and called her 'Spitting Cobra', giving Francis a chance to bond with her granddaughter would help Lucy too. He decided not to hang around and drove down south to the farm. That evening, when Johnny left, Emma was already asleep. Lucy sat in the kitchen, desperate, fighting her inner demons. She felt imprisoned; she drank half a bottle of Jack Daniels and Coke and got drunk. She stumbled to her bedroom, tripped on a loose carpet, and hit her head on the corner of the bed. Numb to self-inflicted pain, she barely flinched, took a sleeping pill, and fell asleep as morning approached.

The following day, Lucy woke when Francis rang the bell. She had a throbbing headache and walked half-asleep to the kitchen for coffee. Suddenly, Francis screamed in panic. "What happened to your face?"

"I tripped over some clothes on the floor," Lucy said casually; no big deal.

"You are lying to me. That crazy Johnny did this to you. We have to report this to the police." Francis was beside herself with anger. "Where is that bastard?" she wanted to know.

"He drove down south to his parents' place to cool down. Johnny threatened to take Emma to his parents' farm, but I wouldn't let him."

Francis immediately started packing Emma's clothes into the suitcase.

"What are you doing, Mum?" Lucy asked, surprised.

"We need to leave this place before Johnny returns. His parents are rich. If they get involved, you will lose Emma. I can help you take care of her," Francis said, firmly grabbing Lucy's hand and leading her to a sofa.

"Now listen to me, Lucy! We have to outsmart that stupid boyfriend of yours. First, we must get a temporary restraining order against him. We have to say Johnny did this to your face. This bastard would've probably done it, anyway," Francis said firmly. She was in charge of the whole situation. She held Johnny responsible for Lucy's reliance on drugs. Francis was adamant that when Johnny returned, he would not find them at home.

Lucy simply nodded, unable to talk or resist her mother. A few hours later, two social workers knocked on the door. They carefully studied Lucy's swollen, painful-looking black eye.

"What happened?" one of the social workers asked, nodding sympathetically. "That looks nasty.

"Johnny was drunk; he did this to my poor daughter. Then, like a coward, he ran to his parents' farm. Luckily, I was here, so he did nothing to the baby." Francis sounded very convincing.

◌

Returning from the farm, Johnny discovered an empty house. Little did he know, his life would turn into a nightmare. Restraining orders prevented him from approaching Francis's home or seeing his daughter. Johnny understood this was Francis's handiwork; it was a fait accompli. There was nothing he could do or say to change the situation.

Lucy and Johnny met with a family dispute resolution practitioner a few weeks after their separation to help them develop a parenting plan that prioritised their child's best interests. Johnny tried to gain custody of their daughter but eventually gave in to their terms after Lucy again threatened to report him to the tax department for unpaid taxes.

From that moment on, Johnny was deemed Francis's arch enemy. Driven by a Sicilian vendetta, fuelled by hatred and lies, Lucy refused to have any contact with him. Francis continued spreading rumours that Johnny was a violent wife basher.

Meanwhile, Johnny's life started to go downhill. He could not repay the loan, his business went into receivership, and his reputation suffered among the bike gang members. With few options left, Johnny returned to his parents' farm, and settled into a small granny flat behind the house. He was disheartened and defeated, his only consolation the anticipation of seeing his beloved daughter Emma every other forthright. That was the only time when Johnny found peace, joy, and reward for his lonely existence.

❧

A few months after splitting from Johnny, Lucy found herself trapped in her mother's modest Fremantle house. Finding herself without alternatives, she consented to undertake a complete rehabilitation program for her cannabis addiction.

Lucy finally said goodbye to Mr Pot.

However, living under the same roof with her mother, their relationship worsened. Francis constantly interfered in her life and living together became unbearable. When Emma started attending daycare, Lucy decided to move out. She approached a business associate of her father's, who owned a two-bedroom duplex near the beach and secured a long-term lease at an affordable rate. This gave her the independence she needed. Lucy was now eligible for the single-parent pension and rental assistance, which provided the financial security and stability she required.

Chapter 31

Trouble in Paradise

Lucy had been enjoying a year of happiness with Ricky until they ran into Dennis at the shopping centre. Ricky had previously met Dennis at Andy's drug-infested home. He tried to avoid him but Dennis approached them anyway.

"Wow, mate, no wonder we haven't seen you for nearly a year. Who is this gorgeous lady you are trying to hide from your friends?" Dennis smiled.

Ricky wished he could disappear. He felt cornered with nowhere to hide. He tried to hurry Lucy along because 'their ice cream would melt'.

"This is my girlfriend, Lucy," Ricky responded, holding Lucy's hand tightly. Lucy smiled shyly and lowered her head, blushing as Dennis stared at her.

Tall, slim Dennis wore tightly fitted jeans, black boots, and a leather jacket with the Harley Davidson logo. He casually held on to his helmet and lifted his hand to stroke his sun-bleached blond hair.

"Listen, Ricky, why don't you and Lucy come to Andy's place one weekend for a barbeque," Dennis said, smiling.

"Well, mate, I'm a family man now. Lucy has a ten-year-old daughter, so socialising is difficult," Ricky said.

But Lucy cut in. "Sure. We could come over when Emma visits her father. It would be nice to meet some of Ricky's friends." Her senses came alive the moment she made eye contact with Dennis; they transported her back to her past, where memories of her first and only love were frozen in time. In that instant, she recognised the scent of cannabis, which awakened all of her senses. Despite being clean for the past eight years, she reignited her need for cannabis. Meeting Dennis had brought back all the happy memories of Mr Pot. This time, Lucy was determined never to let him go.

After an uncomfortable silence, Ricky apologised for their abrupt departure and explained that Lucy's daughter was home alone.

As they drove home, Lucy grew increasingly anxious and asked. "You never mentioned that you have friends. Dennis seems such a nice person. How did the two of you meet?"

"What is all this? I already told you, I was lonely and hung around Andy's place. I left that group of friends when I met you," Ricky said, waiting for her response, but Lucy kept quiet. "But Lucy, I haven't seen Andy or his mates since we met. I don't want to be associated with that group."

When they reached home, Lucy went straight into the bedroom. Ricky unpacked the shopping bags, and Emma watched TV. When Ricky finished preparing dinner, Emma helped to set the table. Ricky went to the bedroom to get Lucy.

"Come on, Lucy. Dinner is ready. What is wrong? I told you the truth. I never want to see those people again. What have I done? You seem upset."

"Please leave me alone. Go ahead, have dinner without me. I have a terrible headache. Let me rest for a while," Lucy said, her voice muffled as she pulled the blanket over her head. Ricky knew not to press further, which would aggravate her more, so he left her alone, and she stayed in the bedroom.

After Emma went to bed, Ricky had a few more beers and was even more upset, wondering what had just happened. Eventually, he knocked on the door and asked Lucy what was wrong. After a moment or two, Lucy abruptly opened the door. "You are a lousy liar. You told me you can't get me any weed, but you have friends who smoke it."

Dismayed at her outburst, Ricky retreated to the kitchen to wash the dishes, but Lucy followed him, firing another vocal barrage. "Tell me … why did you lie to me? I could smell marijuana on Dennis. Why can't you get some weed from him?"

"Dennis belongs to a bikie gang and lives somewhere north of the river. He runs a tattoo parlour to cover up his drug deals. Andy is only a middleman – he gets his supplies from Dennis."

"Why can't you get some weed from Andy? We could smoke a joint together," Lucy pushed the point.

"I told you I want nothing to do with these people. My dad calls them 'sewer rats'. My life has changed since I met you. I am a family man now and no longer want to associate with such a crowd. Every weekend in Andy's house, druggies congregated; most of them looked like zombies. I've seen what drugs can do to you; they mess up your brain. That is why I never used drugs and only drank Vodka or Bourbon.' Clarifying his stance on drugs; Ricky paused momentarily, wanting to see Lucy's reaction.

"Yeah, you drink alcohol. That is just as bad," she bit back.

Ricky remained silent. Lucy had touched a sore spot. He hadn't understood the severity of his alcohol use until he suffered from alcohol poisoning. Aware of his dependency, he limited his drinking to when Emma visited her father.

But that night, when Emma was asleep, Lucy continued to prod Ricky, jabbing his arm playfully but with added meaning.

"We could have some fun nights together like you've never had before," she said, smiling cheekily.

Ricky shook his head. "No, I won't have that shit in my house." He tried to break away, but Lucy pressed his hand against her bosom.

"Please, Ricky, just once, for me, if you love me," Lucy beseeched in a silky, sexy voice. Ricky, however, wouldn't budge. "Why won't you make me happy?" Ricky's mind and emotions were conflicted. He could not decide. Lucy noticed the cracks in his resolve, so she pushed harder.

"If you love me, you will make me happy, Ricky. Our life together is good. If I have some weed, it will be perfect. You know how much I love you. You are my soul mate. Please, just this once."

Feeling overpowered, Ricky caved in.

"Okay, Lucy, I'll get it for you, but only if you promise never to ask me to do this again. I'll get you one weed pouch; when you run out, that's it. No more. You know that because it's addictive. You must promise, never to put me in this position again. Do you agree with that?" Ricky stated his terms, waiting for her answer.

"Oooh … yes, yes. Can you get it when Emma is at her dad's this weekend? We will be alone. You can drink a few, and I can smoke, only one joint. This is all that I am saying."

After some soul-searching, Ricky drove to Andy's place, and exchanged cash for cannabis.

"Give your girl a few joints; she will be happy all day and all night, too." Andy laughed.

"Yes, but Lucy has a ten-year-old daughter – smoking weed in front of kids is wrong. Our relationship is serious, and I don't want to ruin that."

Andy nodded. "Yeah, mate, but she will love you even more if you give a joint or two. Besides, it settles their mood swings, too," Andy advised his old friend.

"Smoking weed is addictive. I prefer if we have a few drinks together," Ricky said with concern.

"Don't be silly. Alcohol is worse than weed; look at my legs. They swell up when I drink. I shouldn't drink because I have diabetes. Good luck, mate. I miss you; come around so we can have a drink together. It will be just like old times," Andy prompted.

"Thanks, mate, but I don't want to buy any more of this shit. I don't want Lucy to get addicted. Besides, I am trying to give up drinking," Ricky said politely.

Ricky dreaded the thought of Lucy meeting anybody from that group. He didn't want her to know where Andy lived; he had to keep her away from the 'sewer rats' if he was to have any future with her. So, for now, at least, Ricky felt safe.

That evening, while Lucy was in the shower, Ricky quickly hid half of the packet in the garden shed, thinking the amount he'd purchased should last for a while – long enough to detach Lucy from thinking about his druggy associates. After dinner, she smoked a joint and shared a bourbon and coke with him, which helped her relax. Later, they rolled on their king-size bed and made love. Lucy felt extremely happy. She knew Ricky loved her deeply and would do anything to make her happy.

The following weekend, when Lucy asked to smoke another joint, Ricky told her that he had no money to buy any more weed. She fumed and started yelling, shouting abuse. Then she went to her bedroom and hastily started packing her bags.

"What are you doing? "Ricky asked, shocked.

"What does it look like? I am packing and going back to my duplex. I told you that if you don't bring me weed, I don't want to stay with you." She slammed the bedroom door in his face.

Ricky pleaded with her to stay, but she ignored him, telling him she would come back to collect Emma's school bag and her books.

That same evening, Ricky arrived at his parents' house, visibly drunk and distressed. He went straight to the point, his voice trembling. "Lucy has left me. She packed her belongings and moved back to her dingy duplex. She is not responding to my phone calls, and I don't know what to do," he cried.

Tom and Donna looked at each other, and then Tom disappeared into another room. It was clear he didn't want to get involved.

"Tell me what happened," Donna said, then let out a big sigh.

Ricky kept the main reason for their arguments a secret. Instead, he expressed his frustration with Lucy. He complained that even after living together for almost a year, she still paid rent for her run-down duplex. Ricky was tired of Lucy's demands to drive Emma from his place to the duplex every other weekend to maintain the illusion that she and Emma still lived there when her father came to pick her up. When Johnny arrived, Emma came out from behind the building. She greeted her father with a casual hug and a smile, covering up for her mother's lies.

Ricky finished his tale with a heavy heart. "I couldn't tolerate such dishonest schemes. Lucy got very upset; she grabbed her belongings and went back to her duplex, ending our relationship." He hung his head low. "What do I do now?"

Troubled by Lucy's deceptive actions, Donna felt something was wrong but didn't wish to discuss this with Ricky. Instead, she advised him to give Lucy space; her rented duplex was her safety net. She urged her son to be patient and buy her flowers, which might help to mend their differences.

After taking his mother's advice, Ricky begged and pleaded with Lucy to give him another chance. She finally agreed to return to him but clarified that she would only return on the condition that Ricky promised to buy her some cannabis.

Ricky readily agreed to her terms; he also recognised that alcohol fuelled his aggression, and promised to change. They came to a mutual agreement: Lucy would move back to his place, and peace between them would be restored.

ॐ

Donna offered to help take care of Emma. This allowed Lucy and Ricky to work on improving their relationship. Emma was a shy girl who lacked confidence and avoided making eye contact. Donna tried to engage Emma in various activities, such as going to the movies, visiting the zoo, and spending playful days at the playground. She also enrolled Emma in swimming and sports and attended school events and holiday festivities.

Donna excitedly told Tom she was glad Ricky and Lucy had reestablished harmony in their home.

"Believe me, you are fooling yourself if you think you will make any difference. Don't come crying to me when things get out of control. I don't want to say I told you so," Tom said, walked into his study and closed the door.

ॐ

On weekends, Donna visited Ricky and Lucy's home. She would bring homemade meals, clean the kitchen, and tidy the garden. They would all take a walk on the beach. They would build sandcastles together with Emma. This lifted their spirits, and Donna was pleased to see them as one happy family again.

She knew though that mental illness was an endless pit that required severe professional intervention to prevent things from getting worse. She encouraged Lucy and Ricky to attend counselling, and for a few weeks, she saw some signs of improvement. However, Lucy eventually stopped attending, and Ricky soon followed suit. Their volatile relationship collapsed with a loud crash.

Consumed with problems at home, Donna's work performance deteriorated. She felt emotionally and physically drained, and her career ambitions started slipping away. When she confided in Tom about her inability to change the situation, she felt helpless and tired. Tom responded with another one of his lectures.

"I warned you against meddling with this matchmaking business. Inevitably, it would backfire spectacularly. You've been steering the Titanic, and now you've struck the iceberg. It's only a matter of time before the ship sinks. I suggest you get on the last lifeboat and row as quickly as possible to save yourself and us. If you don't, you will surely go down with the ship."

"Oh, Tom, don't talk rubbish. I can't give up. Both Lucy and Ricky's mental illness is their biggest problem, but with counselling and medication, they could have a normal life. There must be something we can do to save these poor souls from drowning," Donna said, determined.

"Well, my dear, they don't want to be saved. We better jump on the last lifeboat, or we will all sink together." Tom didn't even bother to listen. With a forced smile, he walked away and closed the door behind him. Donna felt suddenly annoyed with him, thinking Tom always avoided solving problems.

☙

Over time, Emma became increasingly demanding and cheeky, which caused additional tensions in the house. Lucy's dependence on smoking weed exacerbated Ricky's inability to cope with the situation, leading to him excessively drinking which resulted in more arguments. This led to both verbal and physical abuse, further worsening the problem.

Johnny, Lucy's ex-partner, had a visitation agreement that stated Emma should visit him every other fortnight. However, the visitations became inconsistent, and Johnny's concerns about this were ignored. On some occasions, Johnny travelled 120 kilometres to pick up her up, only to be told that Emma was sick and could not see him. This significantly affected the father-daughter relationship.

Donna had driven Emma to her father's farm a few times and discovered that Lynn and Ian were hardworking farmers and caring grandparents to Emma. Contrary to what Francis and Lucy had portrayed, Johnny was not an aggressive monster. Donna suggested Johnny could pick up Emma from her house in the future to avoid any conflicts with Lucy or Ricky.

℘

Right before Easter, Donna received a phone call from Ricky's neighbour. The neighbours were fed up with the disturbances, dubbing Ricky and Lucy 'the neighbours from hell.'

Margaret often called, but this time, her tone was frantic.

"Donna, you come as quickly as possible. Those two lunatics are on the verge of killing each other."

When Donna arrived, she found out what had happened. Ricky had locked Lucy out of the house on the back patio. She was drunk and had been aggressive towards him. He had told her if she cooled off, he would unlock the door and give her another joint. However, when Lucy realised Ricky had hidden marijuana from her and locked her out of the house, she went wild and smashed her fist through the kitchen window, cutting herself. Ricky called the police, and an ambulance transported Lucy to the local hospital. Ricky couldn't afford the ambulance bill, so Donna paid for it.

While Lucy's hand was wrapped in a bandage, Donna came by to help with household chores, cook meals, and care for Emma. Ricky joyfully told his mother they had resolved some of their issues and that they were a happy couple again.

During school holidays, when Emma stayed on her father's farm, Lucy and Ricky lived without a care in the world; they partied until late at night and slept most of the day, Lucy under the influence of drugs, and Ricky usually drunk and barely aware of their surroundings. When lunchtime arrived, the couple groggily emerged from their slumber, feeling miserable and dishevelled after a night of heavy drinking.

Their home fell into disarray, with a kitchen sink piled high with dirty dishes and the floor littered with empty takeaway containers. Lucy and Ricky, too exhausted to converse, carried on in silence. Lucy spotted a leftover joint on the couch and decided to light it while Ricky nonchalantly opened a can of baked beans and began eating them straight from the can.

Lucy paid no attention to him, concentrating instead on smoking, squeezing the last lot of pleasures from the overnight leftover joint. He returned to the kitchen and continued eating. His mouth was full of beans; tomato sauce ran down his unshaven chin, which he scooped up with his spoon, leaving a smudge on his face.

"Open the windows! The house stinks from your smelly sneakers and your dirty clothes are scattered all over the floor."

"Oh ... shut up! My house always stinks of your dope. You should get off your arse and do some washing and cleaning. But, let's not argue. It's too early in the day." Ricky tossed the empty can into the bin with a noisy clank. Then he hauled himself out of the kitchen and sank beside Lucy with a deep sigh, followed by a loud, satisfied belch.

"Why do you always find something to fight about? We used to have heaps of fun. Why can't we have some fun?" Ricky smirked.

Lucy suppressed a yawn. "I need to smoke a joint or two to have some fun. I'm miserable being stuck with you." Lucy gave Ricky a dark, annoyed look.

"Why do you say that? I do everything for you," Ricky responded.

"If you love me, you will get me some more weed," Lucy said, more than just teasing him.

"Of course, I love you, but I don't want you to be hooked on that shit."

"I don't think it's fair to blame me for wanting to smoke weed. When we met, you lied to me about drinking. You stink when drunk. I need to be stoned to make love to you," Lucy exclaimed.

Ricky felt as if she had stabbed him right in his heart. Then anger welled up and shot through him like a high-voltage electrical current. Without thinking, he slapped her hard across the face.

"You filthy bitch, you're a bloody freeloader. I am sick and tired of spending money to buy you an endless supply of pot. I don't want to do it anymore. You can buy your weed!" Ricky pushed her off the couch.

However, Lucy stood her ground and, ignoring her bleeding mouth, she hit him back even harder with clenched fists. She went berserk and started ripping his shirt as Ricky tried to move away. He broke free, but she followed and again savagely lunged at him. Reaching the kitchen, he opened the fridge door as a shield. In the fridge, Lucy saw an unopened bottle of champagne.

Without hesitation, she grabbed it by the neck and threatened Ricky. They furiously fought for the bottle. Ricky wrenched it free from her hand and tried to move away from her. The entire bottle smashed, and the broken glass cut Ricky's leg. At that moment, the fight-or-flight physiological reaction kicked in and the fight went out of control.

Ricky kicked while limping and bleeding. Lucy grabbed a knife, and Ricky instinctively grabbed a towel and disarmed her, throwing the knife out of the back door and over the fence. With his arse exposed in his oversized flapping underpants, he ran down the street as fast as his legs could carry his lumbering bulk. Freaking out, Lucy followed him outside and started running after him, yelling and shouting obscenities, but couldn't catch him.

The neighbours called the police.

❧

Donna finally sought Francis's cooperation to care for Emma. Spending more time with her grandmother allowed Lucy and Ricky to concentrate on repairing their relationship. However, these visits were infrequent, and Emma's school attendance suffered.

With Emma's safety compromised, and Donna knowing that no child should live in a violent home exposed to domestic violence, Donna suggested that Emma should live with Francis, but Lucy instantly refused. Donna had no choice but to contact Emma's father and report to him that his daughter was exposed to domestic violence. Eventually, with Child Safety Department intervention, Lucy agreed for Emma to live with her paternal grandparents, Lynn and Ian, on the farm in Coolup, which proved to be the best outcome for Emma.

Feeling better knowing that Emma was in a safe home with loving grandparents, Donna remembered Tom's words that the ship was sinking and she was powerless to save Lucy and Ricky from drowning. He had told her Ricky and Lucy couldn't be saved; he had told her that mental illness could not be cured, only kept at bay; he had warned her that she should focus on preserving their own relationship.

"Let them sink or swim. It is now up to Ricky and Lucy to manage their relationship. It will be up to them to stay together or break up. Donna, you have to accept that you have hit a brick wall. You have been defeated by mental health; this is beyond you. Only these two misfortunate souls can save themselves. The time has come for you to focus your energy on your career and on our own relationship," Tom said.

Donna looked at her husband, knowing that he was right, but it was hard to let go.

ʘ

Eventually, Lucy's situation deteriorated further. She stopped paying rent for her duplex, and received an eviction notice. Now without a safety net, she had no choice but to permanently reside with Ricky. Unfortunately, this allowed Ricky to exert control over her, leading to a cycle of verbal and physical abuse. When Lucy found out that Donna was the rightful house owner, she felt betrayed and trapped.

Donna decided that Lucy and Ricky should start paying rent as tenants in common. The minimum rent amount for a three-bedroom, two-bathroom home within walking distance to the beach was a reasonable request. Donna would be able to cover the cost of house insurance and maintenance. Ricky agreed to this arrangement and signed a formal lease at the real estate agency. However, Lucy was not entirely pleased with the agreement but eventually decided to share the rent with him.

Since Emma was now living permanently with her father and her grandparents, Lucy and Ricky had no more responsibility, so they reverted to drinking and smoking weed. Regrettably, Lucy kept demanding Ricky to bring her more weed.

"The bag I bought you should have lasted you a few weeks. I am not willing to throw my money away like that anymore," Ricky growled. But Lucy ignored him and continued smoking her last joint.

She stretched lethargically. "You know the deal. No weed or I am walking."

"I refuse to be your drug supplier. You should give me some money – cannabis is expensive," Ricky responded, determined not to spend another cent.

Lucy then opened her purse and tossed a hundred dollars on the kitchen bench.

"Okay, here, take my money. Bring me two big bags of weed. That should last for a month. Otherwise, I will move back with my mother," Lucy sneered.

"But you hate living with your mum."

"Yeah, I do, but living with you in this house makes me miserable. I am bored; we never go anywhere. Why can't we go together to Andy's place? Dennis invited us for a barbeque," Lucy reminded Ricky.

Without uttering a word, he grabbed his keys, slammed the front door and drove to Andy's place. When Ricky arrived there, Dennis and a few old mates were sitting in the backyard, drinking, smoking weed, and discussing some sort of business dealings.

"Hi mate, how did you score such a sexy chick? Bring her along next time. We could have a good time, just like the good old days." Dennis pulled up another chair and offered Ricky a beer.

"Thanks, mate. But I'm trying to give up drinking. Besides, Lucy is not interested in this kind of partying," Ricky lied, desperate to keep Lucy as far away as possible from the 'sewer rats'.

Andy, pleased to see Ricky back, rose slowly and together they walked to the kitchen. The house was pitch dark, only the TV light lit a corner next to the couch, where Mark and Steven sat, stoned and oblivious of their surroundings; zombies out altogether.

In the middle of the room, on a beer-stained carpet, stood a small coffee table with a few empty cans of beer and an ashtray full of cigarette buds and leftover joints. The windows were shut, and the torn-up curtains were barely hanging on. The entire house reeked of stale cigarettes and cannabis smoke.

Andy walked to another room; Ricky followed, ignoring Liam who was stretched out on the double bed with a few used needles on the carpet. Andy got a key out of his pocket, opened a cupboard, and pulled out a few drawers. It was full of all sorts of drugs, and money. He pulled out a packet of cannabis, saying to Ricky, "Listen to me, mate, this batch of cannabis is top grade; this will keep your woman happy. And don't forget, you can always rely on me for a good supply."

"Thanks, mate; this may be the last purchase. Lucy has promised to stop; we are planning to have a baby together."

As he was about to leave, Andy nudged him with an elbow, his broad grin exposing yellow tobacco-stained teeth. "Some chicks get horny while smoking pot. Give Lucy what she wants; she will love you for it and beg you for more sex. I bet you, she will fall pregnant immediately."

When Ricky arrived home with two bags of cannabis, Lucy was overjoyed. She smoked a few joints, and they shared a few Jack Daniels drinks then made love. Somehow, miraculously, Lucy was delightfully happy again. In the throes of her joy, she promised Ricky that if he continued to supply her with regular weed, she would give him what he desperately wanted. Ricky was determined not to be shortchanged by Lucy's manipulative bargaining arrangements.

His ultimate desire was to become a father. This now was his only dream.

Chapter 32

The Swan has Landed

On one of many pleasant afternoons, the sea breeze came in early. Tom and Donna, sitting on their balcony, decided there was no point discussing the endless topic of Lucy and Ricky's yo-yo relationship, which they seemed to thrive on.

"Tom, I can see now that you were right. No matter how hard I try to help, they are unwilling to change and stick with counselling, which never lasts more than a few sessions." She was tired of false promises.

"Don't blame yourself. You had the best intentions, but don't forget that the path to hell is paved with good intentions. I say again, put your energy into your career and focus on our relationship," Tom reminded her in his usual philosophic way.

Donna agreed. She sipped her wine and watched the sun slipping towards the horizon and pushed her thoughts back to the short holiday they were now planning in Thailand.

"We will spend the upcoming weekend at the Hyatt. And we have to attend to support Mike and Antoinette, who have been nominated for another gold plate award. This year's theme is Chinese, which celebrates the Year of the Dragon, so I will have to find a suitable evening gown."

She smiled, reminiscing about last year's French theme, where all their friends attended and had a great time. Tom chuckled when she mentioned it, reminding him they had ended up on the back of the newspaper's social pages as one of the best-dressed costumes.

Both absorbed in conversation, relaxing next to each other, they gazed out at the distant horizon, the sun now settled behind the vast Indian Ocean – the nearby lake surrounded by native bushes still in full bloom reflected pink.

Tom pointed out towards fluffy cumulus clouds. "We need some rain to top up the lake; this year, the water level is unusually low, and the gardens are desperate for rain, too."

Absorbed in watching people walking their dogs and a few ducks picking hidden bugs from the surrounding lake grass, others fleeing back into the water when some of the dogs barked, Donna sat back enjoying the strains of a soft Chopin piano composition as the sun disappeared. A wind gently rustled the leaves of the nearby tree branches close to their balcony and toyed with their hair, tousling it and relaxing their minds.

Ring. Ring-ring! Ring-ring! Ring!

Tom concealed a frown as Donna lethargically rose and went inside to see who was calling. She picked up the phone and merrily said, "Hello."

It was Ricky.

"Mum, happy news: Lucy is pregnant. You're going to have a grandchild."

A sudden burst of intense emotions flooded through her: shock, numbness, panic, worry, excitement, delight, and euphoria, all in a tumble. She silently whispered, "Thank you, dear God." She stood breathless for a moment, then said, "Congratulations, my son. I'm so happy for you and Lucy." Trying to hide her deeply conflicting emotions, she slowly put the phone down. Truly stunned, happy, euphoric but also worried, she hastened back to the balcony.

"Tom, you're going to be a granddad. Ricky just phoned us with the happy news that Lucy is pregnant."

Tom's immediate reaction was a shortening of breath. Then, with his voice full of unease, he said, "Do you know what this means?"

"Yes, I know," Donna said quickly.

"I'm not sure you do."

"Oh, Tom, it means a turning point in Ricky's volatile relationship with Lucy, a change for the better."

"I hope you are right. I don't want to dampen your enthusiasm, but from now on, we'll have to adopt a whole new perspective on our future because a single act like falling pregnant can have ramifications beyond one's imagination. We know that. That's why this happy news concerns me."

Donna pushed her own concerns aside. "Tom, don't spoil today because of what may happen tomorrow. Instead, let's celebrate. Lucy's pregnancy is great news!"

Seeing Tom still unmoved, the frown creasing his forehead, Donna said, "Tom, dear, this is when we should open that bottle of champagne to celebrate this special occasion." She quickly ran down the stairs to the cellar but could not find it. She grabbed a 24-year-old single-malt Scotch whisky and two bubble-based tumbler glasses instead. After getting some ice from the fridge, she returned to the balcony.

Tom confronted her with scorn. "Where is the champagne?"

"I couldn't find it. I saw one bottle on the shelf, but it was not cold." She handed Tom the bottle. His head lowered, and with a grin, he capitulated and poured a celebratory drink. Relaxing, he considered Donna's outlook, and tried to see a positive outcome. To cheer himself up, he said, "Let's hope that God has answered your prayers. A child will bring peace to Ricky's family. It might be precisely what Ricky and Lucy need to live together like a decent couple, and their child should bring them closer together."

The evening was perfect. The sun went down, and the view from their balcony was majestic, full of changing colours. Donna turned her head to Tom and tried to sound casual, "I wonder if it will be a boy or a girl."

"I sure hope it's a girl," Tom said with a steely, cold voice, leaving Donna in no doubt that he meant it. And, of course, she knew the reason why – Tom was disappointed in his son. Ricky had never measured up to his expectations.

Suddenly, as they looked towards the pond, a single black swan with its majestically extended wings slowly descended in a silent, graceful motion. It touched the water with its outstretched feet and then, gliding serenely for a moment, stopped. Swans always fly in pairs; they mate for life. The female was hiding in the bushes, preparing the nest for her chicks.

Tom and Donna were taken aback by the lovely sight, almost like a good omen of things yet to happen.

As they merrily discussed their possible good fortune, Tom finished the last of his Scotch. Then he tossed the last bits of ice left in his glass over the balcony's handrail. But, as he flung the heavy glass, it slipped out of his clammy hand and followed the falling ice cubes two floors down to the brick paving below.

Instantly, he went rigid. Then, slowly, he turned and looked at Donna as if he had seen a ghost. "Oops," he said with great seriousness.

Donna, realising what had just happened, sat stunned. It seemed their good omen had just gone over the balcony with Tom's glass and had shattered to smithereens on the hard pavers below. She had an overpowering urge to let out a piercing shriek, unable to believe how unlucky they were. It spoiled their evening. It certainly ruined hers since it had been perfect up to that moment.

Thoroughly downcast, Tom and Donna went downstairs to sweep up the broken glass. They froze in total astonishment as they opened the front door to step outside.

Tom's whiskey glass not only had not shattered but also sat upright without a chip or crack as if someone had carefully placed it there.

"Oh, my God," Donna heaved a short sigh.

Taken aback, Tom was just as amazed. Then he turned to face Donna and triumphantly raised his hands.

"What do you say about this for a good omen, my sweet? A glass falling on the brick paving from the second-floor balcony and then finding it like this?"

Donna laughed joyously as she spotted a beautiful dove sitting on the top of the letterbox, not startled by all the noise. Donna stopped, went closer and gazed at her beautiful dove. She felt a liberating sensation with the rebirth of her desperate hopes, which seemed so lost a moment ago.

"Tom, this is truly a miracle. It's a good omen; this beautiful dove brings peace and hope for good things coming our way. First, we saw a majestic swan landing on the lake, and this beautiful dove brought us a grandchild. This is a sign of good things to come. I know this is it. I know our life will never be the same." Donna smiled.

Tom looked at his wife, indeed knowing that this was it. All his dreams about owning a yacht and sailing around the Adriatic and Mediterranean coasts were over. When the pressure and stress hit home, Donna would have to quit her job, too. This was a game changer, a scary prospect that these two lunatics had conceived a child.

Tom turned around and hugged his wife, remembering a proverb: "A human being is such a precious and complicated being that any fool can make."

That night, slightly worried about how this pregnancy would progress, Tom and Donna went to bed as the happiest couple in the world.

ભ

The following weekend, Ricky and Lucy came for dinner. The expectant mother looked radiant, and the couple seemed so happy together. Unbeknownst to Donna, Lucy's pregnancy meant she wanted to reward Ricky. He would have done anything to become a father, and he never complained about her devotion to Mr Pot.

In the next few months, Donna spent every weekend at Ricky's house cooking and cleaning. Their house was always filthy and covered with leftovers, dirty dishes, greasy takeaway food boxes, beer bottles, and crumpled clothes. But Donna found the many empty bottles of hard liquor the most worrying.

She continued to advise them, suggesting counselling, Alcoholics Anonymous and drug rehab. She felt like the United Nations, trying to bring peace to a war-torn environment.

They both wanted a new start and to create a happy home for their baby. So Donna arranged for them to attend rehabilitation and counselling. During that time, Lucy was diagnosed with bipolar and personality disorder. Sadly, she gave up treatments, which as usual, only lasted a few weeks.

For a few weeks, Lucy and Ricky occasionally had enjoyable moments when Lucy had enough marijuana. Their relationship was fragile, like glass legs that could break anytime. The few happy moments were often short-lived and would cause bitter arguments the following day.

Lucy's behaviour could change drastically from being calm and relaxed one minute to becoming aggressive and destructive the next. She would often throw and break plates, scream, and even physically attack Ricky, who would retaliate.

When Ricky reneged on his promise to Lucy and started restricting her supply of cannabis during pregnancy, all hell broke loose. He pleaded with her, "Consider the baby's wellbeing; smoking that shit will harm our baby."

"I'll quit weed once the baby arrives," she repeatedly promised. Ricky, observing her sadness and hollow eyes, attempted to comfort her. Fearing the risk of a miscarriage, he reluctantly agreed to let Lucy have a limited amount, only a tiny dose of weed to smoke.

But Lucy hated being controlled, and started drinking instead. Furious, Ricky took charge of Lucy's alcohol intake to protect their unborn child. This caused more chaos in the household as Lucy struggled with depression and regret over her pregnancy, often threatening to harm herself and the baby.

To escape arguments at home, Ricky spent hours drinking with the 'sewer rats', and his alcohol problem spiralled out of control. He stayed there until late at night, drowning his pain with a bottle of vodka, as he used to do, sobbing to Andy about how much he loved Lucy, telling him that all Lucy loved was smoking marijuana.

Without a steady stream of cannabis, Lucy had intense mood swings, which worsened because of Ricky's alcohol abuse. He had his own struggles with mental health, which caused him to behave unreasonably and obsessively because of his bouts of depression and paranoia.

Once, when Lucy was highly depressed, she locked herself in the bathroom holding a knife to her stomach, threatening to kill herself and the unborn baby if Ricky refused to bring her some weed. As far as Ricky was concerned, he didn't care about Lucy's withdrawal symptoms. All he cared about was the safety of his unborn child.

Tom and Donna became desperately worried. When they drove them to the hospital for a test, Lucy had to be restrained, the car door safety lock in place as she threatened to jump out of the car onto the busy freeway.

When they discovered they were expecting a girl, Donna hoped this might bring them closer. Occasionally, Ricky would allow Lucy to smoke half a joint to keep her calm. Once, when they came for dinner, they discussed the girl's name and chose Isabella – the name meant 'devoted to God and being eternally beautiful'.

In the later stages of Lucy's pregnancy, Ricky's home remained troubled. Lucy felt betrayed as Ricky failed to uphold his promise of providing her with cannabis. The resentment escalated into deep-seated hatred because Ricky continued drinking, and domestic violence seemed inevitable.

Lucy would shout and yell at him, "I hate being pregnant. You don't deserve to be a father. I wish I never agreed to have a child with you. I hate you. I hate you."

Ricky turned a deaf ear to Lucy's requests for marijuana and kept all alcohol out of her reach. His primary concern was the wellbeing of his unborn child. The love between them faded; they merely tolerated each other's presence. As her pregnancy neared its end, Lucy often isolated herself in the bedroom, consumed by depression and yearning for weed, wishing for an escape from her life.

When she was due to give birth, Ricky patrolled the house, pacing up and down, worried sick about what she might do. During the night, he went on Google searching for information, wanting to know how to handle the situation when Lucy entered labour.

On the day Lucy's water broke and she went into labour, she was extremely depressed and refused to get out of bed and go to the hospital. Ricky, beside himself with fear, threatened her.

"Get up, your lazy fucking bitch. You must go to the hospital," he yelled, pushing her out of the bed.

When she fell on the floor, she shouted at him, "What do you know about giving birth? I already have one child. Get the fuck out of my sight. I hate you," she screamed back.

But Ricky was not moved. He instinctively knew what he had to do. "This is it. I am calling the police to escort you to the hospital." Angry, and determined to ensure his daughter got the best care, Ricky knew only a hospital birth could provide such assurances.

Ricky dragged Lucy to the car, and they arrived at the hospital just in time. The nurse scolded Lucy for procrastinating. Immediately, she was rushed into the delivery room.

Panic arose when the baby was born. "Help! We have a still one," the nurse called for the doctors.

Isabella was born blue and unresponsive, but the doctors and nurses pumped the amniotic fluid out of her lungs, reviving her. When Isabella started to cry, Ricky also cried. He was over the moon when he first set eyes on his baby Isabella.

Donna was thankful that her guardian angel was present in the room. Isabella was meant to be born; nobody could stop that from occurring.

Doctors advised Lucy to stay a few extra days in the hospital as the baby needed extra care with antibiotics, but she refused. Her only wish was to go home and spend time with Mr Pot. Ricky promised that as soon as their baby was born, she could have as much marijuana as she wanted. He had promised her the world to ensure his daughter was born healthy and safe.

Once at home, Ricky encouraged Lucy to breastfeed, but she refused and chose formula instead. When Ricky realised Lucy was unwilling to budge to keep peace and harmony in the house, he returned to Andy's place and brought her a bag of marijuana.

As soon as Lucy was reunited with Mr Pot, peace and tranquillity were restored in their home.

A day after his daughter's birth, Ricky visited his parents and said," My daughter is my angel, and she will save me from myself. Who knows, maybe she will save Lucy too. But I doubt it because Lucy loves Mr Pot more than her child."

Tom and Donna hoped that Isabella was the angel who would save her parents.

After Isabella was born, Donna noticed a transformation in her son that she had never seen before.

A week later, Ricky, Lucy, and Emma came to their home to introduce Isabella to her grandparents. Tom was the first to hold her in his arms, looking at that small bundle, her slim wrists still holding the intravenous injection, a slow release for the antibiotics to help her fight the infection in her lungs. Baby Isabella looked so vulnerable that Tom was instantly smitten; a jolt of electricity went through his veins and he immediately became her protector. He vowed to himself that he would never allow anything to happen to her.

Donna, too, was overjoyed. A sense of calmness engulfed her entirely. She finally understood her desperate obsession with saving her son. She felt her guardian angel had guided her to Lucy, that Ricky and Lucy's meeting was pre-ordained. It was a miracle; Lucy was God's vehicle that brought Isabella to this world.

Donna was emotional; she knew her task of keeping Ricky and Lucy together was over. Isabella, that beautiful little angel, could save her parents. She finally learned that all her searching had led to her finding her. Isabella's spirit was now the shining star that guided her. She had arrived just before her parents' lives fell apart. Donna hoped Lucy would love her, but first, she had to learn to love herself.

Donna nicknamed her granddaughter Izzy, and that name stuck. One big hurdle was over when Izzy recovered well from her birth. She was strong as steel and soft as a feather. Donna remembered her mother's words and thought these exact words belonged to Izzy, too. Holding little Izzy close to her heart, she felt her warmth and instantly knew she would never let her go.

Still, she was fearful. Her instinct, her gut feeling told her their lives would never be the same. Tom's and Donna's lives now belonged to little Izzy.

Chapter 33

Fight to Save Little Izzy

Part 1

When Lucy and Ricky couldn't care for their newborn baby, Tom and Donna felt a strong moral obligation to step in and become temporary caregivers. Although they believed a child needed both a mother and a father, they had no other option but to seek help from the Department of Child Protection, which had the authority to determine what was in the child's best interest.

In the beginning, Tom and Donna found it challenging to adjust to their parenting roles again, but changing nappies was more straightforward this time. Because Tom and Donna had no family in Australia, they were grateful for their supportive friends who provided them with baby clothes, a pram, a cot, toys, and anything else they needed for the newborn.

With a heavy heart, Donna decided to retire. Her nearly twenty-year career had given her great satisfaction and fulfilment, but now she knew it was necessary to take on her role as a grandmother and caregiver.

It came as no surprise for them to take care of Izzy, given the tumultuous relationship between Ricky and Lucy, which was still plagued with mental health and substance abuse issues. The situation worsened when their newborn baby arrived, and everything fell apart.

Lucy was increasingly frustrated with Ricky for refusing to supply her with marihuana, so one day, when Ricky drove to Andy's house, Lucy followed him there. Ricky had always been afraid that Lucy would leave him if she got involved with the 'sewer rats', and sadly, his fears became a reality. Lucy found herself surrounded by the sweet smell of cannabis that she so desired. After spending most of her days there, Andy and Lucy became lovers. Soon, she started spending the nights with Andy, and eventually, she never returned home, leaving Izzy with Ricky. After Lucy's betrayal, Ricky resorted to drinking, and his mental health issues resurfaced.

Concerned for the child's safety, Tom and Donna approached the Department of Child Protection (DCP) for help.

When a parenting agreement couldn't be reached, the DCP referred the matter to the Family Court for resolution. Tom and Donna applied for a temporary safety order from the Family Court to safeguard the innocent child, the court issuing temporary orders that would remain in place until the final orders were determined.

Tom constantly supported Donna as they navigated this new era of modern parenting. Once Izzy started attending a local daycare centre, Donna met many young mums who offered her advice on new parenting skills, which immensely helped her.

Tom and Donna were relieved; they believed the child's safety would be given priority over the biological parents' needs. They thought the law was clear-cut, and the evidence that the biological parents were unfit to raise the child was clear. They were confident that the custody battle would not take long, so they searched for a lawyer to represent them.

Alpha & Co., a legal firm specialising in family law, had an excellent reputation. According to their glossy brochure, they provided clients with top-quality legal services and aimed to resolve matters as early as possible to save their clients' money. The firm had served clients in the city's southern suburbs, across the Swan River for over thirty years.

After reading the brochure, Tom told Donna, "This is the law firm we need. Let's proceed with them."

Donna agreed.

During their office interview, Tom and Donna were greeted by a senior lawyer, William, a sixty-year-old, plump, stocky man with thinning hair, a slightly hooked nose, and a broad mouth. He introduced himself as "Bill" and made them feel comfortable.

Bill informed them that their case involving child custody was simple since an interim order was already in place for their granddaughter. He further added that the Family Court would likely deem both parents unfit because of their mental health issues, alcohol and drug addiction, and domestic violence.

Tom and Donna were happy to have found a lawyer who assured them they shared the same beliefs.

"I usually take on challenging cases, such as complex divorce issues, dealing with property settlement, and monetary evaluation of how the couple will split family income and pay alimony.

"Your family matter is simple, a piece of cake," Bill said again, full of confidence. "Your case will be handled by my son, William. He is a Junior Legal Counsel, much cheaper, and his hourly fees are only three hundred and fifty dollars. However, don't worry; I'll ensure everything runs smoothly."

Tom and Donna were bemused by William's nonchalance. However, after speaking with William Junior, they were optimistic. He seemed very knowledgeable about family law matters, and they thought he must be as good as his father. Assessing his words, he made an encouraging impact.

Before leaving the office, Bill added somewhat indifferently, "If it's not bothersome, could you deposit six thousand dollars into our account as soon as possible? It's a standard procedure for all new clients."

The agreement was sealed, and Bill advised Tom to complete and return Form 13 Financial Statement to his office to consider whether any or all parties were eligible to pay for the costs of an ICL, an Independent Children's Lawyer. Bill informed his new clients that an ICL would represent Isabella during the family court proceedings. His role was to protect a child's safety so the child would have a voice, too.

Bill stood up and shook Tom and Donna's hands heartily. Then he escorted them, with some well-established pomp, out of the premises, or the 'Dragon's Den', as Tom would derisively call the Alpha & Co Legal firm a few years later.

They rushed home to complete the form as their new and trustworthy lawyer instructed. William convinced them their financial status would show the Family Court that they had sufficient funds to care for all the child's needs. Tom and Donna were deemed eligible for contributions towards legal costs for the ICL. This reassured them that Form 13 would become a valuable tool in their fight to save their little angel.

In the beginning, Tom and Donna viewed everything through rose-coloured glasses. At the first court appearance as a preliminary to the court trial, Alpha & Co.'s legal firm got a further Interim Order endorsed by the Court, making Isabella's current custody arrangement official for the time being. To the satisfaction of Tom and Donna, Alpha & Co. safeguarded their right to continue caring for Isabella's daily needs.

A few months later, the mediation process recommended that parental responsibility for the child be shared equally between Tom and Donna and Ricky and Lucy in consultation with each other. However, Tom and Donna disagreed if the parents were unwilling to change their drug and alcohol intake.

In the subsequent Family Court proceedings, all parties and their legal representatives were requested to attend mediation to resolve parenting issues, followed by a Case Assessment Conference. Genuine efforts to determine Isabella's custody had failed. Of course, Lucy and Ricky engaged Legal Aid lawyers for free. Only Tom and Donna, who physically provided the day-to-day care for their granddaughter, had to pay lawyers' fees. Accordingly, their case dragged on through the Family Courts for much longer than necessary. As far as Alpha & Co was concerned, their clients were their 'cash cow'.

಄

Lucy wanted to avoid being drawn into a long Family Court dispute that would have been bad for Andy's shady drug business. She approached her mother for help, and Francis confirmed Lucy lived with her and that the address was her legal residence. Lucy didn't care about formalities and hated paperwork. The only documents she ever filled out on time were her Centrelink documents. Wasting time on Family Court documents was not on her priority list. She ignored all the deadlines and disregarded all the Magistrate's requests.

Donna and Tom were shocked that such flexibility was allowed for a biological mother but not for the father. Ricky complied with all the rules, as requested by the Magistrate, but it was not that relevant in the grand scheme of things. Within months of moving out, Lucy stopped coming to see her baby daughter. To entice Lucy to come along and bond with her child, Donna started sending Izzy's photos to her maternal grandmother Francis and her half-sister Emma, hoping that when Lucy saw her little princess, she might change her mind, visit her child, and reconnect with little Izzy.

But Lucy never came, and that broke Donna's heart.

Donna and Tom were sick and tired of attending mediation meetings. It was all a waste of time and money. The only beneficiary was, of course, the lawyers. The ICL's only interest was how to reunite mother and child. However, Tom and Donna would not budge on demanding that the biological parents had to test for drugs, alcohol, or mental health issues.

Tom had forwarded a letter to the ICL, desperately trying to convince him. "Lucy argues she has an undeniable right to Isabella simply because she is her mother. However, this claim supersedes Isabella's inherent right to health, safety, and well-being. Regarding ensuring Isabella's future, we as grandparents will never be tempted toward a comfortable but wrong judgment instead of the one that is difficult but right. For that reason, we have to and indeed are at this very moment obliged to seek custody of Isabella to protect her from harm and ensure Isabella's health, proper education and future."

However, the ICL was not convinced. He firmly believed efforts should be made to reconnect the mother with her baby. Tom and Donna insisted that both Lucy and Ricky should be drug tested. Ricky complied with magistrate orders, but Lucy never did. When Tom and Donna told the ICL that Lucy didn't want the child, he didn't believe them. Instead, he labelled the paternal grandparents with a lack of tolerance towards the biological mother because of being 'culturally entrenched.'

When Lucy turned up with her mother for the first hearing, she had to carry on with her charade; she was stuck in a difficult situation. She had to appease her mother and her new lover, too. To get Andy's sympathy, Lucy had to show she would never let go of her baby. She had to fight the two 'rich horrible in-laws' who had stolen her daughter. Lucy was convincing as a grieving mother, desperate to get her baby daughter back. Lucy always put on a good show.

However, Donna had seen Lucy in action many times before. Lucy relied on her personality disorder, able to change her behaviours like a chameleon. She was highly skilled at fooling and manipulating people. Sadly, what upset Donna the most was that Lucy never once asked to see her baby. Accompanied by Francis, Lucy portrayed herself as a victim to both her mother and Andy, claiming her depression caused Family Court duty lawyers, sympathetic towards Lucy as they believed her to be a mother struggling against prejudiced in-laws, to offer her assistance.

Although Tom and Donna were just as strict with Ricky, their concerns were not seen as genuine. Consequently, one of the duty lawyers represented Lucy's interests before the Magistrate.

"Please, Your Honour, this poor mother needs our help to hear her voice."

Donna felt she was going to be physically sick when she heard that. For Tom and Donna, the custody dispute was now more of a life-or-death situation – protecting little Izzy was their only aim. *One step at a time*, they thought. Indeed, once the Family Court enforced the drug testing, it would all be over, or so they believed. But once again, they were proved wrong.

Tom and Donna had many sleepless nights, worrying that if the Family Court granted Lucy unsupervised visits, she would take little Izzy to Andy's drug-infested home. This was a place for a child's innocence to be stolen by decadent men without shame or decency.

ʘʘ

Eventually, more than a year later, Lucy's paperwork was finally submitted, and the Family Court never penalised her for non-compliance. The other parties involved followed the

Family Court's stringent rules. To their disappointment, the Alpha & Co. lawyers made little fuss about it.

However, Tom and Donna believed that drugs and safety could only be seen as black-and-white issues, with no other shades applicable. No matter what financial and emotional pressures were put on them, Tom and Donna were unwilling to budge, as that would compromise Izzy's safety.

❧

One year later, Francis insisted that Lucy, with help from a legal aid lawyer, prepare the documents and affidavit on Lucy's behalf. Even worse, that same lawyer helped Francis. Both their affidavits were full of lies. Lucy claimed she lived with her mother, which was a deliberate lie since Lucy now lived with Andy, her drug supplier. Francis and Lucy's affidavits were never questioned, nor did the system apply any penalty for submitting them one year late, and the facts were never verified.

Alpha & Co informed their clients that lying in affidavits was common practice and not a significant concern. However, Tom and Donna found this to be a considerable issue, and it caused them great distress. One agreement recommended by the Independent Children's Lawyer and approved by the Magistrate stated that Ricky could spend time with Isabella at his parents' home, provided he did not consume alcohol or use prohibited drugs during his time with the child or for twelve hours before the child was in his care.

The ICL suggested Lucy spend time with Isabella at her mother's house during the day on Fridays and Saturdays, provided she did not consume alcohol or use prohibited drugs during her time with the child or for twelve hours before the child was in her care, providing that Francis did not allow Izzy to go to another place or home, particularly not to Andy's drug-infested house. Tom and Donna were shocked at how flimsy these statements were made. Francis lied to protect her daughter, not her granddaughter. That was the critical issue: Francis couldn't be trusted.

William and his senior lawyer, Bill, encouraged them to make some concessions. Still, when Tom and Donna wouldn't budge on drug issues, their lawyer, William, told his clients in no uncertain terms, "You can't possibly think that the court will remove a child from a mother. If the courts take all the kids away from mothers using drugs, there will be more orphans on the street today. The court would never agree to that. It is best to find some compromise that must be decided upon.

"They may consider Francis a viable supervisor. If that is not okay, maybe Emma, who will soon be of age; she may be seen as a supervisor …"

Hearing this, Tom's face drained of colour, and thought even his lawyers needed more confidence to win. He couldn't bear the thought of Izzy being taken to Andy's house to be with Lucy. The mere idea tore at his heart and made him physically ill. Despite this, he did his best to conceal his emotions.

Tom and Donna remained firm in their stance that specific conditions must be met to ensure compliance. They only agreed to give their consent if the ICL recommended that Lucy and Ricky be mandated by the court to undergo drug testing before allowing Isabella to have contact with either of her parents. If the ICL did not make this recommendation, access to the child would be withheld until further notice or direction from the court.

Tom and Donna, the paternal grandparents, stood firm, insisting that the Independent Children's Lawyer conduct a drug urinalysis test within 24 hours and follow up on the outcomes of these tests. Their primary concern was the child's protection, above all else. Enforcing this requirement on the biological parents, however, presented a challenge. Tom and Donna received criticism for being overly stringent, particularly towards a mother who consistently cannot meet these expectations.

Tom and Donna experienced a sense of déjà vu, recalling a similar ordeal they had previously endured with the Department of Child Protection, where they had encountered issues related to drug and alcohol abuse. These issues had been largely overlooked in many letters expressing their concerns about Lucy living with a drug dealer, believing that the illegality of drugs would prompt serious action. Unfortunately, they ultimately realised their efforts were in vain.

Feeling bewildered and lost, Tom and Donna struggled to comprehend the complexities of family law, particularly its stance on biological mothers.

They were charged exorbitant money every time they visited or sent a letter to Alpha & Co. The only constant they could rely on was the punctual arrival of bills from Alpha & Co, which kept coming and coming. The arrangement didn't work. Lucy refused to take a drug test. For Tom and Donna, that was not acceptable. Hence, the Independent Children's Lawyer blamed the paternal grandparents for being 'entrenched.' However, for Tom and Donna, that was the only legal card in their hands. If they had gone soft on drugs or alcohol abuse or compromised on mental health issues, it would have been detrimental to Izzy's safety.

Against all odds, Tom and Donna objected to Francis acting as a supervisor, knowing that little Izzy would end up in Andy and Lucy's drug-contaminated household. Tom and Donna would not let Izzy out of their sight. One positive sign was that Ricky was still committed to attending AA and counselling, as well as following his drug and alcohol program. Lucy had promised to provide drug tests but had yet to follow through; it was clear that something needed to be done to ensure accountability. However, Lucy knew she would never pass a drug test and didn't want to implicate Andy.

To make matters worse, Francis pushed Lucy to attend every Family Court appearance, hoping to get a win against Tom and Donna. Francis told Alpha & Co. lawyers that she wished Tom and Donna would have to sell their house and go bankrupt. Donna knew that Francis's Sicilian mantra of never forgiving or forgetting, a vendetta against her enemy, would last until 'death do us part'. Alpha & Co, the family lawyers, were happy to drag out the proceedings, knowing they would earn more money that way.

The next suggestion was to connect Isabella and her parents through the Supervised Child Contact Service closest to their home. This was where children and biological parents could meet in a friendly and safe environment. Family Court granted another extension followed by many more delays before these formal arrangements were put in place. Tom's and Donna's legal fees continued accumulating, tapping into their savings.

Then suddenly the unforeseeable health development spun their lives out of control when Tom's doctor called him regarding his latest blood test results, which wasn't good news.

When Tom arrived home, he told Donna that he'd been diagnosed with blood cancer, a non-Hodgkin's lymphoma and would start chemotherapy immediately. Tom's oncologist reassured him that his blood cancer was in its early stages and had not spread to his lymph glands. With chemotherapy, he would recover.

Tom and Donna embraced tightly. They knew they had to confront and overcome this challenge together. Donna tried to remain brave; she had to be strong for her granddaughter, who needed her more than ever. Little Izzy assisted in shaving her Granddad's hair while Tom playfully teased Donna that she had also lost more hair than him due to ongoing stress with the Family Court.

The only positive thing, the silver lining, was that Tom's diagnosis happened while they didn't have to attend any court hearing or mediation. It happened when Lucy and Ricky had eight mandatory weeks scheduled at the supervised centre. After that, if requested, it would be extended further. Ricky had no plans to quit, so that gave Tom extra time to recover from the onslaught of the chemotherapy.

Tom demonstrated remarkable perseverance during his chemotherapy sessions, even though he had to deal with exhaustion, breathlessness, and nausea. The days after the treatment were particularly tough for him, as he felt discomfort and pain. Despite experiencing good and bad days, Tom never grumbled and stayed determined to overcome his health issues.

Tom wanted to keep his health issues private, worried that it may jeopardise their Family Court outcome. He was elated when he received news that he was in complete remission. However, after chemotherapy, his immune system was compromised, which made him susceptible to other illnesses. Regular visits to the hospital to boost his autoimmune system would be necessary.

Donna was grateful that God had answered her prayers and that Izzy's granddad would be around for a long time.

The arrangements for the supervised contact appointments at the Child Contact Service between Isabella and her parents started positively. Ricky attended every week as per the court order. When Lucy attended, Tom or Donna brought Isabella to the contact centre ten minutes before the appointed time, left her there with a supervisor, and then exited the premises through the back door unobserved, not crossing paths with Lucy approaching the front door. Tom and Donna hoped that this might produce some positive outcomes.

Donna believed that the goal of the Children's Contact Service was to provide a neutral environment focused on the child and not the parents' dispute. However, the coordinator proved that idea wrong. She took Lucy's side against Ricky, who had a bad temper and was a violent man supported by his wealthy parents.

Tom sent a letter of complaint to the Counsellor Branch Manager. After that, there were no more problems or issues with the petulant coordinator. Tom and Donna finally understood that the system favoured biological mothers above anybody else, and delays would only benefit Lucy. The delays squeezed their hard-earned savings. Everyone hoped that Tom and Donna would have to give in. Alpha& Co's lawyers told them asking the mother to give up drugs was unreasonable. They explained Lucy was sick and that the only way forward was to be patient and help the poor mother rehabilitate.

For Tom and Donna, that was a scary thought. They knew Lucy didn't want to be rehabilitated. They feared that if she gained custody of their daughter during the next court hearing, she would take her to Andy's house – 'the house of horrors'– where Isabella's innocence would be shattered and her childhood stolen. Tom vowed that this would never happen as long as he was alive.

This determination to protect Isabella from a bleak future consumed Tom. Day and night, he couldn't find peace. That determination gave Tom and Donna strength to keep fighting the system, which saw grandparents as a temporary solution. Pushing to reunite a poor child with biological parents who were afflicted with severe mental illness and substance abuse was plainly wrong.

The only consolation, an array of sunshine, was that Ricky loved his daughter and would rehabilitate and change his life. Lucy however chose not to. She still loved Mr Pot more than her daughter. Lucy remained unwilling to sacrifice her relationship with Andy, who held the key to the sweet candy shop, where she could get whatever sweet delights her heart desired.

However, the show must go on.

Francis pushed her daughter to fight, and Lucy had to make Andy believe she was a victim so he would feel sorry for her and allow her to choose any candy she wanted. Therefore, Lucy continued the charade; it didn't cost her anything to appease her mother and kept her from interfering in her life. All Lucy truly wanted was to be left alone in her sanctuary, where she could find solace with her drugs.

Part 2: A Spy for hire

Tom spoke up after feeding Izzy and putting her to sleep. "Donna, we need to take drastic action. Our current situation is not improving, and it's draining our finances. I'm tired of constantly worrying. So, I've hired a private investigator to monitor Lucy's activities and relationships. We need to gather evidence for the Family Court that proves Lucy doesn't live with her mother but with a drug dealer named Andy instead. I understand it will cost us money, but please don't argue with me about this."

"Okay," Donna replied and sat at the table, looking at Tom. "If that's what you want, I'm with you. Darling, we will never give up on Izzy. I promise you … never. Please, calm down."

Tom felt relieved. He slowly walked to Donna and gave her a long, tender hug.

After spending a day scouring the web for a Private Investigator, Tom believed he had finally found the right one. Spy for Hire boasted of providing effective, efficient, and transparent services. Crucially, they claimed their gathered evidence was admissible in court, which mattered greatly to Tom. Consequently, he decided to give them a call.

The man replied affirmatively and confidently, assuring Tom that the requested investigative services were available. He specified that an upfront fee of two thousand dollars in cash was necessary at the initial meeting, with subsequent charges of one hundred dollars per hour. He projected that collecting evidence on Lucy's location might require more than fifty hours. Tom agreed immediately, while Donna stayed quiet.

Tom and Donna went to the Spy for Hire agency the following day. Upon locating it, they arrived at a modest, grey office between a fish and shop and a Chinese massage parlour.

Tom's stomach plummeted, and his immediate impulse was to run. Donna responded similarly, but a man at the office entrance noticed them before they could exit and beckoned them over. He presented himself as Bob and welcomed them inside. The office's interior was as uninspiring as its facade.

One corner was occupied by a modest desk with three chairs circling it, while a shelf beside it was cluttered with files and folders in a disorganised pile.

Bob was a former police detective. His tall, thick-set frame exuded masculinity, dominance, and strength. His square-shaped head balanced atop his powerful neck, with a small mouth, the curved upper lip set in a permanent smirk, shallow cheekbones, and small, deep-set eyes.

When Tom explained what they wanted from Bob regarding Lucy, he said without a trace of civility, "We'll nail the bitch!"

This sudden vulgarity startled Tom and Donna. Tom stared at Bob blankly, unsure of how to respond. Donna seemed uncomfortable. Tom tried to be more specific while recovering his composure.

"We only want Lucy observed and followed on days of supervised contact at the Child Contact Service and randomly on weekends to establish and get a record of where she lives, whom she gets in touch with and whether her mother, Francis, goes to Andy's house."

Bob waved his hand. "That won't be a problem. Only it will take a lot of working hours to get that. By the way, have you brought the two thousand dollars we agreed?"

"Yes," Tom said, handing Bob the money envelope.

Saying nothing else, Bob took the money out and counted it.

"Don't worry; I'll get that lying bitch and her mother, too. Just give me a few days, and you won't have to worry anymore. It won't cost you much; I guarantee it. Drugs are destroying our society, and I hate them," Bob declared with a smug laugh. A speck of spit flew from his lips as he spoke. His pockmarked face twisted into a sneer as he looked at Tom curiously. Donna looked sullen.

Tom rose from his seat, and Donna quickly followed, standing beside him. Bob remained seated as he reassured them once again that their needs would be met to their satisfaction; he guaranteed it. With hurried thanks, Tom and Donna left the room.

☓

On his first visit to the Child Contact Service, Bob waited near Andy's house, with his camera eager to spot Lucy. Lucy appeared, accompanied by Andy. She got into Andy's well-worn pickup truck in the driveway, and he joined her. Bob turned on his dashboard-mounted video camera and snapped photos with his handheld camera. Shortly after, Lucy headed for the Child Contact Service, Bob trailing her inconspicuously.

He conducted surveillance from various locations for the following two months, remaining undetected. Despite his efforts, he realised he needed to be more cautious. One day,

Andy emerged from the house and rode his bicycle past Bob's car, giving it a curious glance. Then he turned and rode back home.

Within minutes, tattered sheets covered all the windows of the house. Realising his cover was compromised, Bob left the scene. Subsequently, a female private investigator in an unmarked car assumed surveillance duties. The switch was successful; Andy never detected the new tail. He likely sensed ongoing surveillance, as he would cautiously peek outside before exiting his home and scanning his surroundings. Seeing nothing amiss, he'd retreat indoors. Shortly thereafter, Lucy would emerge, with Andy following closely behind. Such scrutiny was troubling for Andy, mainly if his drug contacts, fellow bikers, or even the police took notice.

Observers witnessed Francis picking up Lucy at Andy's house. On a few occasions, Emma accompanied them while they went shopping. Francis frequently drove to Andy's house to pick up Lucy in her car, and then they went to the Child Contact Service.

Lucy fulfilled her obligation by attending all eight mandatory sessions at the Child Contact Service to get a supervision report for the court. However, following these initial visits, her mother ceased providing transportation, resulting in Lucy's sporadic attendance and fourteen absences thereafter. The Child Contact Service was compelled to suspend her visits with Isabella because of her apparent disinterest in seeing her daughter.

In the letter, the Contact Services Centre manager explained that the waiting list was long and that a place was needed to keep it open for other clients.

Tom felt relieved upon securing evidence that Lucy and her mother had been dishonest about Lucy's location. Tom notified their lawyer, Alpha & Co., about engaging a private detective to gather this crucial proof.

"We now have ample evidence to demonstrate that Lucy and her mother perjured themselves in court with fraudulent affidavits," Tom declared, thrilled to possess irrefutable evidence of Lucy's and Francis's deceit. "The Family Court will have to consider the video evidence of their falsehoods."

William's demeanour changed suddenly, his voice taking on a stern tone as he scolded Tom for obtaining the evidence without consulting him first.

"Why did you feel the need to hire a private investigator? You should have come to me first for advice. I am strongly against it. And even if we have this evidence, judges won't look favourably upon it. They are known for being uncompromising when it comes to the rights of the biological mother."

Disillusionment hit Tom and Donna hard. What was the point of fighting so hard to save the child when the court disregarded the child's rights in leiu of the mother's.

℟

During a stormy night, two police officers arrived at Tom and Donna's residence, searching for Lucy. They were following up on a missing person's report. Having already checked the homes of Lucy's mother and Ricky without success, they turned to Tom and Donna, who unfortunately had no new information to offer. Despite this, Tom and Donna felt a sense of gratitude and relief, knowing that Isabella was safe and sound, sleeping in their home.

A few days later, Lucy returned to Andy's house. Donna speculated that Lucy's abrupt absence might be connected to the recent police raids in their area, which resulted in several drug arrests. Despite the grandparents' concerns that unsupervised visits might endanger Isabella, Tom's efforts to seek assistance from the Independent Children's Lawyer was dismissed.

When Lucy became tired of the constant court hearings and meetings, she thought about giving up custody of her daughter to Tom and Donna, yet Alpha & Co. recommended she speak with her legal aid before taking such a step. Alpha & Co. was financially interested in prolonging the case, as it would bring in more revenue. Meanwhile, Lucy had no choice but to maintain her facade while dealing with her mother's persistent complaints.

A church regular confided in Donna that Francis had vowed to battle the malicious grandparents until they were penniless and compelled to sell their home, and be left destitute, just like her dear Lucy. Consequently, the Family Court skirmish dragged on. Amidst the turmoil, the sole beneficiary was Alpha & Co, who clung to their lucrative client--the proverbial goose laying golden eggs that sustained their bank balance.

Donna still naively believed that she might convince and persuade Lucy to keep her contact with Isabella. It would be beneficial to establish a civil relationship with Lucy.

"I hope Lucy can come to our home and spend time with her baby. She could come and see Isabella's dancing performances or attend some fun activities at Izzy's daycare centre." Donna wanted to do something.

Donna sent copies of her letters, but disappointingly, the Independent Children's Lawyer had yet to respond.

Meanwhile, efforts continued to settle the matter out of court. A Legal Aid Dispute Resolution conference was arranged, yet Lucy disregarded the summons. Further attempts were made to involve her in seeking a peaceful resolution; all parties participated except Lucy, who remained unresponsive. Additional calls were made to Lucy's number. She was at Andy's house and consented to travel by train. The dispute resolution facilitator assured her that a Legal Aid-sponsored car would wait for her at the train station.

Accompanied by her legal aid lawyer, Lucy arrived nearly two hours late, and the conference commenced.

With glassy eyes and a detached demeanor, she consented to all the proposals. Donna pondered whether the same terms would have been extended to the child's father had he been absent.

During the discussion, Lucy swayed back and forth in her chair, seemingly entranced. Across from her, Ricky and the Legal Aid lawyer kept their gazes down, fixated on the table, avoiding any eye contact with Lucy. All overlooked this behaviour, but Tom and Donna exchanged glances of disbelief. Despite prior assurances, Tom and Donna were still perceived as inflexible and uncompromising. They insisted on drug and alcohol testing for both Lucy and Ricky, disregarding the fact that the agreed-upon rehabilitation records had not been reviewed or acted upon. It was yet another fruitless meeting, squandering time and resources without advancement.

After the conference, the attendees remained seated while the chairperson assured them, he would create a document summarising the agreements reached during the meeting. He promised to send the document to everyone for approval and signatures within a week. This document was a record that could be used in the final court hearing. Tom and Donna waited for almost three months for the requested documentation, but they saw no sign of it.

Outraged, Tom and Donna refused to sign anything without proper recordings. As per the Legal Aid information pamphlet, the conference chairperson provided feedback to all participants and made recommendations to all parties involved. Tom and Donna were supposed to receive a certificate of attendance, but they had yet to receive it. On the other hand, Lucy's last request to see her daughter was over four years ago.

Tom and Donna alleged that Lucy and Ricky suffered from severe mental health issues. The ICL contested this assertion, maintaining that it was unjust to the parents and that privacy in mental health should be upheld. Despite this, when Tom and Donna insisted on subpoenaing medical records, the family court appointed an expert witness to conduct comprehensive interviews and provide a professional evaluation of Lucy and Ricky's parental capabilities. Following this, a psychiatrist would present their assessment, upon which the Family Court would base its decision.

Lucy had always harboured a deep-seated fear of doctors, but during her younger years, she was diagnosed with multiple personality disorder and genetic bipolar disorder. Ricky had struggled with severe mental health challenges, so much so that he depended on a disability pension for his livelihood. An appointed Single Expert Witness could evaluate whether Isabella's parents could meet her needs. Again Tom and Donna firmly asserted that the needs of a child should always be prioritised over the wants or needs of their biological parents.

After endless hours and numerous payments to Alpha & Co. lawyers, Tom and Donna became disenchanted with a system that overlooked grandparents as key figures in children's well-being. Depression gradually enveloped Tom, leading him to talk to himself in a futile attempt to make sense of his dark thoughts. He would sit, watching Izzy play, considering all else insignificant. Furthermore, he was haunted by recurring, horrific nightmares of drunkards harming a little girl for sport, his cherished Isabella, his dear sweetheart, and his little angel. The thought of such horrors befalling Izzy during a visit to Andy's house was unbearable.

Tom and Donna dedicated themselves to Isabella for many years, often neglecting their needs. As a result, their social life dwindled; friends visited less frequently, and the festive gatherings ceased. Their lives were completely transformed. They fulfilled the role of parents in every aspect, yet they possessed no legal recognition. The ordeal with Family Court deeply impacted them. To recover and rejuvenate, they began sleeping in separate rooms. Their lives were entirely centred on meeting Izzy's needs.

While Izzy was at daycare, Donna realised that many other grandparents were in a similar predicament. The system used them to provide temporary care for their grandchildren until their parents were rehabilitated. This temporary solution often lasted for decades. Tom and Donna didn't want that. They needed certainty so they continued their quest to protect Izzy, now and forever.

It was clear to Tom that their lawyer was just another part of a more extensive system that operated like a well-oiled machine. But what could they do about it? After much deliberation, Tom and Donna decided to change their lawyer. They couldn't continue with this charade, or they would go bankrupt. After facing continuous frustration and expenses, Tom had had enough and notified Alpha & Co. that their services were no longer needed.

William countered sharply, "You won't get better results with another lawyer. If you think you can take the child away from their biological parents, you must be from another planet." Overcome with irritation, William's face flushed red as he insisted, "You're simply too old. Stop deceiving yourselves. You must confront the reality of aging. Who will care for your cherished granddaughter when you kick the bucket? Keeping biological parents involved is a child's only safety net; in their absence, the children would be orphaned."

With those words, William stormed out, likely upset over losing a lucrative client who had significantly contributed to his firm.

Making the final payment to the receptionist was a bitter pill to swallow, yet there was no option for retreat. Donna gathered all the files and documents and exited the office without glancing back.

Both Tom and Donna were relieved. They felt that Alpha & Co. lawyers had used and abused their innocence. However, William's crude but honest words resonated with Donna. She hoped they would live long enough to see Isabella grow into adulthood.

Part 3: A Lawyer with a good heart

Tom appointed a new lawyer a week later. This time, he chose a Queen's Council (QC), a barrister with specialised knowledge and experience in procedural hearings before a Judge. The new lawyer, Douglas, was an imposing and handsome man with an open face. He accused the ICL of deliberately delaying the trial date and intended to expedite the process. This marked a significant change as there would be no more court delays.

The Independent Children's Lawyer took Douglas seriously, and his footwork quickly changed from a slow tango to a tarantella. Things happened fast, and both Tom and Donna were pleased. At last, they could see the light at the end of the tunnel – the eventual trial and closure to this arduous saga.

Douglas advised Tom to send all the evidence, including photos, videos, and reports compiled by the private investigator to Lucy. Tom then sent this proof to Andy and Francis's address by registered mail. This would frighten Andy and Lucy, as it would expose their drug-dealing activities. Additionally, Lucy and her mother, Francis, would be worried that their affidavits to the Court, which contain lies, would be revealed.

Douglas advised the Legal Aid lawyers to bring the case to a determination without any further delays. Donna provided Douglas with business cards and contact details of Lucy's doctors, psychiatrists, and counsellors and requested he subpoena their reports for the Court. Douglas complimented Donna on her record-keeping abilities and suggested that she should have pursued a career in law. The collected files were sorted chronologically, and all the documents and evidence were easily accessible. Douglas found it easy to determine how things had unfolded over the past five years.

In the next few weeks, Douglas suggested to Tom and Donna that Consent Orders might be the simplest and most economical way to resolve their family dispute. After consulting with all parties involved, including the Independent Children's Lawyer (ICL), Lucy, Ricky's lawyer, and Tom and Donna themselves, everyone agreed to review the Consent Orders before signing them. Once all parties had the opportunity to examine them, the Consent Orders were accepted and signed.

Douglas requested the court to allocate a date for a short hearing since the minutes of consent orders had been accepted for filing. He listed the case as a Special Appointment, which was a specific request to complete the proceedings. On the day of the hearing, Lucy would be served the minutes of consent orders. However, it was uncertain if Lucy would accept the final draft, given that Isabella would stay and live with Tom and Donna permanently.

Douglas made sure that Lucy's legal representative fully understood the consequences of not signing, which would result in the case going to trial. In the event of a trial, everything in Lucy's life would be revealed in an uncompromising manner, and her partner Andy would be called in as a witness and served with a subpoena to give evidence. As a seasoned barrister, Douglas would be the one to question all witnesses, and it wouldn't be a pleasant experience. He assured them that he would make sure of that.

Therefore, everything was in place for the big showdown, which would take place in three weeks, D-Day. Tom felt edgy, his nerves tight as violin strings. Tom and Donna carefully examined all the records in his binder daily, checking and re-checking every document, memo, email, and letter to ensure he had everything necessary. Their sleeping was worse than ever. For them, this was a do-or-die mission.

Tom and Donna sat at the table the evening before D-day, hardly talking, each lost in their thoughts. Downcast, Tom suddenly lifted his head and looked at Donna in despair. "I hope God hears me," he said in a low voice.

Tom bowed his head and said nothing, and then Donna remarked, "After nearly fifty years of marriage, you never cease to amaze me. My prominent scientist is now turning to God."

On the morning of the big day, Tom rose early. Donna and Izzy were still in bed downstairs. Izzy got up in her floral bunny pyjamas, holding a teddy bear. Tom outstretched his arms, and Izzy ran into his embrace.

"Good morning, my little bunny," Tom said with tenderness. Izzy snuggled against Tom's chest and giggled with delight.

Donna smiled. She had to hurry to get her ready for kindergarten. Tom made a strong black coffee, pacing in the kitchen endlessly. Izzy had a bowl of cereal with milk and berries. Tom only had a croissant with jam and another black coffee. Donna had a cappuccino and a slice of raisin toast; both were extremely nervous. They had to hurry. Izzy was going to child care, and they had to be at the Family Court in three hours.

"We have to stay positive," she told Tom, and he reassured her that today, in the Family Court, the law must prevail. Child safety must be the priority."

Within the next hour, everyone was dressed up and ready. After checking that Izzy's backpack was fully prepared, they were on their way: Izzy went to kindergarten, and Tom and Donna went to the courthouse.

Douglas was already in full swing at the Family Court when they arrived, ensuring everything ran as planned. He waited for the Independent Children's Lawyer and Lucy to come, as he wished to talk to them. This was the key to achieving a successful outcome.

Lucy arrived with Andy, who sat outside in the waiting room. This time, Francis was absent, which Donna thought was good. Douglas immediately approached Lucy and had a private conversation.

The Independent Children's Lawyer hovered nearby. No one saw him come in. He seemed unusually tense. Whenever Douglas approached him, his right shoulder would twitch nervously, bringing a faint smile to Tom's lips. Donna noticed this too.

☙

It was the moment Tom and Donna had been waiting for. Their case was finally called, and they walked into the courtroom. At the entrance, everyone bowed towards the front of the Court as a sign of respect. A few minutes later, the Magistrate entered, and everyone in the courtroom stood. The Magistrate and the people bowed to each other; once the Magistrate was seated, everyone else took their seats, and the court proceeding began.

A moment later, Douglas approached Tom and Donna and whispered almost inaudibly, "Lucy signed; it's over," he said, walking away to the front of the courtroom.

Tom and Donna looked at each other, dazed and frozen. "What did Douglas just say?" Tom asked, wondering if he had heard correctly.

"Douglas said that Lucy had signed the Minute of Consent Orders. My love, it's over, we won. We have what we want. Of course, Lucy can spend time with Isabella when she wishes, but only with consultation with us. Izzy stays with us. Our baby is safe."

Tom experienced a sudden sensation of liberation as a heavy load lifted off him. It made him feel weightless as if he was carrying the burden of Atlas holding the sky on his shoulders. Tom and Donna were relieved after five years of struggle, pain, and misery. They felt they hadn't experienced this freedom in a long time.

The legal formalities promptly followed. The Magistrate asked Lucy why her legal representative was absent. Lucy responded that she didn't want one. The Magistrate asked for a duty lawyer to explain the details of the Consent Orders.

When that was done, the Magistrate asked Lucy, "Are you fully aware of what you are signing?"

"Yes, I understand and accept the Consent Orders, Your Honour," Lucy responded.

"It is understood that you can visit your daughter, but it has to be agreed upon beforehand, and it will take place at the paternal grandparents' house. Alternatively, you can coordinate with them to make other arrangements that suit both parties. Your daughter will be living permanently with her paternal grandparents, but if you want to spend more time with her, you can do so by consulting with them."

The Magistrate then explained the same orders to Ricky. He had the same visitation rights as Lucy. It became clear that Tom and Donna were unbiased, as both biological parents were treated equally. Isabella's father and her paternal grandparents were to share the parental rights. If the birth parents intended to change these consent orders, they had to do so in writing within the next 12 months. All legal representatives agreed to this.

The Magistrate asked Lucy, "Do you understand, and do you have any other requests?"

"I understand and have no requests, Your Honour," Lucy said.

The Magistrate looked at Lucy. She had no paperwork or handbag, not even a pen. Lucy fidgeted and looked somewhat hasty as if wanting to leave the courtroom. The Magistrate looked around, slightly annoyed, and said to the Court Clerk, "Please give this mother a pen to sign these Consent Orders." When the documents were signed, she informed all the parties that the Consent Orders would be posted to all parties within the next few days.

The Magistrate pronounced the Final Court Orders and formalised the terms of the Minute of Consent Orders. The court proceedings concluded. All those present stood and bowed to the bench. They remained standing until the Magistrate had departed.

Tom and Donna looked at one another and wanted to kiss and hug, but they restrained themselves. Instead, they walked to the exit, where they turned around, bowed again to the front of the Court, and then walked out of the courtroom.

Once outside, Douglas came up from behind and joined them. "We have achieved what we set out to do. It was a good day. I'll send you all the final documents as soon as I get them."

Donna was the first one to collect her marbles and express her gratitude. "Thank you so much, Mr Douglas. We are ever so grateful to you for what you have done, not just for us but also for a beautiful, innocent little girl whose good life and future are now guaranteed. Thank you, thank you so much."

After saying these words, Donna wrapped her arms around Douglas's neck and kissed him.

Tom looked slightly uncomfortable. "Sorry, no kisses from me," he said, "but here is my hand." Tom gave him a firm handshake.

Douglas smiled and looked pleased. "Look, I only did what had to be done. But I must go now. I'm in a bit of a hurry. I have another court case to attend to twenty minutes. If you'll excuse me, I'll be in touch."

Tom and Donna were left standing, happy but uncertain about what to do next. Then the Independent Children's Lawyer came over and said a quick goodbye. He stopped short, and brought Lucy and Donna face to face. As a last attempt, he asked, "Please, Donna, help Lucy get to know her daughter."

"Of course, I will," Donna said, looking at Lucy while gently touching her hand. "Lucy, you are always welcome to see your daughter anytime, anywhere," Donna said.

Lucy pulled her hand away and said, "Is it over? Can I go now?'

"Yes, it's over," the ICL responded. Lucy turned around and left, never to be seen or heard from again. Ricky had a last word with his lawyer then hurried off home, too.

On their way home, Donna and Tom stopped at a beach foreshore café, relieved that the trauma was finally over.

"What did you say to Lucy?" Tom asked.

"Nothing much. Lucy didn't care, and she couldn't wait to get away. Andy was waiting for her downstairs. He probably pressured her to end all this as he needed to keep a low profile. By the way, Tom, I don't think Lucy will even read the consent orders. She never opened any of her official mail. That consent order will end up in the bin, too."

Tom sipped his coffee while Donna continued, "Besides, are you surprised that Francis was not here today? Lucy had no witnesses in the Court and refused to have a Legal Aid lawyer. That means that she can tell everyone: Andy, her mother Francis, her sisters, and even young Emma that she fought bravely for her baby but lost it all to the horrible wealthy paternal grandparents. Nobody will ever know that Lucy willingly signed."

Donna's explanation resonated, and it was proven correct when, a month later, a neighbour who lived close to Lucy's mother confirmed that Francis was telling everybody that Tom and Donna had stolen Lucy's baby. In addition, Emma's father, Johnny and her paternal grandmother, with whom Emma lived on the farm in Coolup, heard from Emma that her poor mother, Lucy, was devastated because she lost her Family Court battle. However, Lucy omitted to say that the Family Court allowed her to see Isabella whenever she wanted to and that it was her choice not to see her daughter. Tom and Donna had the Family Court Orders to prove that fact.

For Tom and Donna, this was a bittersweet victory. Sharing parental rights with Ricky was not something they were looking forward to. Knowing Ricky's mental health issues, there were bound to be problems. However, Douglas advised them that keeping one parent involved was inevitable.

Although Tom and Donna's ordeal was over, they felt short-changed after so much wasted money. They wanted to go before the Judge to show how incompetent Isabella's parents were. Donna wanted to ask the Judge to show more respect and gratitude for the grandparents' rights and not take them for granted. Grandparents care for their grandchildren, but allowing biological parents to have all the authority would create many unresolved and ongoing conflicts. Sadly, many grandparents were stuck between a rock and a hard place.

Independent Children Lawyers' practices didn't always represent the children's best interest either. However, the child's interests should always be put above those of the biological parents.

Mr Douglas proved he was an outstanding lawyer and a decent, kind man. He knew well that his clients had already spent a small fortune; he didn't want to take the last piece of the cake and didn't waste time or money.

He wrapped it all up in a few months and advised his clients to save money and accept the Consent Orders. That was the best outcome for all parties involved.

Mr Douglas advised them it would cost a small fortune if they went to an eventual trial before a judge. The Family Court's goal was to keep the biological parents engaged, so Tom and Donna accepted his recommendations and realised that saving money for Isabella's education would be more productive.

Tom and Donna would always remember Mr Douglas for being a great lawyer with a kind heart, one who recognised the important role grandparents played in helping many disadvantaged children. Tom and Donna felt lucky to have met such a wonderful lawyer and exceptional human being.

Chapter 34

Close Encounter and Food Festival

One month after signing the Consent Orders, Donna drove with Isabella in her child seat to a dancing class at the local sports venue just behind the shopping centre. As she was about to park her car, she saw Lucy looking for a parking spot nearby. Donna parked her car close to Lucy's, rolled down the window and greeted her with a hello.

Caught by surprise, Lucy glanced at Donna and then at Isabella, who was only a metre away. Feeling awkward, Donna asked, "Lucy, would you like to say hello to Isabella? I am taking her to her dance class; she is a great little ballerina. Would you like to come and see her dance? I will drop the invitation in Francis's letterbox."

Lucy instantly looked away without uttering a word; she turned her car ignition on, reversed her car, and drove away. Donna remained stationary, shocked, and close to crying but then composed herself. She turned around and looked at Izzy, her heart aching for her granddaughter. Donna remembered the last time Lucy had physical contact with her daughter was at the supervised Child Contact Centre. Izzy was a toddler then, and now she was five years old. Donna took Izzy into her dancing class, and the incident was forgotten. She knew it would be cruel to tell Isabella who they had just seen.

௸

One warm summer afternoon, Donna planned to meet with other mothers from the daycare centre so Izzy could play with her friends. The annual food festival event was so much fun for both children and adults.

Izzy had fun splashing around, building sand castles, swinging and climbing on the playground swings. The foreshore was crowded with people who came to sample various cultural foods and other exhibits. Donna walked hand in hand with Izzy, checking out the variety of food stalls, Izzy's face sticky from indulging in fairy floss; she pointed out the bouncy castle.

Next to the fairy floss on the grassy area, Donna noticed Francis sitting under an awning with her oldest daughter, Paula, and two teenage children; Emma, Izzy's half-sister, was also with them. Without thinking, she instantly thought this would be an excellent opportunity to introduce Izzy to some of her maternal relatives. Francis did not respond to Donna's greeting of "Hello." Donna felt awkward and tried to make conversation by saying, "You've found yourself a lovely little spot."

Paula responded with a smile and said, "Hello, Donna."

"Nice to see you all. This is Isabella, my granddaughter," Donna said, looking at the two teenage girls. Donna looked directly at Emma. "I haven't seen you in such a long time. You have grown so tall! Are these girls your cousins?"

Emma looked at her grandmother. Seeing Francis's frown of disapproval, Emma lowered her head and did not respond. Paula, Francis's oldest daughter, introduced her two teenage daughters. "Every year, we attend the food festival. The girls adore the beach; they will stay with Emma at my mom's house this weekend."

Inspired by Paula's friendliness, Donna proposed taking her daughters and Emma to the nearby kids' amusement area. "Isabella wants to go on the bouncing castle."

The girls jumped to their feet excitedly. "Can we go, Mum?" Francis suddenly stood up and angrily yelled, "The girls will stay right here. Get away from us, you evil woman!"

The girls looked scared, while Paula, their mother, looked down in shame and avoided eye contact, saying nothing.

Donna, who didn't want to upset little Izzy, apologised and quickly left. Later, she noticed Emma and her two cousins at the corner of the food stall munching on chips and ignoring their surroundings while chatting. Izzy joined her little friends and happily jumped into the jumping castle.

When Donna arrived home, Izzy was utterly worn out. Following her bath, she cuddled beside her beloved puppy, Bon-Bon, and soon fell asleep. Sitting beside Tom, Donna immediately told him about her encounter with Francis, recounting first her meeting with Francis's eldest daughter, Paula, and her two teenage cousins. Izzy's half-sister Emma, now a teenager, had grown so much Donna had barely recognised her. Tom listened patiently, seeing Donna's disheartenment.

To soften her disappointment, Tom reminded her to be vigilant. "Listen, love, the sooner you accept Izzy has no family, the less you'll hurt. As long as Francis is alive, she controls her family with her stubborn Sicilian vendetta. She will allow none of her family, including Lucy, to have anything to do with us. Sadly, Izzy is the only innocent party in this messy custody battle, and Francis doesn't seem to care. We must protect Izzy, and there is no point in pursuing reconciliation that will only result in further disappointment."

Donna knew Tom was right, yet she felt compelled to persist; it was Izzy's birthright to be acquainted with her maternal relatives. With a stroke of fortune, she might one day prevail.

Over the weekend, Donna drove to Francis's place and left an invitation in her mailbox. The invitation was for the end-of-year Izzy tap dancing show at the Performing Art Centre. Donna hoped Francis and her immediate family, including Lucy, would accept the invitation and come to the show to support and applaud Izzy's dance recital.

Unfortunately, Francis nor anybody from her family attended. However, on the day of the performance, many of Donna's loyal friends and their families attended. The enthusiastic crowd of friends clapped and cheered loudly, applauding Izzy and her dance group, making the night a magical experience for little Izzy to remember.

A few weeks later, Donna, ever persistent, made another attempt to reconnect Izzy with her half-sister Emma. Donna drove to visit Lynn, Emma's paternal grandmother, at their farm in Coolup. They arranged a meeting nearby to attend the Pinjarra Country Festival.

When Isabella was born, Emma was twelve years old and lived with her paternal grandparents for five years and never spent time with her baby sister. Yet, when they met, it was as if they had never been apart. Emma held Izzy's hand, looked at horses and farm animals, and even rode with her little sister on the farm tractor. In the afternoon, they all sat together; Emma happily shared chicken nuggets and chips with her little sister.

Donna and Lynn, Emma's grandmother, were delighted to see Emma and Izzy's interaction. It warmed Donna's heart. When they left, Donna promised to send Emma photos and movie vouchers for her birthday, encouraging Emma to go to the movies together when she next visited Izzy.

Emma never showed up to visit and didn't even try to reconnect with her little sister. Sometimes, Donna would meet with Emma's grandmother Lyn, who told her Emma regularly visited her maternal grandmother, Frances, during school vacations and special family occasions. Francis had forbidden Emma from visiting them. Emma, along with the rest of her family, had become entangled in Francis's web of hatred and lifelong animosity. Donna realised that nobody would dare challenge Francis. The woman harboured a deep-seated vendetta against Tom and Donna, and nothing could deter her destructive course. It seemed that Francis would never release them from her clutches. She wielded control over her family just like Don Giallombardo the Mafioso Godfather she used to work for back in Sicily.

℣

Six months later, Ricky informed his mother that he had received information from one of the 'sewer rats' that Lucy had left Andy and had started dating Dennis; she'd been spotted driving around town in Dennis's van with the bright red flames painted down both side, massive tyres and a unique with silver tow bar with horns. On weekends, Lucy accompanied Dennis on his country trips, and during the week, she hung around his tattoo parlour in Yunderup. Lucy stuck to Dennis like the glue; she could choose anything she wanted to make her feel high. When Dennis was busy, she was never lonely as best friend Mr Pot was always around.

Donna wasn't surprised by Lucy's betrayal. If what Ricky had told her, she'd fallen for Dennis the first time she glanced at him in the shopping centre, she had probably seduced him while still with Andy.

Andy was as devastated as Ricky had been that Lucy had betrayed him with his best mate. Dennis had stabbed Andy in the back, and their drug-dealing partnership ended for good. Heartbroken, Andy drowned himself in alcohol and drugs. He died alone in his dingy rented home, one of his friends discovering him unresponsive on the floor.

Andy was only forty-two years old. Sadly, nobody attended his funeral, fearing that the police may have been watching. He was buried in a pauper's grave, marking a tragic end to his life.

Donna didn't feel one bit sorry for that low-life drug dealer. Lucy did to Andy precisely what she did to Ricky. However, one good thing happened since Andy's premature death. When Ricky found out that Andy died from alcohol poisoning, he didn't want to end up like him, and started attending Alcoholics Anonymous meetings; he gave up drinking for good and never touched another drop of alcohol.

Ricky wanted to live for his daughter. He had a purpose in life and hoped that, one day, he might assume greater parental responsibility for his daughter as specified in the Court Orders. Lucy had the same right to visit her daughter. However, she has shown no interest or willingness to change her lifestyle.

After Andy's house was sold, Lucy had to move out. The new owners demolished the property and constructed a new home. As a result, Lucy had to temporarily move back in with her mother. Once the interior painting of Dennis's house in Yunderup was completed, Lucy moved in with Dennis.

She was staying at her mother's home for the Christmas celebrations.

Chapter 35

COCO: Izzy's Christmas Wish

In two more sleeps, it would be Christmas Day and Santa would visit her. An excited Isabella helped with tree decorations, Tom lifting her on his shoulders when they'd finished so she could place a golden angel on the top of the tree. Izzy gazed at the beautiful tree full of lights and decorative balls, with silver and gold tinsel brimming. Just a few more nights until Santa slid down the chimney and gave Isabella many gifts.

Tom and Donna were thrilled that, after nearly five years, the Family Courts had allowed Izzy to live permanently with them. They looked forward to the upcoming Christmas celebration. Once the festive season was over, little Izzy would start preschool.

One day, when Donna and Izzy returned home from the beach, they were exhausted. Donna crashed onto the nearest chair and lovingly watched her little angel run swiftly to the fridge for a drink. She looked so cute, with flushed red cheeks, a sweet oval face, and curly golden ringlets resembling Shirley Temple.

Tom helped rinse the sand from Bon-Bon. Then, he went into his study. Donna and Isabella curled up on the sofa, munching scrumptious snacks; they were relaxed and carefree, simply enjoying a lazy afternoon.

"Babba," Izzy pleaded in her tiny voice, "can we watch a movie together?"

"Of course we can, my sweet," Donna replied. "What would you like to watch?"

Izzy shrugged, so Donna took her time flicking through the options before selecting Coco; the Disney animated film had won several awards, including the prestigious Oscar for Best Animated Feature Film. Donna believed this family-fantasy film could spark Isabelle's imagination. Understanding the importance of family was crucial for little Izzy.

The movie highlighted Mexican traditions, celebrating the remembrance of departed family members. The story depicted a young boy who was accidentally transported to the land of the dead. During his visit, he searched for his ancestor, who was desperate for his living daughter, Coco, to remember him so his spirit would be freed. But Coco was now an old woman haunted by her father's disappearance. Not knowing why, Coco sat quietly in her room's corner, surrounded by dimming recollections. When the boy returned from the realm of the dead, he shared stories with Coco about her father, whom he encountered on his odyssey.

When the boy sang 'Remember Me,' a melody her father penned to rouse Coco from her sorrow, the music stirred deep emotions within her, reviving her memories. She began perusing old photographs, reminiscing about the cherished moments and affection she once shared with her father. Coco's tender memories helped heal her father's broken spirit, freeing it to soar in the heavens above.

Donna loved the movie. It had a beautiful story about relationships between parents and children, with themes of death and the importance of memories.

After the movie, Izzy sat quietly. Donna thought she would sleep well that night because of all the swimming, but then she worried that the movie choice was wrong. Skeletons could be scary. She gave Izzy a loving cuddle.

"Sweetie, did you like the movie?" Donna asked timidly.

Izzy lifted her head somewhat slowly and looked at Donna with her beautiful, now sad, green eyes. "Babba, I don't remember my Tummy Mummy. If I forget her, her spirit will never be free," Izzy whispered in her tiny but very concerned voice. Donna referred to Lucy, as Izzy's 'Tummy Mummy'.

Suppressing her tears, Donna said reassuringly, "Oh no, my sweet little angel, you will never forget your Tummy Mummy. Let's look at her photo." Hand in hand, she gently guided Izzy to a display cabinet with a special rotating photo exhibit. After flipping through a few, Izzy's gaze landed on her mother's picture.

Her eyes lit up. "Babba, I remember this picture. This is my Tummy Mummy," Izzy declared, smiling.

"See these other pictures of your Mummy and Daddy? They're smiling, cradling you when you were just born. Your parents were so joyful," Donna said to her.

"Izzy, look at this picture," Donna urged as she continued to flip through the album. "This one was captured on your first birthday; everyone looked cheerful. You and your Tummy Mummy share the same lovely curly hair."

Donna kneeled before Isabella and gazed into her soft eyes, now brimming with warmth and contentment. She embraced her gently, comforting Izzy, assuring her that all was well.

"Sweetie, you'll always remember your Tummy Mummy. You can look at her photos whenever you want," Donna said. She was about to explain to Izzy why her biological mother wasn't part of her upbringing when their puppy, Bon-Bon, jumped between them, diverting Izzy's attention. Izzy immediately started chasing Bon-Bon around the house.

Watching Izzy play, Donna felt a warm sensation in her heart, seeing her so happy and untroubled. She thought it best to postpone the delicate conversation about Izzy's mother to another time.

Izzy's spirits lifted as Donna mentioned ice cream, dispelling the momentary gloom. Joyfully savoring her treat, Isabella watched her beloved lighthearted Disney cartoons. Their antics quickly restored her contagious laughter, capping off the day beautifully. Yet Donna's mind remained troubled.

The festive season was approaching. Even though Christmas was still quite a few weeks away, the household countdown had already started. The Christmas preparations were a time of delight. Izzy's friends gathered at Donna's place for holiday festivities, making Christmas decorations and Christmas cards for loved ones.

They used last year's recycled cards, pasted fancy stickers, and liberally applied glitter, resulting in a joyous disarray. This chaos was part of the charm, yet for some younger children, writing cards was daunting.

With resolute diligence, Izzy was keen to show her skill in penning a letter to Santa, asking for her special wish. However, Izzy's demeanor changed abruptly, and she became quiet.

"What's wrong, sweetie pie?" Donna inquired with a hint of concern.

"Babba, I made a Christmas card for my Tummy Mummy. I've decorated my card with lots of glitter, smiley faces, and love hearts," Izzy said, beaming with pride at her creation. "Do you think my Tummy Mummy will like my card the most?" Izzy asked hopefully.

"Of course she will, sweetie. We can go together and put the card in a letterbox. I am sure she will be delighted when she receives it," Donna said reassuringly, yet she suddenly felt anxious, wondering if she'd done the right thing by telling Isabella that her mother was not dead. Had she opened Pandora's Box with unforeseen consequences?

Despite the challenges, Donna clung to the hope that Christmas would bring much-needed miracles and that everything would turn out fine, especially for Isabella. Like Izzy's beautiful Christmas cards, the festive season could mend broken relationships and shower them with a touch of magic and the spirit of Christmas. *Indeed, Santa may grant Izzy her secret wish that she had penned in her card to her Tummy Mummy.*

On their way to church the following morning, Donna took Izzy's hand, and they walked through the park to drop a Christmas card into Francis's mailbox. The morning air was refreshingly crisp, the sky a clear blue, and the shrubs by the lake teemed with birds' musical chirping.

Together, they walked down the narrow path. In her new bright bubble-gum pink silk dress adorned with a large pearl white bow at the back, Izzy frolicked in her ivory white shoes with small heels, playfully hopping from one side of the footpath to the other. "Babba, look at the beautiful flowers. Can we smell them?" she asked.

"Yes, aren't they beautiful?" Donna remarked, leaning down for a closer inspection. With her tiny, delicate fingers, Isabella crouched and swiftly picked several of the most vibrantly coloured flowers; gardenia whites and daisy yellows peeked out from among the native shrubs. Turning, she presented Donna with a petite cluster. Donna gratefully accepted the flowers, inhaled the bouquet's scent, and released a theatrical sigh of pure joy. Inspired by Donna's display, Isabella twirled back to the flowerbed and mimicked the gesture, taking in the aroma again. Content and unhurried, they continued their stroll around the lake. Izzy attempted to mimic the aquatic sounds, giggling when her frog imitations fell short. Their attempts at duck sounds left them in stitches, laughing heartily at their playful silliness.

As they were about to cross the road and take a shortcut to the church, Donna noticed further down the street Izzy's maternal grandmother, Francis, coming out of her house and placing Christmas presents in the back of her four-wheel drive. Lucy followed closely behind her. Donna's heart missed a beat and suddenly started racing at a hundred miles per hour. Impulsively, and without thinking, she approached them to deliver Izzy's pretty Christmas cards, which could be a good icebreaker.

Donna thought, *Why not? What do we have to lose? This is a God-sent opportunity to bring Izzy and Lucy together again. The festive season is when people are kind to each other. This is the right time of the year to heal the brokenhearted and kindle the love between mother and child.*

As soon as they approached the driveway, Donna encouraged Izzy to say hello to her Tummy Mummy. Then she stepped back to give them space.

At first, the situation looked tense, and time stood still. Then Lucy went down on her knees and, gently stroking Isabella's curly locks, spoke to her in a sweet, tender voice, telling her daughter, "Isabella, you are so grown up. You look just like a princess." Her voice was soft and soothing as she gently caressed her baby daughter's face.

"Come on, sweetie, give your mummy a hug, just a little kiss," Donna encouraged Izzy.

Lucy spoke gently to her girl and embraced her tenderly. And Isabella looked at her mummy with love and affection. This beautiful, heartfelt moment would stay with Donna forever.

But Donna's initial euphoria quickly turned to despair as Francis reappeared. "Get in the car, Lucy. We have to be in Wanneroo on time!" she spewed in a hateful voice.

Reluctantly, Lucy pulled away from her daughter. But Francis grew increasingly agitated and resorted to vulgar language directed at Donna. "Leave us alone, you wicked woman! You took Isabella away from her mother and me," Francis yelled.

Lucy's tender moment with her daughter immediately deflated, while Isabella froze and was now visibly scared and confused. She didn't understand why her Nana Francis yelled so much, telling her she had been stolen from them.

Izzy turned her head with tears in her eyes; she clung to Donna, pleading, "Help me …"

Donna stood dumbstruck, then angry. *How could Francis be so heartless! How could she hurt an innocent child so cruelly?* She fumed inwardly.

Donna excused herself, realising this chance meeting was getting out of control. She wished them both a Merry Christmas, took Izzy by the hand, and started walking toward the road. As they were moving away, Francis suddenly changed from violent Hyde to friendly Jekyll and approached them in two or three steps. She hugged Isabella.

"I love you, Isabella. Your mummy loves you, too. Tomorrow is Christmas Day, and your Mummy and I will come and visit you at your house, and we will bring you lots of presents."

Then, changing back to Hyde, Francis straightened and gave Donna a sharp, scathing look. "Is it okay with you if we come to your house tomorrow, Christmas Day, early in the morning?" Francis asked caustically.

"Of course it is; you are most welcome," Donna said placidly. This was hope for Isabella, and as pleasantly as she could, she managed a courteous smile.

Francis abruptly nodded. "Okay, see you tomorrow."

Donna and Izzy continued their walk, hand in hand, through the park. At first, Izzy seemed quiet, but soon her mood turned somewhat positive. Then, unexpectedly, as they neared the church, she looked up at Donna and said with some confidence.

"Babba, I know why my Tummy Mummy couldn't come and visit me before."

"Why, my sweet?"

"My Tummy Mummy has no car. Nana Francis is driving her to visit family who live far away. That is why she couldn't visit me before," Izzy said.

"Of course, my sweetie pie, I'd never thought of that; you are so smart," Donna said.

Izzy continued to cheerfully chatter in her sweet little voice all the way to the church, telling Donna, "Babba, I am so excited; my Tummy, Mummy, is coming to visit us, and Nana Francis said they would bring me lots of presents."

To change the unsettling and worrying subject, Donna said in a soft, gentle voice, "Yes, my sweet, but let's hurry because we will miss our mass, so we'd better hurry now."

Donna struggled with the notion that maybe she was wrong about Francis. *After all, she goes to the same church as me and believes in the same God. Why not give this troubled woman the benefit of the doubt? A miracle may happen tomorrow, and Santa will grant Izzy her secret Christmas wish,* she tried to reassure herself and stay positive.

⇒

On Christmas morning, Santa arrived early, and all the presents were neatly stacked under the tree. At dawn, Izzy was already awake and brimming with excitement, her laughter and joy filling the room. They all rose and sat around the tree, pleased to see Izzy so happy. She was surprised and overjoyed that Santa had brought her so many lovely presents, and sang and hip-hop danced around the house. Everybody found something special under the tree. Even the puppy, Bon-Bon, got a bone to play with. Just as she opened the last of her presents, Isabella asked worriedly, "Babba, when is Tummy Mummy coming? Quick, let's open the door and have a look!"

Not waiting for anyone's response, she ran to the front door. Not finding anyone outside, she looked pleadingly at Donna. "Can we leave the door open to see when they come?" she said.

The front door stayed open all morning. Now and then, Izzy would go to the front door and look outside to see if Tummy Mummy was there, hoping and wishing that Santa had granted her a special Christmas wish.

Donna was overwhelmed with sadness for her granddaughter, but suppressed her tears and hid her pain. She had to stay strong but was upset with herself, thinking, *How could I get into such a terrible mess? It's all my fault. I should have known better not to give Izzy any false expectations. This is Izzy's special day.*

Sadly, not even Santa could grant Izzy her special Christmas wish. She waited all day for her Tummy Mummy to arrive, but Lucy didn't show up and she probably never would.

Donna took comfort in knowing that Izzy was in a safe home and cherished the deep emotional bond Izzy had with her and Tom, and her Daddy. Donna planned to share her perspective of the truth with Isabella when she was older, more mature, and resilient, hoping it would mitigate any future emotional pain and distress.

Tom and Donna were resolute in their decision to preserve the Christmas spirit. Isabella recounted how Santa had consumed the cookies and milk she left for him and the carrot had also disappeared, presumably enjoyed by his reindeer. The air in their home was alive with cheerful Christmas tunes, easing them into relaxation. The radiant hues of the Christmas tree's ornaments, coupled with the wafting aromas of exquisite treats from the kitchen, enhanced the warm and inviting ambience of their home.

That afternoon, they gathered on the balcony, basking in the shimmering lights that danced through the greenery of the foreshore trees. As the sun dipped below the ocean's horizon, their home seemed to transform into a magical castle, with Izzy as their cherished princess. Come evening, Izzy and Bon-Bon played together, their joyful noise filling the air as they frolicked.

After indulging in a hearty serving of chocolate pudding, Izzy finally exhausted her energy and slowed down. Post-bath, nestled comfortably in her bed, Izzy listened as Donna read a fairy tale of princes and princesses in a distant, magical land.

Before the night's end, Donna paused to tenderly watch over Izzy and Bon-Bon, now a single, serene bundle of sleep. Surrounded by a menagerie of plush friends, including teddy bears, unicorns, and ladybugs, Izzy and Bon-Bon lay snug and content.

Every night, just before Izzy would fall asleep, the ritual was always the same; Izzy would say, "I love you to the moon and back."

"But I love you all the way to the universe," Donna would fondly reply, standing at the doorway, looking at Izzy and Bon-Bon curled up together, content and at peace with the world she lived in.

Chapter 36

A Chesterfield Chair

After the Christmas celebrations ended, Tom removed the outdoor Christmas lights while Izzy helped Donna dismantle the Christmas tree and store everything away for the following year.

During the summer, Izzy had many activities. Donna enrolled her in swimming lessons, and once she learned how to swim, Izzy wanted to spend all day at the beach. Donna often joined other younger mums, and their children played on the beach together all day.

In the new school year, Izzy started pre-school. Tom and Donna looked at her dressed in her school uniform and carrying a backpack on her shoulders. How grown up she looked – the years had disappeared in no time.

Tom and Donna wanted to get their life back to normal and grew excited that they could start travelling again. Sharing paternal rights with Ricky was complicated, but thankfully, he finally agreed that Isabella could have a passport so they could take her with them on holidays.

However, just as they were ready to pop the cork on a bottle of champagne to celebrate their freedom from the endless Family Court custody battle, an unexpected incident disrupted their holiday plans and turned their lives into turmoil.

◌

Tom was very fond of his roses and took great care of them. He would regularly spray them to keep them healthy and beautiful. However, during one of his pruning sessions, he accidentally pricked himself on a thorn. Although it was just a tiny prick, he paid little attention to it.

Tom had previously undergone cancer treatment and was now in remission. Since then, he had been relatively healthy and thought there was no need to worry about the slight injury.

However, when his hands swelled, Donna convinced him to see a doctor about his arm. After a thorough examination, the doctor advised him to take anti-inflammatory pills, rest, and drink plenty of water.

Within twenty-four hours, Tom's condition worsened. His arm swelled, turned purple and red, and became hot and painful. Donna took him to the emergency department as his fever spiked. Tom was isolated and given intravenous antibiotics. The doctors suspected a staph infection. However, the initial antibiotics did not work, and Tom's fever persisted. The doctors feared the disease could spread to his lymph glands and bone. Despite trying different antibiotics, the bacterial infection continued to spread. Tom was diagnosed with MRSA, a superbug resistant to antibiotics. If the treatment fails, the blood infection could be fatal.

After enduring two nights without sleep, Donna went to the hospital to see Tom. His hand was now a grotesque shade of blue and alarmingly swollen. He fought for every breath, and his blood pressure had plummeted to dangerous levels. With his body starved of oxygen, Tom had never appeared so fragile. The look of defeat etched on his face silently conveyed to Donna the severity of the situation. His survival hinged on innovative experimental drugs that the doctors administered with urgency.

Days later, the doctors delivered a grave ultimatum: "Should the antibiotics be ineffective, we will be left with no option but to amputate his arm above the shoulder."

This was uncharted territory for Tom, who had never undergone surgery before. The prospect was daunting. He understood the stakes and signed the consent forms for the surgery scheduled for the following afternoon. As a last resort, a renowned hematologist from the city's clinics was consulted. He suggested a combination of antibiotics administered intravenously throughout the night.

The doctors told Donna, "Go home. Prepare for the worst but hope for the best – this is our last effort to save his arm, perhaps even his life. Let's hope the treatment is effective. We'll be closely monitoring his vital signs, as this treatment poses risks of blood clots, internal bleeding, or low blood pressure, which could lead to a heart attack."

When Donna looked at Tom, her thoughts reeled. *Is this it? It can't be. He can't leave me now. I need him. Izzy needs her Didda.* She pushed her emotions away, fearing her pain would show. *Stay focused*, she told herself. *Do not cry!* Instead, she smiled, hugged Tom, and reassured him. "Have faith in the medicine. It will all work out just fine."

Tom and Donna chatted for a while, mainly about Izzy. Tom missed his little princess and longed to see her, but the hospital environment was unsuitable for a child. And Tom preferred Izzy to keep memories of him as a healthy, playful, and cheerful Didda.

"We owe it to Izzy to keep her happy memories intact," he said.

As Donna was about to leave, she forced another smile. "Look on the bright side," she said to cheer him a little, "you look good in short sleeves, and short sleeves will cost us less." Tom gazed at her with fondness and returned a weak smile.

Donna fled the hospital so Tom wouldn't see her crumble. She couldn't believe it. How did a simple rose prick lead to this life-or-death battle? No one knew where the super-bug came from, but the fragile, beautiful rose bush was the culprit. Donna remembered their trip to Sicily's wine regions. The winery owner, Sergio, said roses may look delicate but harsh, sharp, and unpredictable. Donna believed Tom was tough, too. He'd survived chemotherapy, so surely, he could beat the monster bacteria and pull through.

That was their darkest twenty-four hours; Donna had never prayed so hard.

They had been married for nearly five decades, and she had hardly ever cried in front of him. Once or twice, while watching a sad movie, a few silent tears would smudge her face. Besides, she always knew seeing her crying or sad would upset Tom.

While at home, in the evening, when Izzy slept snugly, Donna sat in her dressing gown in Tom's study. To calm her anxiety and worry about Tom's condition, she played a classical CD of Adagios, a baroque cello composition. Donna thought that nothing cries better than the sounds of cellos and violins, she let herself be carried away by them. The cello's slow tempo calmed her, and the violin's notes ascended like a majestic eagle, lifting above the sombre clouds of despair towards the luminous horizon of newfound hope.

The office served as Tom's regal domain, his niche in the cosmos. He revelled in the company of his world history books and the eminent historical figures within them – mighty conquerors, generals, philosophers, and scientists he knew intimately during his scholarly pursuits and relentless reading. Donna's hand, quivering slightly, brushed over the books' shiny spines, meticulously arranged in the towering Jarrah bookcase.

Donna cried silently, wondering if Tom's fingers would again grace these volumes.

ೞ

When Izzy returned from preschool the following day, she noticed a small bird in distress on the front porch.

"Babba, look, the baby chick is sick; she must have fallen out of her nest."

"A neighbour's ginger cat is jumping on our fence; that is why this little chick is hurt," Donna said, comforting Izzy.

"Babba, can we help the little chick get healthy again?" Izzy asked, with a sad look in her eyes.

"Indeed, there's no doubt that we can. Let me find a soft towel and a cup of water." Donna glanced sideways and spotted a mother dove perched on the letterbox, not frightened, just peacefully sitting there.

Izzy then gently picked up the little chick and carried her inside. She gave her some water and put her on a soft pillow in the backyard. "Let us nurse the baby bird so her mother will come and rescue her. It's best to keep Bon-Bon inside so he doesn't scare the little chick," Donna reminded Izzy.

Not long after, late in the afternoon, a silver dove flew into their yard; she appeared not scared and started dancing and hopping around her little chick. Donna and Izzy transferred the little chick to a soft cotton wool padding and hid her in a big bush. "When the mother dove builds a nest, the chick will survive." *That is a good omen*, Donna thought. *What if this is the same little dove? Has she come here to live with us and save Tom?* Donna's hope rejuvenated.

The following day, just as Donna had predicted, the mother dove built her nest under the house eaves, shaded and hidden by the Hibiscus shrub that Tom had planted a few years prior. Izzy was overjoyed that her little chick had survived. She began sprinkling some bread crumbs, and the mother dove and her chick didn't fly away, even when Bon-Bon barked. The dove's

444

nest became their new sanctuary.

The next day, after dinner, Donna briefly visited the hospital; Tom's condition had not changed. He looked grey and weak, with the intravenous drip still attached to his arm. The nurse informed her that he was sedated and sleeping. Donna knew not to disturb him; she didn't want him to sense her worry. Barely keeping it together, she left the room and returned to her car, relieved that Tom was still stable.

The car park was nearly deserted. She rolled down the window and took a deep breath, savouring the familiar scent of eucalyptus trees that filled the evening air. Dark clouds loomed overhead, adding to the weight already pressing on her chest.

Taking a deep breath, hoping it would calm her racing heart and soothe her aching chest, Donna longed for tears to fall and release her pain, but she let out a raw, high-pitched moan instead – a haunting sound of pure agony. She sat motionless in the car, forcing herself to listen to soothing music as she prayed and pleaded with God not to take Tom away. She felt unprepared for such a loss and couldn't bear the thought of it happening so soon. They had many plans together, and she couldn't imagine facing the future without him. And then there was little Izzy – Tom's granddaughter – who loved him dearly. She would miss him terribly if he were gone.

Donna sat in the car for what seemed like an eternity, thinking that it would be lovely if she had family member to cry on their shoulder. This was her most desperate hour and she felt so alone. Nobody would comfort her during these tough times.

The thought of losing her soul mate was devastating. Married for almost fifty years, they were a perfect match. All of her friends envied them – Tom was intelligent, loved reading, and had vast knowledge in many areas, and he was also incredibly generous. Donna had a sharp business mind, was dedicated, positive, and passionate, with a kind heart. Together, they formed a great team, like a shining gold coin with two sides. Tom would often tell her they were 'The Dream Team'.

Although their lifelong friends were understanding and supportive, they had not much in common any more. Most of their friends enjoyed their retirement, travelling and having fun. Tom and Donna now had the responsibility of raising Izzy, and their lifestyle had completely changed. No more cocktail parties or elaborate dinners. Going out, dancing and romancing had become tiring, hence their friends now found them boring.

Donna sat in the hospital car park, in solitude, thinking and listening to soothing melodies on the radio for what seemed an age and all the while dark clouds gathered in the sky. She hated driving when it was dark, so she hurried home. But the moment she exited the car park, a sudden downpour flooded the streets, making the road slippery.

She put on her glasses but visibility was still poor, so she proceeded cautiously, seeing little. Cracking open the window for fresh air, she turned the radio up, letting the music lift her sombre mood. Once home, she parked in the garage, turned on the interior light, and glanced at her reflection in the rear-view mirror. *No wonder visibility was an issue*, she thought, *it's not the rain's fault.* In her distress, she hadn't realised she'd driven with her sunglasses on. That realisation brought a chuckle at her absent-mindedness.

Composing herself before entering the house, where Ricky was watching Izzy, she avoided discussing Tom's condition with him as it seemed futile; he appeared indifferent to his father's plight, the bond between them having long ago completely eroded. Ricky also still harboured bitterness towards them, unable to forgive them for gaining custody of his daughter. Despite complying with every mandate from the Family Court, including undergoing gastric stapling surgery and permanently abstaining from alcohol, Ricky felt powerless because they were still in charge. His mental illness was now worse than ever, and he'd become a hermit obsessed with conspiracy theories; he was self-absorbed, and full of self-pity. Since Lucy had left him, he hated all women and didn't even remember Mother's Day or birthdays.

What Donna needed right then was to be alone in peaceful tranquillity and she needed to spend time with Izzy. Like most nights, Donna sat on the bed next to Izzy and started telling her another story from her childhood experiences. The story revolved around a playful dog. Izzy chuckled, and couldn't believe that her dog was called Lucky.

But that night, however, Izzy was restless. She asked, "When is Didda coming home? I miss Didda, and Bon-Bon misses him too." Izzy stroked her puppy that was curled up next to her.

"Soon, sweetie. Didda is recovering." Donna couldn't utter another word as she suppressed her tears. Her chest tightened as she tried to block her emotions from surfacing, a sharp, piercing pain making her gasp for air to suppress that familiar choking feeling. Taking a few deep breaths, she pushed away the crippling feelings that had buried in her core.

Desperate to hide her emotional pain, her watery eyes blurred her vision, and she tried to hide behind the bedside lamp that illuminated Izzy's favourite, soft Disney toys.

Izzy's smile cheered her up as she continued chatting. Then, out of nowhere, Izzy came up with a question that shocked her. "Babba, my friend Lilly told me that her granddad died; he was old and had grey hair. Didda is old and he has grey hair too. Is Didda going to die?"

"Oh no, your Didda won't die. Don't worry, sweetie, and I won't die for a long time either," Donna said.

"Babba, I don't want Bon-Bon to die," Izzy said next.

"Don't worry; Bon-Bon will live a long time; she is only a very young puppy." Donna smiled faintly, but Izzy continued chatting.

"Babba, heaven is so far away, up in the sky, close to the moon. When you and Didda die, how will I find you?"

As Donna gazed at Izzy, she let a smile settle back on her face, and gently caressed her. "Don't worry, my sweetie pie, we will always find each other. Nobody ever gets lost in heaven. But that's enough chatting, and you must sleep now."

Donna lay next to Izzy, her fingers gently caressing her curly hair as she listened to her soft breathing; it was food for her starving soul. Izzy turned around, her little hand stretching over her shoulders, her soft curls smothering her face. Donna relaxed, and a few tears cascaded down her cheeks – one, two, then several more. Donna felt the familiar saltiness on her face and a sense of relief. As her emotions swelled, she was careful not to disturb Izzy. She muffled her sobs with her hand, taking deep breaths to calm the lump in her throat as she tried to stem the flow of tears. Then Bon-Bon began to lick her tears away gently, the endearing little fur ball snuggled up so close that Donna could hear the puppy's heartbeat. That night, Bon-Bon was indeed her best friend in the world.

☙

The next few days, while Tom barely held onto life, Donna struggled to hold it together and to keep her faith. Emotionally drained, all she wished for was a restful sleep but her mind her started wandering. *This is all so unfair; it is too soon to lose Tom.* Donna's life without him would be unimaginable. Her vulnerability and the accumulation of stress left her feeling desperate, alone, needy. She needed Tom; he was her rock. What if he never came home to Isabella and her? She couldn't imagine living without him and wondered why life could be so cruel.

Donna forced herself to push these negative thoughts from her mind. *You must not give up hope. You have to stay strong and positive for Izzy.*

☙

Tom remained in the isolation ward for more than a week before a ray of sunshine entered their world. The doctors reassured Donna that Tom had improved from the latest round of antibiotic cocktails. Finally, her prayers showed some hope. Not all was lost. Her beloved husband was going to pull through this. Tom was as strong as some of the warriors he read about in his books.

☙

While Tom was in hospital recuperating, Donna decided to surprise him and try to fix his broken Chesterfield chair, which broke a few months back when Ricky sat on it. His more than ample weight was too much for it, and the steel frame that held the legs had snapped and one leg had broken off at the base. Donna mused on the irony of how their son's mental illness seemed to shatter everything in their lives. Tom had attempted repairs but to no avail; the chair was over twenty years old, and the manufacturer recommended purchasing a new one.

But Tom was extremely attached to the old chair; it was a part of him, a companion during endless hours of reading. The old Chesterfield, with its premium leather and dark knobs shining like rubies, boasted shades of crimson, a touch of purple, and a deep burgundy wine colour that only grew richer with time.

449

Donna contemplated: *What if I repair the chair back to its original glory? This act could symbolise the mending of other fractured parts of our lives.* With this thought, she decided to do precisely that – fix the chair and, in doing so, attempt to restore their lives to the state they were in before the unfortunate rosebush incident.

With such thoughts, she became resolute in repairing the chair, believing that, if she could restore the steel frame to its former strength, Tom would return to her as resilient as the steel of his cherished chair. After an extensive search for the welding business Donna had used years earlier, the Irish couple who ran the shop always kind and accommodating, she finally located it. The receptionist, however, informed her that the Irish gentleman had passed away a few years back, and the current owners were boat builders who did not offer that type of service. Donna's heart sank. This place was her last hope. The old Irish man repaired anything that was broken.

Feeling hopeless, she turned to leave, but the receptionist stopped her. "Hold on, I'll call my husband and ask him."

A few minutes later, a big man in overalls came out. "Let's see what you got, lady. I don't know, but I'll have a look."

He followed Donna to the car, took the chair out of the boot, looked at it and said, "It's unusual to weld something like this. This might be tricky as it's a swivel chair, but we weld sailing swinging sails. Leave it with me; let me talk to my crew. My tradesmen are good welders; they may figure out how to mend this."

"Thank you so much," Donna said.

"Don't thank me yet. Come back tomorrow, and we will see. No promises though, okay?" he said.

Donna was on tenterhooks and not expecting too much. She had taken the chair to many places and been disappointed too many times. When she returned to collect the chair the following day, she was greeted by a friendly smile from the same giant bloke dressed in greasy yellow overalls. He wiped his hands as he walked towards her.

Donna didn't know what to expect, but the big grin on his face was a good sign.

"Lady, you're in luck," he said. "My boys did brilliant work. Your chair is as good as new. Our business is boat building; everything must be strong enough to hold the sails in extreme weather. Nothing is as strong as the big yachts sailing from Sydney to Hobart on Boxing Day, which we have worked on. Lady, I'm telling you that your chair is now that strong. It will never break. I guarantee you that."

Donna's jaw dropped in happy disbelief. "I am so grateful. I've spent days searching for a repair shop that could fix my husband's favourite chair. I feel so fortunate to have found you."

The big fellow smiled back, seeing she was ecstatic with the news.

"Lady, the chair is fixed. I am sure your husband will be pleased," he said. The gentle giant of a man put the strong-as-steel chair into Donna's car boot.

"How much do I owe you? Would you prefer cash or a credit card, sir?" Donna said, prepared to pay any price he named; the chair was her lifeline, and no amount of money could replace that. She envisioned Tom smiling, swinging back and forth in his Chesterfield chair, even as it scratched the wooden floor, but it didn't matter.

The tradesman's face lit up again, and he wiped his hands on a dirty, oil-streaked cloth. "No problem, lady. This job is on the house. Free of charge. I'm sure your husband will be delighted to have his chair back," he said in his deep, soft voice that brimmed with sincerity and empathy.

Donna immediately thought about the cycle of good karma. Ray, the old Irish fellow who had passed away, must be smiling down from the heavens, pleased that he sold his business to such a kind man.

As the gentle giant of a man closed the car trunk and bid her farewell, he took a few hurried steps towards his workshop before abruptly stopping and turning around, shocked to see Donna crying. She was equally surprised, pondering on the sudden onslaught of tears that cascaded down like a thawing glacier, saturating everything in its wake.

Donna's weeping was intense, unleashing a torrent of tears akin to Niagara Falls. Her body quivered, and her hands trembled as she struggled to open her car door. When she observed the worker awkwardly attempting to comfort her, she felt pity for the kind-hearted colossus of a man beside her. She thought, *This poor man doesn't know what's going on, probably wondering, 'What's wrong with this crazy woman?'*

Seeing Donna so distressed, the worker grew concerned. "Are you alright? What seems to be the problem? Your chair has been repaired; you should be smiling instead of crying."

Donna could only nod. "Yes, I am so happy. I have never felt this good. You can't imagine what this means to me," she said, forcing a smile. Then she thanked the worker, and drove away.

That same afternoon, she went to the bottle shop, bought an expensive bottle of wine and a thank-you card and drove back to the boatyard. Without explanation, she left the gift at the reception desk and ran as fast as possible before anybody saw her. She had never been so embarrassed and so extremely grateful at the same time.

ᘓ

A few days later, the hospital rang, asking Donna to pick Tom up. Izzy and Bon-Bon wanted to participate in this special happy occasion. And indeed, it was a splendid occasion. Tom was surprised and overjoyed to have his chair back, while Donna was equally thrilled to have the love of her life return home. Watching Tom contentedly spinning in his Chesterfield chair warmed her heart. Tom was finally back where he belonged. The chair rejuvenated his health, and the life-threatening ordeal was behind them. Their life and love for each other would be as enduring and strong as that new chair.

༄

After Izzy and Bon-Bon were asleep that night, Donna made a pot of lemon and ginger-flavoured tea and apple pie. She sat beside Tom and held his hand.

"Has my little princess fallen asleep?" Tom wanted to know.

"Both of them are fast asleep. You wouldn't believe it but Bon-Bon and Izzy are both snoring."

Tom, seeing his wife unsettled, asked, "So what's bothering you?"

"While you were in hospital, I realised that life could be so fragile. Izzy was worried that you might die. I think she knows we are getting old and is worried about who will look after her if we do die."

"Don't worry; I'll be here for at least another decade, and since you're ten years younger than me, you'll see Izzy mature into adulthood. You're resilient; you might live to be a hundred, so there's a chance you'll meet your great-grandchildren."

"May I remind you, Tom, that we are in the autumn years of our lives? Time is running out." Donna feigned a smile.

"There is no point getting sentimental about age; it is only numbers. But we have to accept the situation for what it is,"

Tom said, sipping his tea and taking a bite of his warm apple pie. He placed his plate on the coffee table before continuing.

"I now understand why the Family Court battle lasted almost five years. It was essential to keep both biological parents involved, just in case one of us kicked the bucket. I certainly had a very close call with the Staph infection. Life can be so fragile at times," Tom chuckled and carried on talking.

"But who will take care of Izzy if we are no longer around?" Donna asked, waiting for her philosophical husband's reply. However, she was pleasantly surprised this time, as Tom's reply was much more realistic and down-to-earth.

"The one person who can bring you some hope is Ricky. He loves his daughter, which I am sure of. He inherited a home from us, which is a huge plus. Ricky is your only Plan B." Tom chuckled.

"I agree with you. Ricky made some changes in his lifestyle, but he is still struggling with mental health issues. Knowing that he loves his daughter and she loves him back is encouraging news. Sadly, Izzy's mother hasn't seen her since she was a toddler. I heard from some churchgoers that Francis is spreading rumours that we stole Izzy from Lucy. Donna's look showed that she was concerned about this."

But Tom cautioned her. "You are aware that Francis and some of Izzy's maternal relatives could show up here one day. We must always shield Izzy from potentially harmful and unstable adults. We must teach Izzy to be observant and wary of avaricious family members who may try to attach themselves to her and take advantage of her inheritance. You must teach her to remain alert, rely on her rational mind, and trust her instincts to avoid being deceived by those greedy relatives. We must remain vigilant in this matter."

Donna's nerves were eased as she sipped her tea and lovingly watched her husband. Tom was like an anchor for her, always knowing how to ease her mind.

"Tom, I've been thinking about how Izzy will handle that her mother abandoned her. It breaks my heart to think about it. Losing a mother at such a young age is a significant loss, and I can relate to it personally. Not knowing my mother left a massive void in my heart."

"Why are you feeling so down? Your situation was different. When your mother passed away, you were placed in an orphanage. Izzy, on the other hand, lives in a safe and happy home. You have been like a mother to Izzy, and she hasn't missed out on anything," Tom said, smiling at Donna. "The most important thing is that Izzy loves you. You have filled the void in her heart. We all need you, and even though I hate to admit it, Ricky needs you, too. Hopefully, one day, he will realise how valuable you are, but don't be disappointed if he doesn't. But don't' lose sight of the bigger picture – remember that the buck stops with you."

"Tom, dear, sometimes I feel frustrated with God for making us endure so much pain and suffering. Raising a child is already difficult, and dealing with external pressures from biological parents only adds to the challenge."

"Blaming God for our situation is not fair. If you're looking for someone to blame, it is Francis and her crazy Sicilian vendetta towards us. She is a bitter and hateful old woman who caused all this trouble for us and her family. However, we should focus on the fact that God has given us the responsibility to take care of our granddaughter. Izzy deserves a safe and happy childhood, which is every child's right, and we are providing her with that."

Tom couldn't stop himself from yawning. He was ready to go to sleep. Without fail, for nearly half a century, it had been a nightly routine before bed. Tom would consistently express his affection by saying, "I love you, my dear."

And Donna responded with joy, saying, "I love you, too."

Tom, with his cheeky smile, would always say, "But, my dear, I love you even more."

"Yes, I know. I am lucky to have you and Izzy in my life." Donna gave him an affectionate smile and sent a goodnight kiss his way.

❧

All was good in Donna's life again. God had indeed smiled upon her and all her prayers had been answered when Tom's health was restored and he came home. That was the greatest gift Donna had ever received.

Chapter 37

Easter Celebration

Donna cherished her Easter festivity memories from her childhood. The cultural and religious tradition of egg painting symbolised rebirth and new hope for the future. It was a time when the European spring breathed life into everything around. Donna continued to celebrate these traditions with her granddaughter in Australia. She wanted Izzy to have similar happy Easter memories.

The festivities started on Good Friday with a trip to church and eating only fish that day. On that day, Donna and Izzy started decorating hard-boiled eggs. When the eggs were cool, Izzy helped to put them into food colouring water to soak overnight.

On Saturday morning, Donna and Izzy spent hours decorating and wrapping over a dozen eggs, Izzy planning to give some to their neighbours. Their fingers were stained from green, blue, purple, red, and yellow dyes. They carefully wrapped each egg in designer cellophane paper and tied them with pink or blue ribbons. Finally, they placed the eggs in small Easter boxes, one egg per box.

After completing that task, Tom assisted Donna and Izzy in preparing the garden for Sunday's children's party, adorning it with colourful ribbons and balloons attached to the trampoline. They arranged the table with arts and crafts, and Easter bunny-themed paper cards designed for each child attending Izzy's party, with everything in place and ready for the guests.

Izzy was exhausted. She snuggled up with Bon-Bon, eager for another tale from her grandmother. As Donna tucked Izzy in, she shared memories of the Easter festival, the story from her own childhood, as she reminisced about the Easter celebration she'd spent with her beloved Aunt Pavica.

"I spent Easter in a tiny village with my Aunty Pavica. Children from the neighbourhood would gather in her courtyard and celebrate Easter. The kids had so much fun. We soaked our boiled eggs in natural colours, made from brown onion, green grass, seaweed and blueberries. Then we would wrap them up in a fig leaf and gift them to our family." Donna finished her story.

"Babba, did you put on lots of glitter and stickers? Did you eat lots of chocolate eggs?"

"Sweetie, back then, people were very poor. They didn't have glitter or stickers, and chocolate was a delicacy that my Aunt Pavica couldn't afford. But we still had a lot of fun. We played games and, at night, we sat under the stars by a fire. We roasted corn on sticks and listened to Aunt Pavica's stories. It was so much fun. Sweetie pie, it's time to go to sleep now. Tomorrow is Easter Sunday, and all your little friends will come to celebrate with you. But after the party ends, I promise to tell you another story."

CR

On Easter Sunday, Donna's house was typically brimming with children; they would decorate and paint eggs, creating quite a mess. The atmosphere was noisy yet joyful.

Once the eggs were dried, they were wrapped in decorative paper and adorned with delicate gold or silver bows. Inviting Izzy's friends over was a key part of the festive celebration. The children delighted in finding chocolate eggs hidden in the backyard, which they would then take home, along with the hand-painted eggs, to their families. The next day, Izzy's friends would arrive, and the backyard would be abuzz with excitement. Izzy used a spectrum of colours to create a special rainbow design on each egg, then wrapped them and placed them in little decorative baskets topped with a pretty bow. These were transformed into individual gift packages extending best wishes for the Easter celebration to all her friends and neighbours who were unable to join the party, unlike previous years.

"Can I paint some eggs for my preschool friends who couldn't come to my party? When Lilly and Connor receive their Easter eggs, they'll be so happy. Babba, what do you think of my decoration?"

"I'm really fond of it. You are such an artist."

"I'll put lots of gold glitter on it. This egg I made for my dad. His favourite colour is blue, and I put heart stickers on it," Izzy said happily.

Donna thought how lucky Ricky was to have such a loving, thoughtful daughter.

The children were engrossed in decorating their eggs and taking pride in their artistic creations. They delighted in chocolates and fairy bread, their faces smeared with sprinkles. Donna set up various activities. The children paraded through the garden, balancing eggs on wooden spoons. Whoever came first was rewarded with an additional chocolate egg. Sticky chocolate handprints adorned the table and sliding door.

Before their parents collected them, the children strolled by the lake, feeding ducks and admiring the baby birds in their nests. The children were in awe as they witnessed two magnificent black swans floating gracefully around the lake. Under the shrubs, amidst the water lilies, ducks hid their nests, protecting their newly hatched chicks.

Finally, when all the children had gone home, Izzy and Donna gathered all the colourful Easter eggs in a basket. They walked around the neighbourhood, handing out decorative eggs wrapped in cellophane with pink and blue ribbons. The neighbours reciprocated and gave Izzy chocolate eggs, which excited her the most because she loved chocolate.

When all the deliveries were done, they went home and found a pleasant surprise waiting for them, too.

"Look, Babba, what's that?" Izzy said, noticing a cardboard box at the front door; she was keen to see what was inside.

"Babba look. It's Easter bunny chocolate," Izzy said opening and peering inside the box.

"Let me see the card. This chocolate box came from your godmother Margaret; she often looked after you and protected you as a baby."

On Easter Sunday, many friends left messages of goodwill, neighbours expressed gratitude for such a thoughtful handmade gift. The Easter celebration worked its charm, strengthening Isabella's friendships and bringing the neighbourhood closer together. Donna was pleasantly surprised to find that Tom had already cleaned up all the mess. He had little patience for screaming kids or chaos but cherished seeing Izzy so happy; that was what mattered most to him. Sweeping up glitter wasn't easy, nor was picking up scattered arts and crafts from the floor, and wiping children's fingerprints off the outdoor furniture.

After indulging in all these hectic fun activities and eating so many chocolate eggs, Izzy crashed. After another short story from Donna, she and Bon-Bon fell asleep.

Ↄ

On Easter Monday, Tom, Donna, Izzy, and their dog visited the beach. Izzy joined some children, building sand castles.

Bon-Bon, the dog, would tentatively wet her paws before quickly retreating from the gentle waves she disliked. Yet, beyond the shoreline, she enjoyed swimming. After frolicking with the puppy, Izzy would challenge Bon-Bon to a race back to the shore.

Donna stood at the water's edge, laughing, applauding, and urging Izzy not to fall too far behind Bon-Bon's doggie paddle. She could swim as a toddler, and she loved competing with Bon-Bon. Later, when dry and comfortable, they sat on the sand, building sandcastles and digging a big hole to cool down their feet.

Bon-Bon looked more like a lamb than a dog. Bon-Bon and Izzy were inseparable friends from the first moment that Izzy had held her in her arms.

In the late afternoon, everybody was exhausted. Even Bon-Bon went quiet, ignoring the noisy seagulls swooping around her. The golden sunset illuminated the sky, bringing in the refreshing sea breeze called the Fremantle Doctor. It was time to pack up and walk home.

Returning home, slightly sunburned, lethargic, and thirsty, Izzy still mustered the energy to chase Bon-Bon around the backyard. As Tom bathed Bon-Bon, who was covered in sand, Izzy and Donna scattered breadcrumbs for a dove and her chicks. The dove and her chicks had established a permanent nest in the hibiscus bush, which bloomed with bright yellow flowers, as though woven from rays of sunshine.

After dinner, a quick shower and a hot Milo, Izzy was ready for her bedtime story.

"Tonight, I'd like to share a story ..."

The bedroom was warm and cozy. Izzy turned to face her grandmother, eagerly expecting the start of the story.

"Many years ago, during a visit to my Aunt Pavica's village, there was a large fig tree in her courtyard. In that tree, my little dove built her nest, and I would feed her chicks with crumbs of cornbread. Later, with my guardian angel's guidance, I moved to Australia. That's where I met your Didda, and we fell in love.

"I love feeding our dove and her chicks too. Babba, did your little dove follow you to Australia?" Izzy said, yawning and stretching her arms.

"I don't think so. It is such a long way to fly for such a small bird. But her spirit may have followed me all the way here."

"Babba, what is spirit?"

"The spirit is unseen, it's a part of our being, but only those who believe in it can see it. Can you remember the Coco movie? During one scene, a boy set out on a search to find a spirit that had been lost. I can still recall when he sang 'Remember Me' and Coco examined her father's photographs. Coco's remembrance of her father allowed his spirit to be released.

"You're a bit too young to comprehend stories that are so complex. It's important to hold on to the memories of our loved ones, as their spirits will forever be free.

"When you get older, I will tell you a story that took place long before you were born, in a distant land. Some of these stories are so old that even your granddad hasn't heard them yet. When you fall asleep, these stories will help you have pleasant dreams."

"Babba, I love listening to your stories," Izzy replied with a smile, stretching her arms as she yawned again.

"I hope you will remember my stories. One day, when you grow up, fall in love with someone special, and have children of your own, you can tell them all about us."

Izzy was exhausted from the day's activities, and Donna's storytelling soon put her to sleep. Donna took a moment to see how Izzy was doing, and she put on another blanket on her. For a brief moment, she stood there, captivated by the sight of Izzy and her snow-white puppy snuggled up in a picture-perfect moment.

She quietly exited the room on her tip-toes and walked to the lounge room to join Tom. They finally spent some time alone together, which was very special. They cherished these moments when they could truly connect. Donna made chamomile tea with lemon, and they enjoyed slices of her walnut cake, leftover from Easter Sunday.

"During the Easter celebration," Donna told Tom, "I told Izzy about my Aunt Pavica and how she taught me the true meaning of Easter. I shared with her my fondest memories of listening to Aunt Pavica's stories and my bond with a little dancing dove that built a nest for her chicks on top of our giant fig tree. I explained to Izzy that Aunt Pavica's spirit would remain free as long as I remembered her and shared her stories with future generations.

"I want to tell Izzy stories that will bond us. It is essential to keep these memories alive, and creating a spiritual connection is so important."

Tom turned to her and smiled. "You're such a wonderful storyteller. Please continue to tell Izzy these stories. As she ages, she can piece together the truth, and all the parts will come together. The future belongs to her; she can pass on the stories you told her to her children. That is the only way for humans to claim immortality." Tom smiled wider. "And of course, you and I will always remain in her memories, as she will have the opal shell necklace to remember us by."

Donna managed a fleeting smile. "You are right. I once read that human beings die twice. The first occurs when the spirit leaves the body, and the second happens when no one remembers them. By keeping Aunty Pavica's story in my memory, I remember her spirit accompanying me to Australia. When we leave this beautiful blue planet, Izzy will remember us, so our spirits won't have to travel far."

Donna's smile spread with the realisation.

"We are all here on this earth on borrowed time; let us enjoy one day at a time," Tom said sleepily.

"I have been trying to understand my obsession for years as to why I was desperately searching for the right partner for Ricky. I know that Lucy was that person; she was meant to give birth to an angel, and Isabella is that angel. She is a gift from heaven and has already saved her father. Maybe one day, she can save her mother, too."

"Yeah, maybe I agree with you. Izzy has a kind heart, and she will understand her parents' human frailties. Despite her young age, she has already demonstrated empathy, which will help her to understand her mother. As she grows older, she will come to realise that her mother's mental illness and drug addiction were significant factors that led to her abandonment."

Donna poured herself another cup of chamomile tea to calm her emotions, which were flooding back. She recalled her Aunt Pavica's words about her mother's prediction that all five daughters, including Donna as the youngest, would grow up to be "strong as steel yet gentle like a soft feather." Donna believed that her granddaughter Izzy would become just that. Her future was not predetermined, and how her story would unfold would depend entirely on her.

CR

About the Author

Croatian-born Nada Lubay, at the tender age of twenty-two, emigrated to Australia. She has lived in Perth, Western Australia, for more than forty years and would never live anywhere else.

Nada had a successful career in Vocational Education Training, working for a Registered Training Organisation (RTO) and was passionate about helping young students gain employment.

Nada's life dramatically changed when she battled the court system to secure a safe environment for her granddaughter, and then worked tirelessly to gain recognition and equal standing for the thousands of grandparent carers who are also raising their grandchildren.

The Silent Heroines was Nada's first novel. *Tears of an Angel*, her second novel, is the prequel and outlines Donna's personal story.